The Footstop Café

The Footstop Café

Paulette Crosse

SIMON & PIERRE FICTION
A MEMBER OF THE DUNDURN GROUP
TORONTO

Copyright © Janine Cross, 2007

All rights reserved. No part of this publication may be reproduced, stored in a retrieval system, or transmitted in any form or by any means, electronic, mechanical, photocopying, recording, or otherwise (except for brief passages for purposes of review) without the prior permission of Dundurn Press. Permission to photocopy should be requested from Access Copyright.

Editor: Michael Carroll
Designer: Erin Mallory
Printer: Webcom

Library and Archives Canada Cataloguing in Publication

Crosse, Paulette
   The footstop café / by Paulette Crosse.

ISBN 978-1-55002-716-7
   I. Title.

PS8605.R68F66 2007   C813'.6   C2007-902050-X

1 2 3 4 5   11 10 09 08 07

Conseil des Arts du Canada   Canada Council for the Arts

ONTARIO ARTS COUNCIL
CONSEIL DES ARTS DE L'ONTARIO
an Ontario Government Agency
un organisme du gouvernement de l'Ontario

Canada

We acknowledge the support of the **Canada Council for the Arts** and the **Ontario Arts Council** for our publishing program. We also acknowledge the financial support of the **Government of Canada** through the **Book Publishing Industry Development Program** and **The Association for the Export of Canadian Books**, and the **Government of Ontario** through the **Ontario Book Publishers Tax Credit program** and the **Ontario Media Development Corporation**.

Care has been taken to trace the ownership of copyright material used in this book. The author and the publisher welcome any information enabling them to rectify any references or credits in subsequent editions.

J. Kirk Howard, President

Printed and bound in Canada
Printed on recycled paper

www.dundurn.com

Dundurn Press	Gazelle Book Services Limited	Dundurn Press
3 Church Street, Suite 500	White Cross Mills	2250 Military Road
Toronto, Ontario, Canada	High Town, Lancaster, England	Tonawanda, NY
M5E 1M2	LA1 4XS	U.S.A. 14150

To my children, again and always

Acknowledgements

Apparently, the English word *crisis* is translated by the Chinese with two little characters; one means "danger," the other "opportunity."

Many thanks to my editor, Michael Carroll, for seeing *The Footstop Café* through interesting times and persevering. Thanks also to Laurel Hickey for great support and friendship way back when. And thanks, too, to the book club at the North Vancouver District Public Library in Lynn Valley, and Olivia, who ran the club when I first started this novel, for enlightening me on how non-writers read books. As someone once said: "The universe is made of stories. Not atoms." So I add: "God must therefore be a librarian."

I don't ever recall any accidents. We practically lived at the canyon. We just loved it down there, especially the Thirty Foot Pool. We respected that canyon and we knew exactly what we could do with it. Whenever there was any accidents down there, it was always the children from out of town or Vancouver.

— *Peggy Hunt, daughter of one of the original pioneers of Lynn Valley*

Chapter One

Karen Morton keeps her microwave in the bathroom. She does this because she's afraid to get zapped by its radiation. The way she reasons it, she's never in the bathroom while cooking and is therefore out of harm's way. Before she hit upon this solution, whenever she used the microwave she could feel her ovaries writhing and shrinking somewhere in the vicinity of her kidneys, behind the bony flare of her pelvis, either side of the small of her back.

Her nine-year-old son Andy has inherited this terror of microwave radiation.

One evening while his mother is zapping a butternut squash for dinner, Andy has to defecate. It is the kind that can't wait, the bloated-stomach kind that comes after eating porridge all day in an attempt to put muscle on a skinny frame.

A butternut squash takes approximately fifteen minutes to cook in the microwave; Andy can't wait that long. He is desperate, but not desperate enough to risk cancer of the prostate by straining into the toilet alongside the microwave. (The microwave sits on a small, olive-coloured table that Karen purchased from the Salvation Army explicitly for this purpose.) Nor does he dare go into the bathroom to turn the microwave off — just standing before the activated device those scant few seconds, with his gonads right at radiation level, is a prospect that makes his wee hairless testicles shrivel.

Yet Andy has to go badly. He looks outside his bedroom window and scans the gloomy yard, then decides he also doesn't want to risk Mrs. Baroudi seeing him crouch behind one of the rhododendrons that separates her yard from his. He needs a room, a room with a lock on it. The hall closet.

The hall closet has a lock because of Candice, who showers two to four times a day, depending whether it is a weekday or a weekend. With each shower, she uses a dozen or so towels to dry her budding body. Karen has installed a lock on the closet door in an attempt to reduce the massive laundry loads this shower fetish produces. Everyone in the house has a key to the door save Candice, a fact she resents as vocally as possible.

Andy needs something to poop in, a container of sorts. Preferably one with a lid, so he can whip the makeshift toilet outside and into the battered metal garbage can without someone smelling him out. He needs something like a margarine tub. Such a tub sits on his bookcase, where used batteries collect dust until his mother disposes of them.

A contraction grips his lower bowel. With a strangled gasp, he dumps the batteries out of the margarine tub and runs from his room. He slides to a stop outside the hall closet and pauses: Candice is in her room, listening to the radio and talking on her phone. Satisfied, Andy unlocks the closet, shuts himself in, and yanks down his pants.

There is something deeply gratifying — a monk-like contentedness — about producing a large, solid stool. Like everybody who's ever spawned such a specimen, Andy feels the bigger his stool is, the more he has achieved.

In much the same way Dairy Queen employees fill cones with ice cream, he gently swirls the tub beneath him so the stool can fit completely inside. Through the tub's yellow plastic he can feel the stool's warmth. The stench is strong and worrisome — until now he he had no idea how much the water in a toilet bowl dampens such odours. Moving carefully in his crowded, dark quarters, he snaps the lid over the tub. Done. Relief.

Except ...

He forgot toilet paper! Panic descends upon him, the cold, clammy panic he feels during gym class as he waits, as if on a firing squad, to be chosen last *again* between two teams. It is the kind of panic that makes him stutter and blink repeatedly. It is the kind of panic that has started to elicit contempt from Candice, who once thought him so funny and smart, a cross between a Muppet and Albert Einstein. Better than a puppy, she used to say, ruffling his hair.

As panic injects adrenaline into his veins, he hears footsteps: Candice is walking down the hall in his direction, talking into her phone.

"No, I mean, she locks it. Honest to God, *locks* it. It's like I'm not even a person in this house anymore, you know?"

Andy gropes wildly about him, finds something soft and cotton, gives a few vigorous wipes across his bum, and yanks up his pants.

"I mean, it's so totally unfair. What am I supposed to do, go around — oh, my God, what is that *stink*? What? Just wait a minute. No, just wait a minute."

Andy freezes in terror, margarine tub of stool cooling in his palm, eyes transfixed on the knob just visible from the light under the door. The knob turns.

In a blinding, horrifying flash, he realizes the flaw in his plan: the door locks only from the outside. Somehow his distracted mind overlooked this simple, devastating fact. His whole clever scheme shatters as Candice wrenches the door open.

He screams. Candice screams. He bursts into tears and darts by her.

Candice spies the poop-smeared towel. "Oh, my God! Andrew Morton, did you *shit* in the closet? I don't believe this! Mother! Mother! I do *not* believe this! Gloria? Guess what? My moronic little brother just *shit* in the closet! Yes! No, I'm not! *Mother!* Look, I gotta go. I can't handle this. No, forget it. Bye."

From where she hovers over a pan of frying mushrooms, gently sprinkling garlic powder onto their golden backs, Karen winces. *What now? What, oh, what now?*

Sputtering and crying, Andy stumbles into the kitchen, fumbles with the back door handle, and flings himself outside.

"Candice!" Karen cries in alarm. "What did you do to your brother?"

"What did *I* do? What did *I* do? For Christ's sake, Mom, he just *shit* in the closet!" Red-faced, Candice marches into the kitchen, waving her cordless phone in the direction of the hall.

Karen grips the serving spoon beside the stove. "Don't swear, please."

"Jesus, Mom, are you deaf? Don't you care that your precious son just shit in the closet?"

"I said don't swear!" Karen lashes out without thought. The serving spoon makes a wet, slapping noise as it strikes Candice's cheek. It leaves behind a smear of brown mushroom juice. Karen stares at the mark in horror — she doesn't believe in spanking, has never struck her children in her life.

Candice stands still for all of three seconds, then bursts into tears. "I'm sick of living here! I hate it, I hate it, I hate it!" She hurls the phone to the floor. The plastic battery cover flies off and hits the fridge. *"And I hate you!"* She storms from the kitchen.

Karen waits — one, two, three, four, *wham!* The whole house shudders as Candice slams her bedroom door shut.

Swallowing, Karen places the serving spoon on the stove, then switches off the mushrooms and moves the cast-iron pan from the burner. She takes a slow, deep breath, turns around, picks the cordless phone off the floor, and retrieves the plastic backing. One of the little tabs that snaps it into place is missing. She puts both the plastic backing and the phone on the counter and leaves the kitchen.

As she walks down the hall and passes the bathroom, the microwave beeps. The butternut squash is ready.

Why? she wonders as the smell of stool grows stronger the closer she draws to the closet. *My dear sweet Andy, why?*

Karen leans on the closet door and stares at the pink cotton towel on the floor. Streaks of brown slick its fuzz like oil on cat's fur. Moving methodically, she picks it up by one unsullied corner and carries it to the battered metal garbage can squatting at the back of the kitchen, adjacent to the teahouse.

Then she scrubs her hands with Pear's Transparent Soap, goes into her bedroom, and masturbates.

When Karen masturbates, this is what she does.

She chooses a carrot, an organic one, from within a cello bag in her fridge. The carrot must not be too slim at the tapered end, or it will break off during its employment (she has learned this through experience, and there is nothing so sensuously dampening as poking around in one's vagina in search of a lost carrot end).

Chosen carrot is then peeled and both ends are chopped off, being that the tapered end occasionally has wispy filaments attached to it and the blunt end is far too reminiscent of manure and farmers' Wellington boots.

Thus amputated and denuded, the carrot is placed in the microwave for twenty-six seconds. This takes the refrigerator chill off the vegetable and endows it with a stimulating heat. Occasionally, the tapered end will sizzle at this point, sometimes steam. If in the correct mood, Karen likes to imagine the carrot is protesting, weeping like a virgin, and that she will ignore its feeble cries and thrust it into herself with a dominance that will silence it.

Into the bedroom Karen goes. She closes the drapes. She kicks off her sandals and socks and moves the full-length bedroom mirror (the same that has been in her possession since she was seven) in front of the bed. Then she lifts her cotton skirt up, pulls her panties down to her ankles, and half lies, half sits on the edge of the bed.

Her knees flop to either side, thighs spread. Exposed to the mirror, she slowly, soothingly, begins rubbing the warmed, peeled organic carrot over the fleshy pink bud that brings her such release, such frustration, and such despair. After a few languorous rubs, the carrot is inserted. Karen's stomach muscles strain, far more so than they ever do while sweating through sit-ups in front of Susan Powter's fitness videos.

Eyes fixed on the mirror image of the lodged carrot, her right hand comes into play. And mouth. Hand to mouth, to wet the fingers, to make them slippery. Hand to pink bud. Fingers moving fast, face the apoplectic red of an infant freshly squeezed from the womb. Such *desperation* written on her contorted face, such *need*. No, don't look at the face — concentrate on the carrot, the sensations, the fingers.

Her fingers strum fast and hard against her clitoris, battering the tiny protuberance until it swells and hardens. When climax comes, her legs stiffen. She doesn't cry out, not in pleasure. She chokes, a dry, despairing sound. Occasionally, if she's in that frame of mind, she will laugh for the joy of having independently brought herself to this pinnacle of self-indulgence, laugh for the sheer ridiculousness of her situation. But the laugh is always brief.

The carrot is withdrawn, panties tossed into the laundry basket (it is night, after all, and she will not need them much longer), and cotton skirt pulled back into place. Socks on, feet jammed back into sandals. Carrot washed in the bathroom sink. (Aptly, it is always limp at this point, which satisfies her: she has conquered the carrot completely.)

On her way back to the kitchen, she gives the carrot to Yogurt, Andy's albino guinea pig. Waste not, want not, being her motto.

Karen's husband, Morris, knows nothing about his wife's masturbation, though this evening would have presented him with a prime opportunity to Learn a Thing or Two about his wife, for he lies upon the living-room sofa a mere room away, his evening newspaper scattered about him.

As usual he's preoccupied with feet. In his mind he is back at the office, healing ram's horn nails, diagnosing bunions, treating plantar's warts. He wears the soft, rapt look of an antique dealer discovering a Chippendale in a farmer's barn.

The same expression appears on his face while examining his patients' appendages. It is noticed by everyone, men and women alike, but especially the women. The men — and there are few of these, Morris would be the first to admit — receive his attentions as they receive their morning coffee: it is a right due unto them for the money they have paid. No more, no less.

But the women, they each believe that no one else receives such tender touches, such reverence, from Morris. They need to believe this, need to believe that their podiatrist recognizes their fragility, their individuality, through the soles of their feet. His soft, dry, manicured hands sliding gently over the cracked calluses on their heels declare: *You, my patient, are a creature like no other, and I treat you accordingly.*

Now the smell of poop swirls towards his nostrils, mingling with that of fried mushrooms and baked butternut squash. Frowning, he sits up. "Karen? What's that smell?"

Karen pauses on her way down the hall and sticks her head into the living room. "The cat had an accident in the closet. I've cleaned it up."

"The cat?"

"Dilly."

Alarm flickers across Morris's cheeks, and he sits up straighter. "Good grief, you can't let it into the teahouse anymore if it's going to do that sort of thing."

"I'm sure this was a onetime accident —"

"We can't take any chances, though, can we? Imagine if it starts defecating all over the sculptures!"

"That won't happen. Cats need something soft —"

"No, Karen, I'm sorry. The cat can't go into the teahouse again. You understand, don't you?"

Karen swallows, fingers twining around her skirt. Of course she understands. The shrine cannot be desecrated. She nods once, tersely, and returns to the kitchen. Deliberately, she burns the tofu burgers.

The teahouse: a shrine settled back among towering hemlocks and stately cedars. It exists because of Lynn Canyon Suspension Bridge.

Only a quick drive from the bowels of downtown Vancouver, the bridge draws an endless number of tourists each year. Made of rattling wood, it is suspended by enormous wire cables draped across a fern-dripping gorge some 150 feet deep. Marilyn Monroe once crossed its creaky planks.

The North Shore, separated from downtown Vancouver by Burrard Inlet, boasts two such suspension bridges. One, Capilano Suspension Bridge, charges an exorbitant entry fee and has plastic tepees, carved Indians, and garish totem poles liberally decorating its grounds. Tour buses constantly clog its environs. The other one, Lynn Canyon Suspension Bridge, is buried amid suburbia and forest, is free to walk across, and has headstones for decoration instead of covered wagons. The headstones commemorate those who have died in the park. There are many.

In 1985 Morris and Karen purchased a tiny house at the very end of Peters Road in North Vancouver. (Actually, Morris purchased it. Being eighteen and pregnant, Karen didn't have a great deal of purchasing power.) The broadside of the small, neglected rancher bared its peeling clapboards to the large gravel parking lot of Lynn Canyon Suspension Bridge. Together Morris and Karen sanded the clapboards and painted them powder blue. Following her husband's instructions, Karen meticulously painted an enormous foot upon the broadside of the house.

"Welcome to the Footstop Café," she calligraphied across the ankle. "Tea, scones, fresh cream, and soothing foot massages inside."

"It should read teahouse, not café," Morris said, chewing on his knuckles in agitation. "Teahouse."

"I didn't have room."

"But this has to be a teahouse, Karen, not a café. A place of leisure and beauty, of learning and comfort. Not a greasy spoon."

"It *will* be a teahouse. I promise."

They planted fuchsias, petunias, snapdragons, and delphiniums on either side of the river-rock path that wended its way to the refurbished potting shed at the back of their house. Above the shed's crooked red door they hung a foot-shaped sign that declared: "Welcome to The Footstop." (Karen, yet again, ran out of room, and rather than offend her husband by inscribing "Café" upon the board, she decided to punctuate after "Footstop.") Quaint flower-print curtains hung in the windows, and red-and-white-checkered tablecloths beamed up from Formica tables. Vases of flowers and walls of sunny yellow invited tourists to enter. Mozart played in the background.

Within five years of opening, the Footstop became such a success that Morris and Karen expanded. The potting shed grew as large as their rancher. Shrouded by trees and shadow, exposed only to the gravel parking lot, the addition to the tiny house brought nary a peep from the local building inspectors. The neighbours watched and, bemused, attended the open-house party where Morris, Karen, and baby Candice personally massaged each and every foot present.

Although Morris was inclined to believe that the success of the Footstop was entirely due to its lofty merchandise, it was instead because most tourists, after the initial gasping at the bridge and canyon, were disappointed that the park was, indeed, little more than a park. They eagerly waddled to the Footstop in search of something to do.

No one left without buying at least one foot.

Control in a life where control is cloud-like, nebulous, blowing like cotton-tree fuzz and catching in snags of wood and piles of clay-clammy pebbles — that is why Karen masturbates. It isn't that cleaning up her son's defecation sparked some fetish deep within her, and it isn't in defiance of the ugliness of his deed; it is a cry, a lifeline, a buoy thrown out from a pitching boat. To masturbate is to connect with herself, with all that she holds secret and longs for. It is mining, core-tapping, plunging into treasure-filled depths. She masturbates to remind herself that she exists. That in something she still has control.

They eat dinner in silence, Candice skewering each marrowfat pea on her plate with angry precision. Andy eats methodically, head lowered, eyes blurred behind smudged glasses. Oblivious to the tensions around the table, Morris savours each forkful of his food, contemplatively rolling it around his mouth before swallowing. Karen watches each of them closely, seeking evidence that she knows these people.

After dinner, Morris retires back to his sofa and Candice to her room. Andy — who never needs to be reminded when it's his evening for dish duty — languidly fills the sink with steaming water.

"It's okay," Karen says, tousling his orange hair with

one hand as she squirts blue liquid soap into the sink. "Your father thinks it was Dilly."

"So?" He whirls on her, his face screwed up in an anger so intense that Karen steps back. "Does that mean I should thank you?" He starts weeping, his neck flushing crimson, his cheeks billowing in and out like the gills of a puffer fish. "What am I supposed to do, anyway, with that stupid microwave in the bathroom?"

"Andy —"

"She thinks I'm a moron! She hates me!" He throws himself against Karen's bosom and blows small bubbles of mucus against her sweater. "She'll never speak to me again!"

"Oh, Andy, that's not true," Karen murmurs, rocking him slightly. "She loves you. You're her brother."

"Big deal."

"I'll move the microwave somewhere else. The furnace room."

"So? How will that fix anything?"

"I'll talk to her —"

"No!" He pulls away and stares up at her in alarm. "You always make things way worse!"

Inwardly, Karen shrivels. She forces her face blank. "All right," she says mechanically. "I won't say anything."

"Promise?"

"Really, Andy ..."

"No, Mom, you've got to promise! Promise me you won't say anything!" His pale fingers embed themselves in her forearms.

"But —"

"Mom!"

"All right. I won't talk to her. Promise."

Andy shudders in relief and releases her. "Good."

Karen washes the dishes in a daze. Beside her, Andy carefully polishes each one dry.

"I think I'll go for a walk," she whispers as she places the last dish in the cupboard.

"You okay, Mom?"

"What?" A bright, brittle smile creases her face. "Certainly. Go join your father now. I'll be back in a bit."

Chapter Two

Moey Thorpe has never been in the Footstop Café. As his mustard Plymouth chortles over the ruts and bumps leading to Lynn Canyon, he wonders what it will be like within the café's cottage-quaint interior. But the thought is only a vague, wispy one without enough curiosity to merit life, and it instantly melts away in the twilight.

Gravel crunches beneath worn Michelin tires as he pulls into the canyon's parking lot. The smell of hot motor oil sours his nostrils as he climbs out of the car. Leaving the doors unlocked (no point in locking them; the rear window is just a sheet of plastic), Moey lumbers towards the bridge.

From the waist up, he is a big, hairy man, his hair the thick black sort that reminds most people of genitals. From the waist down, he's as slim and tight as a delicate transvestite. In shape he resembles a snow cone.

Moey passes the park's first headstone, a bronze plaque implanted in a large boulder. The boulder squats at the top of a flight of low, shallow stairs that leads towards the suspension bridge. The sombre words it bears bless the memory of a woman who was crushed to death by a similar boulder while sunbathing peacefully in the canyon.

Moey next passes three calf-high concrete pylons. Some time ago the District Council of North Vancouver saw fit to erect a large billboard that graphically depicted the various dangers lurking within the canyon. Sketches of bodies decaying in the foamy clutches of whirlpools, trapped beneath submerged logs, or impaled upon rocky protuberances were all realistically portrayed in hopes of decreasing the annual death toll.

Instead, the billboard merely caused a traffic jam of Japanese tourists upon the stairway, and teenagers continued to plunge lemming-like to their deaths. The billboard was therefore relocated to the parking lot. The three concrete pylons remain like an enigmatic sculpture in its original display spot.

Without so much as hesitating — a true local — Moey marches onto the bridge. It shudders and creaks beneath his weight, the entire length of it undulating gently. A cool autumn breeze redolent with dead leaves and rotting bark blows up from the canyon and into his bristle-brush hair. Far below, not yet engorged by rainfall, Lynn Creek runs like a thread of Christmas tinsel between cliffs and boulders.

As always, Moey stops in the middle of the bridge. He glances left, then right; at this time of night, at this time of year, all teenagers should be at home doing schoolwork or drugs. But still he makes sure he's alone.

In the gathering gloom, both ends of the bridge gape black and empty at him. Good.

He takes off his ski jacket (a greasy relic from younger days) and from its left pocket extracts four silver discs that glint wickedly in the moonlight. Using his teeth and fingers, he works the elastic loops attached to each of the discs over his thumbs and middle fingers. From the right pocket of his ski jacket, he removes a length of cloth. It clanks like prison chains and glistens as metallically as the four discs gleaming on his fingers. His breath quickens.

Moey attaches the scarf-like, clinking cloth around his hips, then raises his hands above his head. The cool wind races up the gorge and caresses his body. His nipples harden against his plaid work shirt.

Then, with a flourish, Moey Thorpe begins to belly-dance.

Every culture in the Middle East claims ownership of this exotic dance. But much like religion, each country shares familiar aspects of the dance while at the same time making it wholly unique. The true origins of the dance have been lost in the sands of time.

The Greeks under Alexander the Great, the Turks in the Ottoman Empire, the Romans, and the Nubian dynasties of ancient Egypt all may have shared the crime of disseminating the dance throughout the Middle East. The only fact known with certainty is that the *danse du ventre* was introduced to North America in 1893 at Chicago's World's Columbian Exhibition by a certain Sol Bloom.

Culture and history aside, however, there are three things essential to all belly dancers: skill, suppleness, and a costume. All else can be faked.

Ah, yes, the costume! Again many arguments exist about what constitutes genuine belly-dancing attire. Some adamantly claim that only the Gypsy look is authentic, with its many draping scarves, its colourful flared skirt, its jangling silver jewellery and flounced croptop. Others scornfully declare that a genuine belly dancer wears only gauzy harem pants and a coin-studded bra. But so much more exists! Beaded fringes, gold silk tassels, hip scarves, veils, armbands, headdresses, painted glitter, sequins, stretch lace, gauntlets, Beledi dresses, high heels, Moroccan slippers, bare feet, ankle bells, wigs, capes, turbans! The list goes on.

One thing and one thing alone is consistent (except in Lebanon, for reasons known only to the Lebanese): the zils, also called sagat. Be they bronze or tin, factory-made in Taiwan or hand-hammered in Egypt, the music of the finger cymbals accompanies the hip lifts and shoulder shimmies of every accomplished dancer. It is the music of these that now clamours bell-like through Lynn Canyon from Moey's blunt fingertips.

The jiggling bridge always intensifies his shimmies and makes him feel buoyant. It is a feeling to which he is rapidly becoming addicted.

Although only brief, his dancing routine drenches him in sweat. Panting, grinning, Moey finishes his last ribcage slide and pelvic drop and triumphantly zaghareets. The canyon walls echo from his tongue-vibrating ululation. A raven screams back from the treetops.

Perspiring heavily, Moey removes his zils and coin belt, replaces them in their respective pockets, then shrugs back into his ski jacket. Exhilarated from the dance, he does a samiha to the far end of the bridge and begins to hike to the Ninety Foot Pool.

The Ninety Foot Pool is not, in fact, ninety feet deep. In the summer when bikini-clad babes and testosterone-laden hunks guzzle beer upon its rocky banks, the Ninety Foot Pool is actually about thirty feet deep. That doesn't stop anyone who is trying to impress members of the opposite sex from leaping off the numerous surrounding cliffs into said pool.

Again in its wisdom, the North Vancouver District changed all the signposts within the park, thereby renaming the Ninety Foot Pool the Thirty Foot Pool (which was what it was originally christened back in 1912 when the canyon was first declared a park). This didn't deter the cliff-jumpers one iota, nor did it stop the rising death count. And locals still refer to the pool as the Ninety.

By the time Moey reaches the pool, his olive-toned flesh has cooled and puckered. With each breath, wisps of white flutter from his mouth. He perches upon his favourite rock, folds his firm, slim legs to his burly chest, and gazes meditatively at the waters.

He loves this park. A native of the Saskatchewan wheat fields, he loves the canyon's abundance of water and greenery, of buckled land and scoured rock, which differs so vastly from the staid, fundamentalist prairie. For him the exuberant life bursting within the forest represents all that he wants to be: natural, wild, strong, sensual. Everything a belly dancer embodies. Everything his parents despise.

Port and Gemma Thorpe *are* the prairies: stoic, seamed, hard-working, unemotional, and predictable. They expected all of their six sons to become either farmers, carpenters, or mechanics (though an able man, Port often drawls, is all three). Moey became none of these. The Saskatoon Heavyweight Championship belt hanging in his rented basement suite attests to this.

He throws another stick into the water. The ripples spread outward until they touch the far bank and lap against the hooves of a white stag. Moey blinks and sits up straighter.

The white stag snorts steam from flared nostrils and placidly stares back.

You always make things way worse!

How could a child say such a shattering thing to a mother? Karen's guts shrivel like a disturbed slug contracting in on itself. *She* certainly never said such a thing to her stepmom, Mei-ling (aka Petra) Woodruff, however many times it was warranted.

Karen blows Dilly's tail fur out of her mouth, adjusts the cat's position on her shoulders, and stuffs her hands deeper into the gritty wool pockets of her cardigan. She passes the headstone at the top of the stairs leading to the bridge, then, instead of heading across the bridge, turns left and descends a second set of slimy wooden stairs. A large bear-proof garbage can almost blocks these stairs from sight. The can reeks of dog urine; one patch on it is rust-pocked at cocked-leg height.

Few people take this trail, the purpose of most park visitors being to cross the suspension bridge and thereafter, at a loss on how to proceed, visit the Ninety/Thirty Foot Pool.

Karen prefers this side of the canyon, the west, because it has less litter, fewer tourists, and fewer cliff jumpers. Unfortunately, this summer the odds evened a little in the last department; the western banks successfully claimed the life of a thirteen-year-old boy who tried to impress his buddies by diving off a precipice. Even now, rain-shrivelled cards and mildewing flowers mark the spot mourners designated as a shrine to his memory.

The sight of the withered bouquets sheathed in tattered plastic and piled up like so much garbage disturbs Karen. Every day she passes those sad cards and dead flowers and wonders when the park ranger will throw them out. It isn't that she doesn't feel for the parents of the dead child; it is just that the two-month-old shrine now looks like an abandoned grave. The boy's spirit needs to be freed from that tether.

The stairs lead Karen down a narrow path cut between bulging, mossy rock. The rumble of the canyon to her right increases as the trail drops to creek level. Dilly remains motionless on her shoulders, bilious green eyes fully dilated in the gloom.

"How have I ever made anything worse?" Karen woefully asks the cat. In response Dilly sneezes out a strand of Karen's frizzled red locks.

"I admit his last birthday party was a mistake. I've apologized for that. I knew it was a mistake from the start and I should have stood up to Morris on the issue. But damn it, Andy didn't raise a fuss, did he?"

But, of course, he didn't. Andy worships the ground his father walks upon.

No, the responsibility to prevent the birthday disaster fell upon Karen and Karen alone. But she stood by and did nothing, and then it was too late and all the kids in Andy's school began snickering behind his back. Her subsequent attempt to fix things resulted in Andy being expelled.

Karen blames her father, Sandy Woodruff. Throughout her Anglican childhood he stertorously repeated, "You must trust all things unto God, pudding face. Trust all things unto God."

"God!" Karen says scornfully, and immediately shoots a guilty look skyward. Just like her stepmom, Mei-ling, she feels the Almighty needs protection from the harsh facts of life. God, in Karen's experience, couldn't tie a shoelace correctly if He tried. But she would sooner be barbecued in Hell than let Him discover this awful truth.

This disparity between what she's been taught by her father and what she herself believes has created within her a tendency not to act on a situation until it's too late, and then to overcompensate wildly and futilely when God's will proves disastrously different from what she hoped. Alas.

At a fork in the path Karen turns right and begins goat-hopping over the rock-strewn creek bank. The autumn chill carries the green smell of slime, pine needles, and moss. Up ahead at the Ninety/Thirty Foot Pool something plops into the water.

Karen barely glances up from her hopscotch progress along the creek bank; here in the canyon things always plop into the water. Bambi-cute squirrels shake loose hemlock seeds into the pool. Small fish that have survived the urine and beer cans of summer frequently flip from the surface to smack their gums around hapless water skeeters. Crows defecate into the pool with similar plops. Pebbles jarred loose from scrounging raccoons likewise plop into the pool. The surface of the pool is always going plop.

But this time Dilly doesn't like it. It takes Karen a moment to realize that the nails of her feline companion are now painfully embedded in her flesh.

She immediately stops. Always dreading that her luck might run out and a pervert will catch her in the deserted canyon, Karen trusts Dilly to warn her of the existence of such deviants much as most women trust their overweight, arthritic Labradors to protect them should such a hazard appear.

Her eyes promptly fall upon the white hart.

That's what she thinks as soon as she sees it. Not stag or reindeer or wapiti, but hart. Not albino or grey or silver, but white. White hart.

And there is no question, from its gently heaving flanks to its muscled hindquarters, from its majestic antlers to its water-submerged hooves, that this is a white hart. It swings a dripping, bearded muzzle in her direction and languorously blinks. Steam fogs its nostrils.

Dilly stiffens, her thorny grip hooking another half inch through Karen's skin. Karen stands rooted to the spot. The birthmarks between her thighs start to tingle.

And that's when she knows: this hart, this flesh-and-blood impossibility from fantasia, is a sign from the benevolent, world-weary God she so recently scoffed. It is a sign that He knows she is avoiding her Destiny, that it pains Him deeply. A sign that it is high time she begins doing something about it.

With a choked cry, Karen spins around to flee. She promptly slips on a rock, twists her ankle, and crumples to the ground.

As soon as the woman appears, ginger hair puffed from her head like quills from an enraged porcupine, neck engulfed by a fluffy white muff, Moey expects the stag to run. Instead, it merely lowers its head to the pool and sucks in a huge draft of water.

Oblivious to the stag's presence, the woman continues to rock-hop along the creek bank across from Moey, drawing steadily closer. In an attempt to get her attention without startling the stag, Moey tosses another, then another stick into the water.

Plop! Plop!

She stops and looks up. Stiffens. Even in the gloom, Moey can see the shock on her pale face as she stares at the stag.

The stag slowly lifts its head from the pool and lazily swings its great neck in her direction. Steam puffs from its nostrils. With a raven-like croak, the woman turns around, hurls her neck muff towards the nearest bush, and flings herself upon the rocky ground.

A second of silence passes.

"Dilly!" the woman cries, and one of her pale hands rises from the rock bed and waves frantically at the muff. "Dilly, come back!"

Moey gawks at the woman as she flounders on the creek bank, trying to get to her feet. An anguished cry brings her to her knees again, a cry Moey knows all too well from the boxing ring: a broken bone given a voice. Leaping to his feet, he clambers to the creek's edge and splashes towards the opposite bank.

Had it been winter or spring or even later in the fall, fording the creek would have been as safe as a blind man crossing a freeway during rush hour. However, it is early autumn, when, thirsted into submission after a dry summer and not yet replenished by the rains of late fall, the creek is at its lowest and most fordable. Moey reaches the woman's side in minutes.

"My cat," she moans, clutching her ankle. "My cat."

A foreign tourist, Moey thinks.

"No, that's your ankle," he corrects gently, kneeling beside her. "Let me see if it's broken. Broken, you know?" He pantomimes breaking a stick in two. "*Crack!*"

Groaning, she permits him to remove the sandal and sock on her left foot. The swelling there and her squeal of pain at his prodding tell Moey all he needs to know.

"Broken," he says smugly. "Thought so."

"Broken? But what about my cat?"

"Your ...?"

She stabs a finger towards the bushes. "My cat. She took off in that direction. She can't be out here at night. The coyotes will get her."

He blinks at the bushes, and it slowly dawns on him that she's talking — in English — about her neck muff, or what he thought was a neck muff. It's a cat. And the woman is obviously no foreigner.

"Could you find me a stick to lean on, please? I have to find her."

"I don't think you should walk on that foot —"

"But I *have* to find my cat!"

Moey shifts. "Look, I, uh, can carry you to my car and drive you to the hospital —"

"But my cat!"

"After I help find your cat."

"Oh. That would be ... thank you."

Unnoticed by them both, the white hart slips between the trees and disappears.

"*Dillyillyilly,*" Karen croons.

A tentative meow sounds from a bush in front of them, slightly to their left. Karen gestures in that direction. "Could you carry me over there?"

After a moment's hesitation, the man nods and picks her up. Despite the agony in her foot, Karen is very aware of the strength in his arms and the muscles of his chest, which is pressed against her cheek. His knee joints pop like embers exploding in a fire as he straightens.

Moving with painstaking care, the man steps from rock to rock until he reaches the spongy forest floor. "Okay?" he grunts as he sets her down.

She closes her eyes briefly against the hot, throbbing pain in her ankle. "I'm fine." Then, lightening her tone, she murmurs to the bush, "Come here, Dilly. Good kitty."

But the bush remains immobile.

"She's hiding," the man says glumly.

"She's scared. I'll have to go in and get her. Could you help me kneel?"

He glances at her foot, opens his mouth to protest, then

claps it shut again. With a nod he helps her kneel.

The pain in Karen's ankle makes her head spin, and she bites her lip to keep from crying out and scaring Dilly away. Damp peat seeps through her skirt onto her kneecaps. Slowly, she crawls into the slimy bracken. A twig snags her hair. A slug elongates beneath her left palm. Something clammy plasters itself across her forehead. She jerks, stifles a curse, shakes off the slug under her hand, and brushes away the leaf on her forehead. A thorn stabs her right knee.

Dilly's white form bobs into view a few feet ahead of her. "Dilly, good kitty, come to Mommy." Karen reaches out gingerly, and Dilly tenses. Mentally ringing the cat's neck, Karen continues to coo soothingly. Gradually, she is allowed to stroke a furry cheek, to slide her fingers around the scruff. She grabs hold tightly.

"Got you, you miserable beast," she grunts, dragging Dilly towards her and shoving the struggling cat up inside her sweater. The cat's furry head pops out alongside her neck. They stare at each other, cat and human, eye to eye. Dilly's tail sweeps back and forth across Karen's stomach. Claws extend into her bosom.

"Don't even think about it," Karen whispers.

The cat's mouth opens in plaintive protest, but Karen pushes the head back down into her sweater. With one hand firmly hugging Dilly against herself, she backs up. Unfortunately, this reverse motion catches the rear hem of her skirt under her knees. Her skirt begins a jerky, steady migration down her buttocks. She stops, tries to lift one knee to free her skirt. The shift of weight causes an excruciating blast of pain up her injured leg.

"Oh, hell!" she cries, and Dilly writhes vigorously.

"Are you all right in there?"

"No, I'm not! Dilly! Stay still, you ungrateful wretch!"

"Do you need a hand?"

"No!" Karen gasps, envisioning the man crawling headfirst into her partially exposed ass. "Stay there! I'm … I'm fine. Coming out right now. Fine."

He mutters something in a doubtful tone, but the bushes behind her don't part.

Karen takes a deep, cleansing breath, then tries to move forward, as if the motion itself can reverse the downward migration of her skirt. No such luck. She attempts to pivot so she can at least come out of the bush headfirst and not preceded by her naked bum. But there's no room among the thorns to pivot.

"To hell with it," she sighs. Then, louder: "Could you close your eyes, please? I've … my skirt's fallen down."

A pause, a grunt from the bushes behind her, then the *shuffle-squelch* of feet moving in the mud. Gritting her teeth, Karen resumes crawling backwards.

Just as she comes out into the open, her skirt skies the rest of the way over the smooth moguls of her buttocks and rests around her thighs. A cool autumn breeze dances across her rump.

Now what to do? She can't stand up by herself, not with her bad ankle. She doesn't look up. The pair of black Nikes to the left of her, facing away, shift. An awkward pause.

Then the Nikes move and the man's knee joints backfire as he swiftly kneels. Karen cringes as he gives an almighty heave on her skirt. He yards it up to her waist with such force that the fabric under her knees separates from the rest of the skirt with a sharp rip. Without missing a beat, the man stands again, lifting Karen onto her feet by her elbows. She almost swoons from the sudden elevation change and the furnace of pain in her ankle.

They avoid each other's eyes as they try to regain their composures.

"Thank you," Karen eventually mumbles. "I couldn't ... I tried ... my hands weren't free. Anyway, thank you."

He studies a hemlock. "You've got your cat?"

"In my sweater."

"Can you walk at all?"

"I ... can try."

Silence.

"I'll carry you," he says, then scoops her off her feet with such dizzying speed that her tofu burger lurches into her throat.

Although Moey is a very strong man (as the thrice-defeated Todd "The Sledgehammer" Dupuis would be the first to admit), the woman is neither small nor slender. By the time he staggers into the parking lot with his burden, breathing like a bull facing down a matador, he feels certain he's torn at least one ligament in his pectorals. He places the woman gently on the hood of his Plymouth and fumbles in his pockets for his car keys.

"You don't have to drive me to the hospital."

"Can't ... drive there ... yourself," he pants.

"Just find me a stick to lean on. Really. I'll walk the rest of the way home and my husband can drive me."

He stops digging in his jacket. "Home?"

"There." She points.

His eyes swivel to the enormous ghostly white foot painted on the side of the nearest house.

"The Footstop," she says. "That's where I live."

"Ah, yes. Well ..." He nods as if confirming something he already knows. "Yes."

The woman sticks out her free hand. "Thank you very

much for your assistance."

"No problem. Any time." His sweaty hand slowly crushes hers. "Any time."

"My name's Karen."

"Moey. Moey Thorpe."

They continue to shake hands, both bobbing their heads like woodpecker toys.

"If you're in the neighbourhood one afternoon, drop by. I can massage your feet or something. To say thank you. You know." She flushes.

"Yes. Well. I'll do that."

They release hands. Moey shrugs at her house. "Maybe I should carry you to the door."

"Oh. Thank you."

Taking a deep breath, he scoops her up again like a praying mantis attacking its prey, and bulldozes his way through the cedar boughs overhanging the rock path to her back door.

"Thank you very much again," she gasps as he puts her down beside the metal garbage can, the same one that contains an Andy-soiled towel.

"Take care of that foot, you hear?" he says. Then, panting like a farrowing sow, he ducks back through the cedar boughs and disappears into the night.

Karen staggers into the house, calling for help. Morris and Andy greet her in the hall with matching dropped jaws. Candice bursts from the bathroom with a towel wrapped about her torso and starts shrieking.

"*Ohmygod!* You've been raped! I don't *believe* this! Don't just stand there, Dad, *do* something! Call the police, call an ambulance! Andy, get him the phone!"

"Candice —"

"It's nothing to be ashamed of, Mom. It isn't your fault.

And you're not supposed to have a shower or anything, 'cause that'll wash away the evidence."

"I wasn't raped."

"That's denial, Mom. Gloria says that —"

"Have you, Karen?" Morris asks, bewildered. "Have you been ... defiled?"

Andy bursts into tears.

"Don't just stand there crying!" Candice shouts. "Go get the phone like I told you!"

Karen takes a deep breath, sticks two fingers in her mouth, and lets loose a whistle. All tears and shouts cease.

"I have not," she says firmly, "been raped. I have, however, broken my ankle. I fell. Simple as that. I fell."

"But your skirt," Candice says.

Karen glances down to where Moey inadvertently shortened the length of her skirt by six inches or so. The ragged hem trails a few twigs and leaves. "It ripped during my fall," she says, a flush creeping across her cheeks. "I'm okay."

Her husband's face turns sallow, however. He stares at her feet in horror. "You've broken an ankle?"

"I think so, yes. My left one."

"Oh, no," Morris gasps. He falls to his knees and flutters his hands over her left foot. "Karen, how could you?"

Andy bursts into tears again.

Chapter Three

With some difficulty, Karen lowers herself into her steaming bathtub. Her left foot, encased in plaster, a plastic Safeway bag, and a pink towel, is balanced precariously on a metal crutch that stretches like a bridge from one side of the tub to the other. Curls of plastic advertisements for Pillsbury Dough peel from the crutch.

At eleven o'clock the previous night, Karen and Morris discovered that the hospital no longer sent crutches home with their disabled outpatients. A nurse sternly informed them that far too many crutches left the emergency ward, never again to return. In the wake of all the budget cutbacks, the hospital saw fit to revoke the privilege of sending crutches home with the lame. Instead, a local supermarket rented Karen a pair of crutches for a nominal fee, thus the Pillsbury Dough advertisements plastered on its surface.

Karen is now indulging in a hot bath because Morris magnanimously told her to take the day off from the teahouse. He wrote a note and stuck it in the window: "Closed for today due to affliction. Will reopen tomorrow. Sorry for any inconvenience." From the sound of the rain battering the roof, Karen doubts that the suspension bridge, and therefore the Footstop, will receive any customers today.

Arms trembling slightly from bearing the brunt of her weight, she levers herself into the foamy water, groaning as her skin turns a delicious scalded red. From the bathroom floor Dilly meows.

"Just wait," Karen murmurs, leaning back and closing her eyes. "It's too hot for you. Wait."

She lets her thoughts drift as tiny bubbles pop and crackle around her, releasing apple-scented steam. She thinks back to the previous night's occurrence, to the indignity of backing out of the bush in front of a stranger with her buttocks exposed. Blushing, she begins to shampoo her hair.

By the time Karen finishes, the water has cooled enough for Dilly to climb in. The cat stretches across her stomach, purring as she kneads her breasts and butts her chin. Bubbles adhere to the cat's fur like foam to a sandy beach.

Seven years ago Karen found four kittens stuffed inside a plastic ice-cream bucket on the doorstep of the Footstop. Two of the kittens were dead, not from lack of oxygen (someone had thoughtfully made holes in the lid of the ice-cream bucket) but from lack of blood: fleas swarmed over them. Karen immediately took control of one kitten and Candice the other.

Upon the advice of a local veterinarian, they purchased a pair of flea combs and spent the next few hours combing the kittens and drowning the captured fleas in a cup of bleach. (Andy, only two, tried to drink it.) Regardless of their efforts, the kittens weakened. The fleas crawled down their ears, up their nostrils, and into their half-closed eyes, hiding from the combs with a canniness that bordered on higher intelligence.

"They need to be flea-bathed," Karen muttered, angrily squashing a flea between her thumbnail and the kitchen counter. It made a satisfying pop.

Candice frowned. "But the vet said we can't do that. The kittens are too young. The chemicals will kill them."

"Chemicals or fleas — either way they're going to die. Watch your brother. I'm going to the pet store."

Karen defied the veterinarian's instructions and bathed her languid, flea-infested kitten in chemical shampoo; Candice staunchly continued with the flea comb. By nightfall Karen's kitten was tentatively sucking on a doll's bottle of milk; Candice's kitten was buried in the backyard.

Since then Dilly insists on sharing the bath with whomever is currently in it.

The bathwater is beginning to cool. Karen lifts a sopping Dilly from her stomach and drops the cat onto the floor, where she promptly shakes like a dog and proceeds to groom. After a great struggle, Karen extracts herself from the bathtub. She scrubs her rosy, rounded flesh with a towel (does the towel smell faintly of Andy poop, or is that her imagination?), sits on the toilet, and works her panties over the bulbous cast on her left foot. It isn't until the black cotton slides over the birthmarks on her inner thighs that she remembers the white hart by the creek.

Immediately, she freezes. Her birthmarks begin to buzz, much as an elbow tingles if the funny bone is walloped.

Ah, yes, those birthmarks. Mei-ling (aka Petra) Woodruff had plenty to say about them during Karen's childhood: "Karma. They are there because of karma. All Buddhists know that a person's physical features are influenced by karma."

And this: "Jesus was very open-minded, girl, very understanding of those who were confused about their sexuality. A prostitute was his closest friend — sex thrives on friendship."

And this: "The Hevajra Tantra says great knowledge abides in the body, though it is not born of the body. Do you know what this means? This means that your body is a telephone between the human and the divine."

Ah, yes, Mei-ling (aka Petra) Woodruff had a *great* deal to say about Karen's birthmarks. None of it comprehensible.

Karen dresses in a daze, eats her scrambled eggs and toast in a daze, finishes mending the hole in Candice's favourite plaid shirt in a daze, and hobbles into the teahouse in a daze. Yet she isn't so dazed as to forget Morris's edict to keep Dilly out. That she consciously chooses to ignore.

A door in the kitchen leads directly into Karen's workshop nestled at the back of the teahouse. A heavy brocade curtain separates the workshop from the teahouse proper.

Glue, nails, chalk, papier mâché, sculpting burrs, and glitter spill from shelves; scissors, clay, oil paints, sanding belts, wood shavings, exacto knives, and Magic Markers overflow from stacked boxes. Upon a large, rough-hewn workbench lie beads, leather strips, pencils, hammers, chisels, turpentine, shrink-wrap plastic, and stacks of coloured paper. The room looks like a collision between a stationery store and a hardware depot and smells like the well-oiled wood of an old church.

In a corner of this room cowers a worn wicker basket lined with a hairy wool blanket. With a yawn Dilly walks into this basket, curls up, and proceeds to sleep. Karen flicks on a wire heater, leans her crutches against the workbench, and sinks onto a paint-flecked stool.

Almost twenty minutes go by as she sits and stares blankly at the heater's red coils.

"I can't do it," she finally says aloud. "I can't follow my Destiny. It will ruin the family. Candice will die of shame."

Not true, a voice murmurs in her mind. *Certainly, Candice may never speak to you again, may endure endless torment at school, and may even leave home, but she won't actually die. Not unless, in running away, she ends up a heroin addict.*

"What about Morris?" Karen argues. "It will destroy him. Who will run the teahouse? I owe him more than that."

Why? What exactly has he done for you, other than bless you with an old one-level house, a foot-fetish fair, and two children? And besides, he's been spending an awful lot of time at the office lately. And that honey-voiced, stout 'n single receptionist of his is always with him, isn't she?

"But Andy will never understand! He'll cry, he'll beg me not to do it, it will affect his emotional stability."

More so than the Footstop already affects it?

"I can't do it, okay? I can't." Karen grabs the pillowy portion of her inner thighs and squeezes hard, trying to squelch the tingling in her birthmarks and the voice in her head. "I imagined it. I didn't see the hart. It never existed! Now stop pestering me!"

Pinched into submission, her birthmarks quit prickling. But her long-denied aspirations continue to throb through her veins, newly awakened by the non-appearance of the white hart.

Someone else is likewise unable to concentrate on the task before him as the image of the white hart pops into his mind. But unlike Karen, Moey Thorpe doesn't have the luxury of privacy when the memory of the fantastical beast returns to him. Instead, he stands before the serious, expectant eyes of twenty-four kickboxing students.

He gazes blankly at the far wall where mirrors reflect

an orderly row of white uniforms: it is this sea of poised white that reminds him of the stag.

Jesus, he forgot all about it, what with helping the lady find her cat and all. How could he forget such a thing? (The image of smooth, pearly buttocks glinting up at him from beneath a halo of salmonberry leaves rises briefly in his mind.)

He shifts uncomfortably, then sends the students sprinting around the gym. But he can't rid his mind of the stag. While teaching roundhouse kicks, he thinks about the beast. While demonstrating spinning back kicks, he thinks about Karen. While correcting a student's *epon kumite*, he thinks about belly dancing. The thick, wiry hairs on the nape of his neck refuse to lie flat.

So it comes to pass that after finishing his classes, Moey Thorpe finds himself climbing into his Plymouth and heading towards Lynn Canyon, his skin prickling with presentiment. As he drives his exhaust-spouting car up Lynn Valley Road, the rain is so thick and fast from clouds so white that it seems as if heaven is hurling fat globs of cream onto his windshield. His wipers don't so much improve visibility as draw attention to the lack of it.

Heart thudding hard against his chest, he pulls into the Lynn Canyon gravel parking lot and kills the ignition. His tongue turns into sand as he stares at the alabaster foot painted on the side of the house in front of him. His fingers turn ashen around the steering wheel. The prickly feeling of presentiment increases.

And, for the first time in his life, Moey Thorpe feels truly afraid.

He is scared of making a mistake and looking foolish. He is scared of trying to attain something that really matters to him because he is scared that he won't be able to attain it. If he doesn't voice his hopes, if he never tries to achieve what his heart truly wants, then at least the possibility that he *can* succeed *if only he tries* still exists. But once he tries and fails, then that possibility disappears; he will be faced with the stark reality that his dream is beyond him.

Moey has seen such fear grip kickboxing students prior to competitions. For the first time ever he truly understands their lock-jawed panic, their icy shivers, their loose bladders. "Your fear is only an imagined fear," Master Zahbar always roars at Moey. "It's a negative response that reinforces vulnerability and incompetence. Think positive! Don't *permit* yourself to be afraid. Be victorious!"

For the past three years Moey has repeated those words to his terrified students. And yet now he understands there is nothing imagined about certain terrors, such as the terror that now seizes him as he looks at the Footstop. Trying to think positive thoughts while in the clutches of such a fear is like trying to tell a diabetic to produce enough insulin through sheer willpower. And trying to ignore his fear is like trying to ignore the impending 500-foot drop of a gondola that has lost its brakes.

Breathe, Moey instructs himself. *Breathe.*

This, at least, seems good advice. His watering, fixed eyes and swimming brain certainly agree — breathing is good.

He sucks in another lungful of air.

For a full five minutes Moey relishes the triumph of successfully breathing. Then, before his startled mind can react, his body launches itself out of the Plymouth and into the driving rain. His legs sprint along the rock path to the Footstop as his back obligingly ducks beneath dripping Douglas fir branches. His enormous hands grasp the quaint brass knob of the café and rattle the door. So paralyzed is his mind that he doesn't notice the sign taped in the window, let alone the words inscribed on it. When the knob refuses to turn in his hands, his fingers ball into mallets and pound the door in a frenzy.

A light goes on in the café. A pale hand pulls a lacy drape to one side. A shock of frizzy red hair pops into view.

Only when Karen opens the door do Moey's hands stop their frantic pummelling.

"You teach karate," she says, blinking at his rain-splattered uniform. She is leaning on a pair of crutches.

"Kickboxing," he gasps.

"Oh." She shuffles back a pace or two, the rubber ends of her crutches squeaking on the hardwood floor. "Come in."

Shivering, he does so and shuts the door behind himself.

"I didn't expect to see you so soon. Not that it matters," she adds hastily. "I'm grateful for your help last night."

"No problem," he says through chattering teeth.

"Would ... would you like a cup of tea? Officially, we're closed, so I didn't do any baking. Because of my foot, you see. But I can make you some tea ..."

He wants to say no, to blurt out his purpose before his terror-spiked mind can resume control of his body.

"Tea would be great," he says instead.

"I'll put the kettle on." She crutch-walks to the back of the café and ducks behind a heavy curtain. A moment later Moey hears the soft snick of a door closing.

The urge to flee overwhelms him. Karen doesn't know where he lives, probably can't even remember his name; if he leaves now, she'll be none the wiser to his purpose and he can continue his safe existence as a kickboxing instructor without having threatened the fragility of his dream.

He turns to the door behind him. He imagines the Hand of Fate upon his shoulder, or more aptly, the breath of the white stag upon his neck. With a shiver he twists away from the door. And, for the first time, he becomes aware of his surroundings.

The café looks like a museum currently celebrating a Mexican festival. A flock of brightly coloured piñatas dangles above a French Provincial trestle table. At either end of the table stands a pair of empty cake stands, book-ending an antique cash register, a pair of scissors, a roll of tape, and two rolls of wrapping paper.

Moey slowly surveys the café. A half-dozen pairs of wingback chairs are strategically placed throughout the room. Between each pair of chairs stands an antique coffee table, and beneath each coffee table rest two plastic Scholl's Footbath Massagers. Their electric cords disappear into slits cut into the thick Persian rug covering the hardwood floor.

Here and there sculptures of feet sit on white pedestals. Antique cabinets line the walls. Trancelike, Moey wanders towards the first cabinet. On its mahogany shelves stand rows of beaded moccasins, Dutch clogs, and woollen slippers. The next cabinet contains foot-shaped soap dishes, clay pots of foot balm and soaking salts, pumice stones, foot-shaped towels, and pearl-handled nail clippers.

On the shelves of an adjacent cupboard, scrolled charts of acupuncture, reflexology, and horoscopes-for-the-foot vie for space with handmade address books, each the shape of a foot and bearing the title *Footnotes* on its cover.

Flower vases in the shape of feet, foot-shaped oven mitts, stationery bearing winged feet, DVDs entitled *Foot Care & You*, earrings and necklaces of feet, foot pillows, foot stools, key chains, address labels, plant pots, picture frames ... everywhere Moey looks, he sees feet. Even the piñatas, he belatedly realizes, are bright papier mâché feet.

He picks up what looks like a small jam jar, its lid covered by a square of red gingham tied at the mouth with a big red bow. Aloud he reads the words: "Fresh Homemade Foot Butter." He looks at the brown-speckled stuff in the jar, and his fingers tingle with revulsion.

"Cinnamon spread," Karen says behind him.

Moey almost drops the jar as he spins around.

"Cinnamon spread," Karen repeats, hobbling into the room. "It's very good. Made with fresh butter, cinnamon, and brown sugar. Delicious on hot toast or scones. It's one of our best sellers."

He looks down at the jar in his hand. "Foot butter," he repeats stupidly.

"I had to call it that, otherwise Morris wouldn't let it in the shop."

"Morris?"

"My husband." She flushes. "I convinced him that as part of a balanced diet, essential oils and fatty acids maintain the health of the foot. In the summer I sell an average of twenty jars a day."

"Ah." He thinks for a moment. "How much?"

"Seven-fifty a jar. Costs me less than half that to make it."

"Good profit."

"Yes." She shifts her weight on her crutches. "Uh, the tea is ready, but I can't carry it in. Could you?"

"What? Sure. Of course." He replaces the jar of foot butter on the shelf and, after giving himself a mental shake much as a dog physically does upon rousing from a slumber, he ducks after her behind the heavy curtain.

Dazed, he follows her through a small workshop (*she must make everything*, a small part of his mind computes), through a door, and into a small sun-yellow kitchen. On the yellow Formica table sits a pot of tea in a foot-shaped tea cozy beside a pot of sugar and a carton of cream.

"We could sit in here if you prefer ..."

"No," he replies, so quickly and forcefully that her hazel eyes widen.

"I mean, if it's okay with you," he says, trying to smile reassuringly, "I'd like to go back to the café."

She nods uncertainly. "Of course."

He picks up the teapot, sugar, and cream and together they return to the teahouse. A few minutes of strained silence later, Moey finds himself slouched in one of the wingback chairs sipping a cup of Earl Grey. Karen sits beside him, her broken foot propped on a coffee table. They both resolutely study the piñatas dangling from the ceiling.

When the silence reaches the snapping point, Moey clears his throat. It is time to Listen to Fate. Karen looks at him expectantly.

"You, uh, you get many customers?" he asks. Even to himself, he sounds as if he's been sucking on helium.

"Lots in the summer. Tourist season, you see. Some days there's barely enough room to stand in here."

"Oh." He clears his throat again, trying to lower his tone an octave or seven. His vision jumps erratically, his heart pounds hard against his throat. "And the rest of the time?"

"When a tour bus pulls in, I'm swamped. And every holiday — Easter, Valentine's Day, whatever — it gets busy with people showing their relatives around."

"I see."

Silence again. Moey's thoughts churn. His palms feel as slick as wet lasagna noodles. He gulps down a swallow of tea and scalds the back of his throat.

"*Haugh ...*" he begins, then coughs his throat clear and

tries again. "How are you going to manage with your foot like that if you have to carry things from the kitchen and back?"

"Morris is going to buy a hot plate today to set up in here. And he's going to help me do the baking each night."

"Ah." He sips his tea again. Another long, awkward silence descends. Karen studies the piñatas once more.

Do it, Moey tells himself fiercely. *Ask her.*

I can't, a hitherto unknown portion of his person whines.

Don't be a wimp, he answers, and takes a deep, quavering breath. Puts down his cup. Faces her. "Karen?"

She turns to him. "Yes?"

"I ... I would like ..." He wipes his sweaty palms on the knees of his kickboxing uniform, tries again. "I was wondering ..."

"Yes?"

"I would like ..."

She leans forward. "Yes?"

"I'd like to work here," he blurts. "As a belly dancer."

Magic — what exactly is it? Most people don't recognize it when they see it, but Karen has always known about its existence, has been able to correctly identify it. She's taught her children to recognize it, too.

"Look, Candice, magic! We push this silver thing, and voilà, warm water comes out. Clean, warm water to wash a baby's hands in. Magic!"

And: "Shall we gaze into the crystal ball and see what pictures we can find? Press the magic button, Andy. There! Look, there's Big Bird. You made Big Bird appear in the big glass window! How did you do that, you clever boy? And we can hear him, too!"

And: "With a flick of the magic wand I shall dispel

darkness from this room. Let's count together — one, two, three ..."

Water faucets, television remotes, light switches — for Karen they represent magic. It exists all around her: telephones, automobiles, ice cubes tinkling in a glass of cold tea. Rather than explain these phenomena to her children in the technical language of the witches and wizards who have created them (a mathematical language she equates with spells), she defines them as magic.

A plumber in oil-slicked coveralls is a warlock who threads brass and copper tubes together and commands water to appear at her house whenever she desires. A gas fitter is a sorcerer who combines invisible gas, complex equations, and wire circuits to provide her with warmth on a frosty night. The midwife who assisted at the births of Candice and Andy is an earth goddess; the woman who taught them swimming lessons a water sprite; the Lynn Canyon forest ranger a sylvan deity. Godkins, fays, spellmasters, and shamans — this is how Karen sees car mechanics, nurses, teachers, and surgeons.

For as long as she has lived in her own house, she has left thumb-size portions of food on her kitchen windowsill. Not to please ethereal spirits, and certainly not to ward off werefolk or devilings; these offerings are instead a tangible, visual recognition of the abundance of her universe, of the constant miracles in her life.

Morris has grown so accustomed to this ritual that he reminds her to place a wee saucer of food on the sill if she forgets to do so; its absence makes him uncomfortable, like viewing a crooked picture on a wall. Candice, until she turned fifteen, would occasionally place a pretty feather, a handful of forget-me-nots, or an unusual stone upon that sill. (Now she has matured beyond such superstitions and chooses to ignore the saucer's existence. She doesn't dare deride it, though, beyond rolling her eyes.) Andy—straight A, encyclopedia-loving Andy — regards the saucer on the sill as something sound, something necessary. He justifies this feeling by telling himself that even the astronauts and technicians at NASA respect certain superstitions, especially after the flight of *Apollo 13*.

But the white hart is a magic too unusual for Karen; it's an oddity far beyond the realm of her world. Despite the strangeness of her birthmarks, despite the way she views electricity and automation, despite her eclectic religious upbringing, she cannot accept the appearance of the white hart. It has to be a hallucination; things like that don't happen in the real world. It isn't magic; it's ... imaginary.

Yet listening to Moey Thorpe talk about the connection he sees between belly dancing at the Footstop and the appearance of the white hart, she can't deny that the hart appeared. Here this man sits before her admitting that he saw *her* hallucination. Ergo, it cannot have been a hallucination. That majestic white beast did materialize on the rocky banks of Lynn Canyon.

Ice feathers brush against Karen's skin. Her life, she feels, will never be the same again.

Chapter Four

Egret Van Gorder can't think properly. From the puckish tip of his upturned nose, which exists just below whey-coloured hair and two eyes as blue as God's heaven, down to his sneaker-clad feet, fever grips him. Every inch of his lean, hard body effuses fever — in his sharp replies, in his constant activity, in his Tommy Hilfiger clothes and the snap of his torso as he powers off the board into a one-and-a-half pike. They all speak of fever. Pussy fever.

He has it bad. No amount of jerking off, no amount of partying or diving practice, can drive this wild, raging need from under his skin. As desperate as a junkie looking for a fix, he needs to plunge himself into the warm, wriggling wetness of a woman. This makes him intensely aggressive on the trampoline, makes him drive too fast in his dad's car, makes him steal the Man's custom-built Virago 1100 and take it for a spin around the block in the pouring rain.

Egret Van Gorder can't be held responsible for his state; he is, after all, a teenager, and therefore a slave to his hormones. A *virgin* teenager, to be exact.

Not that Egret isn't attractive. Sure, his fingers have slid into the mysterious salty depths of more than one gasping girl. His lips have closed around sweet, firm nipples while his pelvis has ground the attached, fully-clothed hips into the bleachers at Mahon Stadium. But he has yet to submerge his submarine into the waters of fair Atlantis.

He is certain that out of the 239 guys in Sutherland Secondary School, he is the only male virgin left. And the real bitch of that is his age; because of his intense training schedule, he is in a special half-time program at school. This decelerated learning plan makes him a couple of years older than his classmates, and so here he is, a fucking *nineteen*-year-old virgin.

Once, he could have had Lucy Ng. He was *that* close to breaking down. Instead, Lucy's robust lips nearly ripped his dick from its roots during a vodka-laced blow job, and he actually enjoyed the ordeal, despite the alarming bruises that appeared the day after.

Why did he relish such brutish treatment?

Because while Lucy was trying to suck his intestines out through his cock, he had visions of another pair of lips doing the same thing. Lips that belonged to a slim, aloof creature with green eyes. Lips attached to a body that held a second set of lips nestled beneath a mound of red hair between smooth white legs. Lips that belonged to Candice Morton.

To those fleshy lower lips and those lips alone he vowed to lose his virginity.

With a complete absence of thought that is, in many respects, akin to the fever that grips young Egret, Karen sits at her kitchen table and stares blindly at a magazine. Since Moey Thorpe left her at noon, she hasn't turned a page. It is now 3:15.

On rainy days such as these when nary a customer appears, Karen works in her shop creating Footstop merchandise. If she feels uninspired, she flips through magazines instead, combing the pages for ideas on new products. Today even that is beyond her.

She has a hundred other tasks crying out for her attention: as a volunteer for the North Shore Neighbourhood House, she has pamphlets to deliver; as a canvasser for the Canadian Cancer Society, she has doors to knock on and donations to collect; as a mother to a budding inventor, she has a list of peculiar hardware items to shop for. But again she is incapable of turning her attention to any of these tasks.

Instead, she tries to recall her conversation with Moey, but she can't. All she can remember is his burnt-toast-brown eyes fixed so intently upon her, his pulse pounding so visibly in his thick neck. And that one phrase he used, which keeps tolling like a bell over and over in her mind: *When I die, I don't want to regret how I've lived, and I know if I don't do this, that's how I'll die. Full of regret.*

Her birthmarks still tingle at his words.

A thousand questions now whirl in her mind. Why does he want to dance for tips only at the Footstop? Why not at a Middle Eastern restaurant? Okay, okay, so he believes that the white hart wants him to dance here, at the teahouse, but still ... what makes a kick boxer want to belly-dance, anyway? And how on earth is she going to explain this to Morris?

"I shouldn't have said yes," she murmurs. "Why did I say yes?"

The front doorbell rings, jolting her out of her daze. Wondering irritably who it can be — only Jehovah's Witnesses use the front door — she fumbles for her crutches and struggles out of the chair. The doorbell peals again as she lurches along the hall.

"Coming!" she shouts. "Hold your horses!"

Squeak, lurch, swing; squeak, lurch, swing — breathless and red-cheeked, she makes it to the end of the hall and fumbles with the door handle, crutches lodged under her armpits.

A rain-soaked teenager with startling blue eyes stands on the doorstep, hunched in an Adidas sweatshirt. Like all boys his age, he wears no coat and towers several inches above her.

"Uh, could I speak to Candice?"

"She's not back from school yet. She usually isn't home until four."

"Oh." He shuffles a bit.

A swirl of cold wind shoves the door from Karen's hand, thumps it against the wall, and splatters her with raindrops. She shivers and gropes for the door again. "Well, I'll tell her you came by …?"

"Egret. No, don't bother. I'll hang around till four."

"Out here? You'll catch pneumonia. Come inside and wait."

"It's no problem if I wait out here, Mrs. Morton —"

"Mrs. Morton is my husband's mother," she says reflexively. "My name is Karen."

He grins. "Karen."

"Come in, come in, it's freezing out here. Shoot the bolt across when you shut the door."

She pivots and starts down the hall. A pause, then the door thuds closed at her back. The deadbolt snicks into its slot. Footsteps follow her as she staggers down the hall towards the kitchen.

"How did you bust your foot, Mrs. — uh … Karen?"

"I fell in the canyon. Trying to catch my cat."

"Off a cliff?"

"Nothing so impressive. I slipped on the creek bank. Do you want some tea?"

"Don't, like, go to any trouble."

"I was making some, anyway." She leans the crutches against the counter, hops on one foot to the cupboard, and takes out two mugs.

He scrapes a chair away from the table and slouches into it. "So you fell in the canyon, eh? You're lucky you didn't land in the creek. People die like that every summer."

"I know. Sugar? Milk?"

"Yeah, whatever."

"So where do you know Candice from? You look too old to be in her class."

"We're in the same grade." He bites the words off. She takes the cue and searches for a change of topic. He beats her to it. "She tell you I'm training for the Olympics? Diving. Won the bronze by a half point at the PanAm Games this summer."

"Really? *This* summer? That's ... incredible." She stares over her shoulder at him as she fills the kettle.

He grins and flicks a wet lock of hair from his eyes. "Man, you look totally amazed. Like you didn't think I could be good at anything."

The kettle spills over. Karen hastily switches off the tap and plugs the kettle into an outlet. "Yes, well, you don't look like you could ... I mean, you look so *normal*, so average ..." She blushes.

The telephone rings, loud and shrill.

Saved by the bell, Karen thinks as she leaps to answer the phone, forgetting in her fluster her one-legged state.

As her full weight thumps down on her casted ankle, she slips, grabs for the counter, catches the kettle instead. There is a brief, fragile resistance as the plug halts her fall for a nanosecond. Then, with the alarming image of the silver kettle descending upon her forehead, she plunges to the floor.

Pain and blackness.

She couldn't have been unconscious for long, for the first thing she becomes aware of is the sound of the answering machine clicking on. In fact, as she listens dizzily to her own recorded voice inviting the caller to please leave a message, she speculates that on the whole she couldn't have been unconscious for more than sixty seconds.

"Yeah, Mom, it's me. I'm over at Gloria's, school project, you know? I won't be home till later, so don't make me anything for dinner. Besides, I'm on a diet, a totally serious one this time. Maybe a salad, but that's all. *Ciao.*"

Click.

Then another voice, much closer. "Mrs. Morton? Mrs. Morton? Shit! Mrs. Morton?"

She licks her lips, tastes blood, and carefully opens one eye. She winces at the stab of pain produced by the kitchen lights.

"Karen," she hoarsely whispers. "My name's Karen. Mrs. Morton is my husband's mother."

"Shit! You all right? Want me to phone for an ambulance or something?"

"No, I'll be fine," she says quickly. "I can't go to Emergency twice in two days. They'll think my husband's beating me."

"Yeah, but —"

"Could you just help me up? I'll be fine."

"You sure about that? You got a real double whammy there. The kettle bounced right off your head. I mean, it totally flew across the kitchen. And then you cracked your skull on the floor."

"No, really," she says with as much reassurance as she can muster, for by now she is starting to feel ill. "I'll be fine."

He shrugs. "If you say so."

"Could you help me up?" She extends a trembling hand. He frowns, shrugs again, grabs her hand, and pulls.

Kettle water *all* over the floor ...

Her feet skid out from under her as if she's on ice, and she shoots between his parted, braced legs like a professional skater. He loses his balance, cries out, then topples onto her; this time, instead of seeing a kettle descend upon her forehead, she watches Egret's crotch plummet towards her.

More pain, a great deal more, as his groin lands fully onto her face, and the back of her skull thunks against the floor again. It feels as if a truck is trying to take her head off; hot electricity courses down her spine.

"Fuck!" he yells, and scrabbles on top of her, slipping and sliding like a Jell-O wrestler, the fly of his jeans scraping against her lips. He gets off her, flustered and red-faced. "Slipped," he mumbles. "Sorry."

"S'okay," she whispers, closing her eyes as the vise against her head tightens until she thinks she'll faint.

"Maybe, uh, maybe I'll just wipe up the water first," he says.

She hears movement, followed by swishing sounds.

"Hey, you okay, Mrs. Morton? You aren't looking too good."

"Not feeling good," she croaks, keeping her eyes closed, feeling dizzy, feeling vomit burn against her throat. "I think I should go to bed."

"You sure you don't want me to call the ambulance?"

"No. Bedroom."

There is a pause. Her cranium could be an acorn in a nutcracker; her spine might as well have been scalded with hot oil. He mumbles something; she can't concentrate on what he is saying and doesn't much care to. Then his hands grope clumsily under her armpits and he hoists her into a sitting position. She feels his knees against her back, hears him suck in a deep breath, and then the kitchen turns bright orange and slanted as he whooshes her upright.

"Slower!" she cries hoarsely, and vomits across the floor.

"Shit!"

To his credit, he doesn't release her but continues to hold her upright.

"This is *not* good! C'mon, Mrs. Morton, let me phone someone, a neighbour at least!"

"Stop calling me that! Karen, my name's Karen!"

They stand in silence for a moment. Lightning and thunder rage inside her head. She keeps her eyes fixed on the splatter of vomit on the floor. *At least no peas show up in it,* she thinks inanely.

"Could you pass me something to wipe myself with, please?" she eventually asks.

Without a word — and still holding her upright — he stretches towards the paper towel rack and yanks off a ream. She accepts it without turning and gingerly wipes the sour flecks from her lips and chin. Crumpling the soiled paper, she lets it fall to the floor. Silence hangs between them.

"I'm sorry," she finally whispers. "I didn't mean to snap at you."

"Hey, no problem. You cracked your head. You're not feeling too great."

"It's just that I've had a very strange day."

"Understand totally. I mean, a blow like that would've knocked most people into last year. You must have one tough brain box."

She lets that sink in for a moment, uncertain if it's a

compliment. "Yes, well," she eventually says, "I'm sorry if I shouted at you. And vomited in front of you."

"Forget it."

His chest moves behind her — a shrug, she guesses.

"You still want me to take you to the bedroom?"

"Yes," she whispers. And, unaccountably, she flushes.

As if handling a brittle, unpredictable jack-in-the-box, Egret carefully places Karen on her bed.

Shit, does she look white, a totally unhealthy sort of white, he thinks. *The kind of white that floods the Man's face if he goes without a drink for a couple of days.*

Egret looks down at Karen as she lies there, still as a brick, eyes squeezed shut. The water from the kettle has plastered her hippie-style dress against her breasts — full breasts unencumbered by a bra. He can still feel the mellow warmth of them pressed against his hands where he reached under her armpits to haul her upright. Unwittingly, his eyes travel down the length of her.

Her legs, as smooth and white as shaving cream, shine in the gloom of the bedroom. Nice legs. Like Candice's, only fuller ... *Shit, I'm getting a hard-on!* Quickly, he steps backwards, away from the bed. Her eyes flutter open a little.

"Thanks," she whispers. "Sorry about this."

"Don't apologize." He fidgets, rams his hands into his pockets. "Look, you want me to get you something? Aspirin maybe?"

"That'd be great. Bathroom cupboard, behind the mirror."

"You want the light on in here?"

"No, definitely not. Thank you."

He nods, she closes her eyes again, and he beats a hasty retreat out of the room.

Is he losing his mind, giving the once-over to someone his mom's age? Not that Karen looks as ancient as his old lady — fact is, Karen and Candice look like sisters. Only Karen weighs more, looks like the older sister, the experienced one. The one who really knows what to do in bed ...

"Fuck," he mutters, shoving open a door and searching for the bathroom. He realizes his mistake and starts to back out. Then stops. "Candice's room," he whispers, shooting a look over his shoulder down the hall. Of course, no one is there. His heart beats a little harder, and very carefully he pushes the door all the way open and steps inside.

Posters of movie stars and rock bands cover blue-flowered wallpaper. On top of a white dresser a stack of *Cosmopolitan* magazines competes for space with a regiment of lipsticks. Dirty laundry overflows from a teddy-bear-shaped wicker basket. Ahead of him an unmade bed still holds the imprint of where Candice slept. A black rug with a clown on it sits in the middle of the floor.

Like the needle of a compass swinging north, Egret veers in the direction of the bed.

He can smell her, that heady scent of lemon shampoo, blue jeans, and lilac deodorant. The urge to lie on the bed and jack off overwhelms him.

Quickly, he diverts his gaze from the rumpled bedsheets. His eyes fall instead on the teddy-bear laundry basket. Specifically, on a pair of panties draped over its left eye like a pirate's patch. Black lace panties.

A shiver ripples through him.

There, right in front of him, is evidence of Candice's womanhood. It is nature's statement that she is ready for him. And he wants her, is he *ever* ready for her. Stiffer than a damn crowbar.

He throws another look over his shoulder. What he wouldn't give if the woman lying in the bedroom next door was Candice, Candice waiting for him, Candice all thigh-slippery with expectation ...

"But it's her mother and she's waiting for you to get her some aspirin, so get your ass out of here," he chides himself.

Yet he can't. He can't leave those panties there. Without thinking he steps forward, snatches them off the teddy-bear basket, and stuffs them in his pocket. For a moment he stares at the wicker bear, afraid its unwavering eyes are warning him to put the panties back. His heart bongs against his larynx.

"Forget it, buddy," he whispers to the bear. "They're mine now." He turns and leaves the room.

More than once as he rummages through the bathroom cupboard for a bottle of aspirin, his hand dives into his pocket and he fingers the black lace cowering there. He sniffs his fingers and swallows against the saliva that springs into his mouth from the iron-ammonia smell of her crotch. Totally turned on and partially revolted, he suppresses the urge to lick his fingertips.

Never once does he even notice the microwave by the toilet.

Candice's mother is still stretched out motionless on her bed when he returns to the darkness of her room. He stands for a moment in the doorway, looking at her legs exposed almost to the thigh, at her full hips, her big tits, her smooth neck.

He stumbles forward, slopping water from the plastic bathroom cup over his sneakers.

"Here's your aspirin, Mrs. — Karen. I brought the whole bottle. I didn't know how much you wanted. And water, I brought you some water."

She shifts a little, and the rustle of her skin against the bedsheets makes him break out in gooseflesh. He keeps his eyes firmly averted, keeps talking.

"I'll just open it up for you, okay? Then I'd better get going. My old man'll wonder where I am. Look, I'm putting it down on this table here, right by your elbow. That okay with you?"

"Thank you, yes."

He backs away, looking everywhere but at her. "You going to be okay?"

"I'll be fine. Andy should be home soon. I'll be fine."

"Good. Well, then, guess I'll be going."

"Yes. Thank you, Egret. Sorry about ... all this."

"No problem."

He hesitates for a moment, then turns and flees.

Chapter Five

Panic descends on Andy. More than anything else — well, as much as any of his other phobias — Andy is terrified that his parents will divorce. Plenty of kids in his class have two sets of parents, and they wear that shameful brand with as much dignity as nine-year-olds can muster. Kids desperately rely on their parents for order, for conformity, for equilibrium — *everyone* knows that; divorce screams the opposite.

It is an unwritten rule that the divorce of one's parents should never be targeted during a schoolyard attack, but in Andy's case, he knows things would be different. Kids like to pick on him, even now in the new school where, theoretically, they have no reason to think of him as a wimp, save for his meatless limbs, pearly skin, and telescope glasses.

If his parents divorce, his life will become sheer hell. A lonely hell at that. His father is his only friend. And his mother ... he chokes back tears as he cleans his mother's vomit off the kitchen floor.

To Andy, his mom is a red-haired Marilyn Monroe, an awesome alabaster-skinned vixen. When he first heard the word *vixen*, he imagined a kind of industrious ermine, but a *Concise Oxford English Dictionary* set him clear on that misconception a year ago. Now that he knows the real definition of vixen — a female fox — he *still* feels his mother lives up to the word. The term *alabaster-skinned* dignifies the appellation, gives it a royalness that erases all negative meaning. In his eyes, beyond a doubt, his mother is an alabaster-skinned vixen.

And he knows, with equal conviction and a great deal of fearful guilt, that his father somehow falls short of being an adequate vixen keeper.

So the stark evidence that his mother has been entertaining people this afternoon — a tea tray with two dirty cups on it, and two more cups cradling new tea bags awaiting on the counter — accompanied with the inexplicable vomit on the floor, fallen electric kettle, and his mom's damp dress, sends tears of dread racing to clog Andy's sinuses.

Sure, she *said* she must have caught the flu. Sure, she *said* she heard Dilly knock the kettle off the counter while she was lying in bed. But what about the four cups, the pulled-out chairs? And most damning of all — for it guaranteed that her guests weren't female friends — what about her whispered request to refrain from mentioning any of this to his father?

So Andy not only clears up the vomit while his mother painstakingly hauls herself out of bed to prepare dinner, but he also cleans and puts away the teacups, even washes the unused ones, feeling they have, in some way, been sullied. His guilt at concealing this evidence and agreeing to withhold this information from his father makes him miserable. His mother seems unaware of his misery as she hobbles into the kitchen, looking far too ashen for even an alabaster-skinned vixen.

They peel potatoes and carrots together as the clock ticks towards dinnertime. Not once does either of them speak.

In a way, Candice hasn't lied. She and Gloria *are* collaborating on a school project. Sort of. Like, it is biology, isn't it?

Okay, so sure, she and Gloria are no longer in the same biology class, but hello? Is that her fault? If Candice's demented parents hadn't hauled her out of her high school, then, of course, she and Gloria would still be in the same class, and they wouldn't have to sneak around like this against their parents' wishes. No, not wishes: demands. Like, *court orders.*

"Mr. and Mrs. Vermicelli agree with us," Candice's parents said. "This is the best for both of you girls."

As if! Putting them both into different high schools only guaranteed they *had* to see each other more often, 'cause Candice wasn't able to make friends at her new school. Not award-winning friends, anyhow. Not friends you could *trust*.

As Candice strips off her sweater and casually tosses it onto Gloria's bed, she feels another twinge of guilt for leaving that hasty message on the answering machine at home. She deliberately spoke fast, hoping Karen would still be searching for her crutches by the time Candice got off the phone.

Of course, there would be a major crisis to deal with later for even admitting to being at Gloria's house, but why bother lying? Gloria's rank brother saw Candice come in the back door when he *should* have been out smashing his head against other football players. He had a practice scheduled, Gloria said so, but no, the ignoramus caught a cold, came home straight from school, and it was guaranteed that he would tell his parents, and they in turn would fall all over themselves to phone Candice's parents.

"Don't worry about it, okay?" Gloria now says. She cracks her gum and unbuttons her jeans. "If you stick to the school project story, what can they do about it? Crucify us?"

"Yeah, whatever," Candice says with a shrug. She pulls her Calvin Klein sports bra over her head and drops it to the floor. From the corner of one eye, she sees Gloria — naked, olive-skinned, raven-haired — check the lock on her bedroom door and turn the music higher. Her burgeoning body reminds Candice of one of those Italian sausages Mr. Vermicelli sells — shiny, spicy, stuffed so full it threatens to burst its seams.

Parental-focused guilt flees and instead wet impatience fills Candice. Her nipples go rigid, the skin on her scalp tautens. She continues to undress, taking her time, oh-so-casual ...

But what if Gloria doesn't make the first move? Then what? As if Candice will! No, it has to be Gloria, always Gloria, 'cause Candice is too cool for that, even though between her thighs she is steaming and pulsing like a potato in a microwave.

But what if Gloria *doesn't* make the first move? What if Gloria starts laughing instead? What if all their prior games — none as committed as this — have just been part of a setup to get Candice completely exposed while some hidden camera records her total humiliation?

Gloria approaches her. "You're just so *spinal*," she says, running a finger across Candice's back. "I'd totally kill to be as thin as you."

Candice shrugs, though her skin puckers at Gloria's touch and the baked potato between her thighs releases a jet of steam.

"And your skin is *sooo* white, like a swan or something."

"Yeah, but I burn easily. In the summer, you know." She can't turn around, can't face Gloria. Her heart is a bullhorn in her ears, her legs whimper to sink into the bed. So *bad* she wants to turn around, to press and slide her skin all over Gloria in a wild feeding frenzy, but she can't, no way.

She feels two cool, soft breasts press against her back, feels Gloria's fuzz against her own naked buttocks.

"You sure you want to go ahead with this? You don't have to, you know."

"I know," Candice says calmly, almost indifferently.

"We've got plenty of time to change our minds. Mom and Dad won't be home for a couple more hours yet."

"Do *you* want to change your mind?"

"Do *you*?"

Candice shrugs again, as if she cares less.

"I mean, we've talked about this, right?" Gloria says. "It's not as if we're lesbians or anything. We're just practising, so we don't make idiots of ourselves when it comes time to do it with a guy. Right?"

Candice doesn't want to hear *that* word, not right now when she's burbling and rippling down there, all briny with heat. So she turns and says, "Sometimes you talk too much, Gloria. Let's just fuck, okay?"

And Gloria says, "Okay."

Which is, like, what she's *supposed* to say.

Morris finishes work at 5:15, says good-night to Clara, his receptionist, and heads home. He thinks of Karen while he drives — specifically, how he first met her. His last appointment prompted the memory: Penny Edmonds, a twenty-five-year-old delicately laced with lavender perfume. For a half-second, until Morris noticed her weak arches, her feet took his breath away.

Karen had feet like that when he first met her — slender and smooth, the nails tiny translucent crescents topping perfect alabaster toes. Impeccable cuticles cupped nail bed to toe. The ankles were slim and strong, the heels uncracked, the creamy skin flawless, soft, and cool as satin.

Usually, even the best feet suffer some flaw, some minor imperfection. The big toes sprout a few hairs, or a thick vein protrudes on the ankle bone. Toes can look like squat sausages, not in proportion to the length of the foot, or like thin, groping fingers. Something *always* mars the foot's elegance.

So although Penny Edmonds's weak arches are only a minor flaw, Morris's connoisseur eye noticed them instantly. As he drives, a pang shoots through him and, wistfully, he remembers the first time he saw Karen's feet.

Lying on Ambleside Beach, baring his lean, student-white frame to a lukewarm sun, eyes safely shielded beneath his *Hawaii Five-O* sunglasses, Morris was studying the myriad of feet walking by him. He was stretched out on his belly, of course — so many exposed feet in a constant dizzy parade provoked an impertinent bulge in his blue Speedo bathing suit.

Then they passed him: naked, dusted with sand, a thin band of gold around the right ankle — the perfect feet. He gaped, he became dizzy, a strangled cry escaped his throat. As the feet walked away, he scrabbled from his beach towel and stumbled after them.

Above the smell of hot dogs, coconut oil, and vinegar-doused french fries, the smell of lavender perfume drifted, coming from the owner of those wondrous feet. Like a drunken man, Morris introduced himself, ignoring the fact that the girl was at least ten years younger than himself. He was immune to the derision on the faces of her friends. All he cared about was her feet.

Morris shifts on the cracked vinyl seat of his car, restless from the memory. He carefully applies the brakes as he approaches the corner of Mountain Highway and Lynn Valley Road and admonishes himself to concentrate. This area is rife with hazards, positively rife. Bicyclists cluster around the Starbucks coffee shop to his right, attracted to the heavy, cloying aroma of roasted java beans like hummingbirds to nectar. That's what they always remind Morris of, those cyclists — gaily coloured, spandex-sheathed hummingbirds. And the bicycles are hummingbird wheelchairs.

To his left, smelling of gasoline and grape bubblegum, stands a 7-Eleven convenience store made hazardous by the horde of teenagers lurking outside, dressed in their immensely baggy pants, ski toques, and brand-name sweatshirts. More than once Morris has witnessed an accident between a cyclist, a teenager, and a car at this busy junction. And Morris hates accidents. Getting Karen pregnant was an accident.

He frowns and turns the corner onto Lynn Valley Road a little too sharply.

Morris would have eventually married Karen even if she hadn't ... if he hadn't ... if the Accident hadn't occurred, because as well as her feet, he was infatuated with everything else about her — her bubble-filled laugh, her bizarre religious background, her clumsiness, her attention to his needs, her wildly frizzy hair, her industriousness, her loyalty, her willingness to try anything. This last was his undoing, since it provoked the Accident.

Never once did she flinch, hesitate, sneer, or display shock at his attraction to her feet. Not even the first exquisite time he placed her feet sole to sole and slid his penis into the wonderful, smooth hole her two marble-like arches made. Whether he suggested inserting one of his own immaculate big toes into her, or masturbating himself while she lovingly cradled his feet between her lush breasts, Karen was willing to try anything.

And so when she shyly suggested that perhaps, if he didn't mind so much, they might actually try intercourse ... well, he felt obligated to perform.

Of course, he enjoyed it immensely — he was still able to feel her exquisite feet sliding up and down the backs of his calves as he pumped away. But being a fool, he assumed she was protected. A mistake, that. An accident.

Morris turns — again, a trifle too sharply — onto Peters Road and thinks: *It shouldn't have happened. The odds were against it.*

He recalls something from the biology classes he was required to take to get his podiatry degree, something about a woman being fertile for only twenty-four hours once a month, and out of the twenty million sperm the average man ejaculates into a vagina, only fifty reach the egg alive. The odds of Karen falling pregnant that first time were *entirely* against it. But, nonetheless, it happened.

Morris's fingers whiten on the steering wheel, and the pleasure of the whole memory vanishes, chased away by self-recrimination. He turns too quickly onto his gravel driveway, tires splashing through potholes and kicking pebbles into the street.

No, he can't forgive himself for his oversight, for not ensuring Karen was on the Pill before so glibly agreeing to have intercourse with her. Because pregnancy altered her. Specifically, it changed her feet. Where once smooth, slim ankles existed, stouter ankles marred by small, permanent folds now lived. Curvaceous arches were exchanged for slightly flattened ones; two perfect size 7AA feet were transformed into two size eights. During her pregnancy, calluses rudely took up residence on either side of her big toes, and even to this day, they refuse to leave. In a word: ruined. Morris ruined the only pair of perfect feet he's ever encountered.

Wearily, he climbs out of his Tercel and trudges through the rain to the back door, wondering how Karen can possibly love him after what he did to her.

Andy has fallen into the habit of visiting the suspension bridge every evening as dusk descends. How this compulsion started, he doesn't remember; he's not even conscious that it *is* a compulsion, that within him ticks some clock that guides him to the creaking, slimy planks of the hanging bridge at precisely the same hour each day.

After he finishes his homework, or practises his trumpet, or helps his mother chop broccoli/carrots/eggplant for dinner, he slips into his jacket and shoes and races to the bridge. Every dusk. His mother warns him not to be late for dinner.

If it's raining, he runs, rubber boots splashing through the puddles that pock the gravel road of the park; if it's sunny, he also runs, sucking in swift, deep breaths of moss-and-cedar-scented air. No, he doesn't run; he flies. Occasionally, he flaps his arms, glasses bouncing up and down on his nose and turning his vision staccato and trembly.

In the fall and winter, dusk comes early, almost as soon as he arrives home from school, and the park is silent save for the roar of the creek. Sometimes a dog walker passes him; he knows a few of the dogs by name. There is Bear, the barrel-size black Labrador with ropes of drool hanging from his mouth, and there is Grizzly, the exuberant malamute who stinks like a mildewy raincoat.

But the summer is different; the parking lot is packed with cars and buses. Tourists crowd the park's single, paint-flaking totem pole, attempting to take pictures of one another. The German tourists wear big bellies, big cameras, and big voices. The Asian tourists swarm around their guides like bees around their queen. From the concession stand wafts the smells of Pine-Sol disinfectant, hamburger grease, and spilled orange soda.

No matter the season, Andy's little form is ignored. He expects this invisibility because he is of the canyon, while the tourists are not. They no more see him than they do the purple periwinkle that grows by the roadside in the spring, or the orange lichen that grows like tiny inverted suction cups on the north side of fallen logs in the fall. The tourists are only interested in the bridge that swings above the creek, in satiating their lust for awe. They visit each headstone in the park, they pore over the dangers graphically displayed on the billboard, they jump up and down on the bridge so that the cables creak as white foam crashes on the rocks far below.

Likewise, Andy ignores the tourists.

He doesn't think during these flights, not at all. Not of his tormentors at school, not of his fall from Candice's grace, not of his parents, his homework, his inadequate twig body. He has given himself permission *not* to think of these things. During this special half-hour, he merely flies, inhaling the fragrance of wet rock and decaying leaves, sucking into his lungs the scent of swordferns, hemlocks, and the long tresses of beard moss.

In the spring and summer he runs to Twin Falls, which is relatively free of tourists because it requires a ten-minute hike downstrean from the suspension bridge — too much like work for most tourists. There, he climbs onto the wooden bridge (a stout, short, normal bridge plastered with gum and engraved with initials), leans over its slimy wooden railings, and gazes at the crashing green water below.

In the fall and winter he doesn't need to escape the tourists (there are few), so he heads to the suspension bridge. Here he either watches the swirling water far below or he looks up and gazes at the sky. Either way, he witnesses magic: the magic of the creek or the magic of crows.

Crows, yes. For in the fall, against the smoky lavender of dusk, myriads of black forms wing their way southeast. Their silence is intense, their numbers staggering. Andy tried to count them once and gave up, overwhelmed after reaching a hundred for the seventh time. Only occasionally this creek of feathered black is broken by an empty stretch of sky, marked by a star or a lone, straggling crow.

Andy has discovered that it isn't just here that this phenomenon can be seen. While visiting Nanny and Grampa Woodruff, the exodus of crows can be witnessed from their backyard. While strapped in his parents' Tercel, stuck in traffic on the Second Narrows Bridge, he has also seen this flood of crows.

They appear out of the distant sky, black dots from West Vancouver, North Vancouver, and Deep Cove. The dots resolve into glossy wings and powerful beaks. The crows always appear in the fall, never in the spring or summer, and they always fly southeast, never north or west.

No one seems to notice this bizarre twilight ritual except Andy. He never sees anyone else look up. Crow after crow wings its way southeast, and no one notices save Andy. He wonders what strange, dark purpose the crows have, and how the thousands of people in the city can be unaware of this fantastical sunset journey. It fills Andy with awe and fear: he is surrounded by people oblivious to a great gathering of nature.

Once, he mentioned this phenomenon to his father, even managed to get him outside into the gravel parking lot adjacent to their house to look upward.

"Probably heading to a rookery somewhere, or migrating," was all his father said, and Andy gaped at him, stunned. So many crows heading to the same rookery? So many thousands gathering unerringly each autumn night at the same place? That was too incredible to picture! And migrating, how could that be? Vancouver is no less short of crows in the winter than in the summer, so the crows aren't leaving.

Unless, of course, phantom crows fill their places, shape-shifting spirits that choose to disguise themselves as crows ... It is this thought that currently shivers over Andy as he stands on the suspension bridge, neck craned back, glasses blurred with rainwater, fat cold droplets splattering his pale face and trickling down his neck. He is not thinking about his mother's frightening request that he refrain from mentioning her vomit to his father, nor is he thinking of the fallen tea kettle and the four teacups. Instead, he is merely watching the crows.

And thus he doesn't see something large, antlered, and white moving ponderously along the creek bank, just a few hundred yards upstream from the canyon falls below. Thus Andy misses the only opportunity in his entire life to see a live white hart.

Karen's head aches and her eyes refuse to focus; the last thing she needs is a confrontation. In all honesty, she has forgotten Candice's brief message on the answering machine; all events immediately following her painful fall to the floor have mangled together in a haze. But now that dinner is over, now that Morris and Andy have retreated to the living room with their slices of carob cream cake, Karen wearily remembers the phone message and realizes that a confrontation is inevitable: Candice disobeyed orders by visiting Gloria, and Karen will now have to inform Morris and discipline of some sort will be required.

To her surprise, Candice brings up the subject first.

"Look, I know I'm not supposed to see Gloria except on weekends, okay? But I have this biology project due, and I haven't made any friends yet at Sutherland." Candice scrubs viciously at a pan, soap suds flying like spittle from her scouring pad. "I mean, how can I make friends at that stupid school? They're all retroactive abortion candidates. And so Gloria helped me out, just this once. I mean, Dad doesn't have to know, okay?"

"I can't conceal it from your —"

"Reality check, Mom. I'm not asking you to conceal it. All I'm saying is, because you banished me from the only real friend I have in the world, I wasn't able to finish my homework. I *needed* Gloria's help. Her school is way ahead of mine. I mean, we're still learning about circulation and they're already doing reproduction —"

"Why couldn't you ask a teacher for help?"

"There was a staff meeting right after school, the report is due tomorrow, and it's worth twenty percent of our marks in biology. If I didn't have it ready in time, I'd have flunked. You don't want me to flunk again, do you?"

Candice avoids Karen's eyes and concentrates on removing crusts of baked cheese from the pan. Karen studies her daughter, dishtowel hanging limp and forgotten in her own hands. Something looks wrong in this scenario, sounds wrong: Candice's flushed cheeks, her atypical dishwashing energy, her lack of defiant glaring ...

"You aren't making this up, are you?" Karen asks.

Candice's head snaps up. Her flush deepens. She clenches the scouring pad with white fingers. "That's great, Mom, just great! I didn't have to phone you, you know. Mr. and Mrs. Vermicelli weren't even home. But, no, I decided I'd do the right thing and tell you about it, and what do I get in return? You call me a liar. That's just *great*!"

"But you seem so agitated."

"Of course I'm agitated! Why shouldn't I be agitated? You blame my marks at school on my friendship with Gloria, you separate us, and then when I try to improve my marks at my new school, you call me a liar 'cause I'm honest enough to tell you I met with my only real friend to get help with some stupid homework!"

Karen knows there are a half-dozen flaws in her daughter's logic, but she also knows that the tears of frustration welling in Candice's eyes, the taut quaver in her voice, and the frustration emanating from every pore in her body are more important than the flaws. Not for the first time, Karen feels a pang of guilt at complying with the decision Morris and Angelo Vermicelli made to separate Candice and Gloria.

"Tell me what we should have done then," she says, pressing her fingers against her throbbing temples and trying to concentrate. "We tried everything for you, Candice — tutors, curfews, rewards, mentor programs ... nothing worked. Both you and Gloria failed Grade 11 and it looked like you were going to do the same again this —"

"What has that got to do with anything?" Candice cries. "That's just *so* typical of you to change the —"

"I'm not changing —"

"Yes, you are!" Her voice cracks, and a tear drags mascara down one cheek. "Look, I'm not a liar, okay? I went to Gloria's and was honest enough to phone you about it! I don't know why I even bothered!" She throws the scouring pad into the sink. "You can wash the dishes yourself for all I care!"

Karen watches her barge through the swinging doors, hears her thump down the hall ... One second, two seconds, three seconds, *wham!* The whole house reverberates as Candice slams her bedroom door closed. Karen winces; the sound feels like a cannon placed against her temple. She gropes for the counter, eyes watering, and inadvertently knocks her crutches to the floor. They land with a repercussive clamour.

"Mom?" a small voice says behind her. "Dad wants to know what's going on."

"Nothing," Karen whispers hoarsely. "Nothing. Your sister is having some female problems, that's all. She's feeling a little under the weather."

A pause. "Do you want me to help you finish the dishes?"

"Oh, Andy ..." Karen whispers, and this time it is her turn to release a tear. "What on earth did I do to deserve you?"

Chapter Six

Moey favours modern belly-dance music from Algeria and Morocco as opposed to traditional Pharaonic compositions. As he searches through his CDs for a suitable piece for his premiere performance at the Footstop tomorrow, he puts aside "Ya Raya" (an uplifting little tune) and, as a possible alternative, "Nahawad" (a dramatic, mysterious song). At the same time, in his mannishly cramped script, he writes his monthly Vitality Sermon.

On the last training day of every month, Master Zahbar asks his instructors to deliver unto his students a rousing speech filled with martial-arts wisdom. He has provided his instructors with a self-published manual of Key Elements to be included in these speeches. This evening Moey has chosen Key Element No. 7 (Train Without Music) and No. 17 (Never Feel Relief). He picked both at random.

To say Moey is writing without thought is completely wrong; he is doing a great deal of thinking as his left hand flips through his CD rack and his right hand places inky chicken scratches upon paper. Only he isn't thinking about martial arts; no, he's thinking about double-veil routines versus sword acts. Improvisation versus choreography. Taped music versus a live band.

Moey doesn't feel guilty about this discrepancy in mental acuity, because many years ago he learned that Master Zahbar grows agitated when his instructors embellish on the wisdom inscribed in his manual; therefore, other than the occasional use of a synonym, Moey copies the Master's Vitality Sermons verbatim from the guidebook. More than once he chafed at this restriction, questioned the correctness of it, because some of the Master's philosophies seem rooted not so much in fact but opinion. Yet who is Moey, a prairie-town trophy holder, to question the beliefs of a world kickboxing champion?

So as Moey sweats and frets over the petrifying, exhilarating prospect of doing his first public belly-dancing performance on the morrow, this is what he writes:

> A dedicated martial artist does not train to music. Music is an addictive drug, supplying the martial artist with a false and temporary energy. It creates an unharmonious barrier between the mind and the body, so that the body becomes unable to function adequately without the stimulation of music. What does a martial artist do when in a Real Street Situation? Does he turn up the volume on his walkman? Look for the closest radio? Start singing the lyrics of the latest top-ten song?
>
> No! He must draw on all his resources, focus all his energy, to deal with the threat at hand. He is a warrior! No warrior relies on outside stimuli to perform. If you are training to music, stop now, or I guarantee that when a Real Street Situation crops up, you will be unable to adequately defend yourself!

And he also copies this down verbatim from Element No. 17:

> The path to excellence in martial arts can only be found when the martial artist stops feeling relief. Relief is an indication of both a pre-existing fear and complacency.
> In the first place, the martial artist should never feel fear. If you eliminate all your fears, you will never again feel the relief that follows when that fear is removed. Break down your fears — analyze them, then desensitize yourself by facing them directly and repeatedly. A true martial artist feels neither fear nor relief — be a true martial artist!

As he pens these words, Moey feels uncomfortable, as if he's wearing a wool sweater in a sauna; in fact, for the past six months or so, every time a Vitality Sermon rolls around, his scalp tingles unpleasantly. But as usual he ignores the sensation. Instead he chooses to mentally review another item of importance for his looming performance at the Footstop tomorrow — his costume.

Moey's costume is self-assembled, not self-made. It consists of a red sateen scarf worn pirate-style on his head, a large gold earring, and a curling, fake moustache (all purchased, over a series of months, from Liquidation World). Next comes an enormous black cape of a flowing material that glitters with interwoven threads of gold (part of a Halloween Merlin the Warlock ensemble one of his brothers wore at age fifteen).

A woman's sleeveless bolero, though extra large, fits

him a little too snugly, but it is simply too authentic to replace; reflective plastic mirrors, red tassels, and gold braid decorate every inch of it. He purchased it from a Mexican stall during International Celebration Day two years ago. His pantaloons — a glossy lipstick red — come from Habib's Quality Imports in a section of Vancouver known as Little India. The pantaloons (again, women's apparel) are meant to be worn under a sari. Acquiring them knocked at least a year off Moey's life; the slim, giggling East Indian cashier saw right through Moey's stammered story about it being a present for his wife.

Bare feet and finger cymbals complete Moey's costume. He is aiming for the Gypsy look.

Moey puts aside his plagiarized speech and cracks the air bubbles from his thick knuckles. He closes his eyes and envisions the layout of the Footstop, trying to picture himself moving with grace and passion among its merchandise. Sweat pops out on his palms.

"I'll never be able to sleep tonight," he mutters, and the telephone shrills.

It'll be Karen, he thinks. *She's changed her mind. She doesn't want me to dance tomorrow.*

He hurls himself from his chair in an adrenaline-fuelled trajectory, staggers across his gloomy basement suite (all twenty feet of it), and rips the receiver from its cradle.

"Hello?" he bellows. "Hello?"

"You don't have to shout, Moey! These things work by electricity. It's not a long hollow tube you have to scream down."

"Mom?"

"What, are you joking? It's me, Miranda."

"Oh." He licks his lips and shudders with relief. Not Karen, after all. "Sometimes it's hard to tell the difference."

"What, between me and your mom?"

"Uh ... well, all women sound the same on the —"

"Yeah, well, your mother doesn't suck on your balls, does she?"

He winces. "Miranda ..."

"Look, can I come over for the night? I went shopping today." Her tone drops a little, roughens a titch. "Wait till you see what I bought this time."

"Tonight's not a good night."

"Why not? We don't have any competitions coming up."

Miranda knows the rule: no sex for two weeks prior to a fight. Key Element No. 21: Intimacy Softens the Combative Spirit.

"I just want to conserve my energy for tomorrow," he says.

"What's so special about tomorrow?"

"Vitality Sermon," he lies, his pulse starting to pound like a mallet against his larynx.

"You figure you need extra energy for *that*? You do them every month."

"Yeah, well, I always like to have my wits about me, give a good performance."

"Performance is right. Got to make it sound good in case Hitler's listening."

"Don't call him that."

"Why? You can be such a limp noodle sometimes. Look, do you want me to come over or not?"

He thinks about it for all of three seconds: if he says no, she'll sulk for weeks. She'll misplace his telephone messages at work and overbook his Introductory Lessons. Master Zahbar will notice and take Moey into the office for a Man to Man Talk.

He sighs in defeat. "Of course I want you to come over."

But, of course, he doesn't. Miranda fucks the way she fights — intently, ruthlessly, her sole purpose to conquer. In her twenty-six years of life, she's taken twice as many lovers and won twice as many kickboxing trophies as Moey. The last thing he needs right now is to be conquered.

Oh, to be sure, Miranda won most of her trophies point sparring, not full-contact fighting. At five foot two and 115 pounds, she lacks the necessary mass to knock her opponents' blocks off. Lightness of feet, accuracy of strikes, and unbridled energy can't, in full-contact kickboxing, overwhelm thundering poundage. Not in the competition ring, anyway, where brute force is always combined with deadly skill. Miranda bears this knowledge pragmatically, and what she lacks for in the ring she makes up for in the bedroom.

Once, after an unusual round of celebratory tequila shooters (both of them rarely imbibed alcohol), Moey asked her why she hadn't become a dominatrix.

"Because I don't go for all that sadomasochistic crap," she scornfully replied.

Since then he often wonders how she defines sadomasochism, given her fondness for whips, wrist shackles, and anal beads capable of delivering mild electrical shocks. Not that he ever, *ever*, lets her get anywhere near him with those beads. Or, for that matter, anything else that suggests a back-door entry. Miranda views this as his great flaw, his total abhorrence of even the idea of anything entering his rectum. At least once a month she says irritably, "For Christ's sake, I'll use plenty of lube. A couple of thrusts and you'll be hooked. Come on, you're wasting a perfect pair of balls."

Not the slightest pleat, wrinkle, or crimp mars the taut surface of Moey's testicles, but why this should endow him with the desire for derrière drama is completely beyond him. Miranda can suck on his testicles endlessly, sometimes gently, sometimes a trifle rough, her tongue flicking hummingbird-style to and fro or slinking wet and stealthily over their smooth terrain. She can — and on what she terms her lazy nights, frequently does — climax solely by curling catlike between his legs and sucking contentedly on his privy parts. Those are the nights he likes best.

As Miranda walks into his basement suite a scant fifteen minutes after their phone conversation, her wet Rastafarian braids and delicate Negro features framed by the halogen streetlight a mere five feet from Moey's door, he can tell by the gleam in her eyes that this isn't going to be one of her lazy nights.

Alas.

At least the rainstorm will muffle her screams of pleasure from his landlords above.

As cramped as Moey's writing is, Morris's script is neat and fastidious. Every evening his letters march from his Bic pen with the precision of soldiers on parade.

Morris keeps these obedient alphabetical symbols in a journal. For the most part, his entries describe his unusual podiatric cases, all lovingly and lavishly described. This evening he briefly touches on a case scheduled for surgery tomorrow morning: Mr. P. Chapman, a thirty-eight-year-old man suffering from Madura foot, a fungus infection characterized by chronicity, tumefaction, and multiple sinus formation.

But occasionally the River appears among his meticulous recordings. Morris mistrusts the River, fears it even. Tonight, while his wife lies sleeping on their Sears king-size bed, he writes these words beneath his medical notes:

> Another person drowned in the River today. A fisherman, according to the six o'clock news. He waded in too deep while trying to unsnag his line. I fail to understand why he was fishing during a torrential downpour in the first place.
>
> This is not the only casualty this fall. Five weeks and two days ago, a sixty-four-year-old woman was walking her Chihuahua in Lynn Canyon and failed to realize the danger of trying to cross that River without benefit of a bridge. One wonders if it was a suicide, though apparently this has been discounted. She was wearing heels, too. Outrageous footwear for such an activity. They cause no end of damage to the metatarsus.
>
> What is wrong with people, I'd like to know, that they feel a need to approach that River as if it were immovable concrete. It is a force of nature, unpredictable and therefore dangerous.
>
> I would call it a menace, but that seems inappropriate, as it was here long before we were.
>
> Thirty-three lives have been lost since we've moved into this house. I have kept track. Today was the thirty-third. I don't

know how many more must die before our Council members do something about it. Can't people exercise at a recreational centre? A complete waste of taxpayers' money to erect such centres if people insist on exercising in that canyon instead.

Karen walks along that River. I don't understand it, don't understand it at all. I would talk to her about it — have talked to her many times — but she doesn't listen. So I've stopped. I suppose I could order her to refrain from walking there, but there's no point in issuing a command that will never be obeyed. That only undermines the authority of the one issuing the order. Besides, she's my wife; one mustn't be reduced to believing one's wife is something one can command.

But good God, you'd think she'd show some common sense, some responsibility to her children, and stop entering that bloody canyon! What would I ... [Morris pauses, frowns, crosses out "I," and replaces it with "we."] What would we do with out her?

Perhaps we should move.

The fisherman was only thirty-eight.

Two doors away Andy, too, is confessing his fears, only not in written form and not to a journal. He is sharing them with his Buddha.

The Buddha was given to him as a Christmas present two years earlier by Nanny Woodruff. (Lately, Candice has refused to call her that, saying it sounds babyish; she now calls her "Grandmother" instead.) Nanny Woodruff is Andy's favourite grandparent. Grampy Woodruff simply overwhelms him, the way he heaves his massive bulk to and fro like an active volcano, constantly erupting with deafening bellows of laughter or biblical quotes, and Nanny Morton scares him a little with her embarrassing belches and drool and perpetually gummed-up eyes. Andy has no memory of Grampy Morton, long since buried at the local cemetery behind Capilano College; for some reason this fills him with great relief.

Yes, Nanny Woodruff is his favourite grandparent by a long mile, and the Buddha is his most prized possession. It stands no higher than Andy's index finger, its protruding bare belly glossy and cool. The beaming, bald-headed face carved into the ivory appears merry and compassionate. The hugely swollen earlobes (a sign of great wisdom, Nanny W. says) lend the squat figure nobility.

Most wondrous of all, the Buddha has, casually slung over his back and knotted to a knobby stick, a bag containing all his worldly possessions. To Andy, this hobo's bag represents more freedom, confidence, and wisdom than every Christian symbol contained in Grampy's church.

Staring at the darkened bedroom ceiling, watching moonlight and wind flick hemlock shadows across the ceiling's gyproc surface, Andy rubs the Buddha's smooth belly like a rosary bead. Every night he expresses his fears and desires to the figure through such touch. It isn't anything Nanny Woodruff has told him to do; he doesn't even know if the figure has any function save ornamentation. But from the first moment his fingers touched the smoothness of the Buddha's belly, Andy knew that such an action was right. Was expected even.

So every night through touch the tiny ivory Buddha relives Andy's humiliation of head-swirlies in school toilets, experiences Andy's helpless frustration at having to allow "Big Mac" Ashrani to copy his homework, and shares the looming terror that Andy's mother will one day desert them.

Through touch alone the little Buddha perceives these fears, perceives and soothes them with his polished paunch.

Candice's bedroom is sandwiched between that of her parents and her brother. This situation makes her feel claustrophobic. Even now, burrowed beneath her bedsheets, talking into her cordless phone, she feels the smothering presence of her family. She knows that as soon as her father finishes scribbling in his diary, he'll rap on the wall and order her to hang up. That will be the end of *her* confession: the telephone functions for Candice the way the journal and the Buddha function for her father and brother.

"Hey, Gloria. Yeah. Yeah. I dunno. It was fun, I guess. Yeah, well, what did your parents say when your brother told them I'd been at your place? What do you mean, he didn't tell them? *What* condition, Gloria? Oh, my God, I don't believe it! What kind of a friend are you? There's no way I'm going to the Thanksgiving Dance with your brother. Sure, it's no big deal for you! *I'm* the one who's going to be dancing with him! I'm not freaking out. Well, how would you feel if I set you up with *my* brother?

"That's not the point, Gloria. Gloria ... Gloria ... will you *please* shut up for just a minute? Thank you. Okay. Look, I know my brother's different. I can admit it, all right? But he isn't weird. That wasn't Andy's fault! The whole thing was my father's idea! I am *not* making it up, okay? I was right there. Ask my mom! Of course, she was there. Who do you think made the birthday cake? I don't know why she let him do it. I don't know why she lets Dad do *anything* he does. I mean, it's as if his word is totally the law, you know? That's *exactly* what I was thinking while I was watching him do it. Like, it doesn't take a brain scientist to figure out that massaging a bunch of kids' feet at a birthday party is going to get you in trouble, even if you are a stupid foot doctor.

"Andy came home from school with a black eye the next day, which is totally unfair. As if he can defend himself, you know? Yeah, well, that just made things worse. It was *so* embarrassing to hear her phone up their parents and try to explain it to them. Are you kidding? My mom couldn't explain her way out of a paper bag. And, of course, she phoned up *all* of the parents in Andy's school. Yes! All of them! It took her four days! By then *everybody* in Andy's school was beating him up. I mean, sure he's a milkweed, but he's just a kid.

"Yeah, well, that's when he built the bomb. He was only trying to impress them, win back a few friends. He's so smart that way. I mean, this bomb actually worked. No, the fire department got there before the gym totally burned up. Besides, it's not like a gym is important.

"Look, I've got to hang up now. My dad just banged on the wall. Anyway, tell your brother I'm *not* doing it. I'd rather die than go to that dance with him. Okay, okay, I didn't mean that. Look, I really have to hang up now. We'll talk about this tomorrow. And about that. Yeah, I've got hickeys. I dunno, wear a scarf or something. Yeah, me, too. Okay. Whatever. Bye."

While Karen's family is thus involved in their respective confessions, she lies on her bed, a cold blue gel pack perched on her aching forehead like a small hen upon a large egg. In the semi-lucid state that grips her as she slips off to sleep, the crinkle of Morris's wrist moving over the pages of his journal transforms into the sound of cardboard being dragged over sidewalk and grass. She is transported back in time to when Candice was ten and Andy was almost four ...

On the front lawn of the Parmars' yard, five houses down, the neighbourhood kids were building a fort made from flattened cardboard boxes, a soiled blue tarpaulin, and empty plastic barrels that once contained mango chutney. Despite the July heat, a hive of children frantically buzzed about, shrieking in English and Punjabi.

Candice and Andy showed equal enthusiasm as they dragged their scavenged cardboard to the Parmars' house. Andy shouted out a garble of instructions, frustrated even at his age by the lack of fort-building plans. Candice flapped a bolt of mildewy yellow cloth in the air with her free hand and babbled about curtains, tablecloths, and rugs.

Karen was working in the garden, cutting back the dead stalks of early-summer lupines and watching this activity from the corner of her eye. A glow of intense, warm satisfaction filled her, provoked not just by the children but also by the hickory-smoke smell of chicken barbecuing in Don Willis's backyard, the snap of freshly laundered bedsheets on Mrs. Baroudi's line, the splash of water hitting metal as Jay Osaban lovingly washed his 1926 Model T Roadster Pickup across the street. Morris stood beside Jay, nodding earnestly, discussing the old truck's tires.

With a sigh of contentment, Karen waved to her husband, then looked back at her children. But in that brief glance away from them, something happened. Don

Willis, the potbellied stockbroker two doors down, emerged from his backyard. He now stood beside Candice and Andy, pointing at the edge of his lawn where a corner of their cardboard lay. He gestured angrily, then kicked at the cardboard. It jerked out of Candice's and Andy's hands.

Instantly, Karen was up and running. "Hey!" she cried as she cut through the Baroudis' front yard. "What the hell do you think you're doing?"

Don Willis turned in her direction. "Your kids are wrecking my lawn."

"How *dare* you kick them!" She leaped over a small rock wall. "They aren't doing a damn thing to your lawn!"

"They're flattening it!"

"I'll flatten you, you asshole! I'll rip your balls out and shove them down your throat. You do *not* kick my kids!"

"I kicked the cardboard."

She reached him, breathless, and stood on tiptoe to be level with his face. "I don't care what you kicked. You keep your feet away from my kids, do you hear me? This isn't even your lawn! Your property line starts ten feet back from the sidewalk, just like everybody else's!"

"Look, all I'm saying —"

"I don't give a damn what you're saying. Go crawl back into your house. Go on, get, get!" And she made shooing motions at him, as if he were a dog.

"Jesus, Karen ..."

"And don't take the Lord's name in vain!" Her voice reached a new height. "Not in front of my children!"

He hesitated, clearly overwhelmed, then turned back to his house, muttering and shaking his head. Karen stood there, chest heaving, fingernails biting into the palms of her hands, and watched him go. From across the street someone broke into choked laughter.

She turned around. Jay Osaban had dropped his hose and was slapping his thighs. Beside him, Morris stared at her, his mouth agape.

"'I'll rip your balls out and shove them down your throat,'" Mr. Osaban gasped. "I love it!"

Karen turned back to her children, swallowed, and tried to control the trembling in her limbs. "Are you both okay?"

They nodded, speechless.

She touched them, brushed invisible dust from their clothes, smoothed Andy's hair, tugged Candice's tube top higher. "You're not hurt. You're both fine? You sure?"

"We're fine, Mom," Candice said.

Andy just nodded, still gawking at her.

"Good, good. I'm glad you're fine. Good. Go play then." She picked up an edge of the huge flattened cardboard box and forcibly put it in their hands. "Go play."

Karen gave them a small pat-push on their backs towards the Parmar house. But there, frozen in various positions of play, stood the entire population of neighbourhood children, entranced by her. She breathed deeply, then waved cheerily. "It's fine, kids, just fine. Nobody's hurt, everything's okay. You can go back to making your fort now. It sure looks like it's going to be a dandy."

"God almighty, Morris!" Mr. Osaban hooted. "Can you believe it?"

At that moment Mrs. Parmar came out the front door, carrying a frosted pitcher of iced tea. In the background a Punjabi soap opera star wailed a love song from her television. "Anybody thirsty?" Mrs. Parmar sang out.

The spell broke, and the children unfroze from their positions and raced towards her. After a moment of hesitation, Andy and Candice joined them, dragging along their cardboard.

This is what Karen relives as she drifts into a Tylenol-induced sleep. Meanwhile Morris finishes writing in his journal, the Buddha slips from Andy's sleep-slackened fingers to his pillow, and Candice presses the end button on her cordless phone.

Chapter Seven

Douglas fir, western red cedar, Sitka spruce, and western hemlock rise from the floor of Lynn Canyon and tower into the sky. Among the wind-torn crowns, bald eagles and red-tailed hawks nest. In the hollows of their mossy trunks, downy woodpeckers and squirrels make their homes. These trees are Mother Nature's high-rises.

When he was alive, Frederick Varley — one-seventh of the Group of Seven — knew every species of tree, bird, and mammal that lived in Lynn Canyon. His most famous paintings depict the canyon's exuberant hemlocks and tempestuous waters. "It trembles within me," he once wrote of the canyon, "and pains me with its wonder."

Mirroring the creek's unpredictable nature, Freddy one day up and announced he was leaving Vancouver to move to Lynn Valley and settle there with his mistress, a girl young enough to be his daughter. His wife, to state things mildly, was less than pleased.

Comparatively, Karen Morton can identify only a handful of the trees in the canyon, may be able to name just a few of its most common birds. Although she also draws inspiration from the mossy cliffs and swirling waters, her paintings don't portray her environs. Instead, they depict ankles, toes, and smooth heels — she is, after all, in the business of feet. But she, too, feels the mysterious wonder of the canyon.

But the numinous feeling she experiences upon waking this morning comes from a certain memory: that of the hart. This is swiftly followed by a torrential flood of recollections: a skull-banging kettle, a nose-mashing crotch, a belly-dancing karate instructor.

With a groan Karen Morton — wife, mother, and foot artist extraordinaire — rolls over in her bed and longs for sleep to return.

But it doesn't. After a few minutes, she reluctantly rises from bed.

Morris is always the first to arrive at the breakfast table, emphasizing his punctuality with repeated glances at his watch. Today is no different. Karen places a bowl of instant apple cinnamon oatmeal before him (it is beyond her to cook anything more complex than that; her head still feels woolly and swollen).

Morris clears his throat. "I don't expect you'll get many customers today, not with the way it's raining. The weatherman has forecast showers for the rest of the week."

Karen makes a noncommittal noise and pours him a glass of grapefruit juice.

"Do you need any supplies for the workshop?" he asks. "I have some free time at lunch and could pick them up for you ..."

"No thanks."

"You aren't looking well. Is your ankle bothering you?"

"I'll be okay."

Morris huffs at the back of his throat and frowns, a spoon of steaming oatmeal midway to his mouth. "Why isn't Candice helping you here? You shouldn't be stumping around the kitchen on just one crutch. It places unnecessary strain on your healthy foot."

"I'm fine, Morr —"

"Morning, Dad," Andy mumbles, owl-blinking as he shuffles into the kitchen.

"Ah, son. Slept well?"

Andy sits at the table, and Karen plunks a bowl of oatmeal before him. Using her fingers, she tries to subdue the massive cowlick rising from his head like an inverted cone.

"Ow, that hurts!"

Karen abandons her attempts to defeat his sleep-made rooster comb and turns back to the kitchen counter where a row of half-made cream-cheese-and-tomato sandwiches awaits her attention. "Where's your sister? She's going to be late."

"Candice!" Andy cries. "You're going to be late!"

Karen winces, closes her eyes, and clutches the counter for support, her head pulsating like the thorax of a bullfrog.

"I'm right here, moron. You don't have to scream your head off. *Ohmigod*, is that oatmeal for breakfast? Mom, you know I can't stand oatmeal."

"Sit down and eat your oatmeal," Morris says sharply. "If you'd been out here helping your mother fix breakfast instead of sleeping, you could have made something different."

While Candice mutters under her breath, Karen slowly opens her eyes and carefully resumes making the lunch sandwiches. For a blissful few seconds, only the clink of cutlery fills the kitchen, but the quiet doesn't last.

"I swear I'm going to puke if I have to eat this. I'm not hungry, anyway."

"You can't start the day without a healthy meal."

"Dad, this stuff is hardly healthy. It's ninety percent sugar."

"I'll eat it if you don't want it," Andy pipes up.

"You shouldn't be eating it, either. It'll give you zits."

"I'm too young to —"

"You can never be too young."

"I want you to eat your oatmeal, young lady, and that's final."

"But why does Mom even make this stuff? She knows I can't stand it. It looks like cat vomit."

Andy gags, Morris whuffles in indignation, and Karen quickly pivots and says brightly, "Perhaps you could give the kids a ride to school, Morris, what with the rain and all."

There is a moment of stunned silence, then Candice pleads, "Could you, Dad? Please? That would be *so* great."

"Certainly not! I have to be going in less than two minutes."

"They'll be ready by then, won't you, kids?"

"I'll just grab my sunglasses!" Candice launches herself from the table.

Karen hastily stuffs a sandwich into a cloth bag and shoves it towards her. "Don't forget your lunch."

"Tomato and cream cheese? Mom, you *know* the tomato makes the bread all soggy! There's no way I'm going to eat this."

"Karen, they should walk."

"Just this once, Morris. Andy, go brush your teeth quickly."

"But I'm still hungry."

"Here." Karen snatches the lunch bag out of Candice's hand, retrieves the sandwich nestled there, and thrusts it at Andy. "Eat this in the car."

"What's the point of brushing my teeth if I'm going to eat right after?"

"Oh, great, Mom, now what am I supposed to have for lunch?"

"I have surgery at nine o'clock. I don't have time to drive them to school."

Karen turns, opens the oven, and from its steamy depths plucks out two partially baked blueberry scones. Their hot grease instantly blisters her fingertips. "Here, take these," she says, shoving them at Candice. "Now get your shoes on before your father leaves without you. Andy, go brush your teeth. Morris, you don't have to go that far out of your way."

"Ow, these are hot! And they're still *raw!*"

"How come she gets to have scones and I don't?"

"Karen! That's teahouse merchandise!"

At that moment something snaps inside Karen, a crisp, definitive noise similar to what a potato chip makes when stepped on.

"Put a clam in it!" she shrieks. "All of you!"

They freeze. The kitchen clock continues to tick. It sounds like the timer on a bomb.

Eventually, the red fogging Karen's vision fades and she is able to see again. Her family stands before her, eyes wide, jaws loose.

"Andy, go brush your teeth or they'll rot," she orders. "Candice, either eat those scones or starve. Morris, the longer you stand here and complain, the later you'll arrive at work."

She grapples for her crutches, jams them under her armpits, and lurches towards the kitchen's swinging doors. "Now if you'll excuse me, I'm going back to bed. I have a headache." She is halfway down the hall before anyone in the kitchen stirs.

"Put a clam in it?" Candice murmurs.

"Clam up," Andy translates, a jumble of awe and fear in his voice. "Mixed with put a sock in it."

"Ah," Morris says. "Ah."

A few minutes later the back door closes as they all tiptoe out.

Despite the rigours of his evening, Moey wakes at 5:00 a.m. before the first watery strains of autumn sunlight even think to touch Lynn Valley. Moving carefully, so as not to awaken Miranda, he disentangles himself from his crusty bedsheets and creeps into the living-room/kitchen area of his suite.

Today I'm going to do my first public belly-dance performance, he thinks. *And I'm going to be sick.*

His blood turns to cold slush, his heart to a rabid sled dog. To calm himself he rifles through the kitchen cabinet, finds a can of No-Name mushroom soup and a packet of stale Fig Newtons, and consumes the lot, dunking the Newtons in the cold soup. (He doesn't dare heat the soup in the microwave, lest the noise awaken Miranda and her never-appeased desire.)

Thus fortified, he begins practising his dance routines, using the gentle sleep-rhythm of Miranda's breathing as a metronome. His tension slowly fades with each undulation and pelvic slide. Every time he shimmies, the dried juices of Miranda's ardour peel in delicate white flakes from his chest and thighs and flutter like dandruff to the orange shag carpet. At seven the alarm clock shatters his concentration, and he cries out, startled. Miranda stirs and mutters something in a sleep-fogged voice. Moey flees to the shower.

Half an hour later, leaving no time for Miranda to initiate more sex, he emerges on a billow of steam, looking like a beefsteak tomato. "Ready to go?" he says, avoiding her eyes as he shrugs into his kickboxing uniform.

"Do you mind if I have a shower first? If there's any hot water left, that is."

"Sure, go ahead."

"Christ, what took you so long?" She stalks into the bathroom and slams the door.

Moey stifles a grin, waits until the shower is running again, then hastily retrieves his belly-dancing costume from the darkest recesses of his closet. He stows the costume in his kickboxing duffle bag, under his gloves, mouth guard, towels, padded boxing helmet, jockstrap, Manual of Key Elements, and the Vitality Sermon he copied the previous night. It thrills him to see his glossy red pantaloons nestled beneath his sweat-yellowed jockstrap.

While he waits for Miranda, he mentally rehearses his dance routines and does push-ups to work off his nerves.

Twenty minutes later, scrubbed clean and attired in their crisp black uniforms, he and Miranda pile into his Plymouth, purchase muffins and coffee from the Starbucks on the street corner, and drive to the martial-arts studio. The studio is situated on the upper floors of a daycare centre; cut-outs of Roger Rabbit and Winnie-the-Pooh decorate the dark stairwell and circle the studio's logo of a boxer in mid-leap.

At nine o'clock sharp Miranda lights the incense sticks before the small Buddhist shrine outside Master Zahbar's office and assumes her position behind the reception desk. Moey takes his place on the polished wooden floor of the gym. One by one the members of the adult morning class file in.

They bow once upon entering the door. They bow again to Miranda. They bow a third time to the shrine, a fourth time to the life-size poster of Master Zahbar, and lastly to Moey. The image of Stanley Park Zoo pops into Moey's mind, and it takes him several moments to realize why: all this bowing reminds him of well-trained seals.

The students sit in a silent semicircle on the floor in front of him, folding their legs beneath them with a variety of grunts and grimaces (yesterday's workout was a trifle harsh perhaps). As Moey scans their familiar faces, it suddenly occurs to him that any one of these students might visit the Footstop and witness his performance later that afternoon. The need to urinate rises sharp and urgent, and sweat instantly forms on his palms. He begins to burp mushroom soup, Fig Newtons, and Zimbabwe Blend coffee.

Relax, he tells himself. *The odds that anyone here will visit the canyon today have to be a million to one.*

He has his speech prepared, and he'll recite it. Simple. Then he'll tell them to set up the gym for circuit training so he can stand in a corner and mentally rehearse his belly-dance performance.

You'll be fine, he tells himself sternly, but not with much confidence.

He takes a deep breath and starts to read from the speech. "Today's Vitality Sermon is about Key Element No. 7: Train Without Music." Clearing his throat, he puts on his Assured and Emphatic Voice: "Understand that a dedicated martial artist does not train to music. Music is an addictive drug, supplying the martial artist with a false and temporary energy. It creates an unharmonious barrier between the mind and the body ..."

His Assured and Emphatic Voice wavers, then trails off. After a few seconds, he begins again. "Music is an addictive drug that creates an unharmonious barrier between the mind and the body." He stops again, pulls the speech closer, frowns at his handwriting. "What the hell?"

Around him, his students stiffen.

Although they all communicate outside the gym using a healthy dose of expletives, such words are completely forbidden within the sacred walls of the gym. The students have never heard this kind of unsanctified language pass from Moey's lips before, and the effect of his casual use of such a word is equivalent to hearing the pope declare: "Mother Theresa was a whore and a fake."

Moey is completely unaware of his transgression. All he knows is that before him in his own cramped handwriting trembles a sheet of paper bearing words of utter and complete nonsense. "I don't understand," he mutters. "There must be some mistake. I couldn't have written this."

The students blink at one another, then look back at Moey.

"This is wrong. It must be." Moey flutters the sheet, turns it over, searches the back. Its blank surface provides no answers.

One woman shifts uneasily. "Sir? Are you ... okay?"

Moey glances up and meets her concerned, cow-brown eyes. His mind promptly goes blank.

Once, during a fight against Bulldozer Boris, Moey was on the receiving end of a spinning back kick aimed straight at the heart. How the muscular 280-pound Boris so completely snapped his foot beyond Moey's protective stance, Moey could never recall, but the sensations that followed remain clearly in his memory.

He feels those same sensations now: a consuming inability to think, to breathe, to comprehend. Brain blankness, body loss. Time screeching to a halt. No sounds existing, no smells. A vacuum sucking out his lungs, a void where his heart should be. Total absenteeism from the tangible. Imprisonment in vertigo. All followed by a thunderous vortex of adrenaline that sucks every sensation back into his body — pain, fear, disbelief, anger, shame, determination, humility, wonder. All of it helping him define, in an all-pervasive moment, himself.

Miraculously, he went on to win that fight and accepted the stiff leather championship belt as a changed man. Now, with a damp, wrinkled sheet of paper clutched in his hand, Moey experiences a similar epiphany. He clears his throat and regards the students in front of him. "This —" he waves the Vitality Sermon before him "— is bullshit."

Spines snap even straighter. Eyes grow to the size of ostrich eggs. One fellow, a lank-haired, pimpled youth who always stinks of pot, slowly grins.

"You see, I believe in music," Moey continues. "I believe *strongly* in music. Why? Because everything is music — my heartbeat, my fists on a speedball ..."

He points to the woman who spoke. "What do you think defines music?"

"Sir?"

"How would you explain music to an alien?"

"An alien?" She glances at the rest of the students; they stare at their toes, at the far wall, out the windows. Except for Pimply. His grin shows his tonsils.

The woman releases a quavering breath and looks back at Moey. "Well, I guess music is a series of sounds, sir."

"And what's the point of those sounds?"

"The ... point?"

Agitation sweeps over Moey; he is at the brink of something vital. He feels it shimmering along every neuron in his body. He starts to pace. "Energy, that's what

I mean. Music is energy, and energy is everywhere, all around you, inside you."

He paces faster. "When you go to a rock concert, everybody moves, right? Because of the energy bouncing around, because of the power of being connected to everything else. And when you go ... to a river, or a waterfall, you feel the same sort of power, the same sort of music."

He stops, faces them, and thumps his chest. "It's here that you hold music. It's here that you find your own power. Do you understand?" He waves the speech at them, the speech he copied word for word from Master Zahbar's instruction manual less than twelve hours ago. "Music is *not* an addictive drug. It is *not* a false and temporary energy. This speech is wrong. Key Element No. 7 is wrong. Do you understand what I'm saying?"

They gawk at him, and he spreads his arms expansively. "Music does *not* create an unharmonious barrier between the mind and the body. To hell with that! Music is a combination of sounds that *reflect* the power in your mind and body. We *are* music, we *are* power. Don't let anyone tell you anything different!"

In the stunned silence that follows, the *tap-tap* of a fly batting itself against one of the windows can be heard. Pimply gives Moey a thumb's-up. Then a throat clears, a throat belonging not to a body sitting cross-legged in the semicircle before Moey, but located elsewhere. As one, Moey and the students turn in the direction of the throat.

Master Zahbar stands near the gym entrance, arms crossed over his chest, chin raised slightly, face blank. "Instructor Thorpe," he says into the rigid silence that follows, "I want to speak with you in my office."

Seven times. Egret Van Gorder doesn't know if that's some kind of record or not, but he successfully masturbated seven times during the night. After waking at 6:00 a.m. and completing his seventh feverish salami slapper, the first thing he does is open his bedroom window; even he can smell the sour-milk-and-seaweed stench of his own semen.

Next, he shuffles to the shower, feeling more drained than a can of beer in the hairy clutches of the Man. Using half a bar of Irish Spring, Egret thoroughly soaps his entire body and gingerly cleanses his limp manhood with a mixture of both pride and trepidation. Could his night of vigorous activity have caused some damage?

Back in his room, he dresses to the raucous beat of the Exalted Hellborns, averting his gaze from the sperm-stiffened panties protruding from his pillow. But as he slips his Adidas track pants over his lean legs, the presence of the beleaguered underpants begins to prey on his mind, and not in their hitherto erotic manner. No, it starts to dawn on Egret that he can't leave the panties hidden under his pillow lest his mother choose today to wash his bedsheets.

As he pulls on a clean sweatshirt, he scans his bedroom. Maybe he should hide them among his own clothes in his chest of drawers. But what if his mom discovers them while putting away clean laundry? Okay, what about in his desk? Good idea. But wait! What if she rummages in there looking for a pen or something? In the closet then?

But two weeks ago his mom dug around in that very closet, searching for his old diving trophies to show off to the women in her Gardens Beautiful Club. Sure, he hollered about invasion of privacy and stuff, but who can guarantee she'll keep her promise and not do it again?

Nowhere seems like a safe hiding spot for the stolen panties. Never before has he felt his lack of privacy so keenly. Then a fist thumps on his door, causing him to jump two feet into the air and spin around.

"What the devil you doin' in there? You forget today's a school day?" his father bellows, Dutch accent thickened by impatience. "Get your ass movin'. I got to drive the Man to the hospital after practice."

"Coming, I'm coming." Egret grabs the crusty panties, shoots a wild look around his room, then hastily stuffs them into his swim bag. He'll have to take them with him.

And so it comes to pass that throughout his diving practice he can think only about the panties concealed in the bag in his locker. He worries that his dad might take it into his head to hunt for something in there, or his coach might, or one of his teammates. Combined with a lack of energy due to his night of self-gratification, this distraction is enough to cause Egret to perform one poor dive after the next until at last his father hauls him out of the pool, screaming in apoplectic rage.

"I don't know what's the matter with you, boy," he bellows as they hurtle out of the recreation centre's parking lot and speed down Seymour Parkway. "You can't afford to dive like that, not with the competitions comin' up."

"I just had a bad day, that's all," Egret mumbles.

"That's all? That's all? And how the hell ya goin' to prevent yourself from havin' such a day when the meet comes?"

"I was distracted, okay? I was thinking about —" he flounders for a suitable distraction "— the Man."

His father curses, shifts gears on the Porsche, and runs a yellow light. "Why worry about him? I told you I asked the doctor. You can't catch what he's got if you keep outta his room. If it's gonna bother you this much, I kick him out." He slaps the steering wheel with the palm of his hand. "Yes, sir, I have him out of there so fast his head spins!"

"Forget it, Dad. It was just this morning. I'll be okay tomorrow."

"That better be so. That sure as hell better be so."

His father spends the rest of the drive home muttering about lousy tenants and the stupidity of motorbike tours. Egret barely pays attention. In fact, as he devours the enormous breakfast his mother makes for him, and as he trudges his way along the grassy Grand Boulevard to school afterwards, his thoughts are riveted on the panties in his pocket. He was at a loss to think of anywhere safe to keep them, so they travel next to his left thigh, crammed into his track pants.

Instead of being concerned that he'll be discovered with such an object and taken for a pansy or a pervert, he now worries that the absence of the panties might be noticed by their owner, and that the owner's mother, namely Karen, will link his presence in her house yesterday with the disappearance of her daughter's underwear. Karen will then tell Candice what a fuck-up he is, and Candice will never walk in the same school hall as him, let alone spread her legs to welcome his cock.

How this neurosis has grown, Egret has no idea, but grown it has in great leaps and bounds. By the time the school bell shrills for morning classes to begin, Egret is convinced he has to return the purloined underpants to their rightful owner.

Today. After school. Before Candice gets home.

Chapter Eight

Maduromycosis: a fungus infection of the foot prevalent in the tropics and southern United States. As a resident of Canada, Morris is amazed to see such a case outside a textbook.

Like most people infected with Madura foot, Mr. P. Chapman didn't initially suspect he had contracted a serious disease. The abscesses that occasionally popped up on his right foot always disappeared without treatment. But as the months shuffled into years, damage occurred to the muscles, tendons, and bones of his right trotter. By the time he hobbled into Morris's office, his foot was a club-shaped mass of oily, discharging fistulas.

At first Morris tried to treat the foot with an aggressive regime of tetracycline (Mr. Chapman was allergic to penicillin). Unfortunately, a secondary bacterial infection had already set in, and within a matter of days Morris realized that to prevent the fatal spread of the infection, the foot would have to be amputated. This pained him as deeply as it pained his patient, if not more so.

Morris views the foot as sacrosanct, as a marvellously engineered member that proves beyond a doubt the existence of an omnipotent Creator. That such weight can be supported by a collection of such fine bones! That speed and agility, grace and power, all exist because of the foot!

Whether the foot supplies its possessor with digitigrade

locomotion (as with the five-toed cat or four-toed roadrunner), unguligrade locomotion (as with the hoofed, triple-toed tapir), or plantigrade locomotion (as with the flat-soled raccoon, black bear, and human), Morris uniformly reveres this ground-bound appendage. Indeed, he views the foot the same way Christians consider the faithful donkey that carried Mary to Bethlehem, and years later, Christ into Jerusalem on Palm Sunday.

So it is natural that Morris pauses a moment as his patient lies anesthetized before him, body shrouded in a white hospital sheet. Oblivious to the presence of the nurses and anesthesiologist, Morris gently strokes the swollen lump of fungus granules, fibrous trabeculae, and intercommunicating sinuses.

"The suffering will soon be over," he whispers to the foot. "Rest easy now. Rest. Your work here is done."

Similar words, in a far less loving tone, are currently being delivered to Moey, and not in regard to either of his feet.

"If you don't share my philosophy, you can't instruct in my school. You'll have to stop working here. Do you understand?"

Mute, Moey nods. How else can he respond?

His lack of vocalization only further irritates the Master, who continues to stand before him with arms crossed over chest and chin slightly raised. Red washes the Master's cheeks, turning his delicate Irish complexion as blotchy as a rotten tomato. "What were you thinking out there, Moey?"

"I'm sorry, sir. I hadn't planned on saying —"

"Then why did you?"

"I apologize, sir." He clears his throat and shifts a little. "I realize that what I said was out of place. This is your school."

"Yes, it *is* my school, and nobody tells me how to teach here. You may be an instructor, but you're also my student. You don't question me and you don't tell my other students when you think my ideas are wrong."

"Sir, I —"

"I never said anything against my Master when I was a student. Never. You should know better than that. I *expect* better than that, especially from you. How long have you been with us? Three years now, four?"

Long enough to see you change your name from Seamus O'Grady to Master Zahbar. He doesn't say this aloud. "Three and a half, sir."

"Three and a half," the Master repeats. "Three and a half."

The atmosphere thickens, and Moey gets the distinct impression he is expected to drop his eyes or look away. He feels contrite, yes, but shameful? No. He continues to meet the Master's gaze.

"I don't know how to proceed with this," the Master finally says, eyes hostile. The skin over his cheeks tightens. "I'm going to have to think about this for a while."

"I under —"

"Until I come up with a resolution to this conflict, you'd better take some time off and reflect on what you've done. Understand? I don't want to see you back here until I come to a decision on this."

"Sir …"

"You're dismissed." A pause. "I'll finish your class."

Perhaps from a sense of self-preservation, Karen wakes up three minutes before noon. She immediately grapples for the switch on her alarm clock, flicks it off, then falls back onto her pillow with a shudder of relief. God only knows what it would have done to her hot, spongy head to have been woken by a metallic squawk for the second time in less than five hours.

She stares at the raindrops sliding down her window and remembers how she yelled at her family earlier that morning. Guilt floods her.

A good mother wouldn't have done that, she thinks. A good mother would have endured a few more minutes of squabbling before seeing her family out the door. The memory of Andy's whipped-dog look, Candice's shock, and Morris's dismay makes her skin crawl.

I'll apologize tonight, she thinks. *I'll make them something special for dinner. Potato latkes and fresh salad perhaps.*

Furry-mouthed, she drags herself from bed and crutch-stumps to the bathroom. Without turning on the light, she brushes her teeth, washes her face, and twists her furious red mop into a ponytail. She regards herself in the toothpaste-splattered mirror for a moment, then digs around in the cabinet for mascara. She applies it, reaches for some blush, then grimaces: mascara is plenty sufficient for Moey.

"And tofu butterscotch pudding," she says to her reflection. "I'll make that for dessert. It's Morris's favourite."

And I'll just have to tell Moey I made a mistake, that's all. After today he won't be able to dance here.

Dilly follows her into the kitchen, keeping a wary distance from her swinging crutches. Despite the questionable edibility of the partially cooked scones and muffins inside the oven (Morris switched the heat off before leaving for work), Karen shoves the half-baked goods into a backpack. At her feet Dilly meows.

"What's wrong, Dillums? Did nobody feed a starving pussy? Here, try a carrot muffin."

Karen breaks a hard, dry muffin in two and tosses half to the floor. She eats the remainder herself, even the slightly gooey part in the middle, then transfers a small carton of cream from the refrigerator to her backpack. (Everything else already awaits her in the Footstop: sugar cubes, teaspoons, ground coffee, tea bags, cups, saucers — Morris carried it all into the teahouse the previous evening.)

"Such a diligent man," she murmurs to Dilly as she shrugs into the backpack. "So earnest."

The cat looks up from the muffin on the floor and blinks at her.

"What? You don't believe me? You two never did get along. Come on, it's off to work we go, hi-ho." Humming the tune to *Sleeping Beauty*, Karen leaves the kitchen.

Opening the Footstop for business entails turning lights and music on, flipping the door sign to "Open," plugging in the coffee percolator, and removing the baked goods from her backpack and displaying them on the antique cake stands. Dilly prowls the corners of the teahouse, killing dust balls and munching on dead insects.

To pass the time until Moey appears, Karen hops about flicking dust from countertops and cabinets, inhaling the soothing teahouse scents — mint foot balm, leather moccasins, freshly brewed coffee. (Her nostrils always take on a life of their own in the teahouse, fluttering open and shut like two feeding barnacles.) The entire time her head feels like a plum pudding — hot, thick, and sticky. And one thought keeps repeating: *I shouldn't have said yes. I shouldn't have ...*

As the foot clocks on the wall behind the counter ease towards 12:45, there is still no sign of Moey and certainly no hint of any customers. Not that any will likely appear, since outside the rain continues to hammer the roof like an epileptic carpenter on cocaine.

Karen is both relieved and disquieted; if no customers appear, there will be no reason for Moey to dance and she won't have transgressed against her husband in the least. Yet she also intuitively knows it is very important for Moey to make his first public performance in the relative safety of her little parlour; the boy is coming out of the closet, so to speak, and her maternal instincts want the experience to be one that inspires confidence in him.

"Not that he's a boy," she mutters to Dilly, who has curled up on one of the windowsills behind the lace curtains to watch the driving rain. "He doesn't look much younger than me. Five or six years at the most."

At 1:00 she begins crutch-pacing up and down the length of the teahouse. *I never should have agreed to this. What if Morris comes home early, right in the middle of Moey's performance? Sweet Jesus, the shock will kill him.* Karen breaks into a sweat and lurches faster up and down the floor.

At 1:20, thoroughly disgruntled and bruised under her armpits from the crutches, she collapses into an Edwardian wingback chair and gnaws on the more edible sections of a muffin. She is working on her second when Dilly suddenly straightens on the windowsill, ears swivelling forward.

Karen tenses — customer or belly dancer, which one is wending down the river-rock path to her door?

Customer, customer, customer, she prays.

A hunched, hulking figure in black appears between the drenched hemlocks and cedars, the handles of an army duffle bag clenched in his left fist. Moey. Karen groans, hastily brushes the crumbs off herself, and reaches for her crutches. The doorbell tinkles and a blast of loam-scented air sweeps inside as he enters.

With some difficulty, she works her way out of her chair. "I don't expect we'll get any customers today," she says by way of greeting.

He shuts the door and stands just inside the entrance, duffle bag held before him. Glancing wordlessly about, he slides the worn handles of the bag between his fingers. Despite his muscled bulk, olive skin, and black hair, he suddenly reminds Karen of Andy. It is his stance, that uncertain, apprehensive posture. She experiences another gush of maternal feelings towards him.

"Come in. I'll pour you a coffee." She wedges her crutches under her sore armpits and turns to the counter. "Is that your costume in there?"

"What? Yes. And music. Costume and music."

At the mention of music her stomach somersaults. *Lord, what if Morris comes home and hears Egyptian tunes wailing from his beloved teahouse?* He is so particular about what sort of music she can play here. Mozart, Yanni, Enya ... they all meet with his approval. Ali Baba and the Cairo Cats wouldn't.

"Of course, music." She clatters two cups onto their respective saucers. "That's important. To dance to music."

"Yes."

"'Seek out a man who is skilful in playing the harp; and when the evil spirit from God is upon you, he will play it and you will be well.' 1 Samuel 16:14." Karen wipes sweaty palms on her cotton dress and reaches for the percolator pot. "Not that I'm religious. Spiritual, yes. Religious, no. But my father is a pastor. Anglican."

"Oh."

She glances over her shoulder at him. He hasn't moved from the door yet.

"Come in, sit down, sit down. Do you take sugar in your coffee?" Without waiting for an answer, she turns back and plunks two lumps into both cups.

She hears him move away from the door and shuffle towards a chair. As he lowers his bulk into it, leather creaks and trapped air gushes out the padding. His duffle bag hits the floor with a soft *whumpf* and a muted jingle of coins.

"Yes," Moey says, "music is important."

His tone reminds her of screws and dark alleys and little boys who pull the wings off flies. She smiles too brightly and ploughs on with the conversation. "Sufi master Hazrat Khan once said, 'There is nothing better than music as a means for the upliftment of the soul.' Did you know that? There's trivia for you, ha ha."

"Upliftment of the soul," he echoes.

"My mother taught me that. Though she isn't really my mother. Stepmother." She takes a deep breath and gestures to the coffee mugs. "Perhaps you could carry these for me? Because of my broken ankle …"

He blinks, glances at her cast, then slowly nods. "Of course."

Moey gets out of the chair as if rising from a swamp — sluggish, ponderous, sombre. Karen holds her breath as he wades through an invisible slough to get to her. With an uncertain smile she extends the cups to him. He reaches for them, his eyes meeting hers. Their hands touch; Karen tries not to flinch. A long moment passes.

"I lost my job this morning," he eventually says. His fingers rest on hers — callused, hairy, and incredibly wide. His brow puckers in confusion. "I'm not sure how it happened, but it did. I lost my job."

Relief floods her — *that* explains his funereal tone.

Silence between them. Despite the thunderous rain on the roof, Karen is aware of the rough, sandy sound of Dilly grooming herself. Karen licks her own lips.

"Then perhaps you'd like a little whiskey in your coffee," she suggests briskly. "I have some in the house."

As a teetotaller, Karen doesn't know if whiskey is the correct alcoholic beverage to add to coffee, but it sounds right, and other than a dust-coated bottle of Okanagan red wine, it is the only alcohol she has on the premises. Morris received both bottles of liquor from clients last Christmas, bottles that Karen has been saving to rewrap and give away this year.

As well as the appropriateness of the whiskey, she also doesn't know how much to add to Moey's cup. But she can't deliberate for long; both coffees back in the teahouse are cooling. When she returns, she hastily tips an inch's worth into his cup.

"Is that all right?" she asks.

He pulls his gaze away from the piñatas dangling from the ceiling. "What? Yes, please." He holds his cup up to her.

Karen hesitates, embarrassed to tell him she's already spiked his brew.

What the heck? she decides. *He's a big man. He'll be able to handle a little whiskey.*

She pours some more into his cup, filling it to the brim.

"Thank you, thank you," he says.

She hesitates, then puts a little into her own coffee and sits beside him. They sip in silence for a few moments.

Whiskey-induced sunlight seeps into Karen's limbs; rubies glow in the pit of her stomach. The taste of the whiskey, despite how little she used, burns pleasantly in her nostrils. Her body slackens.

"How did it happen?" she finally asks. "That you were ... laid off?"

Moey stares into his cup. "Music. It happened because of music."

"Ah." She takes another long draft of her lukewarm coffee. The sunlight in her limbs increases.

"Music," Moey repeats. He nods decisively, drains his cup, and sets it down. A single coffee teardrop rolls from the rim to the table. Karen regards it lazily, almost warmly. She knows she should wipe it up lest it stain the wood. And in a minute she will.

Moey fumbles in the pockets of his karate uniform. "Key Element No. 7. May I read it to you?" He withdraws a crumpled sheet of paper and meets her eyes.

"Well ..."

"It won't take long."

"Well ..."

"I'll get you another coffee." He springs from his chair. *Might as well*, she tells herself. *It'll put the poor lad at ease. He's had a hard day. I can't expect him to fling himself right into belly flops when he's in the depths of despair.*

Moey hands her another coffee — liberally laced, she can't help but notice, with whiskey — and reads from the sheet in his hand with a force that pins her to her seat, much like a needle sticks a butterfly to a corkboard. She clutches her mug to steady herself and sips the coffee frequently.

Gradually, his words slide like minnows into her ears and swim through the folds of her brain, darting out before she can grasp much meaning from them. She finds it necessary to lean forward in concentration. An indefinite time later she notices he's finished reading Key Element No. 7 and is instead arguing against it.

Karen spends several moments pondering this fact, staring at the wood grain of the table in front of her. Finding no answer there, she focuses on Moey again. He now stands before her, enthusiastically punctuating his arguments by swatting the air with a roll of wrapping paper.

Good grief, she realizes. *He's drunk.*

Panic thrills through her.

"And that's why I dance!" Moey bellows, striking his chest with the roll of wrapping paper. "I *must* dance!"

He leaps towards his duffle bag, skewers its handles on the roll of wrapping paper, and hoists it into the air. "I shall change into my costume now."

Karen struggles to gather her thoughts. "Really?"

"Absolutely. I promised you a pe'formance and a pe'formance you shall get."

"Oh."

She squints at the blurry outlines of the foot clocks on the wall: all of them read 2:45. *Oh, God, where has the time gone?*

"You can't," she says, turning back to Moey. The room lurches, too.

"Yes, I practised. Don't worry. I am perfec'ly prepared."

Stonewalled by his answer, Karen gropes for a reason why he can't dance, something other than the fact that she doesn't want her children to witness his performance. "You can't because you have no audience."

His face collapses. He takes a deep breath and frowns. His forehead rumples like the buttocks of a Shar-Pei. Then he beams and the wrinkles disappear. "They will come. I have faith. Build it and they will come."

"Build it ..." she repeats blankly.

"And they will come. *You* know."

"Oh."

"I shall change."

"No! I mean, I mean ... perhaps tomorrow would be better, when you haven't had so much to drink."

"Madam, I am not drunk. I do not drink. Ever. I am completely sober. Now where might I change?"

She waves at the curtain that separates her workshop from the teahouse. "Behind there, I suppose, but ..."

"Splendid."

"But you need an audience," she finishes weakly.

"They will come, Karen. They will come!" He zigzags to the back of the teahouse. An elegant snowy foot sculpture rattles on its pedestal as he brushes past it. Karen holds her breath and prays it won't fall.

Moey reaches the heavy brocade curtain that divides her workshop from the teahouse. He draws it aside with a dramatic swirl as the foot smashes against the floor. "Remember the white stag near the creek!" he cries. "We must have faith, Karen!"

She sits there helpless, staring at the pearly shards of ankle. And her birthmarks respond to Moey's battle cry like enraged bees trapped in a jar.

At 2:05 p.m. precisely Egret skips Western Civilization class and boards a bus to Lynn Canyon, figuring it far more important to return the stolen panties to their owner than to learn why Kenneth Clarke believes man is the measure of all things. He disembarks at the beginning of Peters Road at 2:25 and sprints uphill to arrive at the Morton household at 2:38. No one answers his repeated knocks on the front door.

At 2:41 he circles the outside of the house, looking for Candice's window. At 2:45 he finds it — locked. He experiences a burst of panic when he realizes he'll have to break in.

At 2:47, while searching the yard for a suitable rock, he notices the lights of the teahouse shining through the surrounding cedar boughs. With a jolt of logic he decides to enter the house that way without springing alarms, damaging property, obtaining a criminal record, and ruining his chance at the Olympics.

And so at 2:50 he enters the teahouse.

No one will come, Karen thinks foggily, squeezing her thighs to stifle her buzzing birthmarks. *Moey will be crushed when he comes out and discovers no audience, as crushed as that there foot.* She looks from the fallen foot sculpture to the front door. The handle turns. Someone enters.

"Good heavens!" she gasps, rising unsteadily to her feet. "It's a miracle!"

The customer wavers at the entrance of the teahouse, door held ajar as if he might flee at any moment. Or she? Karen isn't certain, is experiencing some difficulty seeing.

"Come in, come in!" Karen cries. "Please be seated. You're just in time."

The customer hesitates, then shuts the door and comes forward.

"Sit, sit!" Karen motions to the chair beside her and plumps its pillow. "Coffee, tea?"

"Uh ..."

"I'll get you some coffee." She searches for her crutches, can't find them, then decides to do without and hops one-legged towards the percolator behind the counter. "I have for you today a specialty. Once you're comfortably ensconced in your chair, the specialty shall begin."

"I ..."

Music blasts over the loudspeakers, then abruptly dies. Both Karen and the customer jump.

"Sorry, sorry!" Moey booms from behind the curtain at the back of the teahouse. "Just figuring out these controls!"

"Do you need help?" Karen calls back.

"No, I think I've got it now. Has the audience arrived?"

Karen turns around, beams at the figure perched on the edge of a chair, and nods. "It has, just like you said! I'm presently serving coffee!"

"Wonderful! I'll wait precisely three minutes before beginning. Howzat?"

"Great!" She nods some more, a sense of elation flooding her. Moey will belly-dance, the audience will clap, and then everyone will leave. Morris will be none the wiser, and Moey will never return. So great is Karen's euphoria that for many moments she can't recall her purpose behind the counter. "Coffee! Of course, you'd like some coffee!"

She searches the countertop and finds tea bags, sugar, spoons, cups, even the coffee percolator. But no coffee pot. "I can't seem to find the pot," she murmurs. "The glass pot. It goes here, right under here. I can't make coffee without it."

"Maybe I should check the kitchen for you," the customer suggests. "Maybe you left it in there in your house."

"Morris specifically brought it in here last night. I remember that." She squints at the table in front of the customer and sees the glint of glass. "Is that it there in front of you?"

"It's a whiskey bottle."

"Oh." She thinks for a moment. "Perhaps you'd like some of that instead."

"Well, I ..."

"No charge, no charge. Consider it compliments of the Footstop." She hops back over to him and collapses into a chair. The person is definitely a him; she knows that now by the timbre of his voice. "Just give me a moment, please. This broken ankle is a lot of work."

Music keens over the loudspeakers: drums and pipes, twangy stringed instruments, shrill ululations, rhythmic clapping, clanging cymbals.

"Good Lord!" Karen gasps. "The performance is about to begin and I haven't even served you!" She snatches her own cup off the table, sloshes whiskey into it, and thrusts it into the hands of the customer. "Drink, drink. You don't want to miss the show!"

"Thanks, but ..."

She squints at the blue eyes bobbing before her. "I do believe I know you."

"It's me, Mrs. Morton —"

"Karen."

"Karen, it's me, Egret. We met yesterday."

Moey chooses that exact moment to enter. He bounds in from the back, his glittering cape swirling, his brawny arms partially raised in a matador stance. His fingers vigorously clack tiny metal cymbals together. Karen's eyes jerk away from Egret and rivet upon Moey instead.

"Holy shit!" Egret breathes beside her.

In time to the music, Moey spins about the room. His hips gyrate while his torso scribes circles in the opposite direction. His abdomen ripples, his back sways. One moment he is slinking sinuously before Karen and Egret, the next he is whirling like a hamster in a washing machine. He moves with the undulating walk of a camel; he quivers like a bowl of pudding in an earthquake. Moey flourishes his cape over their heads, gracing them with the smell of patchouli oil and male sweat. He emphasizes strong, mannish moves with deep-throated bellows. It is both dance and battle, private and shared. Everything about him dazzles.

As the tempo of the music increases, as the drums hammer towards a crescendo, his mesmerizing, intoxicating energy spreads through Karen. She wants to leap up and join him. To vibrate, to scream, to twirl with such feverish energy ...

This is life, she thinks in wonder. *This is life.*

The first movement of the song abruptly ends with a mighty blast of horns and clash of cymbals; Moey triumphantly throws up his arms, tosses back his head, and zagareets. When his shrill cry finishes echoing around the room, absolute silence reigns. Beads of sweat run down his chest and splatter onto the rug.

Karen takes a deep, cleansing breath, then jumps to her feet. "Bravo! Encore, encore!"

Moey bows and swishes his cape about him with one hand. With his other hand he makes an Arabic gesture of thanks from his forehead to his heart. "Perhaps," he gasps as he straightens, "madam would join me in the next dance."

"Yes!" Karen cries, forgetting her casted ankle, her husband, the imminent return of her children. "Oh, yes!"

Behind her someone clears a throat. "Mrs. Morton?"

She turns. "Oh! The audience! How remiss of me!" She fumbles for the whiskey bottle, smiles radiantly at Egret, and refills his cup, which he emptied during the course of Moey's dance.

"Karen," she gently corrects him. "You *must* call me Karen."

Chapter Nine

In 1866, at the age of sixteen, a lad named Jack Daniel discovered a freshwater spring hidden in the wooded hills of Lynchburg, Tennessee. Being an entrepreneurial type, young Mr. Jack lost no time in starting his own bourbon whiskey distillery. To this day that same spring water — fermented with cornmeal, rye, and barley malt, mellowed through ten feet of maple charcoal and aged in charred oak barrels — continues to inebriate millions of people around the world.

Nearly 150 years later, also at the age of sixteen, a lad named Egret Van Gorder is feeling the full power of such whiskey for the first time in his life. Not that Egret hasn't indulged in fermented liquid pleasures before — he has, and he possesses a repertoire of stories to back up such a statement. But never before has he imbibed with the freedom and accessibility currently available.

Nor with such need: with a purloined pair of sperm-encrusted panties in his pocket, surrounded by manifold foot products, and confronted with two drunken, gyrating adults, Egret feels way out of his depth. So he drinks, bolstering his courage and calming his composure in a means honoured long before Jack Daniel ever added his first batch of yeast to his first batch of sour mash. It isn't long before the charcoal-mellowed brew encourages and relaxes Egret to the point where he does backflips off the floor and somersaults off the counter to the raucous applause of the two gyrating adults.

Flushed and unfettered, Karen watches Egret perform another neat salmon flip from atop her antique French Provincial trestle table. The boy has recently stripped off his Adidas sweatshirt; the white cotton tank top he wears underneath accents his muscles the way sweat highlights the sleek, firm muscles of a racehorse.

"Another, another!" she cries out. "Bravo!"

But the music dies as the cassette winds to the end of the last song, and everyone momentarily comes to a stop. They regard one another blankly, chests heaving, cheeks glowing.

Karen turns to Moey. The room tilts slightly. "Is there another side to this tape?"

He slowly strokes his fake moustache. "There is indeed another side to this tape. The B side."

"Great! I'll flip it over." And before her responsible mommy mind can click in (*don't look at the clocks, don't think who might be coming home soon!*), Karen hops and staggers to the back of the teahouse.

As well as she knows her cluttered workshop, it takes her a few moments to find the tape deck among the hammers, paint pots, glue guns, and sculpting burrs on her shelves. When she does so, she is startled to find Egret at her side.

"Mizz Morton —"

"Karen," she corrects. She jabs a thumb at the eject button and watches the tape slowly slide out.

"I mean, Karen. Can I use your washroom? I gotta take a leak."

"Sure, sure." She waves a hand over her shoulder, then

carefully reverses the tape and pushes it back into the deck. "Through there."

He sways beside her for a moment, and she notices the warmth venting from his body the way it does from an overheated car radiator. It is a sweet, clean, salty heat.

"Thanks," he says after a pause, then lurches through the door that joins the Footstop Café to the Morton household.

The cassette begins whirring through the tape deck with a dry, whispery noise.

Aha, Karen thinks triumphantly, *I have successfully inserted the B side.*

Softly, slowly, the eerie strains of a single stringed instrument resonate throughout the teahouse.

"Yes!" Moey cries from the front of the shop. "'Nahawad,' a dramatic, mysterious song! Mystical, sensual, the true essence of the belly dance!"

"Different from the other side," Karen calls back to him, but he doesn't reply. She hears the *shuffle/tinkle* of him dancing on the other side of the curtain.

"Much different," she murmurs to herself, leaning against the shelves and closing her eyes. The wild energy of the whiskey starts to seep from her, replaced by a delightful drowsiness, a pleasurable earthiness. Eyes still shut, listing heavily against the shelves, she sways to the haunting strains of the music.

A horn joins the string, then a pipe, then a drum. Slowly, slowly, the pulse of the rhythm intensifies, yet barely quickens. More horns and pipes join in, trembling, straining. And drums in the background, always drums. Drums of hot deserts, drums of veils. Drums of lean limbs glistening under a relentless sun. Drums of sabres, of reckless courage, of billowing capes and steamy tents.

Animal skins, roughly taken pleasures, jewels, silks, bullwhips, sandstorms: the drums speak of these. They speak of climbing need, of increasing desire, of fluttering hands and shuddering skin.

Her left hand slides across her belly, along the crimped-cotton fabric of her dress. She opens a button, then another. Her fingers drift between the folds of her dress, glide across her breasts, and stroke a nipple to hardness. A groan escapes her. She tilts back her head and aches with the need to merge her flesh with the music, to satiate those drums.

Something creaks out of tune with the music. Her eyes flutter open. Egret stands in the doorway, returning from the house. His eyes freeze on her; her hands freeze on her body. Time lingers and lengthens.

Egret swallows; Karen sees the movement as a mirror of her own need. With her left hand still cupping her exposed breast, she stretches her other hand towards him.

After a pause, he comes to her.

And that is how Andy discovers his mother when he arrives home from school: unclad and creamy white, she is as slick and smooth as wet marble, her body impaled upon a teenager sprawled naked on her workshop floor.

Oblivious to the grunts and jagged sighs issuing from the other side of the teahouse curtain, Moey dances with eyes closed, spirit soaring. He dances with numinosity.

When the tape warbles to a finish, he collapses into a chair and contemplates the way the music stirred his soul. He rests his head against the worn leather. Within moments he falls asleep.

"Tomorrow," Karen whispers against Egret's salty, sweat-slicked shoulder. "Tomorrow we must not feel regret or shame. Neither of us."

Egret stirs beneath her, shifts slightly, and reaches with one hand for his shirt. "'Kay."

"I want you always to feel welcome here. Always."

From where he sits on the edge of his bed, schoolbooks on his left, trumpet case on his right, Andy stares at his tiny Buddha. The glossy figure gazes back, its benevolent gaze expressing sorrow as well as wisdom and sympathy. For the first time ever, its smooth whiteness reminds Andy of his mother. With a choked sob he averts his eyes and contemplates the rug instead.

But still he sees that horrifying image: his mother's white, sweat-slicked buttocks riding a bucking, grunting Teenager. Andy wanted to flee the moment he walked into the workshop, but shock paralyzed him. So he stayed there and watched, rain dripping from his coat to the floor, hardly daring to breathe.

Eyes screwed shut, fingers biting deep into either side of her hips, the Teenager repeatedly pushed himself into Andy's mother. The aggression on his face, the raw need expressed by the veins standing out on his neck captivated, terrified, and repulsed Andy.

Worse was his mother sitting astride the Teenager. Her back was facing Andy, but at a slight angle so he could see her breasts bounce and swing with each thrust. Her casted leg — protruding from her as stiffly as a snowman's arm — thumped dully against the floor with each bounce.

As Andy watched, one of the Teenager's hands detached itself from his mother's hips and clenched her left breast — clenched hard and twisted. His mother cried out.

A scream entered Andy's own throat, and he tensed, ready to leap forward and save her, to batter the Teenager with his heavy trumpet case. Then his mother spoke.

"Harder, yes, oh!"

Andy turned and fled to his bedroom.

Now he sits on the edge of his bed, staring at the rug, not daring to move. Eventually, the weird strains of music from the teahouse die (the same music that drew him from the kitchen to the teahouse workshop in the first place). Even then Andy waits and waits, bladder bursting, stomach growling, chest heaving with held-back emotion. He swelters under his rubber raincoat, pools of muddy water staining the rug under his galoshes. Still, he doesn't budge.

His paralysis doesn't end until he hears his mother stump down the hall an hour later, the rubber end of her crutches squeaking on the hardwood floor. When the bathroom door clicks shut behind her, Andy finally moves. He creeps down the hall, schoolbooks gathered under one arm, trumpet case clenched in his opposite fist, wincing as each floorboard creaks beneath his feet. Behind him, in the bathroom, his mother turns on the sink faucets.

Heart pounding, mouth dry as chalk, Andy enters the kitchen and pushes open the door to the adjoining workshop. Immediately, a strange acidic, salty smell hits his nostrils and he grimaces. He scans the room: he is alone. Taking a quavering breath, he slips inside.

No evidence remains of what he witnessed. He expects to see the equivalent of an earthquake's aftermath. He expects to see his feelings mirrored in his surroundings. But he doesn't. It is wrong that such an event leaves no trace.

Carefully, he tiptoes around the heavy curtain that divides the workshop from the teahouse. Again, everything seems normal. Not a trace lingers of what transpired. In the time that passed during Andy's unnoticed arrival from school, his mother erased all signs that the Teenager ever existed — if, indeed, any signs existed in the first place.

Then something moves, and Andy gasps, stumbles back a few feet. His bony shoulders slam into a display cabinet. The merchandise on it rattles — a foot-shaped spoon rack smacks him on the head as it falls to the floor.

"Meow." Dilly comes towards him, tail fluffed up, eyes squinted in friendly myopia.

"Holy geez!" Andy stammers. "Holy geez, you scared me."

Dilly purrs and rubs against his legs. A few of the foot clocks on the far wall chime: 4:30.

Candice will be home any minute, and not long after that, their father. Andy swallows, readjusts his grip on his books and trumpet case, and quickly leaves the teahouse through the public entrance.

The mushroom-and-rotting-wood smell of outdoors clears the strange stench of the Teenager from his nostrils. Head bowed under the pouring rain, shivering from the blustery wind, Andy slogs through puddles to the back door of the house. Making as much noise as possible — stamping water from his boots, coughing and banging his trumpet case against the door — he enters the kitchen.

"Hi, Mom!" he bellows. "I'm home!"

"That you, Andy?" His mother's voice — normal or frightened? — drifts down the hall from the bathroom.

He dumps his schoolbooks onto the kitchen table, sets his trumpet case on a chair, and shakes water from his raincoat. "Sorry I'm late," he calls. "I forgot something at school and had to walk all the way back again."

"What time is it exactly?"

"Almost five."

"That late? Oh, Lord, I haven't even started dinner."

He sees again her white, dimpled buttocks straddled over the Teenager, and he stifles a whimper.

The swinging doors to the kitchen scrape open and his mother lurches in, crutches squeaking. Briefly, their eyes meet.

Andy flushes and hastily looks away. "I can peel potatoes if you want." He speaks with difficulty, his throat suddenly thickened with tears.

"Could you? Oh, Andy, that would be wonderful."

Feeling nauseated and trembly, he takes off his galoshes, puts on his slippers, wipes steam from his glasses, and begins to peel potatoes for dinner.

Candice has a social conscience and she hates it. Her mother drilled it into her. It concerns litter, and picking it up, and placing it into whatever receptacle is nearest — someone's garbage can left out on the curb, the back of someone's pickup truck, into someone's mailbox. If no receptacle presents itself, the offending piece of refuse must be carried until a receptacle appears. This is as critically disgusting as things get.

Every childhood memory Candice has of her mother involves one of two things: feet or litter. Her mother's feet in sandals at a park, stained by grass, speckled with dew. Her mother bending to check the ankle of the postman when he was bitten by the Wagners' Doberman. A fat man's enormous feet at a bowling alley, where her mother staged Candice's tenth birthday party. Feet, feet, feet.

And litter. A pulpy, wet cigarette pack outside McDonald's on the day Andy got stung by a bee while eating some french fries. A parking ticket stub bobbing in the water near the snout of an alligator at Stanley Park Zoo. An oil-streaked plastic bag half buried in the snow outside Capilano Mall during a trip to see Santa. Litter, litter, litter.

Feet are important and special, Candice was taught, and litter is a defilement. This was drilled into her repeatedly during her childhood. She thanks God that the whole foot-fetish thing passed right over her, but she is cursed, marked for life, by the asinine litter thing. She knows it's become an obsession.

She can't walk anywhere, *anywhere*, without noticing litter. If she doesn't pick up the observed garbage and dispose of it somehow, it lingers in her mind and haunts her every step. It's as if the litter throws out an invisible thread and lassoes her, and no matter how far or fast she walks, the thread gets longer and longer, dragging behind her until at last she can *feel* her footsteps slowing down from the weight of it and she has to turn back and pick up the goddamn piece of litter and dump it somewhere to free herself. Gloria calls this a social conscience, but both of them know that it isn't. It's an obsession, a fixation, a fetish. A *phobia*, for Christ's sake. Like how some people have to wash their hands a hundred times a day or they can't function. That kind of thing.

So Candice tries to avoid being outside when she's around people from school, because for sure they'll think she's mental. If she absolutely has to be outside for whatever reason — like during gym class, when the stupid teacher makes them jog around the block — then she wears dark sunglasses and stares upward a bit, away from the ground. She has learned how to do this and make it seem cool, kind of haughty, which has earned her the reputation of being defiant of authority, which is completely acceptable.

Walking home from school every day is torture. Not that she walks all the way home. Forget that. It's too far. She takes the bus partway. But from where she gets off the bus at the end of Peters Road until she reaches the doorstep of their home, it is sheer hell. There is litter everywhere. And not big litter, either, though there is occasionally a Coke can or a Styrofoam cup, but little litter, like gum wrappers, granola bar packages, shopping receipts. These are always soggy, no matter the weather, and lie in grime in the sidewalk gutter. Most people probably don't even notice these scraps, but Candice has some sort of X-ray vision for them, thanks to her mom. Like that small pink thing at the edge of Mr. Osaban's driveway, for instance. Who would possibly notice that other than Candice?

As her fingers close over the object, she freezes. It feels wrong, too spongy, too juice-laden. She peers at it. Her skin crawls, her mouth turns to limestone. With a shriek she hurls the thing into the street.

"Jesus fucking Christ!" she screams, dancing around, shaking her hand in the air as if trying to rid it of a hornet. "Fuck, fuck, fuck!"

After several more screams, she plunges her hand into a nearby laurel hedge and frantically wipes it on the rain-drenched leaves.

"That's it, that's absolutely fucking *it*!" she shouts. "I have to see a shrink or else I'm screwed for life!"

Head lowered against the driving rain, she marches the rest of the way home, ignoring the tug from each piece of litter she passes. Meanwhile, back at Mr. Osaban's, in the street in front of his driveway, the pink fleshy foot of a bird glistens in the rain. The irony that both Morton fetishes are embodied in the severed object — foot and litter — doesn't escape Candice.

Terrified, Karen tries to perform her housewife duties as if nothing out of the ordinary has occurred. But it has — oh, yes, it really has — and as she and Andy fry potato latkes in the skillet, she thinks of Egret. While Andy tears chunks of crisp lettuce into a bowl and she slices juicy hothouse tomatoes into wedges, she thinks of Egret again. More than once she catches herself groaning, either dismayed or aroused.

Yet everything appears so normal as she sits down to dinner. Morris narrates the details of his day at work, Candice grumbles about the fat content in the potato latkes, and Andy eats with silent gusto. It is almost impossible to believe that Egret and his intense, firm body sweated beneath her less than four hours ago, almost impossible to believe that they stroked and clasped and tasted each other's flesh …

Another groan escapes her, this one not of dismay, and satin heat rushes out between her thighs. A small warm stain spreads across the seat of her dress. She flushes and shoots a look around the table.

First at Morris: she watches a strand of grated fried potato fall from his lips and catch in the day stubble sprouting from his chin. Then at Candice: a clot of mascara trembles at the end of one of her eyelashes as she suspiciously tests a piece of food with her front teeth. Then Andy: olive oil speckles his glasses and makes his chin as shiny as a wet, white pebble as he methodically shovels in food. None of them has heard her gasp or noticed her flush.

Somehow this revelation makes her feel cheated.

Cheated! How can she feel such a thing after what she did? How dare she feel anything but regret and self-disgust?

All these years of carefully keeping her emotions dammed up, of striving to be a correct and proper mother, and she threw them all to the wind. And for what? Nothing more than a fleeting, drunken moment with a teenager. So how dare she feel cheated!

But no matter how she berates herself, the feeling persists.

She puts down her knife and fork and rubs her temples wearily. Again she studies her family: Morris meticulously mopping every speck of salad dressing off his plate with a dinner roll; Candice poking disgustedly at the oily edges of a pancake; Andy sputtering on an onion slice. Slowly, slowly, it dawns on her why she feels cheated.

They all assume her day involved nothing but housework. For them all her days, every day of the year, can't possibly entail anything different than laundry, dishwashing, and vacuuming. She has nothing new and surprising to offer them; she is predictable and bland. And that's why she feels cheated — she, the cheater.

Abruptly, she rises from the table, accidentally knocking over her glass of purified water. Everyone falls silent and looks up, then as one stares at the water cascading onto the linoleum floor and splattering against her cast. For a moment the ticking clock and the dripping water harmonize.

"Still not feeling well?" Morris asks. "Migraine?"

Andy slips from his chair, takes the stained foot-shaped tea towel draped over the sink, and quietly mops up the water. The whites of his eyes as he focuses intently on his task remind Karen of lychees.

"I've got some painkillers left over from my tonsillectomy," Candice says. "Want them? I mean, I don't care if you do or don't. They've probably expired."

"Oh," Karen says hoarsely, "that's very thoughtful."

"Whatever." Candice pushes back her chair and sashays out.

"Go lie down, Karen. We'll do the dishes, won't we, son?"

"Sure, Dad."

"But your dessert ..." she protests.

"I can make it. Tofu butterscotch pudding, correct?"

"Are you sure?"

"Go rest," Morris says. "Get some sleep."

Barely able to hold back tears, Karen wordlessly reaches for her crutches and leaves the kitchen.

I am undeserving of this, she thinks as she stumps down the hall. *I am undeserving of their love.*

Moey wakes up damp and shivering, his tongue feeling like the hide of roadkill, his head one large, pulsating bruise. He blinks in the darkness and listens to the ping of raindrops on metal, wondering where the hell he is.

He shifts, and something tinkles. Slowly, he peels his cheek away from damp vinyl and sits up. Ah, yes, he is in his car. Parked outside the Footstop. Suffering a terrible, terrible hangover.

The urge to urinate woke him. He fumbles with the door handle and staggers out into the driving rain. Shivering violently (dressed only in his much-bedraggled belly-dancing costume), he pisses against one of his car tires and blinks at the enormous ghost-white foot painted on the clapboards of Karen's unlit house. Hemlocks moan and squeak in the wind.

Memory slowly returns. After setting knocked-over chairs and statues upright, after thanking the single audience member profusely for his attention, after finding the lost coffee pot and hiding the almost empty bottle of whiskey in Karen's compost heap (at her behest), Moey reeled to his car and passed out on the front seat.

Now he squints through the rain at the dark sky. Save for the creaking trees and patter of raindrops around him, everything is silent. He guesses it is close to midnight.

Steam billows from his car tire as he finishes his business. Once more he glances at Karen's house. With a sigh he clambers back into his car. After several minutes of searching, he discovers his keys in his duffle bag, starts the engine, and heads home.

Chapter Ten

Reverend Sandy Woodruff and his second wife, Mei-ling (aka Petra) Woodruff, live in a house built in 1938 on the corner of Thirteenth Street and Grand Boulevard. They purchased the house because it was within walking distance of the reverend's church, and it has served them well for more than a decade. But last year its age, combined with the ever-present Vancouver rain, began to wear the roof down. A pair of pantyhose stretched over their heads would have provided the Woodruffs with more protection.

Mei-ling therefore gathered a sheath of estimates from various roofing companies, chose the one with the lowest figure and most promising product, and had the roof re-shingled. Five months later it started leaking again.

Another roofing company inspected the roof (the first company now out of business) and informed the Woodruffs that the house was suffering from excessive moisture buildup in the attic due to the airtight fibreglass shingles that had been used. For just under $1,000 they could install a dehumidifier to rectify the problem. At a loss on how to proceed, the Woodruffs agreed.

The dehumidifier worked with such exuberance, however, that it created the equivalent of a vacuum in the basement. Straining against this sudden pressure, the old gas pipes sprung leaks. For $400, a gas fitter squirted

Sunlight Liquid Soap over the pipes, found the leaks, and fixed the faulty joints.

A few evenings later — the exact time Karen is preparing for bed, her tongue furred with whiskey, her loins scrubbed free of all Egret juice — Mei-ling mentions to her husband that she can smell gas. Reverend Woodruff inhales deeply and repeatedly but can't smell anything more than the halibut his wife cooked for dinner. Appeased, Mei-ling retires to bed, and the reverend joins her after doing his back-strengthening exercises.

At 2:30 in the morning, when the temperature drops outside and the thermostat calls for more heat, a cracked valve in the boiler, accumulated gas, and insufficient combustion air intake in the basement all combine to produce an explosion. Mei-ling wakes instantly and wonders if she's back in Tibet during a bomb raid. Then she smells smoke. By the time she rouses the reverend, the rumble of flames and groaning of timbers in the basement are clearly audible. They flee the house just moments before a second explosion turns their bedroom into an inferno.

Thus, because of a leaky roof, flames devour everything the Woodruffs own (both in their house and the attached garage) and would have set their neighbours' houses alight if not for torrential rain and the swift appearance of the North Vancouver City Fire Department.

And thus Karen Morton is awakened by a phone call at four o'clock in the morning, a mere ten hours after committing adultery with one of her daughter's classmates. The word *retribution* comes immediately to her mind.

The next two weeks pass in a blur. Karen spends her days chauffeuring her father to Bible classes, deathbeds, and christening ceremonies, and Mei-ling to insurance companies, banks, and lawyers' offices. Karen fills out forms, answers the phone, and sorts donations of food, clothing, and furniture left by her father's parishioners. Many of them seem to be under the impression that the good reverend weighs ninety pounds less than he does, and is four feet tall in his stocking feet. Karen saves these clothes for Candice to poke through.

On top of all this she continues her telephone canvassing for MotherWatch (a B.C. Liquor Board–sponsored association dedicated to educating the public about fetal alcohol syndrome), helps Andy create his larger-than-life model of the human tongue (his class is studying taste buds), and bakes orange-cranberry muffins and cream-filled scones for the teahouse, which she opens whenever chance allows.

"Thank God you broke your left foot instead of your right," Mei-ling says more than once. "At least you can still drive."

"I don't know if I *should* be driving," Karen always replies. "It's probably against the law." (Which Morris firmly believes and repeats each morning as they drive to his office together, where he hands her the keys so she can use the car for the rest of the day.)

Each evening Karen prepares two separate dinners, one for the herbivores, the other for the omnivores. Her father insists that grace be said before either meal is consumed, which invariably produces an argument — no one in the Morton family knows words appropriate for such a benediction, save Karen, her father, and Mei-ling. Mealtime becomes a battleground for religious and dietary beliefs.

No comfort after dinner: the children sleep in sleeping bags in the living room while the grandparents occupy their beds. Candice complains about Andy's snoring, about the cold floor, about her lack of privacy. Mei-ling wakes every night from explosion-provoked memories about her youth, while the reverend develops an allergy to Yogurt, Andy's guinea pig. Morris scribbles furiously in his journal until midnight, at all other times taking refuge in podiatry periodicals and tight-lipped silence. Dilly hides under the couch.

Dirty laundry multiplies. Unwashed dishes reproduce. Mail stacks up, dust gathers, jumbo packs of toilet paper vanish overnight.

During all this, Karen thinks of Moey, the white hart, and Egret only ... oh, once every hour or so. Each ring of the phone slicks her with sweat, lest it be Moey inquiring when next he might perform at the Footstop. Each knock on the front door sends her heart galloping into her eardrums, lest it be Egret bearing roses in one hand and condoms in the other, or a letter from his attorney informing her of an impending rape charge. Her fears vary depending on the day.

She embraces the tumult around her, which she views as punishment for releasing passions she should have kept imprisoned, for acknowledging desires both unmotherly and unwifely. By striving hard to maintain peace in her house, by working tirelessly to re-establish order in her parents' lives, she is atoning bit by bit for her terrible mistake. No good can ever come from acknowledging private needs and dreams; that much is now obvious to her. For all these years she did the right thing to ignore her birthmarks, to quash her sensuality, to work diligently at being an obedient wife and conscientious mother.

But a small part of her — and oh, how potent! — remembers the music of the drums. And, if anything, the yearning to fulfill her private aspirations only increases a thousandfold.

"What is it, girl? What?"

Karen looks up from her pottery wheel and blinks at Mei-ling, who sits at Karen's workbench, vigorously chewing tobacco. Six years ago Mei-ling kicked her smoking habit, but after the recent explosion, she succumbed once more to her nerve-soothing, nicotine addiction. To hide her relapse from the reverend and to respect Karen's loathing of cigarette smoke, she satisfies her craving by chewing tobacco.

"I'm sorry," Karen says. "What did you say? Did the doorbell ring? Did someone come in?"

"Nobody's going to come today. Listen to that rain. I asked you what's wrong."

Karen glances down at the platter in front of her and strokes the slimy clay. The wet slate smell fills the entire workshop. "You don't like this?"

"You know I'm not talking about that. Don't be obtuse, girl. Something's wrong. It's as plain as the nose on my face. Something's bothering you."

Karen resumes working on the platter, pinching its edges into a scallop pattern of tiny feet. "It's been a little hectic around here lately."

"That's not it." (*Chew, chew, chew*). "I mean, you've always played the perfect mother, but lately you've become positively indulgent."

"Indulgent?" (*Pinch, pinch, pinch*). "What exactly is that supposed to mean?"

"You treat Andy as if he's a glass ornament. You pander after your husband's every whim as if he's Krishna himself. And Candice —"

"Andy is sensitive. You know that."

"And Candice is on the phone nonstop with that Gloria girl. What was the point of hauling her out of one high school and into another if she has constant verbal contact with that troublemaker, anyway?"

"Mother ..."

"Something's wrong. Something's bothering you. I can see it in your aura."

There is silence while jaws vigorously chew and fingers vigorously pinch.

"And another thing," Mei-ling says, and Karen closes her eyes and grimaces. "The doorbell. Every time it rings you fall over yourself to answer it before anyone else does."

"What have you been doing — watching me like a hawk? Analyzing my every move?"

"I worry about you, girl, that's all. The deities have placed upon you some great task, and I worry about you."

"Oh, for God's sake, don't start that again." Heart pounding, Karen furiously pinches the clay.

"Who are you afraid to find at the door each time the bell rings?"

"I am *not* afraid!"

"Stand up and pull down your knickers. Let me have a look at your birthmarks."

"Oh, for Christ's sake, you're acting like a complete fool."

"Did some Gypsy show up at your door and explain your destiny? Is that it? Because I sure would like to know what you plan to do with your life, with birthmarks like those. You can't hide forever in this foot-fetish farm."

Cheeks aflame, Karen resolutely begins another course of tiny feet around the circumference of the platter.

Mei-ling stands and comes around to Karen's side. "Aren't you going to answer me?"

"Don't hover over me. I can't see what I'm doing."

"Then tell me what the Gypsy said."

"There *is* no Gypsy. Gypsies don't exist."

"They do. The BBC showed a program on them the other night. Russian Gypsies living in trees."

"This is Canada, not Russia."

"If you can find Gypsies living in trees in Russia, you can find them living in Canada." A pause. "So what did the Gypsy say?"

"For Christ's sake, Mother, there was no Gypsy, understand?" She turns and throws her hands in the air. Splotches of clay splatter Mei-ling's pea-green polyester jogging suit. "Can't you leave me alone for just one minute?"

Mei-ling jams her wedge of tobacco into her left cheek. "Fine. But I tell you, girl, if you don't get whatever it is off your chest soon, you're going to implode." She turns around and stalks out.

Karen inhales deeply and deliberately, sucking in the gritty smell of clay and the sweet, wet scent of tobacco. Her mother is right, damn it. But who the hell can she talk to?

Moey lies in bed, propped in a half-sitting position by a mountain of pillows hand-knitted by Miranda. Made of yellow, green, and red acrylic yarn, the pillows' stubble pokes through Moey's sweat-dampened T-shirt, giving him a terrible rash. Up until today he dared not voice his discomfort — easier to bear the rash than Miranda's indignation, since the pillows sell well at craft bazaars, the profits of which go to various foundations for skill-challenged African Canadian youth. He should be *grateful* for the loan of them.

Today, however, he vows to tell her to take her pillows and ... stuff them. Or something to that effect. He isn't terribly sure yet how he'll phrase it — fact is, his head is still one shade lighter than empty.

Those few hours he spent passed out semi-naked in his Plymouth outside the Footstop two and a half weeks earlier cursed Moey with a terrible fever, accompanied by delirium, pneumonia, and an infection in his ears and sinuses. Because of the infection, no mucus drains from his nose no matter how vigorously he tries to blow. The subsequent pressure behind his eyes makes him weep at the smallest glimmer of light, wince at the slightest sound, and shun all forms of movement. This last is nearly impossible, because the pneumonia causes fits of razor-like hacking that shake his entire body.

Miranda relishes every moment of his infirmity. Each evening she diligently changes his bedsheets, feeds him soup, and ensures that he take the correct amount of herbal medicine she herself makes. His illness has bestowed upon her total control over his life, and in return for her slavish attention, she nightly requests that he lie pale and still on those horrible, itchy pillows so she can exploit his body.

Sometimes hallucinating, sometimes cognizant in a detached, dreamy way, sometimes feeling brittle and crispy, other times gristly and grim, Moey watches her suck on, jiggle over, scratch, shackle, nibble, and whip every inch of his frame from his neck down. She moves with such precision, such coiled, taut care, that never once does she jostle his pounding, viscous head. It seems that his frail immobility has only inflamed her passion to new heights, and combined with her position of power, her creativity flourishes.

Subjected nightly to such exploitation, Moey has begun to view his penis as completely separate from himself. It continually responds to her leather cock rings and jelly rubber prostate stimulators regardless of how nauseated, delirious, or unconscious he is. There it rises from its tangled nest of black hair, traitorous, like a mesmerized rattlesnake emerging from a reed basket to a piper's tune. Once he even saw it, not imagined it, as a chicken, beady-eyed and empty-headed, allowing a fox to close jaws around its neck.

The thrill of orgasm belongs completely to his penis; Moey is merely a hapless, sensationless bystander. If he had the strength and clarity of mind, he would resent the way it ejaculates without him.

But today things will be different. For one, the pillows will go. Those scratchy, gaudy pillows will plague his rash-riddled skin no more. He's certain about that. The decision came with dawn, following smoky, disjointed memories of being violated.

Violated. A strong word but warranted, for over the past few weeks, not once, not twice, but repeatedly, Miranda has abused her power and deflowered him in his feeble, delusional state. She has ignored his most ardent aversion and actually *slid* things into him.

Of course, he can't recollect any of it clearly, wonders even if he hallucinated the events: Miranda inserting a dolphin-shaped vibrator into him; Miranda strapping a leather harness around her hips to repeatedly thrust a metal dildo into him!

But hallucination or recollection, fiction or fact, today Moey has resolved to end their relationship. To hell with the memories of his celibate, pre-Miranda days. To hell with the loneliness, the *Hustler* magazines, the unpredictable and unfulfilling one-night stands. To hell with all that: at least he'll have his dignity.

More than dignity, he'll have music. For that is what is missing, has *always* been missing, in sex with Miranda —

music. Her hot sexuality, her fierce eroticism, completely lacks music. It doesn't matter how many interests they share (kickboxing, licorice ice cream, Woody Allen movies), and it doesn't matter how comfortable they are in each other's presence. Between them there exists no music. And Moey wants music in his life.

So he prepares himself to end their relationship. He totters to the shower for the first time in nearly three weeks and gingerly washes his sour, festered flesh. He then dresses in clean clothes, fortifies himself with two cans of Campbell's Chunky Steak & Potato Soup and, exhausted, props himself back against that mountain of horrible pillows.

As he waits for evening to approach, he envisions how he'll take each pillow, one by one, and drop it at her feet as he breaks the news to her.

Egret has also spent the past couple of weeks in torment. No matter how hard he tries, he can't flush the image of Karen — pale, naked, and sweaty — from his mind. Slowly, her image has melded into that of Candice, and he is now convinced, in a desperate way, that this is because mother and daughter are identical. Screwing Karen is therefore tantamount to screwing Candice.

He walks around school bow-legged from a constant hard-on. Before diving practice each morning he has to jerk off a couple times just to fit into his swimsuit. His elbows bear bruises where he whacked them against the black metal doors of the cramped toilet stalls. The smell of chlorine and the feel of wet, hair-streaked tiles beneath his feet has become an intrinsic part of orgasm.

From the looks and snickers following his back, it is obvious that if he doesn't do something soon, he's going to lose his status among his peers. And his diving is suffering; no matter how much he tries, he can't nail even the simplest combination. His father now eats nothing but Tums for breakfast; his coach wears a perpetually bewildered expression. Both are hoarse from shouting at him.

It is the Man, holed up in his basement suite, who finally says what no one else dares to. One day, when Egret brings him his mail — the Man can't walk yet after his operation — he says quite simply, "It's a gal, ain't it?"

Egret pauses in the doorway, blinking in the candlelit gloom. (The Man and Egret's father came to some sort of agreement about reduced rent, the agreement focusing on no use of lights during the day.)

"What do you mean?"

"Christ, kid, look at you. Walkin' about as if your dick is about to explode. Your old man, that's all he talks about these days, jawin' my ear off. I'm sick of it, you hear? Can't concentrate on a lousy hand of poker if his life depended on it."

"Fuck!"

"That's exactly it — fuck! Fuck the girl, or else you're going to fuck up your life. I don't know squat about the Olympics, but I do know that if you blow the next couple of meets, you ain't gonna qualify. That right?"

"I can win 'em."

"Bullshit. You can't even look me in the eye when you say that. 'I can win 'em,'" the Man repeats in a falsetto. "You sound like a goddamn pansy. Want my advice? Get her stoned or drunk —all women loosen up when they're shit-faced — and screw her good. Screw her every night for the next week or so, get it right out of your system. Then get your mind back on your diving, so I can get a decent game of poker out of your old man. Understand?"

"It's not that simple."

"'It's not that simple,'" he mimics. "Christ, when I was your age, I got laid twice a night by a different girl each time."

"Bullshit."

"You're milk-livered, kid. Face it. All that diving's made you into a hen. Either that or you're a fag."

"She's married."

Silence, during which Egret has plenty of time to build up a huge, foamy head of regret.

"Shit," the Man says, breaking into a yellow-toothed grin. "Shit."

"Look, just forget I mentioned —"

"You done it with her already?"

"None of your business."

"You have, ain't ya? I can tell by your face. Shit, the way I hear it, married women —"

"I said forget —"

"Go ape over studs your age. How many times you done it with her?"

Egret clenches his teeth and refuses to answer.

"Just once, eh? What's the problem? You rabbity about her old man?"

"I said forget it." Egret backs out of the room. "Mention this to anyone and I'll tell Dad about your stash. You'll be out of here so fast ..."

"My lips are sealed." The Man's grin turns wolfish, his eyes pink in the candlelight. "But take my advice, kid. Don't worry about her old man. That's *her* problem. You got to worry about makin' it to the Olympics, know what I mean?"

And, unfortunately, Egret does.

Candice skips the last class of the day — Cooking 101: How to Make Gingered Melon Balls — and catches the bus down to Lonsdale Avenue. With its Iranian bakeries, Greek restaurants, and Chinese grocers, Lonsdale is the heart and soul of North Vancouver. It begins at the waterfront and ends at the foot of the mountains. Somewhere in the middle is the Mortons' family doctor.

Candice hates going to the doctor. She detests the stale air and fluoride smell of the office and she loathes the wheezing, bony old people dozing in the waiting room. She hates the dog-eared tabloid magazines on the coffee table and she can't stand the kids fighting over the plastic Fisher-Price telephone in the play corner. It never fails that by the time the receptionist ushers her into the exam room, she feels in dire need of a long, long shower.

Steel canisters of tongue depressors and cotton balls, a blood pressure cuff, weight scales, a Norman Rockwell print of a boy with a bandage wrapped around his head, a small metal garbage can — Candice leans against the exam bench (she won't sit on it; that's just too *required*) and surveys the contents of the tiny room. She knows everything by heart. Nothing ever changes in here.

A *rat-a-tat-tat* on the door and Dr. Dyer steps in. "How are you, Candice? Haven't seen you since —" she glances at the chart in her hand, then looks up "— since the tonsillectomy two years ago." The doctor smiles quickly and professionally, an expression that doesn't quite extend to her eyes. "So what's up?"

Candice shrugs nonchalantly, her heart pounding against her throat. "Not much. School. Homework. You know." She picks at the paper sheet covering the exam bench.

"How's your mom and dad? Your brother?"

"They're okay."

"I read about that fire in the newspaper. That was your grandparents' house, wasn't it?"

"Yeah, but no one was hurt. They're okay."

"Glad to hear it."

Silence.

"So what can I do for you?" the doctor prompts.

Candice swallows, flicks her hair out of her eyes, and looks up. "It's like this. I want to see a shrink. I mean, I'm not crazy or anything, but if I don't see one soon, I'm going to end up that way." Her face flames and her throat tightens.

Dr. Dyer nods. "Okay. I can refer you to one."

"Thanks," Candice croaks, releasing her breath and crossing her arms in front of her.

"Do you want to tell me what it's about?"

"Not really."

"It would help to know what I'm referring you for."

Candice shifts her weight and stares at the Rockwell print.

"I need to know where to refer you, Candice. To a psychiatrist, to a psychologist, to someone who specializes in certain areas …"

Candice focuses real hard on the stupid picture. "I just need to talk to someone, okay? Someone who can straighten out the mess in my mind."

"What kind of mess?"

"Just … mess, all right? Mess."

There is a pause, and Dr. Dyer shifts gears. "I know this is hard for you. It took a lot of courage to ask me this, and I respect that. I *am* going to refer you to someone, but I need to know who to refer you to."

"Why?"

"There are different doctors available depending on the conditions."

"Jesus Christ, I'm not, like, anorexic or anything! I'm not taking drugs or suicidal or anything!"

"I understand."

"All I need is to talk to someone! If it's going to be such a big deal, just forget it!"

Dr. Dyer nods, reaches for a box of Kleenex, and quietly hands a tissue to Candice, who grabs it and angrily wipes at her face.

Goddamn it! she thinks. *My mascara's running all over the place and everyone in the reception room will know I've been bawling.*

"A lot of women your age come in and ask me questions about birth control," Dr. Dyer says. "Do you want to talk to someone about that?"

"No. That's not it."

"I can put you on a two-month trial of the pill if you want. Free samples."

"No."

"I've got a pamphlet you can take home to read. It explains the different contraceptives available ..."

"I'm a lesbian, all right? I don't *need* birth control!"

Silence again. Candice can't breathe, can't move, and a huge, cold weight descends on her chest. Dr. Dyer's brown eyes swim in front of her, and the room goes white and starts to melt.

"Sit down on the bench behind you," a tunnel-distant voice says. A hand takes hold of her elbow and guides her. "Put your head between your knees. Take deep breaths. It'll pass. There you go."

Candice never noticed the floor before. Mottled black and white linoleum tiles. Very ugly.

Her breathing returns to normal. She doesn't want to straighten up, though. She doesn't want to budge from this position ever. She wants to die here.

Then, realizing that Dr. Dyer is the type who will stand there as long as it takes, and that the longer it takes the more humiliating it will be when she finally *does* break down and look up, Candice sighs heavily and straightens.

Dr. Dyer toys with the stethoscope around her neck. "Feeling better?"

"Yeah."

Another pause.

"You know, it's nothing to be ashamed of, Candice."

"I'm *not* ashamed. I mean, it's just that … Look, that's not why I came here. That's not my problem."

"Okay."

"It's garbage, litter. I have this phobia thing with litter. Every time I see some I have to pick it up, and it's driving me crazy."

"I see."

"You don't believe me. You think it's the … the lesbian thing."

"I don't know. Is it?"

"I just *said* it wasn't."

"Okay." Dr. Dyer nods a few times, then turns to the file on the counter behind her and briskly scribbles on a pad. "I'm referring you to Dr. Alana Bronte. She works out of an office on Thirteenth, above the Motor Vehicle Branch. Do you know where that is?"

Candice nods. *Great. Now I'm being sent to a sex specialist or something.*

"I'll get my receptionist to set up the first appointment for you. How's that? Any time after school okay?"

"Yeah, but can she help me? With this litter thing?"

Dr. Dyer switches on the bland, professional smile

again, rips the front sheet off the pad, and hands it to Candice. "She's very good at what she does. I wouldn't refer you to her if I didn't think she could help."

"Yeah, but —"

"It's nothing to be ashamed of." She puts her hand on Candice's shoulder and squeezes. "Don't worry. Everything's going to be all right." With a final nod, she slips out the door and leaves Candice alone again.

"Jesus. *Now* what have I got myself into?" Candice says out loud. She pushes off the exam bench, stoops slightly, and stares at her reflection in the row of stainless-steel tongue-depressor canisters. Her mascara is a mess.

"I *cannot* get onto a bus like this." She pulls her sunglasses out of her purse, jams them on, and scowls at her reflection. Then she starts to cry again.

Furious, she crumples the paper the doctor gave her and throws it into a corner of the exam room. As if she would see a sex specialist called Bronte. What the hell did she expect? Why did she even come here?

She leaves the room, more miserable and more alone than when she arrived.

Chapter Eleven

With her stepmother in the house, Karen can no longer utilize carrots in the intimate act of self-gratification. Mei-ling watches her with the eyes of a gecko tracking a fly, and Karen knows that if she takes a carrot into her bedroom, Mei-ling will guess that something other than snacking is afoot.

Never before has Karen so intensely craved a shopping spree at The Love Shop, but that, too, is completely out of the question, for to visit a sex-toy store is to confront her failure: she hasn't acknowledged her birthmarks, hasn't followed her Holy Destiny.

So, under the pretense of having a bath, she seeks relief in the washroom, which has a lock on the door (her bedroom doesn't). She brings Candice's CD player in with her, both to drown out the chanting of her mother in the living room and the splashing of her own finger play.

Over the past two weeks she has developed a routine: she gets her morning chores out of the way, then brings the CD player into the washroom. She plays a jazz disc borrowed from the library, fills the tub with steaming water, adds a generous portion of Strawberry Shortcake Bubble Bath, strips, sets up one crutch as a bridge upon which to balance her cast, and eases herself into the tub. With guilt-edged fantasies of Egret running through her head, she applies soap-slippery fingers to expectant clitoris.

The Footstop Café

By day eight, the mere smell of Strawberry Shortcake Bubble Bath is enough to arouse her.

But today as Louis Armstrong sings, the bath steams, and her fingers strum, she is unable to bring herself to a pinnacle. No fantasy helps. She misses her carrots. She desires insertion. After fifteen minutes of frustration, she gives up, heaves herself from the tub, and searches for something clean and appropriate.

Awkward because of her cast, she sits on the floor and rummages in the cabinet underneath the sink. It smells of wet plywood and mint toothpaste, and as she reaches into its depths, she expects to be bitten by a spider. Dilly stands at her elbow, peering into the gloom with luminous, dilated eyes.

Karen finds an empty box of Kleenex, a broken hair dryer, a toilet plunger, a jumbo pack of Pears Transparent Soap, two rolls of toilet paper (only two? she bought a pack of sixteen less than a week ago!), and a box of tampons. The tampons are for Candice; Karen uses homemade sanitary pads.

Aha, Karen thinks, *tampons!* A little short, a little slim, but one might work as a carrot stand-in ...

Sadly, the box of tampons is empty. *But wait, what's that jammed behind a drainpipe at the back?*

Squinting, Karen wedges her shoulders into the cabinet. Her head bangs against the steel underbelly of the sink and she curses. She gropes in the gloom and her fingers contact glossy paper. With a frown she pulls the object out.

A rolled-up magazine. Specifically, a *Penthouse* magazine, resplendent with full-colour photographs of thigh-spread, buxom women. It must belong to Morris.

Karen feels a pang of sadness that he has been reduced to this; there isn't a single shot that includes a close-up of the models' feet. She thinks briefly of Morris's receptionist, Clara, and her dowdy ankles and stout calves. If Morris has been reduced to reading skin magazines for a thrill, then perhaps he's even turned to Clara's feet for intimacy. After all, he *has* been coming home from the office late with increasing regularity ... At first (a year or three ago) Karen assumed their dwindling passion stemmed from stress over Candice's failing grades. Or the increasing demand of the Footstop on her energy resources. Or the increasing demand of his clinic on his. Or ... but no, Morris stopped reaching for her feet long before all that.

Okay, maybe he *did* make a few attempts over the years, but they were just that — attempts. Undertakings lacking real substance, devoid of real desire. Efforts too tinged with duty for Karen's taste. So she stopped responding. She doesn't want Morris to feel *obligated* to pleasure her, for God's sake.

When exactly did his desire become drudgery? Has she lost her sexual zing, and if so, why? It's not as if she's lost her looks. Maybe she's put on an extra pound or two over the years, but she was never slim to begin with, and Morris always says he prefers the lush Marilyn Monroe look to the present-day anorexic fad. Her hair is as vibrantly red and curly as when he first met her. She has a few wrinkles, but they are small, crinkly smile wrinkles. Her skin is still unblemished. Perhaps her feet aren't exactly what they used to be, but she manicures the nails and lotion-balms the heels and snips away dead skin and pushes back the cuticles as zealously as ever. So it isn't her looks.

But sexual zing doesn't come just from looks, does it? It comes from confidence, from a sense of achievement. Karen knows that. Women who have sexual zing stride down the street, heads held high; they are breezy and bright in manner. Or they slink through life, their eyes sultry, their voices low and rough and certain. Women with sexual zing have a sense of purpose, take pride in their daily affairs. They are nobody's fool, even when they're uncertain or on unfamiliar ground. They are productive.

But I'm productive, Karen thinks as she stares at Miss October. *I have an entire teahouse filled with merchandise I've made. And I'm an exemplary mother. I attend to my children's every needs. So where is my sexual zing?*

Her birthmarks tingle, and her eyes slowly focus on the brown smudges. Resignation coloured by anger washes over her.

Ah, yes, her birthmarks. *That* is where her sexual zing is — locked up in those light brown marks on the insides of both her thighs, just below the cradle of her sex, almost hidden beneath a blanket of reddish-blond pubic hair.

It isn't fair that she's branded so! Other people have aspirations and dreams and blithely live their lives without ever fulfilling them, so why does she have to be singled out, nagged at daily, by these symbols stamped onto her flesh? Why can't her dream die unfulfilled like everybody else's? Especially since hers is so different, would take such a toll on her family. No decent mother could ever follow such a Destiny!

Karen is now cold from sitting naked and wet on the bathroom floor. She replaces the magazine behind the empty tampon box, closes the cabinet doors, and awkwardly pulls herself to her feet. Then she climbs back into the tub.

The bathwater is lukewarm, a spiritless, uninterested entity, as limp as a wilted carrot. The few remaining pink soap bubbles look like faded petals. They disappear with weak pops as Karen comes into contact with them.

Thoroughly despondent, she begins shampooing her hair. From the CD player Louis Armstrong begins singing "What a Wonderful World."

During these bathing sessions, Mei-ling is in the living room, reciting Tibetan mantras in worship of the goddess Tara. In fact, she is declaiming one at the precise moment Karen discovers the *Penthouse* magazine: *"Om amrtakundali hana hana hum phat. Om ah hum."*

As she chants, Mei-ling is transported back to K'am, eastern Tibet, to the small township of Lhat'og. With each *hana hana hum phat*, she again sees the sparse forest that surrounds the hamlet, can once more smell the thin, dusty scent of its low-lying grassy mountains and hear the wind whistling over the bare white-rock summits. And because she hears this, her hometown wind, she doesn't heed the ring of the doorbell. But when it rings a second time, she frowns, trance broken, and cocks her head to the side. Her frown deepens, then she shouts, "Karen, someone's at the door!"

There is no answer, save the warble of Louis Armstrong's trumpet. With a sigh of irritation she rises from her cross-legged position, hitches her teal nylons up to her breasts (they just don't make designer-coloured nylons with short women in mind), and snaps the crotch of her pink leotard shut. Truthfully, she hates all-in-one bodysuits, especially the way the crotch digs into the tender flesh of her groin, yanks out her pubic hair, and creeps up the crack of her buttocks. But somehow she doesn't feel right chanting in anything else, save her saffron Tibetan habit, which sadly succumbed to furnace flames several weeks earlier.

As she leaves the living room and pads down the hall, she tugs and toys with her leotard, unconsciously snapping the crotch open and closed, open and closed, which is why she always leaves it undone during meditation.

"And I think to myself, what a wonderful world," Armstrong sings as she approaches the bathroom.

The doorbell rings a third time, accompanied by a volley of sharp, neat knocks.

"Haven't you heard that patience is a virtue?" she cries at the door.

"What?" Karen shouts from inside the bathroom. "Did you say something?"

"Yes. Someone's at the door."

"I'll get it!"

"Don't bother. I'm almost there."

Frantic splashing. "Mother, wait ..."

A delicious thrill courses down Mei-ling's spine. "You expecting someone? A Gypsy maybe?"

"Mother ..."

There is a thud, followed by the clatter of crutches and a strangled curse. Mei-ling pictures bubble bath glugging across the bathroom floor, thick and red like strawberry syrup.

"It's too late, Karen. I'm already there. Look at it this way. The gods obviously want me to discuss your future with —"

The doorbell rings again.

Mei-ling stops in her tracks and places both hands on her hips. "Impatient Gypsy wanderer," she shouts, "you must have faith that your knock will be answered! As Jesus said, 'If you have faith and do not doubt, you shall say unto this mountain, be thou removed and cast into the sea, and it shall be done!'"

She nods to herself, snaps her leotard shut one last time, and opens the door. Mei-ling is completely unprepared for the person she finds on the doorstep. Not a Gypsy with hoop earrings and a gold tooth, nor a soothsayer cloaked in tattered robes. The individual standing before her is merely a teenager, a distressingly normal teenager.

"You aren't a Gypsy."

"I ... sorry?"

"Where's the Gypsy? What are you doing here? You should be in school."

The teenager takes a half-step backwards and glances at the address on the boot-shaped mailbox. Behind Mei-ling's back the bathroom door bursts open.

"Goddamn it, Mother!"

"It's not the Gypsy."

"Gypsy?" the teenager says.

"Friends shaking hands, saying how-do-you-do," Armstrong sings.

"Who is ... oh, my God!" Karen splutters. "Egret!"

"Uh ... hello, Mrs. Morton."

"Karen. My daughter's name is Karen."

"Daughter?"

"Mrs. Morton is her mother-in-law," Mei-ling continues, "a drooling fossil who wouldn't know the Torah from the Koran if it bit her in the butt."

"Mother, for the love of God!"

"They'll learn much more than I'll ever know," Armstrong sings.

Mei-ling turns to face Karen, who stands halfway down the hall, one crutch under her arm. Soap suds drip from her head to her shoulders. She's thrown on Andy's *Star Trek* bathrobe, which barely covers her. The belt hangs like a broken tail behind her, sodden with bubble bath.

"Will I *what*, girl? And what exactly do you think you're doing coming to the door half-naked like that?"

"Christ, Mother!"

"And stop taking the Lord's name in vain."

"Mother!"

"*What?* You keep saying that over and over. What exactly do you want?"

"What a wonderful world," Armstrong croons. "*Oooooooh, yeah.*"

The song ends, the music stops, silence falls.

Mei-ling blinks, and realizes she's been bellowing at the top of her lungs. How annoying, when only moments before she achieved the contemplative mood required for mantra recitation.

After several moments, Karen speaks, cheeks flaming. "Will you stop being so rude. That's what I was trying to say. Invite him in, make him a cup of tea, while I get changed. He's one of Candice's friends."

"Why isn't he in school?"

Karen doesn't answer, just turns around, stumps back to the bathroom, and shuts herself in.

"Who's being rude now?" Mei-ling mutters. She turns back to the teenager. "Well, are you going to come in or just stand there and get soaked? You can't vaccinate against pneumonia, you know."

"I'll, uh, just come back another time. Thanks."

"What do you mean, 'come back another time'? What's wrong with right now?"

He gestures down the hall where Karen disappeared into the bathroom. "She looks busy."

"Nonsense. If she was busy, she wouldn't have time for a bath, would she? She's been in there half the morning anyhow. Time she came out." Mei-ling reaches forward and pulls the teenager inside. "Come in, come in. It's too wet to stand in the door arguing. She wants me to invite you in for tea, so in you come." She shuts the door and flips the lock into place. (Karen insists on keeping the front door locked, as if they live in New York, but the back door, does she lock that? No, never, as if the back door exists in safer country.)

"I don't believe in baths," she says, turning back to the boy. "Not healthy stewing in your own juices like that. Do you? Bathe?"

"I, uh, usually shower."

"Good." Squinting in the hallway gloom, she sizes him up again, up and down. Of Hitler's Aryan race, this one. And not Candice's age. He seems closer to twenty, this lad, not seventeen. "What exactly are you here for, anyway? Not her birthmarks, I warrant."

"Birthmarks?"

Disgusted, Mei-ling swats the question away. *Kids these days sound just like parrots*, she thinks. "Into the kitchen with you, or else Karen will accuse me of being inhospitable."

"Really. I can come back later."

"Nonsense." She firmly spins the boy and marches him in the direction of the kitchen. "I didn't know she had any. Keep walking, keep walking. Through the swinging doors. There you go. Take a seat. Friends. Candice. Didn't know she had any. Other than that Gloria."

"We go to the same school."

Mei-ling snorts as she rifles through the kitchen cupboards. "Except you don't go to school, do you? I mean, is it or is it not a school day today? It is, as far as I know. Cinnamon apple or camomile?" She brandishes two boxes of Lipton Herbal Tea.

"Uh, cinnamon."

"Good choice. So why aren't you in school?" She

examines him over her shoulder as she fills the kettle with water. He's still wearing that hellishly daft look on his face, as if he's never seen a Chinese woman in a leotard before, but her question makes him blink and brings his eyes back into focus.

"I'm on a sports program. I study half-days and don't take electives."

"Electives?"

"Woodworking, auto shop, you know."

"And why are you on a sports program?"

"I'm training for the Olympics. Diving."

"As far as I know, Karen doesn't have a pool in her backyard."

"I'm finished for the day."

"So you thought you'd drop by and ...?"

"Uh, I need to make some money. To pay for my coach. I thought I'd ask Mrs. Mor — Karen for a job. In her café."

"Teahouse. Her husband catches you calling it a café and he'll flip."

"Right. Teahouse."

Mei-ling pulls out a chair across from him and sits down. She studies him, drumming her fingers on the table in concentration. He shifts, and after a valiant attempt to refrain from doing so, looks away.

The kid is lying, Mei-ling thinks. *That much is obvious. Ah, well, what else can you expect these days?*

"'You are good when you are fully awake in your speech,'" she murmurs under her breath, "'yet you are not evil when you sleep while your tongue staggers without purpose, for even stumbling speech may strengthen a weak tongue.'"

He glances at her again, this time with the slightly derisive you-can't-be-for-real expression that belongs wholly to teenagehood. If it wasn't for that look, Mei-ling would have let him off the hook, but Khalil Gibran is not to be sneered at.

"So why aren't you hunting for work at a gas station or a concession booth?" she says, narrowing her eyes. "Why here?"

"Because I like it here."

"You do, do you?"

"Yeah."

"Why?"

"The atmosphere."

"The atmosphere?"

"Yeah."

"Huh?"

Impasse. This time he fastens his gaze on her. The kettle begins to shrill. Mei-ling shrugs, rises from the table, and pulls out the plug. The kid has moxy, that's certain. Neither of them speaks as she pours the bubbling water into two mugs.

"The atmosphere," Mei-ling repeats as she plops a tea bag into his mug and sets it before him. "The atmosphere."

He sighs, clears his throat, then asks politely, "You were exercising?"

"Ah. Change of subject. Your parents brought you up right." Mei-ling nods approvingly. "I was, yes, but not that sweaty aerobic stuff. I was exercising my spirit. Do you?"

"Does diving count?"

Mei-ling grins. "I like you, do you know that? You're smart. Yes, I imagine diving counts — for you, anyhow. You're dedicated to it, right? That's a sort of faith. And it's rejoicing in the body the gods gave you, which is a kind of worship. Drink your tea."

She takes a sip herself to demonstrate and scalds the tip of her tongue. "So," she says, eyes watering, "I was contemplating the divine virtues of Tara. Ever heard of her?"

"No."

"I shall enlighten you." Mei-ling steeples her fingers. "Tibetans are the simian descendants of a union between a rock ogress and a monkey. The monkey was an incarnation of Avalokitesvara and the rock ogress was an incarnation of Tara."

"I'm sure he doesn't want to hear about that, Mother," Karen says, shoving through the swinging doors to the kitchen. The scent of strawberry bubble bath and apple shampoo clings to her, as humid as a tropical fog.

My daughter, creator of Parfum de Fruit Salad, Mei-ling thinks. She frowns at Karen. "Why not? The legend of Tara is a story of seduction. Teenagers revel in that sort of thing. Don't roll your eyes at me, girl. What were you doing in that bath, anyhow?"

Karen colours. "Shampooing my hair."

"I mean that music. Why weren't you listening to that disc I bought you the other day? Nine-ninety five it cost me." Mei-ling glances at Egret. *"The World's Best Round Dance Songs,* by assorted North American tribes."

"Interesting," Egret says cautiously, then tries to catch Karen's eye.

Karen takes a deep breath. "Would you like to go for a drive, Egret?"

The boy rises far too quickly from his chair, and Mei-ling revises her opinion of his manners. "You haven't finished your tea. What was the point —"

He grabs his cup and empties the contents. "Great," he gasps hoarsely, setting the mug back on the table.

"Thanks." Moving around the table to Karen's side, he wipes the back of a hand across his mouth and bobs his head at Mei-ling. "Nice meeting you, Mrs. ..."

"Woodruff, the original being long dead." Mei-ling cranes around in her chair to watch him disappear through the swinging doors with her daughter. "I'm glad you liked the tea."

No answer as the two scurry down the hall, visible in snatches between the swinging doors.

Anybody would think I'm Shiva the Destroyer the way they're leaving, Mei-ling thinks sourly.

"You'll get an ulcer drinking hot liquids that fast," she calls out. Still no response. She raises her voice above the *flap-squeak-flap* of the doors. "People can die from ulcers, you know! You'll be dead before the age of thirty if you aren't careful!"

But still there's no answer, save for a meow from Dilly, scratching in the litter box by the back door.

Safely ensconced in her Tercel, Karen circles the neighbourhood, halting at stop signs, obeying traffic lights, and heeding posted speed limits with the exactitude of a traffic warden. Egret sits in the passenger seat and talks about diving.

He talks about stance and takeoff, flight and entry. He talks about five-metre and ten-metre high boards, one-metre and three-metre springboards. He talks about the six groups of dives (forward, backward, reverse, inward, twist, and handstand), and the four body positions (straight, pike, free, and tuck). He is about to launch into an explanation of the tariff values used in judging when Karen interrupts him.

"I suppose this might get noticeable driving around

and around the same streets. Not that we're doing anything wrong."

"No," Egret agrees, nodding at the windshield. Not once since jamming Karen's crutches into the back and assisting her into her own seat has he looked at her. "Maybe we should go somewhere."

"Oh, well ..."

"Just to talk, of course. I didn't mean ..."

Silence, and Egret watches the same bus stop flash by for the sixth time. "I mean, only if you want to. We don't have to."

"No, no, of course. But where? People might see us. Not that we're doing anything wrong." Karen keeps driving.

"No."

"No."

Silence again.

Egret clears his throat as they approach the junction of Lynn Valley Road and Mountain Highway for the seventh time. When he speaks, Karen thinks he sounds reasonable, casual, almost indifferent. Not at all like her thoughts, which are chaotic, colourful, and contradictory.

"We could go to my place. My parents are out."

"Oh, well ..."

"The Man's out, too. The place is empty. His brother picked him up this morning."

"The Man?"

"Our tenant. You've heard of Puckley's, the travelling circus, right? His brother owns it. They're in town, pulled in a week ago."

"Oh, I see. Still ..."

"I only thought —" here he develops a toadlike voice "— I only thought you might want to see my trophies. And the room where I work out. That's all."

Karen slows to a stop in front of the traffic lights. Beneath her fingers the steering wheel feels tacky like old cellophane tape. The spiced grease smell of the local Kentucky Fried Chicken swirls through the car's heat register and mingles with the scent of apple shampoo. On the sidewalk to her left a woman carefully arranges an assortment of enamel chamber pots into a pyramid in front of an antique store.

A horn blares, and both Karen and Egret jump. The lights have changed. A decision has to be made: *where to go, where to go?* But Karen can't move; she's completely paralyzed, body and mind.

"Turn left," Egret says.

And, after only a moment's hesitation, Karen obeys.

So they go to Egret's house, and he shows Karen his weight room, and Karen unobtrusively and with many conflicting feelings admires the muscles knotting in his forearms as he demonstrates half-knee bends with his barbell, which he says strengthens his leg and chest muscles and increases his lung capacity.

Then he leads her through his parents' house, which is opulent in its spacious sparseness and makes her feel grimy, despite the hour she just spent soaking in her bathtub. Somewhere between the stainless-steel kitchen and the forest-green dining room, she finds herself explaining how her birth mother, Petra Pedersen, abandoned her father when she was only three to play the sitar for a San Francisco band called the Tranquil Needle. She tells him of their subsequent trip to Tibet (of which she remembers only spilling Clamato juice on herself in an airplane), and of her father's subsequent marriage to a nineteen-year-old Tibetan-Chinese named Mei-ling.

"So she isn't my mother, not really. She's my stepmother.

For the longest time, until I was seven, I tried to believe she was my mother, just with a different hairstyle. Silly, huh? I refused to call her Mei-ling. I told all my friends her name was Petra. So," she says, barely pausing for breath as she follows him up a winding copper-and-mahogany staircase, her crutches squelching and squeaking, "tell me more about diving."

So he does. As he takes her into his bedroom and pulls trophies and medals out of his walk-in closet (a closet bigger than some people's bathrooms, Karen notes in a vague, bewildered way), he talks about Klaus Dibiasi, one of the greatest high-board divers in the history of the Olympics, and Pat McCormick, who trained throughout her pregnancy, gave birth to a baby boy, and five months later achieved the greatest winning margin ever recorded in Olympic competition. He also talks at great length about Fernando Platas, a gold medallist in both the tower and the three-metre board, and who ranks as Egret's main competitor.

Throughout this recitation Karen's thoughts are in a terrible muddle. Those are the exact words that keep running over and over in her mind — *terrible muddle terrible muddle* — as if the words themselves hold the secret to understanding exactly how she has arrived in the bedroom of her daughter's classmate, despite her vows to refrain from just such a thing. She is swamped by panic, desire, and horrified guilt. All coherent thought escapes her. Simultaneously, Egret is thinking how the whole situation is a fucking mess, a big screw-up, one mother of a mistake. *He* is swamped by uncertainty, misgivings, and burgeoning lust. As with Karen, coherent thought is light-years away.

But again the actions of both Karen and Egret are far clearer than their thoughts and emotions: their fingers brush, their hips graze, their shoulders bump, their pheromones flutter flags of invitation. Their bodies can see the situation clearly for what it is, even if their minds can't. And so, with some awkward fumbling, some elbow knocking, some slightly graceless pulling off of garments, their bodies take control of the situation.

What is it about the salty taste of the male collarbone, the perfumed taste of a woman's thighs, the abrasive feel of molar teeth underneath a tongue, the slippery warmth of lips meeting lips that is so compelling? How can the delicious shock of invading another being, of being invaded, overrule thought, moral conduct, and familial duty? To have naked flesh pressed against your own, to have muscles straining against you, around you, and into you, becomes all-consuming, all-important.

Passion is a black hole that consumes everything but the need to thrust and rub. Passion is a nuclear bomb flash that blinds you to responsibility and the pubic hair snagged between your teeth.

Afterwards, as hot skin turns clammy, as warm sheets disclose cold, damp spots, as your calf draped over a knee begins to bruise and a strange film forms on your teeth not unlike the kind that develops over boiled milk, your eyes, ears, and mental faculties slowly recover from passion's detonation.

Karen tries to stave off the return of her sanity if only for a little while. Guilt slowly laps at the edges of her consciousness, threatening to muddy the clear, warm bliss in which she is currently bathing.

Egret lies half beneath her, half beside her, stretched out on his back, one arm flung over his head, the other curled loosely around her shoulders. His eyes are closed and a filled, pleased look glows on his face. Karen lies half sprawled over him, one leg entangled deliciously between his lean, sweaty legs, the other jutting out from her at an odd angle, which causes her body to be twisted slightly like a piece of red licorice. The excluded leg is the one that ends in her unwieldy cast.

Her face rests against Egret's smooth, hairless chest, which rises and falls quickly enough to make her feel smug. Her limbs feel cream-filled and velvet-coated, her mind as lush as purple lavender in full bloom. She refuses to let anything mar this rich, buttery feeling, not the guilt trying to sully the edges of her contentment, nor the slow realization that Egret is perhaps substituting her for her own daughter. (Candice, he cried, arching away from her, forearms quivering, eyes screwed closed, penis buried deep within her.) Certainly, Karen won't let words like *adulterer*, *slut*, or *irresponsible* turn her warm serenity rancid. Not yet, anyway.

She runs her hand — stained with India ink despite her bath — over his chest, delighting in its vibrant, harnessed-power feel. His skin is smooth like the soft, sweet thighs of a baby, only firm and defined with muscle.

"No hair," she murmurs. "None at all. Not even on your legs."

He stirs beneath her. "S'waxed off. M'old lady does it for me. All divers do it. Looks better under camera lights."

Good heavens, what a world away from her is this boy's life! Talking of TV cameras with ease, referring to his mother as his old lady! Suddenly, she feels every inch her age. And then some.

She thrusts the feeling away and searches for a response. "What made you decide to dive competitively?"

He moves beneath her again. That slight shifting of muscle, that small resettling of sinews and limbs, stirs desire within her and surprises her with its intensity.

"Dunno. I like it, I guess. I'm good at it. My old man, he swam competitively when he was my age. Didn't make it to the Olympics, though. Came down with mono and never recovered."

"Really?"

"Not so that he couldn't compete. But he kind of lost his ambition for it."

She digests that for a moment. "And you? You're ambitious?"

"For diving? Shit, yeah. It's my life."

"But how do you know? How do you know that maybe you wouldn't be better at swimming or some other sport?"

"I just know, that's all. It's just one of those things you know in your gut."

"This gut?" She tickles his abdominal muscles and he wriggles slightly. His pale, shrivelled penis responds by twitching its sleepy head, and her smugness increases. She tickles some more. He pushes her fingers away and leaves his hand on top of hers.

She marvels at this, seeing a hand so unfamiliar to her, so unblemished by work, weather, and years, resting so intimately on top of hers. A gush of something fills her. Affection? Trust?

"I want to show you this," she hears herself say, disentangling from his sweat-warm embrace. "My birthmarks."

She sits up and he props himself on his elbows. They avoid direct eye contact, awkward now that Karen has broken their nearness.

"Here," she whispers, smoothing the insides of her sticky thighs. She plucks off a stray pubic hair plastered to her skin by drying sperm and viscous juices.

Egret sits up, bedsheets rustling around him, and leans closer. His breath is warm on her shoulder; she doesn't dare look at him. In fact, she bends over her own lap a little farther so that her long, frizzy hair acts as a shield. Embarrassment that she is drawing attention to the snowy, doughy dimples in her thirty-five-year-old thighs courses through her.

"They're nothing, really," she says dismissively. "I don't know why I mentioned —"

"Those are *birthmarks*?" Quite unconsciously, he scrapes a fingernail along the inside of her left thigh. The colour remains steadfast. "Wow!"

"Yes, but ..."

"J," he says, slowly tracing a finger over the first pigmented letter. "C. JC. With, like, an arrow ..."

"Those aren't arrows, not really."

"Pointing to your ... your —" he grins and meets her eyes through the veil of her hair "— to your cunt."

"Yes, well ..." She flushes, tries for a light-hearted tone. "Nature does some strange things."

"Yeah, but *that* is harsh. I mean, you've got the initials of Jesus Christ on your ... pointing to ..."

"Yes, well ..."

"Shit, that's wild!"

Now she *does* regret revealing the stupid birthmarks — profoundly. His reaction to them is so teenager that it brings to the fore of her consciousness the brown stain of emotions and thoughts she is trying hard to keep at bay. Okay, maybe her regret isn't *that* profound. His eyes now glitter and his penis perks up, and the excitement exuded from him turns her on despite her discomfort.

"So this is what your stepmom was talking about, eh?" he says.

Karen jerks her head up. "She was talking to you about my birthmarks?"

"Not really. Just when she answered the door. She was expecting someone else — a Gypsy or something."

"And?"

"She asked me if I was there 'cause of your birthmarks."

"That's all she said?"

"Yeah …"

"Are you sure?" She ignores his breast-roving gaze, his birthmark-tracing fingers, his impertinent, fully awakened penis.

"Yeah. What's the big deal? Don't worry about it."

"It may not seem like a big deal to you, but it is to me," she says. *How can a person feel peevish and passionate at the same time?* she thinks. *I must truly be depraved.* "I've had to live most of my life listening to her nonsense about these marks."

"What sort of nonsense?" he mumbles, his caresses becoming a little more determined.

"Nonsense about them meaning something."

"Course they mean something," he says.

She shivers as he clumsily caresses the back of her neck, parts her hair, and buries his face against her sweaty nape.

"S'not every day something like that happens," he adds. "The thing is, what exactly does Jesus want with your pussy?"

Karen sinks into the pillows beneath his weight, feels her hips rising to his. Their lips meet mushily and unevenly. They exchange saliva in a long, warm, writhing way, hands now busy seeking muscle and wet, hair-hidden hollows.

"Perhaps," she whispers into his neck, arching against his gloriously firm chest, "perhaps He wants me to guide the lost and enlighten the uninformed. About sex. Perhaps He wants me to open a Spiritual Sex Store."

There, she said it. Has finally told someone, has voiced her dream aloud. Her clitoris swells into a firm nut. She is giddy with release and freedom.

Egret fumbles between her legs and enters her. She groans, closes her eyes, and relishes the anguish of expectation.

"Enlightenment," she repeats. "About sex."

Chapter Twelve

How a man might best celebrate his reclaimed bachelorhood:

- Dig up the phone numbers of old flames.
- Take the guys from work on a pub crawl.
- Assert one's manhood by jumping out of an airplane, scaling a sheer cliff, walking on hot coals, and rafting down whitewater.
- Take up cigar smoking.
- Fix your mother's sagging porch.
- Move to another continent.

Intrepid Moey does none of these. *He* celebrates his release from the shackles of partnership by subscribing to *Sahda* (the newsletter of the Middle Eastern Dance Association) and, despite his weakened condition from his illness, also signs up for a series of dance workshops at Ballet BC.

The first workshop is devoted to *raks sharki* (oriental belly dance), the second to *debke* (traditional line dance from Lebanon), and the third to transformational drumming and chanting designed to help him explore his inner goddess. This last worries him a little: is it a gender-specific workshop, or does every belly dancer, regardless of sex, need to get in touch with an inner goddess? He isn't sure, so he tries to dismiss the thought.

To be honest, though, the whole thing terrifies him. Never before has he participated in a workshop. Everything he knows about belly dancing, he learned from videos. (Dalia Carella's are his favourite.) He's never been to a belly-dancing *hafflah* — indeed, he's only been close to real live belly dancers while at Persian or Greek restaurants. But at the workshop, lo and behold, he will be shimmying hip to hip with them.

Will they snicker at his costume? Will they gawk at his bulky body? Will he commit some terrible faux pas and forever be branded an outcast?

Moey isn't concerned about the feminine atmosphere associated with the dance. He isn't distressed about dropping his sword on someone's foot during balancing exercises. He *certainly* isn't worried that his rhythm will be off while playing his zils, for his kickboxing has given him excellent timing and equilibrium. No, what Moey frets about is looking gauche, doing something unpardonably wrong, or simply being unacceptable. And he *desperately* wants to be accepted by the belly-dancing community, especially now after the devastating double blow of being excommunicated from Master Zahbar's studio and then ruining his opportunity for a long-term dance gig at the Footstop Café. (He is certain Karen won't take him back after this unexplained, unprofessional hiatus. If there's one thing a restaurateur hates, it's an unreliable dancer.)

So to bolster his courage and improve his health in time for the dance workshop two weeks hence, Moey decides to hike through Lynn Canyon. It will be a gentle hike, a get-in-touch-with-nature hike. An I'm-goddamn-single-again-shit-but-I'm-not-bored hike. Feeling a little unsteady on his legs, he leaves his basement suite, protecting himself from the rain and chill by a much worn K-Way tugged tightly over his equally worn ski jacket.

Pulsating within him is the hope that he might come across the white stag, which would reassure him that the shattered windows, damaged gyproc walls, and eviction notice that followed his confrontation with Miranda are all part of some divine plan for his future.

Andy always walks home with his head down and his eyes pointed at the ground. That way if kids from either his present school or his former one pass him, he can pretend he hasn't noticed them or heard their jeers. It is in such a manner — head down, eyes glued to the sidewalk as his trumpet case bumps rhythmically against his bruised calves — that he sees the slug.

Although rain-bloated slugs and worms deck the pavement with the profusion of tinsel and ornaments on a Christmas tree, this slug is different. This slug is lithe and eager. This slug has purpose and drive. This slug is anything but sluggish. Indeed, it is so intent on its journey that Andy stops to gape at it in wonder, ignoring the steam that immediately fogs his glasses.

The slick black creature, in its eagerness to reach its destination, has stretched out to a slim taper. The entire front half of its body rides through the air like the prow of a motorboat zipping over a lake. Its eye stalks quiver as it strains forward.

Never before has Andy witnessed impatience and excitement in a slug — indeed, until that moment he could have sworn such animation was beyond gastropods. But as he watches this one virtually race forward, its body trembling, he is struck breathless by the realization that these slimy, disgusting things must actually be capable of feelings. And if they can feel expectation and excitement, what else can they feel? Hope, love, disappointment? Desolation, frustration? What exactly does a slug feel at the end of the day as the sun sinks out of sight? All of a sudden Andy feels a little smaller in the world. A little smaller, yes, but also a little less lonely. He looks about, trying to find the source of the slug's zeal.

Ah, there it sits, about four feet away from his galoshes: a fresh, steaming pile of horse manure. The North Shore boasts two riding stables; the original possessor of the manure must have been carrying its rider to one of the popular horse trails in Lynn Canyon.

"Dinner, huh?" Andy mutters. (The prospect of excrement as food doesn't seem revolting with so much innocent gustatory anticipation displayed before him.) He sets his trumpet case down, wipes his glasses free of raindrops and steam, and crouches on his haunches. "You know, you could get squashed on this sidewalk. People are walking up and down here all the time. Don't you know that?"

A raindrop tickles his nose, and he wipes it away. He rises and searches beneath a nearby laurel hedge for two twigs. Holding them chopstick-style, he approaches the manure pile. The stuff stinks like weeds decomposing in the bottom of a pond. He holds his breath while carefully selecting a manure nugget.

After several attempts, he manages to pick the nugget up, but by then its perfect coal shape is marred from all his fumbling. He drops it twice while transporting it to the laurel hedge, which further damages and diminishes its physique. By then the slug has reached its destination.

Andy doesn't feel defeated: it is only a matter of time before someone's Doc Martens turn sidewalk slug café into sidewalk slug graveyard. His intention has been to relocate the gastropod's eatery, not to bring it Meals-on-Wheels. He crouches over the slug. "I'll try not to hurt you, okay? Trust me, this is for your own —"

"Hey, kid, you playing with shit?"

Andy shrieks and leaps to his feet. His chopsticks fly into the air.

"Hey, look, it's the new kid."

"Yeah, pansy Four-Eyes."

Andy's blood freezes and his bladder tingles. He blinks rapidly at the two boys standing in front of him. "H-h-hey, Troy, Kyle," he stammers.

"How come you're playing with shit, pansy?" Troy demands.

"Yeah, how come?" Kyle echoes.

"I wasn't ..."

"You hungry?" Troy asks.

"Yeah, you trying to eat it?"

"N-no."

"Me, I l-l-love shit for dinner," Troy squeaks, fluttering his eyelashes. "I ... I ... I *love* it!"

Kyle laughs.

Panic flares through Andy. If rumours spread that he was caught trying to eat horseshit, life will become more miserable at his new school than at his old.

"I w-w-wasn't trying to eat it, okay?" he blurts. "I was just s-s-saving a slug." As soon as he says it, he realizes what a colossal mistake he's made.

Troy and Kyle gape at him.

"You were what?" Troy barks.

"I was ... I was ..."

"Trying to save a slug? Did you hear that, Kyle? Four-Eyes is a slug lover."

"F-f-forget it, okay, guys? Let's just all go home."

"What, this slug here? Was this the slug you were trying to save?" Troy pokes at the dining slug with his boot. The soft, shell-less body immediately contracts in on itself.

"Just leave it alone, g-g-guys."

"Looks like a good hackey sack to me, hey, Kyle?"

"J-just leave it!"

"Here, catch." Troy boots the curled-up slug towards Kyle. The toe of his boot flicks manure onto Kyle's raincoat, but Kyle doesn't notice.

"Crosby intercepts the puck!" Kyle shouts. "He winds up for a slap shot!" Kyle draws back his foot. "He shoots." Kyle kicks the slug back at Troy, and it makes a soft, wet noise as it lands on the pavement. "And he scores!"

"Stop it!" Andy shouts. "J-just l-leave it alone!"

"Hey, pansy, did you know these things bounce like rubber balls? Watch this." Troy takes a couple of steps back, then runs forward and punts the curled-up slug towards a parked car. It hits the passenger door with a splat, stays glued there for a brief moment, then slowly slides to the gutter. Glistening white protrudes from its slick black belly.

Molten rage erupts in Andy. "Asshole!" he cries. "You killed it, you killed it!"

He lowers his head and charges Troy.

Surprise takes Troy off guard as Andy slams into him and drives him against the car door.

"Asshole, asshole, asshole!" Andy shrieks, pummelling Troy with his fists.

"You little motherfucker!" Troy shouts. "You think you can fight me?"

He turns, slipping in the gutter a little, and shoves Andy off him. Andy staggers back a few paces as Troy knocks his glasses to the ground. One of the lenses pops out.

With a choked sob, Andy rushes forward again and flails at Troy with his fists.

"Why you little fuck!" Troy bellows.

Something incredibly hard slams into Andy's stomach. The air disappears from his lungs with a *huhhn*, and his knees soften like whipped cream. The neck of his raincoat is suddenly yanked up and his feet leave the ground. The zipper of his coat digs into his neck. He claws at it, unable to breathe.

"You don't mess around with me," a voice growls as a fist smashes into Andy's nose.

Green lights pop before Andy's eyes. For a moment he thinks the rain has turned into sparkling shards of glass. Then something slams into his jaw, snapping his head back. Hot electricity speeds all the way down his spine.

"Hey, lay off, Troy!" Kyle yells. "Cool it!"

Troy releases Andy, who falls to his knees, hands skidding through the manure pile. A boot lands in a soft, fleshy part between his hips and ribcage.

Andy tries to suck in air but can't. Then he can, and that just makes everything hurt. Even worse, he can't see and he's going to puke.

At that moment Troy makes a strange *oomp* noise, and someone else begins screaming, using unbelievable cuss words. Andy retches, mucus splatters from his nose, and his partially digested avocado-and-alfalfa-sprout sandwich erupts in chunks from his mouth. The pain in his side surges and burns hotter.

The screaming cuss words continue, accompanied by a *cludthunk, cludthunk* against the hood of the car. A man bellows, "What the hell's going on out here? Get away from my car!"

The cussing and *cludthunks* stop.

"Jesus Christ, what are you kids ...? Hey, don't I know you? Aren't you the Morton girl?"

"I'm a boy," Andy sobs, then vomits again.

Someone kneels beside him, someone panting and radiating heat like a stove element. A hot, trembling hand touches his forehead, his cheeks, his forehead again.

"*Ohmigod*, Andy. Are you all right?" The voice turns away. He knows that voice. Who is it? Then the voice shrieks, "You goddamn motherfuckers! Why don't you pick on someone your own size?"

"I didn't know it was you, so I called the cops," the adult says, drawing closer. "What the hell's going on out here, Candice?"

"My brother, look what they've done to my brother! I'll kill those cocksuckers!" The hot, trembling hand abruptly leaves Andy's forehead.

"Hey, hey, hey!" the adult cries, and there is a brief scuffle in front of Andy. Someone cries hoarsely. Feet kick a spray of manure into his eyes, erase what little sight he has.

"Settle down!"

"Let me go! Let me go! Those pricks deserve to die! Let me go!"

Someone bawls, choking out between jagged, snot-filled sobs. "My dad's ... going to ... sue you! My dad's ... going to ... sue you!"

Andy retches some more. Pain rips up and down his body like a saw-toothed blade. In the distance a siren wails.

Morris bends closer to his patient's diabetic foot and clucks in dismay. It is riddled with welts, pocketed with pustules, and devoid of the smallest toe. "Mrs. McDevitt," he says reproachfully, "you haven't been following the instructions I gave you."

"Ah've told you, Doctor. It isn't my fault. It's m'bowels. How can I concentrate on m'feet when ah'm backed up to the eyeballs?"

"Yes, yes, but you must understand that you're going to lose more toes if —"

"But *m'bowels*, Doctor!"

He sighs and is about to launch into his usual speech about the difference between a general practitioner and a podiatrist — namely that the former deals with all body ailments, be they of the rectum or the septum, and the latter deals only with the foot — when a quiet, polite knock on the door pre-empts his response.

"Dr. Morton? Telephone call, line one."

"I'm with a patient, Clara."

"It's urgent."

Morris sighs again and turns back to his patient. "If you'll excuse me, Mrs. McDevitt."

"You go right ahead, love. Don't mind me. I always bring a bit of knitting with me no matter where I go."

"I'll be right back."

Huffing in the back of his throat, he leaves the exam room. Clara has already vacated the hall and returned to her reception desk. She knows how fiercely he hates interruptions. So left with no recourse but to deal with the intrusive phone call himself, he shoves his hands into his lab coat and enters his office.

The office is a narrow grey room made narrower still by the overflowing bookcases covering the walls. An ancient steel filing cabinet, dented and scratched, juts between two of the bookcases, leaving little room for the swivel chair pushed against a heavy oak desk. Papers, open medical books, a buzzing computer, and an empty flower vase vie for space on the desk's top.

Morris can't keep this place tidy. He doesn't know why; everywhere else in his life, neatness reigns supreme. But here, in this tiny hovel that is his alone, chaos is chief. He resigned himself to the situation a long time ago.

Unable to find his telephone in the mess, he locates the cord instead and follows it to the instrument. "Yes, hello?" he says, gripping the receiver like a weapon.

"Morris, is that you?"

"This is Dr. Morton, yes."

"I don't know where Karen is. That's why I'm calling."

The voice is irritatingly familiar. "I'm sorry, this is …?"

"For heaven's sake, it's me, Morris. Your mother-in-law."

"Oh." His annoyance increases a thousandfold. "What are you phoning for, Mei?"

"I don't know where Karen is and I need to get home."

"I'm afraid I can't help you," he says stiffly. "I am *working*."

An irritated cluck; Morris can picture those flinty brown eyes narrowing. "Morris, I'm at the police station with Candice. I came without my purse and I need your credit card number to pay the taxi driver. He won't take us back home without it. Andy's going to be okay, but they're keeping him in the hospital overnight. Contusions of the spleen, they say, and a broken nose and sprained neck."

Morris blinks, and something cold and heavy lodges in his esophagus. "I don't follow you," he says huskily.

"He was attacked by thugs, and Candice stopped them, only it seems she damaged Mr. Osaban's car in the process. She had to make a statement."

"I'm afraid you have the wrong number," Morris says, and hangs up.

He stands there for several minutes, blinking at the spine of the thirteenth edition of *The Merck Manual*.

Clammy sweat surfaces in his armpits and slides down his arms in a tickly sort of way. His heart pounds slowly, loudly, eerily.

Why have I got The Merck Manual *on my bookshelf?* he wonders. *Must be Clara's. I should take it back to her.*

Out in the reception foyer, the telephone rings. Clara's muted professional voice drifts down the corridor.

"Good afternoon, Dr. Morton's office."

Silence.

"Oh, dear. Oh, no. Is he going to be ... what? Of course, certainly. Yes, right. We're on our way."

A muffled click is followed by the brisk *slap-slap* of Laura Ashley sandals against linoleum. Clara appears in the doorway. "Morris," she says, fingering her pearl necklace with one hand, lightly touching his doorknob with the other, "get your coat on. I'll see Mrs. McDevitt out."

He swallows; the cold, hard object in his esophagus grows larger, sharper. "The appointments ..."

"There are only three left for the day. I'll come back and cancel them after I've driven you to the hospital."

"But ..." Morris coughs and tries to say, *Thank you. What's happened? Is my boy all right?* But all that comes out is a croak. Then Clara helps him into his raincoat.

Karen awakes with a violent start, heart hammering, panic cleaving her tongue to the roof of her mouth. Wide-eyed, she surveys her surroundings: a rock band dressed in Viking horns glares down at her from a poster on the ceiling; rain splatters against an unfamiliar window framed by unfamiliar navy curtains; a black motorbike helmet, a disconnected computer keyboard, and a stack of magazines lie on top of a bureau.

Where am I? she wonders, and the panic that jolted her awake intensifies. She flails, throws bedsheets off herself, and sits up. Beside her someone groans. For one terrifying minute she gapes at the lean young man stretched out beside her without recognizing him. Then everything falls into place.

Oh. My. God.

She scrambles off the bed, snatching at the pieces of her clothing she can find in the tangle of blankets. The lean young man — Egret, that's his name — cracks open an eye.

"Hey. You don't have to go yet."

"Yes, I do." She sits on the edge of the bed and fumbles with her panties, trying to work them over her cast. They catch on the plaster heel. She yanks, and they tear. To hell with it, she doesn't need panties, anyway. With a curse she pulls on her skirt, the little waistband bells tinkling.

"Where's my blouse? Can you help me find my blouse? Is that it underneath you?"

"Uh, I don't —"

She grabs the corner of cloth he's lying on and tugs. It's a pair of Calvin Klein jockeys. "Get up! Help me find my blouse."

"Jesus, what's your hurry?"

"I have to get home. Something's happened. Is that it under your pillow?"

She snatches at the garment. He rolls out of her way, eyes widening. It's her blouse. She slips it over her head, ignoring the sharp wrench of hair catching on buttons and being pulled out.

"Sandals, sandals, where are my sandals?"

"You were only wearing one."

"Yes, but where *is* it?"

"Will you calm down a little?"

"Egret, for Christ's sake, will you help me find my sandal!"

They stare at each other, he still in bed naked, she at the foot of the bed fully clothed. The panic in her is still growing at the speed of a supersonic jet about to lift off.

"It's there, by the closet," Egret says without taking his eyes off her. "You going to tell me what's going on?"

She lurch-hops towards her sandal. "I don't know. I can't explain it. Something's wrong and I have to get home. Where's my crutches?"

"Are you feeling, like, guilty 'cause of what we did? I mean, you can trust me not to tell anyone …"

"I know. It's not that at all. It's nothing to do with you." She breaks the strap on her sandal, curses, and flings it aside. To hell with it, she doesn't need sandals, either. She straightens, then pauses.

Egret stands before her, still gloriously naked and not in the least shy about it, her crutches in hand. "Here."

"Thanks."

But he doesn't release them. "Is it me? Something I did?"

"No. At least I hope not. Oh, Egret …" She breathes deeply and shrugs. "I'm sorry, I really am. I shouldn't be here. Something's happened. I can feel it in my blood. I have to get back home to my family. They need me."

"What do you mean, you hope not? You mean, maybe it *is* me, something I did?"

"No. What I mean is, maybe it's *me*, because of what *I* did. My father would call it retribution." She leans closer, kisses him on the forehead — perhaps too matronly a gesture, but it's too late; she's already done it — and takes the crutches from him. "I've got to go. Really."

He follows her out of the bedroom and lingers on

the landing, watching as she hastily hops down the winding staircase.

"Can I see you again sometime?" he calls after her. His hopeful tone makes her stop for the briefest moment to glance back up at him. He stands under a skylight, bathed in misty, watery light. Golden-haired and naked, he seems like an angel, a sexy seraph encouraging her to follow her Destiny and open that Spiritual Sex Store.

"Of course you can. Come by the Footstop sometime. But not until my parents are gone, okay?"

"Sure thing." He grins. "Then we can take a closer look at those birthmarks of yours, eh?"

She nods distractedly and turns away. She has to hurry. Her family needs her. She's sure of it.

The creek roars in Moey's ears as the rain *plunk-plunks* steadily against his K-Way. Around him the woods are moist, mossy, and rich with decay. He inhales as deeply as his recovering lungs allow: bracket fungi breaking down dead trees give off an earthy, mushroom scent; wet ferns smell sharply verdant; fallen hemlock needles and rotting stumps reek of minerals and nitrogen. He wonders why he hasn't come here sooner.

As he winds his way along the root-gnarled trail towards the Ninety/Thirty Foot Pool, he catches flashes of movement in the berry bushes: squirrels foraging for winter stores, wrens and black-capped chickadees flitting from branch to branch, the dart of something small through ferns and bracken. So alert is he to movement, seeking, as he is, the white stag, that he even notices the activity of bark beetles and carpenter ants chewing their way into fallen trees.

But he doesn't get even a glimpse of the beast he seeks. A sort of desperation fills him as he loops through trail after trail, labouring up rutted paths awash with runoff water, ducking through salmonberry overgrowth, and scrambling over fallen, rotting logs. Thorns snag and rip his K-Way, rocks shift beneath his feet. His breath rasps along his burning throat.

Moey searches for hoof prints, spore, bark-stripped branches, anything that might indicate the presence of the stag. He finds nothing. Dusk approaches, cloaking everything in grey and shadow.

His legs tremble and he shivers, soaked through to the skin. Just as he finishes descending a flight of slimy wooden steps, he gets warm all over — no, not warm, hot. *Very* hot. Fat-fingered, he pulls off his K-Way, drops it to the ground, then unzips his sodden ski jacket and flaps it briskly, trying to put out the fire scorching his skin.

Just as quickly as it started, the fever ends, leaving him dizzy and feeble. Belatedly, he realizes he's ill and isn't thinking clearly. It's time to head home.

How stupid, he thinks as he staggers back to the suspension bridge, eyes partially closed against the vertigo gripping him, knees like Vaseline, lungs as hot as coals. *I'm never going to make it home. Going to have to call a cab.*

But he hasn't brought his wallet with him, and even if he had, he probably wouldn't have found anything in it. He refuses to admit defeat, however; he is a victor, by God! (The image of Master Zahbar cheering him on rises in his mind like a virus cloud.) Wheezing like an asthmatic in a hayfield, he makes it out of the forest, across the suspension bridge, and to the pay phone attached to the park's shuttered, dark concession stand.

Ah, wonderful! Some jerk's cut the receiver off. Swaying, he stands for a moment and tries to think. *Park ranger's office.*

They'll have a phone. But it, too, is shuttered for the season.

"Walk. Gonna have to walk," he mutters through chattering teeth. He drags his feet over to the rutted road and stumbles along it, tacking from left to right like a sailboat attempting to catch the wind.

Then he stops, blinks, and passes a clammy hand over his clammy brow. An enormous white foot looms before him.

Ah, the Footstop! A telephone! Karen!

With a whimper of relief, Moey puts his head down and doggedly ploughs towards the café.

Chapter Thirteen

Morris views the hospital as a place of healing, a sanctuary for the wounded, a haven in the chaos of life. But as he enters the hospital's main foyer, he suddenly sees the place as nothing short of hostile.

The thin, bland carpet at the entrance swallows the sound of his footsteps and muffles the voices of those around him. The paint on the corridor walls looks cold, the white corkboard tiles on the ceiling institutional. From the cafeteria comes the salty smell of chicken broth fused with the astringent odour of disinfectant.

Moving as if in a vacuum, a nondescript brown elevator carries him up to Andy's ward — he feels no motion, hears no sounds, is just suddenly deposited, with mechanical indifference, on another floor. At the nurses' station the telephone rings with a smothered, broken sound; the nurse who points him towards Andy's room seems creased and watered-down. As she turns away from him to riffle through a stack of dog-eared files, the squelch of her rubber soles against the linoleum floor sounds like clenched teeth squeaking against one another. Even the light issuing through the rain-splattered window in Andy's room appears ill and cranky.

"Dad?" Andy croaks at him from a stark white perfectly rectangular bed.

Morris stops in the doorway, unable to enter. His son,

his Andrew Ethan Morton, born at 3:15 in the afternoon, weighing only five pounds, two ounces, is shrouded in bandages, tubes, and mottled purple flesh.

"Christ," he gasps, clutching the metal door frame for support.

"There you are. About time." Mei-ling leaps up from the orange vinyl chair beside Andy's bed.

Morris stares at her. She is dressed in a pink leotard, green nylons, white tennis shoes, and a yellow rain slicker.

"He's on painkillers," his mother-in-law says, toying with her crotch. "Can't remember what kind, something intravenous. Keeps falling asleep, then waking up and asking where you are. What took you so long?"

"What?" is all Morris can manage, looking back at his son.

"Dad?" Andy whispers hoarsely.

"Move nearer. He can't see. Those fuckheads broke his glasses."

Startled, Morris glances at the corner of the room, the origin of the angry, clipped voice. It's Candice, her black Boca pants splattered with mud, her black oversize corduroy jacket heavy with rain. Her hands are jammed into her pockets, her shoulders hunched.

"Watch your language, girl," Mei-ling says sharply. "I heard enough of that filth from you down at the station."

"Don't call me girl, okay? I don't call you old woman, so don't call me girl. My name's Candice. C-A-N-D-I-C-E."

Mei-ling vigorously snaps her leotard open and shut a few times. "Well" is all she can muster. *"Well."*

"Dad?" Andy murmurs sleepily. "Is that you?"

"Christ, Dad, will you move *closer*? He can't *see!*"

A hand touches Morris's elbow and he jumps again.

"Is everything all right in here?" a nurse asks with a frown.

He shakes his head slowly, then with more vigour. Anger builds in him, sparking like a lit fuse on a stick of dynamite.

"No, everything is not all right," he hears himself say. "That —" he points with a long, trembling finger "— is my *son* over there, my *son*. What exactly is he doing here, I'd like to know. He's ... he's eight years —"

"Nine!" Mei-ling, Candice, and Andy say in unison.

"He's nine years old, and look at him! You've got him hooked up on intravenous drugs, throttled by a neck brace, and ... and ... and what exactly have you done with his glasses?"

"He didn't come in with glasses, Mr. Mor —"

"*Doctor* Morton to you, Nurse. *Doctor* Morton."

The nurse — Abigail, according to her name tag — scrutinizes him up and down. "I didn't know you were a doctor."

"Dad?" Andy says from the bed, only this time his voice is fainter, with a slight tremor. "Dad?"

Morris inhales deeply and crosses the room in three strides. He bends over his son, picks up a hand, and enfolds it in his own. Resting on the bedsheet, Andy's free hand looks like a starfish washed up on a beach.

"I'm here, son. I'm here. Everything's going to be okay." As Morris rubs Andy's knuckles, he peers back at the nurse and says stiffly, "Be so good as to explain what's going on."

And so she does, though Morris catches only one word in ten, words like *concussion*, *hematuria*, and *dislocated collarbone*, which set him reeling. While she talks, she adjusts the drip rate on Andy's Ivac pump and checks his blood pressure, pulse, and pupils. Throughout her recitation, Morris absently continues to rub his palm over Andy's knuckles as if polishing an apple.

"Why?" he asks hoarsely when the nurse finishes. "Why would anybody do this to him? He's only a child."

The nurse folds her stethoscope into one of her uniform pockets. "The way I understand it he had an argument with two school —"

"It wasn't an argument, okay?" Candice cuts in. "Jesus, what's wrong with everybody? I told you, they were beating the shit out of him!"

"Language!" Mei-ling cautions.

"Am I to understand," Morris says disbelievingly, "that his attackers were *children*?"

"Fucking psychopaths, that's what."

"Language!" Mei-ling warns more sharply. Then, to Morris, she says, "And they were hardly children. They're three grades ahead of Andy — twelve years old at least."

"So what?" Candice snaps. "What difference does their age make? They're total, absolute fucking maniacs whether they're seven or seventy, and if Mr. Osaban hadn't shown up, I would've splattered their putrid brains —"

"Morris, will you please get control of your child?"

But all Morris can do is gape at Candice, unable to grasp that this enraged, tear-streaked teenager *is* his daughter. Since when has she taken to wearing makeup and swearing like a fishwife? Why is she dressed in a man's coat and plaid work shirt? And where have her pigtails gone? He can't understand all this, much less comprehend the battered little body that is his son in a hospital bed.

"I think ..." he begins, but the thing that lodged in his throat when Mei-ling first called now returns, chewing fiery holes into his throat. He looks at the nurse.

"I think Dr. Morton would like to be alone with his son for a while," she says, placing a hand on Mei-ling's shoulder and staring pointedly at Candice.

Morris feels a rush of gratitude towards her, so excessive it brings tears to his eyes.

Sometime later, still alone with Andy, Morris glances down at his son, now asleep, chest rising and falling beneath the thin hospital sheet. Slowly, he forces himself to assess the ruins of Andy's face. The left side of the boy's chin bears a row of strange red welts, evenly spaced and uniformly wavy. It takes Morris several moments to realize they are the imprint of the sole of a shoe.

Andy's bottom lip, crusted with blood, looks like an oil-oozing wiener, swollen and split from roasting in a too-hot oven. The flesh around his left eye is the size and colour of a rotting plum, the eyebrow replaced by a raw road rash glistening from a Vaseline-like ointment. His nose is hidden beneath a fat white bandage.

Helpless rage overwhelms Morris. He wants to rip the IV from Andy's arm, the brace from his neck, the bandages from his cheek. He wants to howl, crush the boy to his chest, heal him with rage and love. He wants to tear the window curtains from their hooks, smash the glass, hear the clatter of shards on the floor. He wants to bellow at the idiot honking his horn in the street below, wants to rip him limb from limb because this is a hospital zone and doesn't the man know that?

Morris closes his eyes, lips pressed together so tightly they ache.

Where was I, he wonders bitterly, *when my son needed me? With what patient, chattering about what inconsequential thing, while Andy lay bleeding on the road? I should have been there, picked him up from school, organized a taxi, something, anything. My fault. This wouldn't have happened at his old school, no. The birthday, the feet, the bomb, the expulsion, it all led to this. My son is suffering because of me. I did this to him.*

A thin, high cry comes from his lips, like the sound of air rushing from the pinched end of a balloon.

He has failed his son, terribly. More than failed him — he has betrayed him, and not for the first time, either. As Morris huddles against the hard plastic chair beside the bed, still rubbing Andy's knuckles with his palm, he recalls the first devastating time he betrayed Andy's trust. It happened a long time ago, almost nine years earlier ...

From the moment of his birth, Andy was a quiet, content baby with a perpetually surprised expression on his pale pixie face. He never cried, not after the first few shocked wails he uttered upon gushing from the womb, grey with thick vernix. If he was hungry, he merely waved his clenched fists in the air, like a flag boy delivering signals to a passing plane. He murmured and chuckled at Karen's breasts, droplets of milk spraying his cheeks as he greeted her nipples by rubbing his tiny snub nose Eskimo-style on them. If he was anxious about something — the sudden ring of the doorbell, a car backfiring in the street — he merely froze, eyes wide, head cocked slightly to the side as if listening for further signs of danger. No, Andy never cried. He was a quiet, content baby.

And then ...

Vaccination time came, not at two months of age as scheduled but at four months, due to Andy's tiny size. Morris was completely unprepared, even though he knew, obviously, that vaccinations involved needles. He hadn't been there for Candice's vaccines, didn't know exactly why, must have been involved in a conference or surgery or something very important. But he was there for Andy's. Watched, speechless, heart thudding, as the GP casually slipped the needle between the soft, fat folds of Andy's exposed left thigh.

A moment of silence followed during which Morris held his breath. Andy's eyes widened in shock, darted about the exam room, then locked onto Morris. A look of betrayal — utter, bewildered betrayal — encompassed the boy's elfin face. Then he opened his mouth wide, sucked in a quavering breath, and howled.

For twenty minutes he shrieked out his fear and abandonment, barely taking time to suck in his breath. Every second of that twenty minutes was forever scorched into Morris's soul. With one needle he permitted Andy's whole safe, trust-filled world to be shattered. After that Morris detected hesitancy in Andy's smiles, uncertainty in his laughter. The scars of betrayal.

"Dad?" a mushy voice now asks. "Dad?"

Morris swallows rapidly a few times, his Adam's apple a chunk of quartz grating against his thorax. He blinks, concerned that Andy not see him with tears in his eyes, then feels guilty relief that Andy isn't wearing glasses and therefore can't see clearly.

"I'm here, son, I'm here."

"Sorry, Dad."

"Sorry?" He stares down at that grossly swollen, taut and shiny purple swelling that hides Andy's left eye. *"Sorry?"*

"I started the fight. S'my fault."

"Well, I hardly think ... I can't see ... what on earth do you mean?"

"They killed th's'g." Andy's good eyelid droops again

from sleep and his words slur. "Th'killed it."

A thrill of horror courses over Morris's skin. Had his son witnessed a murder, is that why he was beaten?

"Did you tell the police, Andy? Did you tell the policemen what you saw?"

"No one. Jus' you." The eye closes, and Andy sighs heavily. "Laugh at me."

"Murder is nothing to laugh at! It's a very serious offence, a crime —"

"Shlug, Dad, for a shlug."

"What?" He bends closer to Andy's swollen lips.

"Y'know. Gastropod. Mollusc."

"You ... I don't understand, Andy. You started a fight ... you witnessed the murder of ..."

"A slug."

"A slug?"

"Yeah." Another sigh, this one clouded in sleep. "But this one was different. This one ... was ... diff'rent."

And then he falls asleep again.

Morris studies his son, trying to make sense of everything, but he can't. There is no way he can. His son risked his life for a *slug*?

He straightens and sits back in his chair.

Well, Morris thinks, *whatever the truth of the matter is, Andy didn't want to tell anyone. In fact, he fought the sleep-inducing painkillers until I arrived, so he could confess and reveal his burden at my feet. I can't very well ask Candice or Mei-ling what the hell Andy's muttering about, can I? He's entrusted me with this secret — albeit a wondrous strange one — until he regains consciousness. And that's okay.*

Morris stands, takes off his raincoat, and hangs it on the back of the chair. Then he sits back down, crosses one leg over the other, and contemplates the precious face of his son. He can wait for him to wake up and explain it all. However long it takes, he can sit and wait.

Karen pulls into her gravel driveway so fast she sprays a wave of pebbles against the house. She pops open her car door even before turning off the ignition. Not bothering to retrieve her crutches from the back seat, she launches herself from the car and hop-lurches towards her back door.

She doesn't know what this panic erupting in her with volcanic force is. All she knows is that it's flooding her veins with urgency. Just as she's unable to explain the feeling to Egret, she can't explain it to herself. It's something instinctual, a primal reaction, a certain and irrefutable thing: her family is in danger and needs her.

In short, it's a maternal thing.

Karen expects the worst, the very worst. She expects dismembered bodies, blood-splattered walls, and idling, gore-drenched chainsaws. So when she comes around the rock path, bare-footed, ducking under hemlock boughs, grasping rain-drenched branches for support, and sees a body slumped on her back doorstep, her cry isn't of horrified shock but of terror and dismay.

"Oh, God, no!" she gasps, stopping for a moment as every hair on her skin stands on end. "Oh, God, no!" she repeats, then stumbles towards the slumped figure. "Morris? Morris?" Her bare knees thud against pavement as she drops beside him.

He groans, then breaks into a hacking, phlegmy fit of coughing. She grabs a fistful of his hair and jerks his face up from his chest and stares at it, completely bewildered as rain tap-dances on her head and plasters her dress to her back. Finally, she locates her voice. *"Moey?"*

"Karen?" he murmurs.

"What are you doing here?"

"Hiking. Sick. Real sick."

"And my mother won't let you in?"

His eyes roll into the back of his head and he shudders, then goes limp. Still gripping his thick black forelocks, Karen shakes his head from side to side in alarm. "Moey? Moey?"

He makes a noise halfway between a grunt and a gasp.

"Lord," Karen whispers, releasing his head rather too abruptly, letting it thump against the door. She winces, mumbles an apology, and stands. "Mother!" she cries, banging on the door with a fist. "Come out here and help me!"

No answer, save for the *dribble-pit-pat* of rain running from the eavestroughs into the downspouts.

"Mother!"

No answer. She kneels, finds the keys she dropped, inserts one into the door, leans inside. "Mother?"

Still no answer. The damn woman is out somewhere, doing who knows what.

"Where the hell are you when I need you?" Karen mutters.

She crouches beside Moey again. "Moey? Can you hear me?" His forehead beneath her palm feels hot and clammy; his cheeks are a horrible puce. "Moey, can you stand? I think you need to go to the hospital. Moey?"

"Couldn't find it," he groans, moving his head slightly, eyes rolling aimlessly. "Couldn't find the stag."

Is he hallucinating? She holds his face between her hands. "Look at me, Moey. It's me, Karen."

"Eh?" His bloodshot eyes briefly focus on her, then he shivers, his teeth clacking against one another like wooden beads. "Karen. I'll change into my costume …"

"You're not dancing today. You're sick. Do you understand me? You're very, very sick."

"Yes. Yes, I am."

"I'd like to take you to the hospital, okay? But I need you to stand and walk to my car. I've got a broken ankle. I can't help you much."

"No," he says, and his eyes veer away from hers and swim about again. "She's been giving me medicine. I don't need the hospital."

"Who's been giving you medicine, Moey? Your doctor?"

"Miranda. Herbal medicine. Made it herself."

"Herbal medicine? Jesus! I'm just as Mother Earth as the next person, but there comes a time when antibiotics —" Karen cuts short her lecture as Moey breaks into another chest-wracking cough. "This is *not* good," she says, pulling away slightly, out of the stream of his contagion. She waits until he finishes coughing. "Put your arm around my neck. You're going to the hospital."

He doesn't protest this time, and after a great struggle, he eventually rises by himself.

The subsequent journey to the car is a long, difficult, wet one. Moey mumbles incessantly under his breath, eyes wide open one minute, reeling into the back of his head the next. On three separate occasions, peculiar convulsions shake his body, and when the fourth starts, Karen is just about to pray to the God she hitherto believed incapable of tying His own shoelaces when Moey turns to her and snaps, "You're not paying attention, Karen. This is a basic Egyptian box step and single double shimmy. *Please* refrain from doing pivoting hip circles during this movement."

Ah, not convulsions then, but dance moves. To appease him, she mutters an apology, which he graciously accepts.

Then, meek and weak as a lamb, he staggers the rest of the way to her car in silence.

By now Karen is so soaked the plaster of her cast is melting, leaving behind a trail of chalky residue. Her drenched dress, spackled with hemlock needles, clings to her skin like adhesive tape. Her feet are bright red and numb from cold.

Before Moey can get into the back seat of her Tercel, she has to prop him against the hood and yank, jiggle, and twist her crutches out. Once liberated, she throws them into a rhododendron bush, bangs the door closed on him, slips into her own seat, and guns the engine to life.

"You're going to be okay, Moey. You're going to be okay." She hits the gas pedal, her bare, numb foot gliding over it like an oyster. The car jerks violently forward and abruptly stops. In the back Moey pitches forward and smacks face-first against the back of her seat.

"Sorry! Sorry! I'll be more careful!" She takes a deep breath to calm her nerves.

That wretched, roaring sense of panic is still all-pervasive, try though she might to mentally talk herself out of it. Obviously, somehow she picked up on Moey's distressed state, perhaps because he collapsed on her very doorstep, and now that she's found him, the urgency is over. It is her duty to pass that message on to her adrenaline-saturated nerves so she can act sensibly and alertly. If Mei-ling were present, she would have suggested reciting the Four Noble Truths or, more specifically, spoke seven and spoke eight of the dharma wheel, seven being right-mindfulness and eight being right meditation.

"Okay, here we go," Karen says, gingerly applying foot to pedal. "You might want to strap yourself in, though. Just in case."

"Fucking dominatrix!" Moey roars, bolting upright. "You won't shackle *me* again!" The top of his head thunks into the roof of the Tercel.

Karen shrieks and slams on the brake. Moey lurches forward again. His face, as it slaps into the back of Karen's headrest, sounds like an enormous wet lasagna noodle hitting a platter.

Heart hammering, Karen peers in her rearview mirror, waiting for him to groan, stir, curse, or even bolt upright again, but he doesn't.

"Moey?" she asks cautiously. "Moey?"

She cranes around in her seat and looks at the floor of the Tercel. Moey lies there, immobile, eyes closed. His chest rises and falls shallowly but regularly.

"Perhaps it's for the best," she says grimly. She faces forward again and backs out onto the street. Carefully.

Reverend Sandy Woodruff doesn't believe in sin. At least not the way he was taught in theology school and certainly not the way his colleagues and peers define it. For instance, take the phrase "living in sin." He sees absolutely nothing sinful about it. What's wrong with living with a person, testing the waters so to speak, before launching into the commitment of marriage? A fellow isn't expected to buy a motorcar without first taking it for a test drive now, is he? Neither should he be expected to bind himself to a woman without first checking out her engine and, er, interior; after all, a woman is a lot more bloody complicated than a few cylinders and pistons. The same holds true for a woman, of course — prod and squeeze the zucchini at the greengrocer's *before* bringing it home to put in your saucepan. You never know if its core is rotten until you do.

The reverend likes the Canadian definition of sin, is tickled pink that all residents of Canada are, in fact, required to have it: a social insurance number stamped on a plastic card and carried around in the wallet. Everyone refers to it as a SIN card, from employment centres to passport offices, and no Canadian can function legally in the country without one. A nation that demands sin from its citizens in capitals — this appeals to the reverend in a deliciously wicked way. Indeed, he views living in sin as living in social insurance numbers, the way birds flock together and live in numbers for self-protection. Yes, that's exactly what living in sin is: living in a manner that provides one with self-protection.

Not that he doesn't believe in the sanctity of marriage. He does believe in it, and most strongly, and *because* he believes in it, he feels a couple should know each other intimately before embarking on that which is the most holiest of unions — lifelong devotion to one another. No, marriage isn't something to take up frivolously; it's something that should be entered into only after careful consideration, inviolable investigation, and exalted experimentation.

This is not something the Anglican Church permits him to preach from the pulpit.

But long ago the reverend discovered that, if worded properly, one's view can be made to reflect the views of others, while still retaining the essence of one's own beliefs. It's an art, getting people to believe you're agreeing with them while simultaneously, ever so subtly, changing their view to match your own. Mei-ling often says that had he never received the calling, he would have made a phenomenal lawyer.

This doesn't make him any less of a clergyman, just a more practical, amiable one. His church is always full, his parish comprised of all sorts of people. True, Mei-ling edits his sermons prior to his reading them, and not a month goes by when she doesn't get into a dish-shattering screaming match with him over what is permissible to preach. But inevitably, he defers to her judgment. She is always correct, always, and in the twenty-some-odd years he's been married to her, he's never once undergone the scrutiny of his superiors for inappropriate behaviour, quite unlike those dizzy, liberated days when he was married to Petra Pedersen.

Because of this he is a happy man, though today his joviality is a little dampened by the death of an elderly parish member. They don't last long once they have a major fall, these old folks, and Mrs. Kendall — daughter of one of North Vancouver's original British settlers — died today in her hospital bed due to complications following a tumble down the stairs. Reverend Sandy Woodruff was at her side during her last moments on Earth.

"Ah, well," the reverend sighs as he rides the elevator down to the hospital's main floor. "Can't a one of us last forever, now, can we?"

The doors wheeze open and he steps out, tipping an invisible hat to the young nurse who takes his place. She smiles bashfully at him. Ah, how delightful these young nurses always act around a man of the cloth.

"It's the uniform," the reverend says to himself as he crosses the main foyer. "There's something appealing about a gent in a uniform. Reckon that's what gives a nun her charm, too. Same could be said for —"

He stops as a sodden, bedraggled woman with no shoes and one foot in a cast hops by him, muttering to herself. It's his daughter.

"Hoi, pudding face!" he calls.

She turns towards him with a startled cry.

"What the devil's happened to you then? Where's your coat and crutches? What are you doing here? Haven't come to pick me up, have you? No, course you haven't. You didn't even know I was here. Old Mrs. Kendall, I'm afraid. Finally bit the biscuit. Well, you going to answer me?"

"Dad!"

"Yes, that's me."

"What are you doing here?"

He frowns. Always a bit slow, his girl, though terribly clever with her hands. "Just told you, didn't I? Mrs. Kendall, the old gal with glasses, always baked cranberry chocolate loaf for our craft fair. Remember her? Died not twenty minutes ago."

"Oh, I'm sorry."

"Why?"

"Well, she, uh ..."

The reverend waves a hand impatiently. "Never mind, never mind. Just tell me what's going on."

"Oh, well, I was just dropping someone off at emergency, a hiker. Sick, pneumonia they think."

"I see." Although he doesn't, not really, but he's learned over the years that the fairer sex isn't always good at summing things up succinctly and that you get farther if you pretend they have. "And where are your crutches?"

"At home. I couldn't fit them in the back seat with him."

"Ah. And you were in too much of a hurry to put on a coat and shoes?"

She gawks at her bare, chilblained feet as if noticing them for the first time. The toes that protrude from her disintegrating cast look like scalded cherry tomatoes. Water drips from her hair to the carpet.

"I guess so," she says, glancing back at him uncertainly. "I was just going to the cafeteria to get a hot chocolate, to warm up."

"And how were you planning to pay for it? You haven't got your purse with you, either." He sighs, takes off his black overcoat, and drapes it around her shoulders. "Never mind. I'm here. I could do with a spot of tea myself. Grab my arm. There you go."

They proceed towards the cafeteria, Karen's cast leaving white round marks behind like hoof prints of some yet undiscovered one-legged beast.

"God most certainly works in mysterious ways, doesn't He?" the reverend reflects out loud. "Kills off Mrs. Kendall just so that I'm here in time to provide you with warmth and nourishment in the form of hot cocoa ... For heaven's sake, don't look at me like that. I'm not saying you caused her death. Ah, that table there is free."

But Karen has come to a complete standstill. "Is that Candice?"

"Eh?" The reverend turns his considerable bulk in the direction indicated by his daughter.

"And that's Mom with her." Panic edges her voice.

The reverend experiences a chill of presentiment. "So it is, so it is," he murmurs, quashing the feeling. "What the devil are they doing here?"

With Karen clutching his arm for balance, they head in the direction of his granddaughter and wife, weaving through the islets of tables and chairs. Lingy has her back to them, hunched into her chair in such a manner as to suggest she's performing a tea-leaf reading. Across from her Candice scowls furiously at the sugar jar on the table, her legs and arms crossed, one Doc Martened foot jiggling up and down in agitation.

A pang of guilt shoots through the reverend. He has been meaning to have a chat with Candice, more of a gossip, really, about Suze and Della. He conducted a ceremony for them five months ago, leading them through their vows, providing his blessings, that sort of thing, and he thinks it might be the kind of harmless conversation that will prompt Candice to speak up. Clearly, the girl needs to. This shower fetish thing, her intolerable moodiness, her difficulties in school, her sudden animosity towards Andy, and her intense attachment to men's clothes and that Gloria girl — are Karen and Morris blind, not realizing what's up?

"Remind me to have a chat with Candice, will you?" he whispers into Karen's ear, but whether she hears him or not is unclear.

"Mother? Candice? What's going on?" There it is again, that note in her voice, as if she just discovered a cavity by biting down on a chunk of tinfoil.

Lingy leaps from her chair — good Lord, what's she wearing? — and spins around.

"It's about time you got here. I've been leaving message after message on your machine. Morris is up with him now. I tried to get hold of you as soon as I could, but what with taking Candice to the police station —"

"You didn't have to come with me," Candice snaps. "You make it sound as if it's my fault."

"What?" Karen says. "What?"

The reverend finds himself holding his daughter upright while all the hairs on his body tingle unpleasantly. "Yes, good point," he says gruffly. "What exactly are you nattering about Lingy, and what are you both doing here? What the devil is *everyone* doing here, eh? Here, take a seat, Karen."

"No! I don't want to sit down!" she cries, surprising them all and drawing the attention of everyone in the cafeteria. "Mother, tell me what's going on."

"He's going to be okay. His collarbone is dislocated and he's got some serious bruising —"

"Who?" the reverend booms at the same time as Karen calls out in a voice that sounds like the weak, high-pitched yelp of a stepped-on kitten.

"Andy!"

Reverend Woodruff looks from Mei-ling to Karen and back again. "Is it? Is it Andy —"

Karen launches out of his arms and grabs Mei-ling by the elbows. "Where is he? What happened? What have you done to him?"

"Karen ... ow! Karen!"

The reverend attempts to intercede, but Karen turns on him, actually spins about and slaps him hard across the face. The sting and the shock root him to the spot.

"It's your fault, you and your crazy, useless God!" She abruptly pulls away, totters, and crashes into the nearest table as if blind. Metal fold-up chairs clatter to the ground. "Will someone please tell me where my child is?"

"Jesus, Mom!" Candice yells, jumping to her feet. "Will you calm down already?"

Karen lunges towards Candice, who flinches, and the reverend holds his breath. But she merely clutches Candice and begins touching her, smoothing her wet hair away from her face, brushing chunks of mud off her corduroy coat.

"Candice. Tell me what happened. Please. Tell your mother what happened."

"I told you," Mei-ling begins, "his collarbone —"

"No! Not you! Are you Candice? No! So keep quiet. I want to hear if from Candice, okay?"

Silence, not just from Mei-ling but from everyone else in the cafeteria, as well. The reverend notices, with a quick glance at the kitchen, that even the cooks have momentarily stopped mashing potatoes and stirring gravy and are watching the drama unfold instead.

"Now," Karen says, releasing a long, quavering breath, "Candice, go ahead. Tell me."

For the first time in months the snide, angry expression on Candice's face disappears, replaced by the young, uncertain look the reverend knows and loves so well.

"It's like this. A couple of older kids from Andy's school beat him up on his way home. I caught them at it, but ..." Her voice falters, she struggles to gain control, loses, and breaks out in tears. "I was too late, Mom. They hurt him real bad. He's a mess, a total mess ..."

Karen pulls Candice close, and the girl buries her face against her mother's shoulder. They look like twins, the reverend thinks, two identical heads of long, wet red hair pressed together.

"I'm sorry, Mom. It's my fault ..."

"Shh, shh. It's not your fault."

"I should have been there."

"You couldn't have known. No one could have known."

"I wanted to kill them, Mom. I really did. If Mr. Osaban hadn't stopped me ..."

"But he did stop you, so it's okay. You did nothing wrong. I would've tried to kill them, too, if I'd been there."

That, the reverend thinks, isn't necessarily the best response.

But he doesn't voice the thought, doesn't so much as allow it to show on his face. He just waits quietly and patiently while mother and daughter hold and comfort each other. Then, when they've both found sufficient strength to let each other go, he follows behind as Mei-ling leads them all from the cafeteria.

And with every breath he takes, he prays fervently for the health of his grandson.

Chapter Fourteen

It's late. The air smells of rotting tree stumps, wet moss, and the sharp, electrical odour that precedes a thunderstorm. A halo encircles the moon, surrounded in turn by schools of sluggish clouds. The streets stand empty, the houses black-eyed. No birds chirp, no dogs whine, no buses wheeze by. Everything seems murky, moody, hunkered down.

In the distance Lynn Creek crashes through gorges and thunders down falls. From where she sits on her back doorstep, knees pulled up to her chest, Karen shivers and wraps her arms tighter about her legs.

The door creaks open behind her, and a crack of yellow light stretches across the ground. She blinks, her lids grating across her eyes like wire mesh. Her father is behind her — she knows it's him just by his breathing pattern, slow and stertorous. The smell of hot cinnamon wafts over her.

"Here," he grunts.

She turns, all muscles stiff. He holds out a mug and she accepts it with mumbled thanks.

"May I join you?" Without waiting for her reply, he lowers himself onto the doorstep, wheezing from the effort. The door shuts on its on accord in one long, thin creak.

"Been out here a while, have you?"

"What time is it?" She sips the cinnamon tea and winces as it scalds her tongue.

"Three-thirty."

"Really?"

"Found it hard to sleep myself," he murmurs. "Think Lingy's still awake. Heard her moving about."

"And Morris?"

"Dropped off a while ago, right at his desk. Didn't want to wake him, though." He shifts his buttocks as if trying to settle them into the concrete step. "Candice is out like a light, too. I found a bottle of red wine in a cupboard and shared it with her around midnight."

"Dad ..." Karen starts to chide, then stops herself. "Thanks," she says after a moment or two. "Thanks."

"Should've saved some for you by the looks of it."

"I'll be fine."

"Uh-huh."

Karen takes another taste of the tea and stifles a shiver.

He reaches down and picks up a fallen maple leaf. "You were right, you know. What you said about it not being anyone's fault. No one could have known it was going to happen."

"That applied to Candice, not me. I'm his mother."

"That doesn't endow you with prophetic powers, pudding."

Karen remembers the bolt of panic that woke her in Egret's bed. "But I *knew* something was happening. If I'd been home, I would have reached him in time."

Her father twirls the leaf's stem between a thumb and forefinger; the leaf makes a wet, fluttering sound as it spins. "You can't blame your —"

"Why can't I? How do you know God isn't punishing me for something I've done?"

"Because I don't think He works that way."

"You're always talking about retribution," she accuses.

"Yes, but concerning people like Hitler and Mussolini and what have you. I doubt that anything you've done is comparable. By and large, I don't believe our Creator is the vengeful type."

"I wonder."

Her bitter tone stops his leaf mid-twirl. After a pause, he slowly runs his thumbnail down the length of the stem, splitting it in two. "Do you want to tell me what this conversation is really about?"

She glances away. This is just like him to see straight through her.

"Is this about you and Morris?"

That causes her to look back at him. "What makes you say such a thing?"

"He's in there. You're out here. I'd have thought you'd be comforting each other."

"I don't see *you* comforting *your* wife."

He smiles. "Touché. Though we both know she derives more comfort from a stick of incense and a chat to a half-dozen deities during moments like these."

"Don't I know it."

"Don't be hard on her. Lingy's greatest strength just happens to be her greatest weakness, that's all. Same holds true for most of us."

"Really? And what would you say my greatest strength is?"

He studies her, ignoring the angry tone. "I'd say the same as your mother's. Petra's, that is, not Lingy's."

She opens her mouth to speak, closes it, then speaks, anyway. "And what was her greatest strength?"

"Would've thought that was obvious to all and sundry. Her passion, of course. God, she was a passionate woman! Either loved a thing or hated it. Nothing in between.

Course, it was her love for another man and his music that eventually took her away from us, wasn't it? And her love for needles that did her in."

"And you think I'm like that?" Karen says, horrified.

"No, not at all."

"But you just said …"

"That you both have passionate natures. Or had, as in her case." He frowns. "But you, your passion is different."

"How?"

"Well … you adore life, that's what. You find joy in all its mysteries. Quite different than dear old Petra. Her passion was an insatiable hunger, a desire for intense experiences."

"And how do you know I'm not like that?"

The reverend lets out a bark of laughter. "Because you're not a thrill-seeker, pudding! Your mother would try anything, whether it was inhaling a line of cocaine or scaling up a sheer cliff with no ropes. You, on the other hand, can't even get on a rollercoaster."

"Mother did cocaine?"

"Does that surprise you?" He seems genuinely shocked. "The woman died from a heroin overdose. Course she tried cocaine."

"Did you? Ever try it?"

He casts a wry look at her, taps the side of his fleshy red nose with one finger, and shakes his head. "There are some secrets a father should always keep from his child. That would be one of them. Let's just say I'm far wiser than I was back then."

"Oh." She digests that and decides she isn't surprised. "Dad …"

"That's me."

"Did Mom ... was that ..."

"Go on. Spit it out."

She takes a deep breath. "That man Mom left with. Was that her first?"

"Did she have other affairs, is that what you mean?"

She keeps her eyes glued on the silhouette of a nearby laurel hedge. This isn't a conversation a daughter should have with her father, not in her books, especially a father so apt at connecting the dots and reading between the lines. But it's too late and she's already asked. The old habit of seeking guidance from him is deeply ingrained. So she nods. "Yes, that's what I meant."

"Thought you knew that," he says shortly. He shifts a little. "Funny what I've taken for granted all these years."

"How many times?"

"Good Lord, I didn't keep track! Too bloody many — with women as well as men."

"What?" Karen stares at him. He glowers at his leaf and decapitates it from the stem. "Why did you put up with it? *How* could you put up with it?"

"What choice did I have? That was Petra, love her or leave her, and I certainly didn't want to leave her." He throws his leaf aside. "Gave me some damn unhappy moments, she did. Yet I kept telling myself that she loved me most, that she had to otherwise she wouldn't have always come back."

"Except she didn't, did she, Dad? She left us."

"Yes, well, I'd like to believe she'd have come back eventually if that bloody needle hadn't taken her." He blows air out his cheeks. "The problem with Petra was that she believed her conscience was a rotten thing. God knows I argued blind with her about it, but she stuck to the asinine belief that her conscience was something to ignore lest it ruin her life. She drove me mad over that." He brushes his hands across his woollen slacks, a donation from his parishioners, one size too large. "Now I'm in a rotten mood remembering all this stuff."

"Sorry."

"What are you apologizing for? Damn it, sometimes you get my knickers in a twist with your abject servility."

"Abject servility?"

He shifts some more and makes a few grumbling noises, then falls still and contemplates the dark shadows and black pockets of the yard. He sighs. "Abject servility. The way you creep about life, terrified to assert yourself. I look at you, pudding, and I feel I've failed you as a parent."

She stares at him, swallows, counts twenty of her own heartbeats before she can breathe again, knows she should say, "That's not true," but can't, is afraid that if she tries to speak, she'll blurt instead, "That's exactly how I feel when I look at Andy."

"I overcompensated, that's what," he barks, startling her. "Felt it was a flaw of mine that saddled you with a dead mother. So I bent over backwards to create a cheerful little world for you, never shed a tear in your presence. Never let you know that most days after I saw you off to school, I crawled back to bed with a hollowness so deep it made me retch my guts up all over the floor. Never let you know I couldn't so much as wash a dish or add soap to the washing machine without old Mrs. Dunmore's help."

He snorts and looks at her with so much self-disgust that she flinches. "D'you know, there were days when I couldn't even decide what to put on your sandwiches — it was as if mayonnaise and mustard required a skill beyond my capability. You never knew all that, did you?"

She gives the barest shake of her head, mute, and thinks, *Who the hell is Mrs. Dunmore?*

"A bloody mistake that," he growls. "Should have just bawled my eyes out and given you the opportunity to do the same. What a fool I was. What a damn fool."

Dumbstruck, Karen attempts to piece this image of her father — grief-stricken, guilt-ridden, falsely jovial — with that of the capable, gregarious man she knew during her childhood. She can't. She feels cheated. Everything about him has been feigned; she didn't know him at all. All she's known is a cardboard cut-out of him, a staged Kodak picture.

He drops a large, meaty hand on her knee, startling her again. "It's a wicked thing, hiding yourself from your own flesh and blood for fear of hurting them. Achieves exactly what you were trying to avoid in the first place. Kids know the truth. They sniff it out somehow. I think *you* knew way back then. So all I ended up doing was teaching you to deny your feelings, didn't I?"

After her father hauls himself back into the house, Karen sits stewing, thinking, remembering, letting her new knowledge shift the memories of her childhood around until they settle into new places.

Around four o'clock in the morning she recalls who old Mrs. Dunmore was. A neighbour, eighty-two years old. Someone Karen only knew in passing, a stranger, was privy to her father's grief, was once a pillar to his crumbling temple.

Her thoughts cohere, turn towards the present: Egret. Showing him her birthmarks. Confessing her dream to him. *Ah.* She *is* following in her father's footsteps. Only with her mother's propensity for adultery. Grand.

She raps her teacup against her thighs.

Could the attack on Andy have been prevented by following the Destiny in her heart instead of the lust in her veins? In other words, if she listened to her conscience instead of ignoring it as her mother had? If she had the courage long ago to tell Morris about the dream her birthmarks instilled in her, might her confidence and strength have been passed on to Andy, and he now be lying in his own bed instead of one in a hospital? In other words, if she never hid her emotions from her own flesh and blood, for fear of hurting them?

Oh, yes, how painfully clear things can look in the murky light of dawn after a cold, sleepless night spent sitting on a doorstep.

Karen can now see the attack on Andy for what it is: a signal of how derailed her own train is from the tracks of happiness. What she needs to do is shunt her locomotive onto the proper rails before all the passengers riding in her carriage are hurtled into the path of an oncoming engine. Before, in a desperate bid to find life-affirming joy, she errs as fatally as her own mother.

Time to follow her Destiny. Time to realize her dreams. Time to plumb her inner depths for that pale, underfed wraith — her own courage.

Time, as Moey declared, to listen to the message of the white hart.

Karen's birthmarks begin to tingle as they never have before. They vibrate like the wings of a locust in flight. They vibrate like a diving board just leaped from. They vibrate like the hips of a belly dancer in full shimmy. This electrical quivering hopscotches all over her body, from her cast-covered foot to her hair-haloed head. Even her curls quiver.

She rises to her feet.

"It's time," she whispers, and before she can talk herself out of it, she stomps into the house, grabs her car keys, and backs the Tercel out of the driveway.

Tucked beneath sperm-splotched sheets, a certain segment of Egret's anatomy is likewise quivering, though not from a sense of destiny. Egret is dreaming of diving, dreaming of training.

Not all of his training takes place at the diving board, swimming pool, or weight room. Indeed, a vast portion of it occurs at the local gymnastic arena where lean, muscled girls in spandex fling themselves over vaulting boxes and stand storklike on balance beams. There Egret and his competitors practise their pikes, somersaults, and flips on trampolines and thick mats.

Egret has never before regarded these girls as anything but gymnasts. For him they are androgynous creatures, their athletic dedication excluding them from the realm of physical attraction. He respects, admires, and even stands in awe of their abilities, but save for an occasional exchange of sportsmanship banter, he doesn't involve himself with them at all.

But tonight as he lies deep in slumber, the scent of Karen on his pillow, his dreams are solely about these lithe gymnasts, and not at all in an androgynous way. He is mounting them in midair on the trampoline, he is skewering them as they perform spread-legged dismounts from the high bars. He writhes and contorts with them in naked ecstasy during tumbling routines on the mats, and he makes them tremble and cry out as he takes them on the balance beam. Each time he dives into their sweet little pools, the judges give him the highest scores: 9.9, 9.7, 9.8.

He is just in the middle of a performance with a girl on the high bar when he wakes up. Blinking, bewildered, he looks around his dark surroundings and tries to hold on to the fantastic erection slowly wilting beneath his bedsheets. His door creaks, and he squints at it. A figure stands there, silhouetted in the moonlight coming through the hall windows. He smacks his sleep-gummed lips together. "Mom?"

"*Shhh.*" The figure slips into his room, shuts the door, and lurches towards him.

Suddenly, Egret is wide awake and sitting upright. "Who the hell —"

"*Shhh!* It's me, Karen!"

She freezes, he freezes, and they both wait with breaths held to see if his cry has awakened his parents.

After several minutes of silence, Egret moves, heart jackhammering against his thorax. "What are you doing here? How the fuck did you get in?"

She moves to his side and sits on the bed. "The patio door was unlocked. You really should be more careful."

"Shit." He knuckles sleep from his eyes.

"Egret," she whispers, "I have a favour to ask of you."

"What time is it?"

"I'm not sure. About four in the morning. I want you to teach me how to ride a motorbike."

He stops in the middle of running a hand through his hair and stares at her, or the vague shadow and cool outdoor smell that passes for her in the darkness. "You *what*?"

"It's important. You do have a motorbike, don't you? I saw one in your backyard this afternoon."

"That's not mine. It's the Man's."

"Your tenant? The one whose brother owns a circus? Would he mind, or could *he* teach me even?"

"He's recovering from an operation."

"Oh, Egret, please. This is so important."

He breathes deeply and tries to gather his wits. "This is weird. Really fucking weird."

"No." She shakes her head, and her hair brushes his arm. "My son was attacked by two of his schoolmates on his way home today. He's in the hospital. It's not weird. It's necessary."

"I'm having a real hard time following you, Mrs. Morton."

"Karen. You don't fuck a woman and then call her by her mother-in-law's name. My name is Karen."

He doesn't know how to respond.

She sighs and runs one of her hands through her own hair. "How can I explain this to you? I want to change my image, change the image that surrounds Andy. I want to give him confidence and verve. I want him to be popular."

"Okay. But …"

"I've always wanted to ride a motorbike. When I was young, I used to dream of wearing motorbike boots and a leather jacket that clanked with steel buckles. I wanted to feel my hair streaming out behind me as I roared down the streets. I figured that would look pretty spectacular — my red hair whipping against all that black leather."

Egret figures it would, too, but he's having a hard time grasping the situation as a whole, so he merely grunts. It's as if he's come into a movie halfway through.

"Then I got pregnant and married, and somehow I convinced myself that what I wanted was no longer important. And I think I've passed that outlook onto Andy."

He waits for her to continue, then realizes that she's finished, that this is her explanation for breaking into his house at four in the morning to ask for motorbike riding lessons.

"Okay," he says carefully. "Okay."

"So you'll do it?"

"Well, I didn't quite say —"

"Thank you!" She flings her arms around him, and he's smothered in soft lips, warm breasts, and the wobbly parts of her upper arms. "Thank you," she breathes against his ear. "Thank you so very, very much."

How to extract himself from that kind of gratitude? How to reject that super-fast heartbeat pressed against his chest? How to ignore the thought that her indebtedness can be utilized to his sexual advantage? Most of all, still encased in sleep-stupor, how to find the words, the motivation, the cleverness necessary to extract him from this powerfully strange predicament?

He tries once, feebly. "Uh, driving your kid to school on a motorbike might not change things for him."

"Course not. That's just the first step." She pulls away, kisses him on the forehead — shit, his *old lady* kisses him like that! — and rises from the bed. "I've got other plans, too. How's tomorrow?"

"Tomorrow?"

"Afternoon? Around one?"

"Uh, no good. I've got school."

"It's Saturday."

"Oh, right. But I don't know if I can get the bike, and I got to practise …" His voice trails off in the dark as he hears her inhale — a tremulous, dismal sound.

He swallows, sighs. "I'll see what I can do."

"Egret!" She bends over him, long hair tickling his bare chest and caressing his back. "Thank you," she whispers, and this time she kisses him in a way his old lady would never do, not in a thousand million years.

It isn't until after she closes the door behind her that he thinks of the one argument — no, statement of *fact* — that might have saved him from the whole situation: a person with a leg cast can't ride a motorbike.

But as he drops off to sleep, he has the uncanny feeling that even that argument would have failed, and that broken bones won't deter Karen Morton.

For the first time in weeks Moey can breathe properly, can sleep soundly. The steady *tick-tick* of the IV pump beside his bed and the muted ring of call buttons on the nurses' board down the hall soothe him, much the same way the *whir-slosh* of a washing machine soothes a baby. As various antibiotics enter his body, drop by miraculous drop, he sleeps, blissfully free of the kaleidoscopic dreams that haunted him throughout his illness. No prickly multi-coloured pillows, no lubricated steel dildoes, no whips, herbal medicines, or kickboxing dogma to disturb him. Instead his sleep is as thick and pure as dark Belgium chocolate.

Until a cold hand touches his arm and a voice hisses his name into his ear.

He wakes up reluctantly, resigned to the fact that being admitted to the hospital has been just another hallucination and that Miranda is about to use his body to her satisfaction yet again. But, no, there is the IV pump beside his bed, the cotton curtains that divide his half of the room from his roommate's, the rubber *squelch-squelch* of nurse shoes out in the hall ...

"Down here!" the voice hisses. "I'm down here!"

Moey stiffly turns his head and blinks at the pale face of the woman crouched beside his bed.

"Sorry to wake you up so early. I guess I should've waited until visiting hours, but I was afraid that if I didn't come right away, I'd talk myself out of this."

Is this or is this not a hallucination? He is fairly certain it isn't, but then once not that long ago he also was fairly certain his penis was a chicken's head.

"I've decided you're right," the pale face whispers. "I've decided to listen to the white hart. But I need your help. You teach kickboxing, right?"

White Heart? Is that slang for one of the Caucasian nurses on the ward? He immediately thinks of Nurse Ratched in *One Flew over the Cuckoo's Nest*.

"I want you to teach my son self-defence. He's in the hospital right now, one floor below us. His schoolmates beat him up."

Moey frowns. As bizarre as this is, he is fairly certain hallucinatory women don't request kickboxing lessons for their sons.

"In return for the lessons I'll let you dance at the Footstop for as long as you want."

Everything snaps into place. With the same sort of delay that sometimes occurs during long-distance calls, Moey hears himself say "Karen" a few seconds after he speaks.

"Is that a deal?" she whispers.

"Uh, okay," he says, trying to recall exactly what it is she just asked him.

"Great! Look, I have to go before they find me in here. I'll visit you tomorrow before I pick up Andy." She gets to her feet and turns to go, then pauses and glances back at him over her shoulder. "You sound a lot better already."

"I'm feeling better," he says. "You drove me here, didn't you?"

"Yeah. You passed out on my doorstep."

"Sorry about that. But thanks for taking care of me."

"You shouldn't thank me, not really. If it wasn't for me, old Mrs. Kendall might still be alive and you might be healthy, but God was making sure He was going to get me and my whole family here when Andy needed us." She shrugs. "As Dad says, He works in mysterious ways."

"Yes," Moey agrees, "He does." Even though he doesn't know what the hell she's talking about.

Chapter Fifteen

With a stiff, aching neck and a spine crackling with crepitus, Morris hauls himself into work (he took a taxi so Karen could sleep in). But it is no good; he can't concentrate. Cuticles and metatarsals hold not the slightest interest for him, not when compared to his wristwatch and the approach of Andy's four o'clock discharge from the hospital.

It is during his 10:30 appointment with Mrs. Bess Bass — a patient with classic Tinea pedis, the web space between her toes covered in macerated scale, the inflammation extending to the dorsum of both her feet — that he realizes his mind is completely elsewhere.

"Nothing to worry about?" Mrs. Bass exclaims, flexing her pudgy feet. "What about all that soggy stuff between my toes? What about the itching that's driving me crazy?"

"Eh?" He blinks at her, then glances at the foot cradled in his palms. He starts in revulsion. "Yes, well, nothing to worry about with, uh, proper treatment. That's what I meant." He hastily puts the foot down. "I'll ... I'll write you a prescription. And you'll have to stop wearing tight shoes."

Morris quickly peels off his examination gloves, tosses them into the bin, and begins scrubbing with Hibitane soap. The pink liquid froths and foams like blood-tinged shaving cream as he lathers up his hands. And his forearms. And his elbows, which he scrubs with a bristle brush. He takes off his lab coat and shirt, hangs them on the exam room door handle, and flips his tie backwards. Spreading a skein of slimy soap over his narrow biceps, he starts scrubbing them, too, using his fingernails to scrape out any spores that might have gathered around the hair follicles in his armpits.

"Is it contagious?"

Morris freezes, covered in pink soapsuds from fingertip to collarbone. Long nail rakes throb on his skin like road-rash. What the *hell* is he doing?

"Uh, as a matter of fact, it is," he mutters. Without turning around he quickly rinses off all the soap and turns the tap off. Then he snaps a few crisp brown paper towels from the dispenser and pats himself dry.

"Exactly *how* contagious?"

"Avoid public swimming pools." He gropes the counter for his prescription pad and knocks over a stack of *Martha Stewart Living*. "Scrub your bathroom tub and floor with Dettol. Don't wear anyone else's shoes."

"Can my cats get it?"

"No." His hand shakes as he scrawls out her prescription.

"Will it spread to the rest of my body? Should I get some of that soap you were using?"

"Not necessary."

"Are you sure?"

"Quite." He tears the prescription from the pad and thrusts it at her.

"But you seem quite concerned that you might get it —"

"I'm allergic to perfume."

"I'm not *wearing* any perfume."

"The patient before you is ... was." He turns to the

door, snatches up his shirt, and bobs his head at her. "Goodbye."

Morris staggers down the hall, clutching his stomach. He's afraid he'll vomit. All he can see are those scales, the fungal growth, the thickened tan-covered surface of her feet. Spongy, fissured, hot, damp — this is his work. This is his life.

He collapses on the chair in his office and buries his face in his hands. With each exhalation, a soft, despairing cry escapes him.

The door to his office carefully clicks open. With great effort he looks up. The blurred image of Clara stands before him. Her plump bottom, encased in the tight sheath of a pleated navy skirt, nudges the door shut behind her.

"Are you all right?" she asks, toying with her pearls. "Mrs. Bass said ... Well, I've seen her out, anyway."

"Why are you doing that?" Morris demands.

Her fingers brake on the pearls. "Doing what?"

"Talking to me like that. You never talk to me like that. Only yesterday did you talk to me like that, after the phone call, and now again today you're talking to me like that."

Purple blotches slowly flower on her face, and her left eye travels slightly inward, towards her nose. "Like ... what?"

"As if we're equals. I mean, you've been working with me for ten years —"

"Eleven."

"Eleven years then. And never once have you talked to me like that. Like this."

"I'm sorry," she whispers, swallowing hard and staring at his filing cabinet.

"It wasn't meant as a criticism. It's just that —" he spreads his hands "— we never talk. I don't know you. Ten years —"

"Eleven," she whispers.

"Eleven years, and I don't even know you."

"Oh."

"Do you have children?"

Her eyes dart from the filing cabinet to his face, then back again. Her fingers dance across her pearls. "One. I think you know that already. We've spoken about Matt before."

"Have we?"

"Yes. When he went to live with his father. During my divorce."

The faint sound of someone coughing in the waiting room travels down the hall.

"Divorce," Morris says, bobbing his head. "Yes, I remember now. Divorce." He lets out an almighty moan and buries his head in his hands again. "I'm sick of warts, Clara. I'm sick of pustules and lesions and fused toes and bunions and fallen arches and oozing inflammation ..." He stops to suck in a breath, to look up at her with all the strength of a wet kitten. "Man has survived for thousands of years without doctors to remedy such things. My work is unnecessary. Unnecessary and unimportant. My work is *ugly*."

Clara stares at him. The purple splotches on her cheeks deepen, take on a life of their own, and gallop down her neck.

I wonder if she drinks, Morris thinks dully. *I wonder if I should drink.*

Clara inhales deeply, and her great bosom moves scratchily beneath her white taffeta blouse. "I think I'll take the liberty of cancelling the rest of your appointments for the day."

"That isn't necessary," he says bitterly.

"It is entirely necessary." She tweaks her pearls one last time.

Egret awakens that same morning feeling the world is a dangerously strange place, a place where a guy can get himself into a shit load of trouble without quite knowing how.

He doesn't let this observation interfere with his morning practice at the gym, though. He can't. The next international meet is less than eight weeks away in Cologne, Germany. There will be seven judges poolside. Fernando Platas from Mexico will be there, plus Jeff Liberty, who as a diver always scores well above the seven-and-a-half range.

Egret is a strong, dynamic diver, and he knows it, but his entries need polishing. He tends to power off the springboard too strongly and therefore tip over slightly as he knifes into the water. The dangerously strange aspects of the world will just have to wait while he sweats on the trampoline, correcting himself over and over according to his coach's barked orders. And he can do that, concentrate on his dives, now that his prick has been placated.

But the strangeness of life comes crashing down around him again when his father — effusive with praise and sage counsel about his competitors — pulls into their polished aggregate driveway. There stands the Man, swaying slightly on his crutches, leaning against the driver's door of a bright orange Puckley's Travelling Circus van. A snarling tiger is painted on the side, but so much paint has flaked off and been replaced by rust that the tiger looks spotted instead of striped. The overall effect is that of a toothy orange Dalmatian.

"Look at 'im," Egret's dad says in disgust. He throws the Porsche into neutral. "Bum, nothin' but a bum. And he wonders why he's livin' in a basement."

"Doesn't stop you from playing poker with him every night," Egret says.

"He plays a damn good game, that's why. Best tenant we've ever had, but that's not sayin' much. Now get out of the car. I gotta work. What are you yawnin' for? Didn't you sleep last night? Christ, I've told you how important —"

"I'm okay, Dad. I'm okay. I just need some food in me."

"Stay away from that chocolate cake your mother baked last night. You gotta be in top condition next month."

"Yeah, yeah." He climbs out of the car, hauling his gym bag with him.

"Five. I'll be back by five and we'll hit the pool."

Egret nods, slams the door closed, and watches his dad squeal out of the driveway. Then he approaches the idling Puckley's van.

"Hey, kid," the Man drawls, "how's your dick?"

The Man's long, greasy hair looks untouched by the drizzling rain, even though he wears no hat. So much oil has built up on his head since his operation that his hair repels water like a duck's feathers. Even his wiry, grey-rippled beard seems waxed.

"Hey," Egret says.

"You humped the old lady yet?" The Man turns to the driver of the van, a bulkier, ruddier version of himself in a dirty, sleeveless jean jacket and a faded red forehead bandanna. "The kid here's been messin' with a married woman."

"No shit," the driver says, breaking into a mirror image of the Man's yellow-toothed leer.

"Shut your mouth, will you?" Egret snaps.

"What? It's only my brother. Shit, who's he going to tell — his friggin' monkeys?"

Egret clutches his gym bag tighter and listens to their chortling. *Yeah, well, let them laugh,* he thinks. *They probably haven't been laid since the Vietnam War.* He would have said something like that, too, only he can't afford to ruffle the Man's feathers right now.

Instead he lets them snort a bit before he speaks. "You going out?"

"Does it look like I'm goin' out?" The Man shifts his weight on his crutches and spits to the side. "My whole damn leg is killin' me. I ain't goin' nowhere. None of your business, anyway."

"I need to ask you a favour."

The Man's rheumy eyes widen. "Reggie, d'ya hear that? The poor little rich boy needs a favour."

"Tell him it'll cost him."

"Hear that? It's gonna cost you."

"Yeah, I figured it would," Egret says.

"Smart ass."

"How's twenty bucks?"

"Twenty? Today a twenty ain't good enough to wipe your ass with."

Egret swallows back a sharp retort — something to the effect that the way the Man smells, he obviously never wipes his butt, twenty-dollar bill or no.

"Besides, I ain't agreein' to a price until I hear what this favour of yours is," the Man growls.

"I need the house to myself for a couple of hours."

"You need the ... Christ, isn't it big enough without you kickin' me outta the basement?"

"I smell a woman in this," the Man's brother hoots, revving the engine of the van and grinning widely.

"Eh? Is that it? You bringin' the old lady back here?"

"Does it make a difference?" Egret asks. "Look, we'll call it thirty-five bucks ..."

"You afraid I'm goin' to sneak up from my hole in the ground and take pictures of you humpin'?"

"This is worth at least fifty," Reggie crows, gunning the engine again and filling the driveway with stiff blue smoke.

"Whaddya say, kid? It worth a fifty to get rid of me for the day?" The Man crosses his eyes and waggles his brows, which is just about the last thing Egret expects him to do.

"Fifty bucks each!" Reggie bellows, stomping on the gas again. The van gives a deafening, gurgling roar, sounding for all the world like an old tiger going over a waterfall.

"All right, all right!" Egret says. "Lay off the gas before the neighbours start complaining!"

With a whoop Reggie gives one last pump on the pedal, then lets it die to a rough idle. Both he and the Man grin at each other, huge pizza-slice grins that reveal every gap and every rotting tooth in their mouths. Egret hasn't seen that much colour in the Man's cheeks since his operation.

"Glad I could entertain you," he says churlishly.

"That hundred gotta be in cash," Reggie says. "Gotta be in cash."

Keep your ugly ass out of this. Egret allows himself to think it, but he grips his bag handle hard and merely grunts, "I'll see what I've got."

He turns to enter the house, but something jabs him smartly in the ass. Furious, he drops his bag and whirls, fists balled, and meets the rubber end of one of the Man's crutches.

"I don't want your money, kid. Shit, what do you take me for?" The Man spits again, a thick, black-veined, milky oyster. He withdraws his crutch. "I'm goin' out, anyway."

"Goin' to the cop station overtown," Reggie confirms, adjusting his bandanna. "Gonna raise us a little hell."

"Some Greenpeace kids busted a buncha Reggie's animals outta their cages a couple weeks ago. The cops still ain't pressed charges."

"So it's time for a little justice," Reggie says. He makes the van cough up a hoarse roar once more.

Cracking a few ribald remarks concerning Egret, the Man circles the van to the passenger side, hauls himself in, throws his crutches into the back, and slams the door shut. Egret watches wordlessly, trying to imagine how justice is defined by these two aging derelicts — one a biker, the other a tourney roustabout.

"Could be we just lost a tenant," Egret mutters to himself.

Reggie throws a jaunty salute and backs the coughing van onto the road, while Egret lifts a hand in response. His wristwatch beeps: 1:00. *Shit, Karen will be arriving soon.* A mix of apprehension and anticipatory lust ripples down his back.

Shaking rainwater from his head, he bends and picks up his bag. A horn toots behind him, and a car pulls into the drive. He turns to see Karen at the wheel of her Tercel, beaming and waving.

Twenty-three minutes later she is sprawled naked on the heated ceramic tiles of his mother's kitchen floor, smeared in chocolate icing and cast-plaster dust.

How did this happen? Karen wonders, staring at the halogen light fixtures above her. *I didn't want this to happen, had absolutely no intention of this happening ...*

And yet here she is again, like a flipped-over turtle, belly exposed.

She is horrified and yet feels incapable of preventing it. How *can* she when it happened so fast, so unexpectedly? *It* being her nakedness and the pumping teenager atop her. She is demanding so much of Egret — to borrow his tenant's motorbike and teach her how to ride it — that surely she has no recourse but to give him these few moments of sticky bliss.

It goes completely beyond her how Egret can be so oblivious to her disinterest, though. Doesn't he notice her lack of enthusiasm, her diminished natural lubricants, her deficiency of grunts and moans?

Well, too late now. She can't very well tap him on the shoulder — the same one currently buried in her throat as he corkscrews himself as deeply as possible into her — and say, "Egret, please don't take this personally, but I really am here for the motorbike riding lessons only."

Or can she? Can it be as simple as rolling out from under him, springing to her feet with a light laugh, and saying, "Okay, *enough* of this!" as if he's a naughty puppy chewing on her slipper?

Only she won't be able to spring to her feet, will she, what with her cast neatly split in two like the halves of some prehistoric bivalve. Earlier, she sawed the cast off, with plans to bind her ankle with rolled newspapers and duct tape instead to give her the necessary flexibility to ride a motorbike yet provide the support her still-healing bones require. Chances are that even if she could slip out from under Egret and neatly leap to her feet, she would slip on all the chocolate icing coating the floor, the same stuff currently making a thick sucking noise between her back and the tiles with each of Egret's pumps.

She doesn't know what caused him to drop that cake. Perhaps the sight of her dress hitched up as she hacksawed her cast off, or more likely, perhaps the purloined pile of Candice's clothes spilling from her backpack like vegetables from a Thanksgiving cornucopia. (The black jeans and Doc Martens are both a size too small for Karen, but otherwise perfect for motorbike riding.)

Maybe, she thinks as she studies the detailed wood moulding around the rim of the ceiling, *my present position is just a misunderstanding. Maybe Egret assumes this is what I want to do. I mean, our relationship did start on a kitchen floor, and he doesn't know that the sight of Andy in a hospital bed has sent my desire winging away at top speed.*

Egret ducks his head, takes a couple of quick, vigorous sucks at one of her breasts as if he's a scuba diver and her nipple is connected to an oxygen tank, then resumes his position of one shoulder buried in her throat, his neck smothering her face, his chin atop her brow, jiggling and wiggling there like a novelty hula doll atop a trucker's dashboard.

The longer this goes on, Karen thinks, *the more I'm misleading him. He's a good kid. He'll take it well if I explain things carefully. And if on the off chance he doesn't, well, I'll just pay for motorbike riding lessons at a proper establishment.*

And then it strikes her: why the hell isn't she doing that in the first place? Why all this sneaking about, this fear of letting anyone into her plans?

By God, this *is what Dad meant about timid servility,* she thinks. *I'm scared to tell anyone until it's a done deal because I'm afraid of how they'll react. My, it's amazing the insights a gal can get while lying on her back in another woman's kitchen.*

Karen sucks in a breath. "Egret ..."

"*Candugh!*" he cries, arching away from her and shuddering. "*Candugh!*"

There is no doubt about it. The boy is using her as a stand-in for her daughter. She licks her lips — the cake frosting tastes of Bailey's Irish Cream, very nice; she files this for future reference — and says in as level a tone as possible, "I'm going to need a shower before we start."

Time — the thing that goes *tick-tick-tick* as steadily as a heartbeat, yet far more lasting. Karen never wears a watch, ever. Why on earth anyone would want to be constantly reminded of life's steady progression of wrinkles, sags, sluggish bowels, and cellulite, she has no idea. As far as she is concerned, wearing a watch is like wearing a miniature tombstone as a bracelet.

And besides, if one lives long enough without a watch, one can tell pretty darn closely what time it is by the shifting of shadows, the smell of the air, the sound of dogs, and the actions of birds. Karen feels people are worse off because of Timex and Swatch, blinkered like cart horses against nature.

At the moment she is very aware of the time — or how little of it she has until Andy's discharge from the hospital — as she sits straddled behind Egret on the Man's Virago. They are racing down Highway 1 towards Cypress Mountain. At this speed the light drizzle of rain feels like translucent, dive-bombing ballpoint pens stabbing through her tight black jeans.

She is suffering from other discomforts, too. Her helmet smells of greasy hair and garlic and wobbles around heavily on her head. Every time Egret shifts gears she lurches forward and her faceplate slams into the back of his helmet, and each updraft of wind that swirls from the slate-grey ocean to her left chucks her under the chin and lifts the helmet to her lips. She tries to keep her chin down against her chest to thwart the wind, but that only increases the instances of her faceplate thudding into the back of Egret's helmet.

And her ankle, splinted with stiff, tightly bound newspapers, vibrates painfully from the engine's thrum. Rather than let it rest on one of the reverberating passenger's foot pegs, she holds it up, a feat that soon has her calf muscles trembling with fatigue.

Beneath her the road whips by so fast she swears she can hear each segment of the dashed white line shooting past. Nothing will protect her if they skid on that slick road, or if some idiot sideswipes them, or if that huge semi up ahead changes lanes right into their path. No steel doors, no seat belts, no headrests to protect her here. She feels small and fragile and exposed with only the cotton threads of Candice's jeans protecting her.

And the cold, the wind! Karen shudders — doesn't shiver but shudders with the vigour of a bull elephant in must — as gusts of rain-laden wind blast her. She clings to Egret's waist so tightly she can feel each individual muscle in his abdomen. His jacket — a leather one borrowed from the Man's basement suite, where he also found the bike key and two helmets — billows out like a canvas sail on either side of him, giving the impression he weighs over two hundred pounds.

She is utterly terrified. Terrified but alive. She feels honed to a dagger point, defiant, primal. She feels like whooping and lifting her arms above her head to give Death the finger.

She feels *empowered*.

Egret takes Karen to the top of Cypress Mountain, to the huge empty parking lot that in a few months will be buried under three feet of snow and a couple of hundred skiers' cars. He explains all the basic parts on the bike first, lets her push and switch and turn things: choke knob, clutch lever, throttle grip, engine stop switch, starter button, horn. Then he sits her astride the bike, its chrome exhaust pipes steaming from heat and glistening with gasoline iridescence.

He shows her how to switch the fuel valve on, gets her to use the gear change pedal while the bike is still on its kickstand, explains how to gradually apply both front and rear brakes while downshifting. Then he has her kick up the side stand so he can slowly push her around the parking lot with the engine off, let her get used to the low, heavy, sleek weight of the bike crouched between her legs.

After that he asks her to climb off, clambers onto the bike himself, starts it, puts it into neutral, swings off, and tells her to hop on again. She hesitates, and he grins at her.

Finally, she gets on. Alone. And experiences something very much like an emotional orgasm.

Two hours later, cold and soaked to the skin, they duck into the ski-loft concession booth. Shania Twain croons in the background. The smell of hamburger grease lies thick and stale in the air. The loft is empty — only one bank of overhead lights has been turned on. A single fry cook slouches behind the food counter, sucking on a pencil and reading a textbook.

"We're out of coffee," he mutters as soon as they come in.

"What else have you got?" Karen asks, bouncing up and down on the ball of her good foot. The other one is killing her; the rolled newspaper splint is as soggy as leftover cornflakes.

"Hot chocolate. Made with water, not milk."

"Egret? Hot chocolate sound good to you?"

"Make it a double," he says.

They drink watery hot chocolate. They talk about disengaging the clutch and closing the throttle before shifting gears. They talk about springboard dives that are a little over at the bottom. They talk about karma and birthmarks that buzz.

And after it is all over — after Egret has returned the Man's key and helmets and leather jacket to his basement suite — Karen climbs into her battered Tercel and drives to her husband's office, feeling that she and Egret have shared something rich, powerful, and rare on that rain-drenched mountain.

She hopes she can share such a feeling with Andy.

Chapter Sixteen

Mrs. Baroudi has lived beside the Mortons for as long as Candice can remember. Her husband died in a sawmill accident twelve years ago, and now Mrs. Baroudi lives more or less alone. More or less because a nonstop parade of Baroudis stream in and out of her house like ants at a picnic — Gino, an Iowa college football player recovering from Lyme disease; Nola, an anthropology student doing a thesis on prostitution; Marco and Rosaline and their screaming kids from Winnipeg; Carlos, the gambler with his umpteenth Las Vegas wife ... The list went on and on. Candice has heard way too much about all of them.

Not that she's friends or anything with Mrs. Baroudi, but each time the woman expects a visit from her relatives, she calls on Morris and Candice to lug her cedar blanket boxes down from the attic so she can air out her bedsheets, and she always talks a mile a minute about her family. Mrs. Baroudi insists Karen can't help. "Your momma has that baby to look after," she says. "Poppa and Candice will do the job, eh? You're a big girl, big strong girl."

Like, hello? Andy hasn't been a baby for seven years now. But does that matter to Mrs. Baroudi? No. In her pruney mind the job calls for Candice. Once Candice suggested — just a suggestion, a completely *reasonable* suggestion — that Mrs. Baroudi keep the blanket boxes on the main floor of her house where she could get at them as often as she liked. But Mrs. Baroudi went spiral, shouting stuff like "You don't want to help, you forget it, you go on home, I don't need your help." Candice's dad stayed to hang the stupid bedsheets on Mrs. Baroudi's laundry line just to lower the old bat's blood pressure.

Now as Candice raps her knuckles on Mrs. Baroudi's heavy wooden door, she hopes that at least ten of the Baroudi brood are present. That way Candice can fill her receipt books and return home. Not that she holds much hope there will be visitors inside; she and her dad haven't moved any blanket boxes recently.

"Candice, how are you, how are you? What's wrong? Where's your father?"

"Nothing's wrong, Mrs. Baroudi. I'm helping Mom canvass this year."

"You're what? What a good girl! Come in, come in. Tell me what charities she works for this time."

Behind her forced smile Candice grits her teeth and steps inside. There is no point protesting; she would just offend the old lady, and offending Mrs. Baroudi would generate dozens of telephone calls to her parents, accompanied by baskets and jars of absolutely injurious homemade laxatives. Mrs. Baroudi is of the firm opinion that all the evils of the world are due to constipation. Candice has heard the story a million times: Mr. Baroudi was constipated the morning of his fatal accident, and if only he'd had a laxative before going to work that day, he would have been more alert when working that band saw.

So Candice obediently follows Mrs. Baroudi down the tiny dark hall of her small damp house and into her Formica-everything kitchen. She wrinkles her nose and tries not to gag at the smell of the house — a closed-in, sombre smell that reminds her of forgotten potatoes sprouting in the back of a cupboard. Dorea, Mrs. Baroudi's obese cocker spaniel, moves her tail once in greeting but remains in position by the refrigerator.

"Tell me. Why are you helping your mother this year? You've never helped her before. Have some cookies. I baked them this morning. Full of fibre, real good for you."

"She broke her ankle a couple of weeks ago."

Candice doesn't mention that Mr. Osaban agreed not to press charges and has let her dad pay for the damage she did to his 1950 Mercury — damage caused by slamming Andy's psychopathic attackers into the Mercury's hood. But the agreement was made on two conditions: the first that Candice do community work and the second that she talk to a social worker or a psychologist about her aggression. Both of these conditions were actually stipulated by the policeman and the community worker involved in the whole mess. Helping her mom canvass the neighbours for charity fulfills the first condition. The second condition would be met later this week during her first appointment with Dr. Alana Bronte.

"That's right. I remember Karen telling me about her foot. Her left ankle, no? Should be better soon, eh? Have a cookie, have a cookie." Mrs. Baroudi lowers her stumpy body onto a green vinyl chair across from Candice and pulls her black cardigan tighter across her bosom. "So what charities are you collecting for this year? Something for the environment maybe? It gets colder and colder every year. Global warming or something. Are you cold? Do you want to borrow a sweater?"

"I'm fine, thanks." Candice takes a deep breath and spreads her receipt books out on the table. "Mothers Against Drunk Drivers. The Multiple Sclerosis Society of Canada. The Canadian Wildlife Federation. The Adult Literacy Contact Centre."

"Four? Only four this year? Last year she did five. Oh, well, you can't expect people to keep up these days. What's the literacy thing? Tell me about that. I never heard of it before."

So Candice does, reading directly off the blurb the ALC sent her mom: "Did you know that a recent survey by Statistics Canada found that 31 percent of adults in British Columbia can't read or have difficulty reading?" Then she informs Mrs. Baroudi about multiple sclerosis. Fact: Canada has one of the highest rates of multiple sclerosis in the world. Fact: we don't know what causes it, but researchers are closer to finding the answer. Next she does pitches for the Wildlife Federation and Mothers Against Drunk Drivers. In the end Mrs. Baroudi gives five dollars to each.

"It's not much — God knows I'm not a rich woman — but I like to help out where I can. For instance, with your grandfather. As soon as I heard about that fire, I offered your mother my guest room. Here, take the rest of these cookies. I'll wrap them for you. Where are they going to stay, I said, in the teahouse? But she said no. That's okay. I understand. Families have to stick together at times like these."

Candice hastily rubber-bands her receipt books together and rises from her chair. Mrs. Baroudi follows her down the hall.

"Who do you have to do next? Mr. Willis? He's a crazy man, that man, a crazy man. Doesn't get enough fibre in his diet. Do you know what he did last month? He cut off all the branches of my cherry tree that were hanging in his yard. Said the cherries got trampled into his carpet every summer. I asked him what he was doing walking around his house with shoes on in the first place. Bachelors! Here, take these cookies. Let me get the door for you."

Candice accepts the cookies with grim thanks and edges out the front door. Shoulders hunched against the rain, she starts walking down the path.

"Watch your step now. Getting dark early these days. Can't see a thing out here past four o'clock. You know, you really shouldn't be carrying all that money alone ..."

"I'm not alone. My mom's doing the houses across the street."

"What? With her ankle like that? Santa Maria! What is she thinking?"

"Goodbye, Mrs. Baroudi," Candice says, ignoring the dire proclamations from behind. Under her breath she mutters, "Christ in a coffin, that woman's mental."

Glowering, Candice stumps across Don Willis's lawn — as if she would ask *him* for a donation — and heads towards the next house. The sooner she gets this stupid canvassing done and over with the better.

The rain is the drizzly, misty, twilight kind that is twice as wet and invasive as normal rain, and her Doc Martens are soaking wet — how, she doesn't know. She swears she didn't leave them outside on the back step as her mom insists. As *if* she would do such a thing — the boots cost her a year's worth of allowance.

Something huge and hairy and fanged flings itself at her throat, exploding into barks and snarls. The impact sends her flying through the air, and she lands hard — *whoomp!* — on her shoulder blades. Her head slams with a dull watermelon *thunk* against the lawn. She slides across the grass, the snarling thing atop her, receipt books scattering like confetti.

With a cry she folds her arms over her head. Fabric rips. She kicks out. Her left boot slams into something. A bruising vise crushes her left elbow. She shrieks, writhes, flails. Black fur, white fangs, cold, muddy lawn, slashes of dusky sky ...

Then another scream, not her own, followed by a slicing *thwack* through the air. A startled, angry yip.

"Get off her!" a voice shrieks.

Thwack, thwack, thwack! Yip, yip!

Candice rolls onto her elbows and watches someone — her mother! — raise something metallic into the air and bring it crashing down on the snarling Doberman. But the Doberman isn't snarling anymore. It's sitting on its haunches, dazed and silent. Candice briefly thinks of Gumby's pal, the ogle-eyed horse thing.

"Mom, stop!" she yells.

Karen's head whips in Candice's direction, eyes as glassy as a china doll's. The Doberman sucks in a huge draft of air and sways drunkenly. Then, as Karen turns back to look at it, the Doberman slowly topples onto its side.

Thud.

They both stare at the creature.

"*Ohmigod!*" Candice breathes. "You've killed the Wagners' dog."

Karen glances at Candice, her crutch poised to strike again. "Did it hurt you?"

"Jesus, Mom, look at the dog! I think you've killed it!"

"What?" Karen stares at the motionless body, then drops the crutch. The screws in the crutch tinkle loosely as it hits the ground. "I didn't. I couldn't have. I only hit —"

"Santa Maria! Is she hurt? Oh, the poor child, the poor —"

As Mrs. Baroudi stumble-waddles across the lawn

towards them, her stout black shoes slipping and sliding on the wet grass, Karen falls to her knees and shakes the Doberman. "Chewy? Chewy? I didn't hit you that hard! Chewy, get up!"

"Forget about that thing, will you! What about your daughter?" Wheezing, Mrs. Baroudi leans over, hands on her knees as she half bends to peer at Candice. "Look at your arm! Is it broken? Is it bleeding?"

Candice studies her arm, and as soon as she sees the ripped corduroy of her coat and the white stuffing spilling out from it, she becomes aware of the intensely hot pulsing in her elbow. She moves it. "Ow! Shit!"

"Keep it still! Don't move it, don't move it. Here, I'll help you up."

Mrs. Baroudi extends a hand. Candice grabs it and is hauled to her feet.

"Devil dog!" Mrs. Baroudi spits at the ground, then wraps her arms around Candice's shoulders.

Pale and shaken, Karen looks up at them from where she still kneels beside the dog. "I ... I think I've killed it. Oh, God, Theresa, I think —"

"Get up, get up, it's pouring rain out here. You come into my house. I'll fix you both some coffee while we look at this arm."

"But the dog, Theresa! I really think it's dead!"

Mrs. Baroudi frowns. She releases Candice, steps forward, and stoops over the furry body, her huge bottom in her shapeless black dress tipping skyward. Then, slowly, she straightens, drawing her cardigan tightly over her bosom. "I think you're right." She nudges the body with one stout shoe. "Yes, you're right."

"*Ohmigod*, Mom! I can't *believe* you did that!" Candice's eyes dart around the gloomy, rain-drenched street. No one is in sight. "Now what do we do?"

"What do we do?" Mrs. Baroudi firmly takes Candice by the shoulders again. "We go back in my house and drink coffee and look at your arm, that's what we do. Stupid dog. Stupid Wagners. I've been telling them for years that dog goes in my garden. Do they ever clean it up? Never. Come on."

"But we can't just leave it here!" Candice and Karen cry in unison.

"What do you want to do with it — bring it back with us?"

Candice has a sudden image of stuffing the body into one of Mrs. Baroudi's blanket boxes. She shudders. "Try mouth-to-mouth, Mom. Try CPR or something. We can't just leave it."

"Don't you dare, Karen Morton! That is a filthy animal."

"Theresa, I have to try something."

"That dog eats cat doo-doo. I've seen it."

They all stare at one another: Karen at Candice, Candice at Mrs. Baroudi, Mrs. Baroudi at Karen. Then Karen clenches her hands into fists, tips back her head, and makes a screaming sound deep in her throat. Mute, Candice and Mrs. Baroudi watch her.

When she is finished, she turns to them and says quietly, "I'd appreciate it if you both didn't watch this."

"*Ayyy, Santa Maria,*" Mrs. Baroudi mutters under her breath. "For a stupid dog!"

Candice and Mrs. Baroudi face the street. The rain drizzles down, beading their hair with cold mist. The throbbing in Candice's elbow grows hotter.

From behind them comes a deep inhalation, then a rubbery, flapping noise. Another deep inhalation.

Another loose-lipped sound. A few hollow chest compressions — *whump, whump*. Another inhalation. More air escaping passes slackened lips.

A heavy human sigh.

"I'm so sorry, Chewy," Karen whispers. "Even if you were a mean bastard."

"It should have been on a chain," Mrs. Baroudi snaps, startling Candice. "Can we turn around now, eh?"

"Yes. I suppose so."

"You suppose so, you suppose so. Look at you, sitting in the rain with a broken — Eh? What have you done now? You've cracked it in half!"

Candice gapes. It's true. Precisely half of Karen's cast lies atop her injured foot. The other half, the bottom, is nowhere to be seen.

As one, Karen, Mrs. Baroudi, and Candice gaze across the street to where Karen was moments before the attack. A white object lies in the middle of the road, soggy and forlorn.

"Santa Maria! Has the whole world gone crazy?"

"*Ohmigod*, it's totally in half," Candice says. "How —"

"You should sue the doctor who put it on you, Karen. Doctors these days, they aren't what they used to be." Mrs. Baroudi releases Candice's shoulders. "Go help your momma pick up those receipt books, eh? Me, I'll get that cast. And hurry up. I don't want that crazy Don Willis coming out and complaining about this dead dog on his lawn. Him and his lawn. Anybody would think it belonged to the pope."

Closing his eyes, Andy inhales deeply, relishing the familiar urine-and-hay scent of his guinea pig, the soft baby-powder fragrance of his bedsheets, the oiled-steel aroma of the half-dozen Meccano sets strewn about his room. Boy, is it *ever* good to be home.

Andy hates sleeping anywhere but in his own bed. He hates waking up in unfamiliar surroundings, smelling unfamiliar odours. The night always stretches on forever in cases like that, as if he's locked in a menacing otherworld where, no matter how many times he falls asleep and wakes again, it is always darkest night. In such instances creeping horrors lurk at the edges of his eyesight, and he dares not look left or right, just stares at one fixed spot, usually the ceiling, until his eyes grow so dry and cold and itchy he has to squinch them shut and burrow under the sheets — *slowly*, so as not to attract the attention of the creeping horrors.

Only once in his entire life has he ever gone to a sleepover — at Pascale Reinhardt's, the only boy invited to the all-girl event — and that turned out to be utter hell: a pile of bodies strewn across a basement floor, squirming, giggling, and sighing in sleeping bags. He woke up in the middle of the night surrounded by walls decorated with Mr. Reinhardt's collection of First Nations masks and screamed his head off.

Sort of like how he woke up screaming at the hospital last night. It was the blinking red light on his intravenous pump that did it — for a disorienting second it looked like the eye of a Cyclops. The nurses were pretty good about it, after they ascertained he wasn't hallucinating or experiencing problems due to his head injury. They even brought him orange Popsicles from the maternity ward, which conveniently led to a discussion about the necessity for a labouring woman to keep hydrated, a conversation that lasted long enough for the creeping horrors in the hospital bathroom to disappear down the toilet bowl from boredom.

Yes, although Andy was only gone one night, it is truly good to be home again. Grampy Woodruff is singing in the shower, the evening news burbles in the living room. Nanny Woodruff is helping Dad bake teahouse merchandise, Candice and Mom are out canvassing the neighbourhood for donations. All is right in the world.

The front doorbell rings.

Yogurt squeaks as he always does at the sound of the doorbell, thinking perhaps it is a fellow guinea pig. Andy listens carefully, straining his ears past Grampy's hearty rendition of "My Wild Irish Rose." He hears the *creak-snap, creak-snap* of the kitchen doors swinging open and closed, hears the characteristic *shuffle-stomp* of Nanny Woodruff moving down the hall, hears the click of the front door deadbolt being drawn back.

Apprehension fills him. Whatever is on the other side of that door heralds no good, Andy is certain. He shoots a beseeching look at the Buddha on his bookcase — *please make it go away.*

Polite voices filter down the hall, barely discernible above Grampy's singing and the rain on the roof.

"Morris!" Nanny warbles. "You'd better come here for a minute!"

Andy's toes curl in on themselves, and he closes his eyes. *Please make them go away, please make them go away, please —*

"Son? Andy? Are you asleep?"

Reluctantly, Andy opens his eyes. His father is leaning through his doorway, frowning uncertainly.

"Yes," Andy croaks, knowing in his gut that the lie won't save him.

"It seems you've got visitors."

"Oh."

"You up to it?"

"Not really."

"Hmm." His dad toys with the door handle. "Well, I really think you should see them."

Ah. One of those non-choices parents are so good at offering. With a sigh Andy shrugs. There is no need to ask who it is. The roiling acid in his stomach, like a premonitory feeler, gives him a pretty good idea of the identity of his visitors.

"I'll show them in," his dad murmurs.

Andy waits with eyes closed, furious that his sanctuary is about to be invaded, sick with an all-too-familiar dread. Without opening his eyes he fumbles by his pillow for his glasses — an old pair, the prescription not strong enough but better than nothing at all — and carefully perches them on his bandaged nose. Then he lies stiff as a fence picket, aware of every bruise and abrasion on his body.

The floorboards of his room creak. Yogurt squeals and gnaws at the bars of his cage, anticipating a carrot. Slowly, Andy opens his eyes.

It is half as bad as he feared. Only Kyle stands before him. A short skinny man with thin blond hair holds Kyle by the scruff of his coat collar. The man struggles and fails to work an expression of horror off his face as he peers down at Andy. Kyle studies his own shoelaces. In the background Nanny Woodruff pounds on the bathroom door, shouting at Grampy to pipe down.

"You must be Andy," the man eventually says.

"Yes. Are you Kyle's dad?"

"I am."

"Oh."

"Kyle has something he'd like to say to you. Don't you, Kyle?"

Without looking up from the floor Kyle makes an indistinct noise.

"Louder, please."

"Sorry," Kyle says, burning a hole into the floor with his eyes. "I want to say I'm sorry."

Andy suppresses another sigh. Parents just don't get it, do they? Can't they see they're making his future a thousand times worse by forcing Kyle into this degrading situation? Can't they remember this stuff from when they were kids?

"Th-that's okay," Andy says, wincing because his nervous stutter causes lemon-juice pains on his split, swollen lips.

"No, it's not okay," Kyle's father says. "I appreciate your willingness to accept Kyle's apology, but that doesn't make things okay. Does it, Kyle?"

"I dunno," Kyle mumbles.

"I beg your pardon, young man?"

"No. It doesn't make things okay," Kyle says loudly.

"Tell him about Troy."

"Aw, Dad."

"*Tell* him."

Kyle waits long enough to make it clear he is doing so under extreme duress, then directs his blowtorch glare at Andy. "Troy's been expelled."

"And?" his father prompts.

"And we're not allowed to be friends anymore."

"That's right." He releases Kyle's coat collar. "Now I'll leave you two alone to talk things over."

Andy almost faints.

Kyle whirls on his father — they are almost the same height. From the swirling depths of his fear Andy wonders what dire threats such a thin, waxen man can possibly hold over Kyle to remain in charge.

"What do you mean, leave us alone?" Kyle cries. "I did my part!"

"You did. Barely. Now I want you both to get acquainted."

"But that wasn't part of the deal!"

"This isn't negotiable." Then Kyle's dad nods at Andy. "I'm sorry we had to meet under such circumstances."

Andy can only gape at his back as he departs.

"Aw, shit," Kyle says, ramming his hands into his jeans pockets. "This stinks."

Andy tries to swallow the jagged hot ruby in his throat. His heartbeat pounds against his bruised brain so hard his pillow pulses beneath him. He stares at Kyle with the same unblinking concentration he uses when staring at unfamiliar ceilings at night and suppresses the urge to scream for help.

"This stinks," Kyle repeats. He slowly surveys the room, averting his gaze from Andy. "Totally and completely. Hey, what's that?"

He saunters over to Andy's science lab — a metal fold-up table currently cluttered with copper pipes, tin shears, a roll of silver duct tape, a can of WD-40, screwdrivers, electrical wiring, needlenose pliers, and metal sheets. Kyle picks up a copper pipe and nonchalantly hefts it a couple of times in one hand. "What are you doing with all this stuff?"

"T-t-trying to make an air c-conditioner," Andy says hoarsely.

"*Why?*"

"To see if I c-can duplicate the first one made in 1902."

"Yeah, but *why?*"

"I don't know. I just like building things, I guess."

"Yeah, but an air conditioner? That's, like, impaired or

something." Kyle puts down the copper pipe and picks up the tin shears. He snips at the air, then runs a finger over one of the blades. "Wow, these things are *sharp*."

Andy's heart flutters. "You can try it on one of those metal sheets if you want," he gasps, lest Kyle take it into his head to test it on Andy himself.

Kyle grabs a metal sheet and bites into it with the shears. It makes a crisp, twangy sound. "Why don't you build a go-cart or something? An air conditioner is stupid."

"I'm on probation. I c-can only build certain things."

Kyle glances at him. *"You're* on probation? What for?"

"I don't know if I should tell you."

"Yeah, right. Sissy. You're making it all —"

"For b-building a bomb."

Kyle sneers. "Yeah, *right*."

"It's true. That's why I got transferred to your school. I was expelled."

"You can't build a bomb."

"Yes, I can. Anybody can. All the information is on the Internet."

"Yeah, but you'd need, like, plutonium or uranium or other radioactive shit."

"No. Just household stuff."

Kyle shifts on the balls of his feet. "Are you serious?"

"Yes."

"Really?"

Andy swallows; the ruby in his throat begins to melt.

"So did it work? The bomb?"

"It burned down the gymnasium."

"No way. You're lying."

Andy doesn't answer.

"It burned down the *gymnasium*? For real?"

"The smoke was so bad they had to close the school for

a week." For the first time ever Andy feels a spike of pride about the whole thing.

"Harsh!" Kyle puts down the tin shears and comes over to Andy's bed. "That's harsh! Could you, like, build another one? We could set it off in Mrs. Beebe's classroom, blow her stupid ukuleles all over the place!"

"I'm n-not allowed to use the Internet f-for a while."

"How come you're doing that?"

"What?"

"Stuttering. You don't always do it."

"Oh." A hot flush starts up Andy's neck. "I s-stutter when I get n-nervous."

"You think I'm going to beat you up again?"

"Maybe."

Kyle doesn't say anything, just looks down at him in the bed. Then one of his hands moves fast, and Andy jerks, heart slamming into the roof of his mouth.

"What are those red marks on your face?"

"Huh?" Andy blinks rapidly and tries to catch his breath. He is still alive!

"Those marks on your face — what are they?"

"Th-that's where you k-kicked me."

"You mean that's the bottom of my shoe on your face?"

"Yes."

Kyle mulls that over for a moment. "But I didn't kick you. Troy was doing all that stuff. I just kicked the slug."

"I'm pretty sure it was you."

"You're brain-damaged, Four-Eyes."

"You could always check the pattern on the bottom of your shoes," Andy suggests.

Kyle wipes the back of his hand across his nose, shrugs, then bends down out of Andy's sight. He comes up a few moments later with a wet and muddy sneaker and holds it close to Andy's face.

"Look, see? Mine doesn't have a Nike logo on the bottom, and there's part of one right there on your face." He points at the lower portion of Andy's left cheek.

"*Is* there?"

"Haven't you even seen what you look like?"

"No." Andy thinks for a second. "But if you held a metal sheet up really close I might be able to see myself."

Kyle drops his soggy sneaker onto Andy's chest, turns back to the science laboratory, and snatches a sheet of metal. He holds it a couple of feet away from Andy's face. "Can you see it?"

"Closer, move it closer," Andy says, squinting.

"Shit, your eyes are bad." He moves it closer. "*Now* can you see it?"

"Almost. A little closer ... Oh, yeah, now I see it."

"Kind of like in *Raiders of the Lost Ark* when that German guy grabs the medallion out of the fire with his bare hands. Ever see that movie?"

"Never heard of it."

"It's an *awesome* one. A classic. My dad's got it in his DVD collection. Indiana Jones kicks ass. Hey, you want to see something cool? Look at this." He cranks his mouth wide open. "'Ee aht? 'Ere?"

"Did *I* do that?" Andy asks in wonder, gazing at the three broken teeth in Kyle's mouth.

"No. Your sister did. Boy, is she crazy."

"Sometimes. Especially when she has her period."

"Gross. Don't talk like that. I've got *three* sisters and they talk like that all the time. I can't wait until I'm old enough to move out. I'm gonna buy a 750 Ninja and go down to my uncle's ranch —"

They hear a *rat-a-tat* on Andy's door, and Kyle's dad

pokes his head in. "Boys? Kyle? Time to go. We've got to pick Brianna up from ballet."

Kyle turns to Andy and rolls his eyes "Ballet. *See* what I have to live with?"

He retrieves his sneaker from Andy's chest and shoves it back onto his foot. "Maybe we can talk later about this Mrs. Beebe plan. We need a code name for it, though. Project Ark or something." Still jamming his foot into his sneaker, he hop-lurches towards Andy's door. "I'll see if I can figure out how to get around the problem with the Net. Catch you later, Four-Eyes."

Without even thinking Andy replies, "Bye, Fang."

Kyle halts in the doorway, and Andy's heart freezes in his chest. *Jesus Lord, what on earth made me blurt that out?*

Then Kyle grins. "Fang. Cool."

And he turns and leaves Andy limp in bed, listening to his heartbeat wind down from doing a thousand zillion beats a second.

Chapter Seventeen

Morris can't work. Oh, he pretends. He goes into the office every day and looks at foot after foot. He writes prescriptions and referrals (a great many of the latter) and presses warm, wet plaster against fallen arches to make moulds for arch supports. But at the end of the day he can't recall a single individual case, and he hasn't written in his journal since Andy was attacked several weeks ago.

Instead of eating lunch in his office he has taken to wandering up and down the rain-drenched streets around Lonsdale Avenue. Each jaunt lasts longer than the previous one. Four days in a row he has missed the first of his afternoon appointments; today he's been walking for two and a half hours and has missed all but the final three. He imagines capable Clara has rescheduled them.

Might as well go home, Morris thinks. From his present location it will take him at least two more hours to reach Peters Road — two hours in rain that is determined to outdo the torrent that caused the biblical flood. Yet two hours in such a downpour seems entirely reasonable to him.

He wants his wife. He wants her friendship, her support, the giddy, savage sexuality she once had so very long ago.

He wants his son, with his round-eyed admiration, his chirrupy giggles, his inquiring, restless mind.

He wants his sassy daughter and her sarcastic wit.

He wants his in-laws out. He wants the rain to stop. He wants that damn creek behind his house to stop claiming the lives of the innocent. A kayaker died yesterday after flipping over and striking his head against a rock — kayaking in *that* creek in *this* weather!

Most of all Morris wants never again to observe another foot in his life. Each time he examines a foot he sees Andy's bruised and broken face and hears Candice's furious expletives and knows they're all connected to a failure of his own.

So let it rain on him. He doesn't care.

Behind the wheel of her Tercel, Karen watches her mother scramble out of the passenger side and skitter crablike across the wet sidewalk to an ATM. She uses the time to think, to assess her life.

I have committed adultery.

I have murdered a dog.

I have spent a decade and a half creating Formica foot earrings for a living.

She measures this summation against her most recent actions.

I have enlisted the aid of a belly dancer to teach my son courage.

I have traded sex for motorbike lessons.

With an epiphany as sudden and painful as a migraine, she realizes that what Egret said is true: she won't be able to change her life, her son, her outlook, by riding a Harley-Davidson. Instead she has to recognize her nearest and dearest aspiration and strive to fulfill it.

She knows this, exactly as she knew it the other night on her backdoor step, exactly as she knew it fifteen years ago when she painted that giant alabaster foot on the clapboard of her home and agreed to operate the Footstop. Yet acting on the knowledge is difficult, is terrifying. Easier to skirt the issue and disguise the symptoms of her timid servility by substituting less-volatile changes in her life for the Big Change.

So she will tenaciously hang on to the idea that karate and a motorbike will empower both her and her son. She will meander around the edges of the decision she reached at 4:00 a.m. the other day. She won't publicly voice her Destiny nor directly pursue it. She won't help others attain sexual enlightenment through the vehicle of a Spiritual Sex Store. She won't heed the buzzing of her birthmarks. She won't listen to the white hart.

Outside it rains and it rains and it rains.

Moey and Andy regard each other with undisguised incredulity. Moey is thinking: *How can I teach self-defence to a half-blind kid with a displaced collarbone?*

Andy is thinking: *Isn't he going to take his belly-dancing costume off and put some clothes on first?*

And Moey is thinking: *I bet Karen hasn't told her husband about me. I bet he doesn't even know I'm dancing here.*

And Andy is thinking: *I'm going to explode with all of Mom's secrets. I think I'm going to puke.*

And Moey is thinking: *The kid must weigh forty pounds at most. I touch him, he's going to shatter.*

And Andy is thinking: *Is he gay? What is Mom thinking?*

Moey wants to dance here, yes. But not furtively and not as part of a seedy bargain. Andy wants to please his mom and make her happy, but not at the cost of wrestling with this hairy, sweaty stranger dressed in bracelets and red pantaloons.

So what do they both do, this adult and child? They choose the easiest course, the non-confrontational route. The passive way. Denial of self.

Moey clears his throat and begins to show the boy a basic strike combination. Andy carefully adjusts his new glasses on the bridge of his recently unbandaged nose and pays close attention. They keep a good six feet between each other.

Overhead the rain hammers on the roof, a ceaseless, deafening din.

Mei-ling and the reverend agree that if they wait for the insurance claims and lawsuits to clear up before they purchase a house they might very well be living in Karen's rancher for the next ten years. They decide they must cash in their RRSPs, humbly accept the monetary donations that have accrued in Our Father's Fire Fund (started by the reverend's devoted parish), and begin house-hunting.

They almost drop dead upon opening the North Shore edition of the *Real Estate Weekly*.

"Blessed Shiva!" Mei-ling cries. "Five hundred thousand dollars for a rancher?"

"What? You can't be reading that right. Give it here." The reverend spreads the ink-saturated, rain-spattered newspaper across his lap. "Good God, they're out of their minds!"

Apparently, the nebulous *they* are not. A modest three-bedroom home, no matter where in North Vancouver, costs no less than half a million dollars, and homes that cheap are far and few between. Most of the listings in the paper use words like *gourmet kitchen, expansive deck area*, and *mature landscaping in a parklike setting* — all euphemisms for exorbitantly priced.

"Five bedrooms and six baths?" Mei-ling yelps. "Why on earth would anyone want more baths than bedrooms?"

"Maybe that's where people put their guests these days," the reverend growls. "That would explain why this generation seems a little wet behind the ears."

After a few phone calls, Mei-ling and the reverend discover there is a flip side to real-estate lingo: a house that needs tender loving care means it needs to be torn down; quaint means uninsulated; and affordable means it needs a new roof, new plumbing, and new appliances.

They pause in their search and stare across Karen's kitchen table at each other.

"At these prices we can barely afford a thirty-year-old apartment, let alone a shabby old shack," Mei-ling whispers.

"I'm not moving into a sardine can or a stodgy old building." The reverend thumps his fist on the table for emphasis. "Not even if we have to live in this house with my daughter until we die."

A particularly vehement gust of wind hammers a sheet of rain against the kitchen windows. Both the reverend and his wife involuntarily shiver.

"So what did you do with the dog?" Gloria asks, staring at Candice with big liquid brown eyes. The intensity of those eyes makes Candice's nipples harden.

Candice shrugs nonchalantly. "Left it there. Mr. Willis found it when he came home from work, and he told the Wagners to get their dog off his lawn before he killed it. He didn't even notice it was already dead. So now the Wagners think Mr. Willis killed Chewy, which serves him right. The guy's a jerk."

Gloria sighs and sinks back against the pillows of her bed. Candice, sitting at the foot of the bed and flipping idly through a *Cosmopolitan* magazine, tries not to look at the sweet, smooth swell of Gloria's breasts beneath her red-and-pink-striped sweater.

"You have the most exciting life, Candice. Things *happen* to you. Not like my life. God, my mother would never kill a dog for me. Not unless she was going to take it down to Dad's store and make sausages out of it."

"Gross."

They both giggle a little nervously.

Gloria and Candice are alone, quite unexpectedly. Mrs. Vermicelli rushed out to help her husband cater an unscheduled funeral, and Gloria's rancid brother hasn't returned home from school yet. Gloria doesn't seem to know how to deal with this unanticipated pocket of time.

Candice knows how *she* would like to deal with it. Boy, does she ever. In a couple of days her period is due, and she always feels as randy as a tomcat at this time, as if the blood that will soon drip from her uterus is dammed up in her clitoris, swelling it to a turgid pea. She shifts a little, and the seam of her black jeans rubs against her crotch, imparting a delicious thrill.

"So what do you want to do?" she asks casually, shifting again (*rub-rub*).

"Oh, I dunno." Gloria sighs. "We could call up Nick or Tyler, I guess."

"Nick? Tyler?"

"*Duh*. Those guys I told you about. From my brother's football team, remember?"

Candice can vaguely recall such names in some conversation or another. But the suggestion nonplusses her. "Why would we call *them*?"

"God, sometimes I wonder if you listen to me at all! Because they're *hot*, and my brother says they both want to ask me to the Thanksgiving Dance."

Candice quickly flips to the next page of the *Cosmopolitan*. "Oh, yeah. *That* Nick and Tyler."

"As if there are others." Gloria sighs again, and her breasts expand and deflate like a pair of perfect soufflés softly collapsing in on themselves.

This time Candice openly ogles; Gloria stares at the ceiling, oblivious.

"I mean, Nick is cute, but kind of dumb, you know?" Gloria says. "I hate his meaningless chatter. It's so juvenile."

"Yeah."

"So you think I should go out with Tyler instead?"

Candice's heartbeat skitters like a cockroach against her ribs, and a hollow panic floods her, cold as mist, insubstantial as the darkness in a sewer pipe. She shrugs, trying for indifference.

She has missed something somewhere: a cue, a covert invitation — she must have, for by now they should both be naked and stroking, giggling and inserting, *not* talking about odious human meat loaves. Candice wants to steer the conversation and mood towards that end but doesn't know how.

"You're really going to the dance then, eh?" she says, flipping another magazine page without even looking at it.

Gloria arches an eyebrow up to her hairline. "Of course I am. We *both* are. We made plans. Remember?"

The thing of it is, Candice doesn't. The panic in her swells, takes substance. She has difficulty breathing. "I just didn't realize you were serious about this dance thing."

"*Candice*. My brother is totally expecting you to go with him. If you don't show up, he's going to blab about us and then our reputations will be totally shot."

Candice's heart does a double flip. "Blab what?"

"Oh, come on. He *knows* what we do in here. Or suspects, anyway. That's why it's time we stopped practising and use what we've learned in the real world. Just like we planned, right?"

"I didn't realize we'd agreed to stop practising."

Gloria frowns and sits up. She pulls her legs into herself and hugs a pillow against her stomach. "Well, don't you think it's time? I mean, what more can we learn from each other? We don't want to do this forever."

Why not? Candice wants to say, and to her horror she realizes that somehow the words have slipped out without her permission.

Gloria really frowns now, and hugs the pillow tighter. "Because it would be just too *weird*. Girls don't *do* that kind of thing with each other, not unless they're lezzies. Which we are totally not."

With a suddenness that startles Candice, Gloria tosses her pillow aside and leans over the side of the bed. The full, meaty roundness of her buttocks stares Candice squarely in the face. "I've got condoms here. Some for you, some for me. Just in case you decide to go all the way with my brother, which would probably be a good thing. I mean, he doesn't expect it. I've made that clear, but for the sake of our reputations ... I know I'm going to do it with Nick. Or Tyler. Whoever I go out with."

Candice gapes at Gloria's buttocks, rubbery and taut as a dark-skinned olive beneath jeans cradling the red pimento of Gloria's sex in the middle. "What are you talking about?"

"Look, just take some condoms." Gloria divides a strip of gold-and-blue foil wrappers and holds half out to Candice. Candice doesn't take them. They fall onto the *Cosmopolitan*, onto the face of Cindy Crawford. "We both know what to do. I mean, come on, my brother isn't *that* bad-looking."

"He's a walking gym sock!"

"Candice —"

"I'm not going to the dance with your brother! Forget it. And what you're suggesting, I mean, to *sleep* with him just to shut him up ... What do you think I am? A prostitute?"

"Don't go spiral on me, okay? Everybody but us has done it with someone by now. I swear to God we're the only virgins left in high school." Gloria's tone changes, becomes wheedling. "Look, Candy, it's important that we both do this. People are starting to whisper behind my back. They know I'm still seeing you all the time. It doesn't matter that you've switched high schools. People *know*. We've *got* to do this."

"I'm a lesbian."

Gloria stares at her, eyes big and glossy as toffee apples. Candice is swamped with the sudden urge to kiss Gloria, to force her against the bed, to rip her sweater from her chest and hear her soft kitten cries as she nibble-licks the salt liquid that drips from between Gloria's thighs. She feels as if she's the star of a direct-to-DVD movie. She feels disembodied and almost drunk.

"I'm a lesbian," she repeats.

"No," Gloria whispers.

"We both are —"

"Shut up!" Gloria hurls her own strip of condoms into Candice's face. It clips Candice across one eye. The foil is sharper, stiffer, than Candice would have thought. "You're sick if you think that! Really sick!"

"It's true!"

Gloria kicks Candice fast and furious. The *Cosmopolitan* crinkles, pages tear. The condoms disappear under a bedsheet fold. Heels strike Candice's knees, gut, throat. She yelps, scrambles off the bed. Gloria braces herself against the backrest and continues to kick as if she's trying to churn milk into butter with her feet. She's red-faced and crying.

"I'm normal! I'm not a freak!" she shouts. "People like you should be shot! Lezzie! Pervert! Dyke! Get away from me! Get out of here! I never want to see you again!"

She hurls her pillow at Candice, lurches across the bed, and throws the *Cosmopolitan* at her. Candice bats the pillow away, dodges the magazine. Wants to say something, doesn't know what. The girl on Gloria's bed isn't someone she recognizes at all. This person's face is so red and contorted.

Gloria scoops up a *Beauty and the Beast* china figurine and raises it to throw. Candice whirls, scrabbles for the door handle, hands wet, eyes blurred, heart pounding so hard her fingers won't move properly. The figurine smashes against the doorframe, inches from Candice's head. Shards sting her ear and cheek. She yanks the door open.

"You better be at that dance!" Gloria screams after her. "You better be there or else!"

Candice flees. Out of the house, out into the driving, wintry rain.

Chapter Eighteen

On the fifth day of Morris's lunchtime rambles, a car pulls alongside him. He stops, expecting to impart instructions to a lost driver. The passenger window, bubbled with raindrops, slowly unwinds. The dark blur behind it is Clara, his receptionist.

The car door pops open.

"Get in," she says.

There is no room for argument in her voice.

Clara, Morris discovers, lives with her mother, who is introduced merely as that: "And this is Mother." A skinny woman with the leathery, wrinkled skin of a Florida vacationer, she greets them on the porch with a stick of Fraser Valley butter in one hand.

"What's this, what's this? Guests?" She shakes her head to and fro, and her entire throat wobbles.

Morris can't help but stare — the woman has no discernible chin. None whatsoever. The flesh beneath her lips just droops away in a loose mass of wattles, joining at some point above her concave chest.

"Don't just stand there. Come in, come in. Wipe your feet first. On this mat." She uses the stick of butter like a concert conductor's baton. "Good, good. Now wipe your feet on this other mat. Yes, yes, just like that." She shuts the door behind them, opens it again, shuts it, opens it, repositions first one welcome mat, then the other, then shuts the door a final time.

Had Morris not been overwhelmed by the smells fogging the house, he would have looked askance at this behaviour. As it is, he only half notices, busy instead with trying to sort out the incredible aromas. Pungent sage, frying onions. Spicy curry, sharp Parmesan. Porcini mushrooms, marjoram. Garlic, nutmeg, hot olive oil, buttermilk, soy sauce, bay leaves, feta cheese. His stomach erupts with a very audible, wet growl.

Clara drops her handbag onto a table stand and walks down the short hall, taking no notice of either Morris's stomach or her mother. "Straight through here, Dr. Morton. If you want to use the bathroom first, it's the door to your right."

He doesn't. Instead he follows her into a kitchen of such vast proportions he realizes it is the entire first floor of the house, save for the front hall. Morris counts the stoves: seven of them. Fridges, three; freezers (of an immense walk-in size), two. Four dishwashers, all churning. Two industrial-size stainless-steel sinks. Rack upon rack of pots dangling from the ceiling. And in one corner, beneath a window beaded with yellow oil and steam, a small table and four chairs.

"It's always hot in here," Clara says, raising her voice above the sizzling, crackling, bubbling sounds issuing from a dozen different stove elements. "Feel free to take off your jacket."

He does so, and at her behest, follows her to the table. Chinese salted black beans, red onions, and eggplant simmer on the stove closest to them.

"Mother has obsessive compulsive disorder, alleviated only while she's cooking, if you can call indulgence in the disease as alleviation. So she cooks a great deal."

Morris blinks at the assortment of mixing bowls and food processors lined up along the counters. "But who eats —"

"She supplies seven delicatessens with the food. It helps pay the bills."

He guesses it would.

They sit in silence while Mother serves them. For starters she ladles sweet corn chowder into two pale blue bowls, accompanied by matching ramekins of perfectly puffed golden-brown goat's cheese soufflé. While they wait for their main course — pistachio pilaf in a spinach crown — she serves them tomatoes fried in a polenta crust along with borlotti bean pâté on triangles of toasted rye.

Awed, Morris watches Mother move about the huge kitchen. Nothing burns or bubbles over, yet there isn't a single timer to alert her when something is done. While greasing a shallow pan to make mushroom *gougère*, she boils potatoes until just tender for a dish Clara describes as Irish colcannon. As she sifts flour and salt into a bowl, she caramelizes onions in butter. After frying leeks, she roasts red peppers under a grill and lays salted eggplant in a colander to drain. Everything is done with efficient precision.

By the time he eats the last piece of pear-and-hazelnut flan from his dessert plate, Morris feels like the tea bag floating in his cup: hot, aromatic, and softly swollen. So long has he been immersed in the pleasurable wonder of observing Mother at work that he jumps a little when Clara breaks the companionable silence between them.

"You understand now why you had to come here?"

He stares at her blankly.

She shakes her head, wearing the same patient yet slightly exasperated expression Karen displays when explaining the concept of why homework is more important than Bart Simpson to Candice. Leaning forward slightly, Clara places one squarish hand on his and gently taps his knuckles with an opal-ringed finger.

"My mother isn't a freak. She's a specialist. A special kind of specialist. Here, in this kitchen, she's turned her obsession into art. Do you understand what I'm saying, Dr. Morton?"

He's forgotten why they came, why she brought him here. Now he remembers. And in the remembering, in the steam and oil and sizzle of her mother's incredible kitchen, he feels ... healed. He didn't cause Andy to be attacked through neglect and the tunnel vision of caring only for feet. Yes, he shouldn't have done that feet massaging bit at Andy's birthday party, and yes, that certainly led to Andy's expulsion from his last school; Morris won't make *that* mistake again. Keep feet with feet — at the office. Feet don't support life; life supports feet. Remember that.

And Candice. Well, she's growing up. Changing. And he has to make more of an effort to devote time to his family, time away from feet.

So it's all right to love feet and improve feet and heal feet. It's all right to be exactly who he is as long as he remembers: keep feet in the office. Home is for the family.

But where does that leave the Footstop?

He frowns, sits straighter.

Surely, that doesn't count, does it? *Does it?* The Footstop *is* his love for feet on public display, most definitely outside his office. Yet Karen's dedication to the teahouse must make it right.

But doubt grows in his mind. Karen demonstrates the same enthusiasm for the Footstop as she does for any of Andy's school projects. Might she regard the teahouse as merely another assignment? He would have to ask her.

Clara taps him on the back of his hand with a finger, returning him to the present.

"We are all ordinary people," she says, smiling. "Ordinary people living ordinary lives. We do our best. And some of us manage to live our ordinary lives in an extraordinary way." She sits back and nods. "And the world is a richer place because of it."

Chapter Nineteen

Ah, Thanksgiving! That wonderful time of year when North Americans count their blessings by overindulging in every combination of saturated fat known to mankind.

Boiled and strained pumpkin is purchased in tins, mixed with cream, and baked in lard-based crusts. Wholesome potatoes are overboiled, pounded to a pulp, and adulterated by dollops of thick yellow butter. The healthy yam is likewise defiled, then baked beneath a topping of marshmallows. Cranberries are contaminated with sugar, Brussels sprouts smeared with salt and butter, and corn mashed and violated by all three. Carnage of a certain species of fowl sweeps across the country, the cadavers of which are stuffed with stale bread and roasted either too slowly or too swiftly, while liquid fat is collected from the cooking corpses and mixed with salt, flour, and water.

Indigestion, heartburn, diarrhea, flatulence, cirrhosis of the liver, gastroenteritis, kidney failure, high blood pressure, and pancreatitis — these are the rewards for the Thanksgiving faithful.

Such an occasion must, of course, be shared with loved ones, all dressed in stiff new cotton or wrinkle-free rayon, and shoes shined with potent chemicals. Anyone not partaking in this gustatory rite with their family is considered unemotional and ill-bred.

Even vegetarians aren't exempt from this ritual.

Karen hates Thanksgiving. Loves it and hates it. She loves the ideal of it: family and friends gathering to celebrate the bounty of nature. She hates everything else: the grocery shopping, the menu planning, the peeling and cooking and presentation of foodstuffs; the washing of cutlery and platters and Pyrex casserole dishes; the vacuuming and dusting required before admitting guests; the requisite necklace and Suzy Sheer dress and pleated protective apron bearing the stains of Thanksgivings past like a reissued bandage during a wartime shortage.

This year is worse than ever.

Mei-ling works in the kitchen alongside Karen, stirring and exclaiming and using the salt shaker with a vigour that makes Karen cringe. Sarah Kay — an old friend of Karen's who performs this pilgrimage from Alberta annually — is, as always, folding napkins into swans, knocking back red wine, and divulging the juicier details of a female stockbroker's life. Mrs. Morton — the *real* Mrs. Morton, Morris's mother in the wrinkled flesh itself — holds court in the living room, nodding, smiling, and drooling, her derrière a damp sponge of urine. Mr. Osaban talks cars at Morris (Karen felt obligated to invite him this year, since his wife is undergoing a hysterectomy and his car is undergoing repairs), and the reverend bustles from kitchen to living room, filling glasses with Sprite and orange juice, a concoction he believes is an integral part of the occasion. Clara, Morris's receptionist (*why the hell did Morris invite* her *here?*), sits quietly in one corner, twisting her pearls and sipping punch. Her presence is unprecedented, which causes Karen to tremble with the anxiety that perhaps her phobia might be right, that maybe Morris and Clara are having an affair. Oh,

God, surely not! Adulterous husbands don't invite their lovers to dinner with their wives, do they?

From Andy's bedroom comes a deep and suspicious silence, punctuated occasionally by even more suspect giggles (that older boy, Kyle, is over again; Karen really should nip in there and see what they're up to), and Candice is skulking around like Zeus with a toothache, openly helping herself to Sarah Kay's wine. Dilly the cat, meanwhile, has taken refuge under Karen's bed.

Clanging pots and steam and laughter surround her, somehow condensed by the greasy smoke of roasting turkey hanging over the kitchen like the pall of a funeral pyre (her father insisted on turkey). Ice clinks in glasses, voices vie with one another for attention, elbows knock elbows, hugs and jokes intermingle with instructions on where to find napkins, serving bowls, and cake servers. And yet loneliness engulfs Karen — loneliness and a sorrow that make her heart race as she tips Brussels sprouts into a pot of boiling water.

Before she has even formulated the thought, she unobtrusively palms her keys into her apron pocket, slips out of the melee, and limps down the hall (she is now officially cast-free). She pauses at Andy's door, about to intrude, then remembers his "you always make things worse, Mom!" and sighs, turning away and feeling abandoned by something she can't define. Karen continues on, pulls back the front-door latch, and ducks outside into the pelting rain.

The cold takes her breath away. A gust of wind shakes raindrops from the surrounding hemlocks and spatters her Suzy Sheer dress. She feels naked. Shivering, she crosses her arms in front of her. Her breath departs in a cloud. Still hugging herself, she ducks against the windblown raindrops and runs to the Footstop.

Inside ... stillness.

Oh! Soothing quiet and roomy gloom. How familiar, yet how comfortless! Karen wanders about the teahouse, running a finger over the foot sculptures displayed on their pedestals, over the neat row of Foot Butter jars, over the antique trestle table.

Not mine, she thinks. *None of it contains an ounce of the real me.*

She steps behind the trestle table and gropes under its coarse top for the dog-eared Post-it Note concealed there. A moment later she dials Egret's number.

"C'mon, Dad! I'll be back before midnight."

"Midnight!" Egret's dad barks. He thumps his fist on the mahogany table, and all the silverware jumps. "Midnight!"

"Neils," Egret's mother says warningly.

In the kitchen the phone chimes.

"The boy has a major competition in two weeks. Two weeks! And here he sits tellin' me he's goin' out drinkin' all hours of the night!"

"It's a *dance*, Dad, a high-school dance. Not a rave. The only thing we'll be drinking is Pepsi."

"Let him go, Neils."

Two times, three times, four times ... Whoever is on the other end of the phone isn't giving up easily.

"It's Thanksgiving, for Christ's sake!" the old man growls. "Whatever happened to tradition, to family values?"

"Neils ..."

"Fine, fine! Let him go. Shake your little booties to that disco crap. See if I care. But don't come cryin' to me when you don't cut the mustard in Cologne, boy."

Egret swallows a hundred appropriate remarks and shoves back from the table.

His dad's hand shoots out and grabs his wrist. "Wait a minute. You think you can go out like that? Here." He rummages in his back pocket, pulls out an eel-skin wallet, and flips out a twenty-dollar bill. "A young man without money is naked. Have yourself a good time. But eleven o'clock, no later, you hear? Ten-thirty. Make that ten-thirty."

"Eleven is fine," his mother says. "Now will someone please answer that phone?"

Stuffing the twenty into his back pocket and ignoring his father's dire mutterings about cocaine and marijuana and to stay the hell away from them, Egret saunters into the kitchen. He knows it's all just a show, this tough father-coach act, but it still pisses him off. Sometimes his old man takes himself too seriously. And disco! What fucking year does he think this is?

Just as Egret reaches the phone, it stops ringing. He waits for a couple of seconds, just to be sure the digital instrument isn't going to emit another dignified warble, and stares vacantly at the illuminated call-display screen. Something about the name and number catches his attention: Morton. Karen.

Egret feels two things in equal measure: relief and guilt. The first because he missed the call; the second because he felt the first.

He frowns. Like most adolescents, he isn't given to copious amounts of introspection. But he takes a scant microsecond to examine his initial reaction to Karen's call: relief.

'Cause, well, she's old. *No way around that one. And married* — there's certainly that to it. And she doesn't want sex with him anymore.

Hey, whoa, where did that come from, buddy?

From the surprised look in her eyes and her lack of participation the last time they did the naked pretzel together, that's where. Couldn't miss that.

Alarm stabs Egret. He isn't ready for her to lose interest in him — shit, it should happen the other way round. *He should lose interest in her first, this woman old enough to be his mom.* He can't go to Cologne and compete with the humiliation of being dumped by a woman double his age hanging over his head.

Egret nods to himself. He'll fix things. Go see her now before the dance. Stroll through the canyon forest with her, remind her of the reason she fell into his bed in the first place. Hell, it will be a turn-on doing it in the bush. *Sex, sex, sex.* He'll lay it on thick and quash the doubt in her mind and the guilt burbling in his own gut.

Shit, it's only until he's back from Cologne with a medal in his hand, he reasons. Then he'll let her dump him.

Still, he feels kind of slimy about it. *'Cause really, regardless of Karen's age, she's okay.*

Karen slowly replaces the telephone receiver in its cradle. Ten times she let it ring before hanging up, and with each ring she stiffened. Now, as she puts the receiver down, the relief she experiences is immense. She has to accept it: she didn't want Egret to answer. She reached for him — an escape, a fantasy — as a buffer against the reality of her life.

What she really needs to do instead is …

Surrounded by cardboard boxes, all limp from exposure to the rain during transport to his basement suite, Moey stares at his karate uniform. It lies like a supplicant across his lap. He can't quite bring himself to pack it; he is fairly certain he never wants to wear the damn thing again.

The telephone rings.

Moey grimaces. It will be his mother, replete with all the sounds of a Thorpe Thanksgiving in the background — squealing nieces, bellowing nephews, Nintendo beeps, and football commentators. He can almost hear the pop of beer can tabs and the rustle of pretzels coming from the wood-panelled living room.

The telephone rings on.

What a noise. What a singularly annoying, penetrating noise. Who exactly invented that noise and why was it adopted as a telecommunication standard? Why not a drum roll, for God's sake, or even a trumpet blurt? Why this harsh mechanical *unreal* sound? If he knew about it, he would have approved of the Van Gorders' expensive and dignified chiming telephone.

Unconsciously, Moey slips one of the copper bangles from his dance costume onto his wrist and lumbers to his feet. He takes his time rooting through the clothes strewn on the floor and is disappointed when the phone continues to ring. Finally, Moey picks it up. "Hi, Mom."

Wavering, jagged breaths on the other end.

"Mom?"

"No, it's me, Karen, from the Footstop." Then, before he can acknowledge her greeting, she asks, "Look, would you like to come over for dinner? I remember you saying you don't have family here, and I was thinking maybe you'd like to come over and meet the rest of my family. And my friends and neighbours. I've got a few of those here, too ..." A big gulp of air. "You could bring your belly-dancing costume. Perform for us."

Moey sits on the floor. "Perform?"

More of those wavering breaths. "Please," she whispers.

And then he realizes she's crying. Confusion and concern compound his dizziness. "What's up, Karen? What's wrong?"

"Nothing, everything, I don't know. I need ... can you ... I just can't ..."

"Take it easy, take it easy."

"I need to see you dancing, okay? Can you come? Please?"

"Give me ten minutes and I'll be there."

You better be at that dance or else! The words Gloria spoke that last, disastrous time Candice was with her echo inside Candice's head.

"Or else what?" Candice mutters to herself, nibbling on a celery stick while perched on a stool in the corner of the kitchen. Beside Candice, Sarah Kay waxes eloquently about something called a reverse mortgage and doesn't seem at all concerned that no one can hear her above the burbling pots, Grampy Woodruff's guffaws from the living room, and Nanny's psycho Chinese music.

Candice takes another swig from her mug of purloined wine and snarls at an imaginary Gloria, "I'm not afraid of your stupid threat. What d'you think you can do to me, huh?"

A lot. Therein lies the problem.

Gloria's odious brother knows some of the jocks at Candice's new school, is, like, good friends with them. And, of course, those jocks know all the popular girls in Candice's grade. Like, *intimately*. And those popular girls cleave together despite their hissing spats and petty jealousies, creating a fanged and clawed creature that rips apart anyone not conforming to the norm. Candice has seen them in action, daily witnessed the barrage of cruelties they enact on some of the more unpopular girls: Kick Me signs taped to their backs, tennis balls fired at their heads during gym class, dirty tampons tied to their lockers, sniggers and snide remarks propelling them down the school corridors and into the solace of bathroom cubicles, only to have digital photos of them snapped while crouched butt-naked over toilets.

Candice already doesn't conform to the norm, but she is borderline acceptable. Her act of haughty disdain around teachers, her black clothes, her sunglasses, and her newness all buy her a measure of acceptability. But that can, with a few words, be drastically changed. Words like dyke, lesbo, lez.

Gloria knows this.

"You're selling yourself out to them," Candice hisses to the illusory Gloria, helping herself to more of Sarah Kay's wine. "I thought you had more principles than that. I thought you were *smarter* than that."

But maybe smart is just doing whatever the hell it takes to survive high school. Maybe being smart means gritting your teeth and allowing a six-foot jockstrap to fumble down your panties and slobber under your bra until you escape to college.

Totally unfair. And totally, *totally* screwy that being a whore could save her reputation. But that was the truth: fucking a few popular guys — not too many, just a select few — would stave off those deadly words: perv, bull dyke, homo.

"Are you cold, honey?"

Candice looks up, startled. Sarah Kay is standing right next to her, squeaking a cork from yet another bottle of red wine.

"You're shivering like a Texan in Alaska. Are you sure

you eat enough? You've lost weight since I last saw —"

"You say that every year."

Sarah Kay laughs as if Candice has just cracked the world's best joke.

"Guess I'm jealous, honey. I mean, look at you!" She runs a perfectly manicured hand through Candice's hair, and her fingers tip-tap down Candice's back and tickle-pinch her waist. "You're drop-dead gorgeous! Long red hair and a figure to die for! Ever thought of being a model?"

Candice gapes at her — at the smart red skirt and black jacket of her, at the crisp white blouse and smooth neck of her, at the sharp, short haircut of her — and her fingers go limp and wet heat rushes to her groin.

"You're going to be *quite* the good-looking gal, m'dear." Sarah Kay taps a manicured finger on her nose. Lightly. Teasingly.

And before Candice knows what she is doing (it's the wine; she's drunk), she has that finger in her mouth. She sucks it s-l-o-w-l-y, watching Sarah Kay's eyes widen. Sarah Kay's lips form a little *o*, and her free hand drops the bottle of wine.

Candice releases the finger (*oh, delicious finger!*) as the bottle smashes on the floor. Sarah Kay stumbles back, her heels crushing glass.

Someone shouts from the living room, "Need a hand in there?" and Mei-ling whirls from the oven with an invocation against bad luck.

Jesus fucking Christ, Candice thinks. *What the hell?* She stands up, fiery-faced and thin-breathed.

"Grandma, I have to go," she gasps as Nanny Woodruff squats before her to clean up the glass. "I just remembered tonight's the school dance."

"Tea towel over there, Sarah," Mei-ling says. "And a broom and dustpan in the closet by the stove. Where's Karen gotten to?"

Candice backs away from them, eyes resolutely avoiding Sarah Kay. She'll go to the school dance, yes. This whole lesbian thing is a mistake. She likes boys, likes Gloria's rancid brother, really wants to have sex with him ...

Mei-ling suddenly snaps upright from the floor, a stained tea towel in one hand and a dustpan filled with glass and wine in the other. "You aren't leaving here until after dinner, young lady, and that's that. You're going to put something in that stomach of yours to sop up the wine. Now go to your room and lie down for a bit. You look positively ghastly."

"Mei-ling," Sarah Kay says softly, touching Nanny's wrist.

Candice flees.

Moey has driven to Karen's house at the speed of a hockey slap shot. He has driven at the speed of an egg-bound turtle. Karen can't decide which is the truth. Each second creeps by like concrete setting, yet the dread that fills her as she realizes what she has done also makes each minute race.

It doesn't matter now, though. He's here. How did he know to avoid the house where lights blaze and music plays? How did he know instead to slip into this dark and silent spot? As he ducks through the door into the Footstop, self-disgust fills her.

Here I am looking again for a solution from someone else.

She wipes her mascara-smeared cheeks. "I'm sorry. I don't know what came over me. Look, the truth of it is, I called you here because, well, you must have guessed by now that my husband doesn't know you're performing here and I think that it's time you, well, stopped. I'm sorry. I shouldn't have told you I wanted you to perform tonight, though I did mean it when I said it."

Silence.

"You're welcome to stay for dinner if you still want to," she adds lamely.

Moey appears instantly stricken, like a mature, muscular version of Andy standing there, fingering the straps of his bag with the exact uncertainty he displayed the first time he arrived with costume in hand. The first time she committed adultery with Egret.

Karen wilts into a chair and buries her face in her hands. "Oh, God, Moey, what's wrong with me?"

He doesn't come over to her immediately, and when he does, he sits a few chairs away. Through her fingers she watches as he carefully cradles his duffle bag in his lap, patting it the way an old man might stroke an old dog. She struggles to gain control of herself.

"I'm not drunk, if that's what you're thinking," Karen says, straightening. This was the truth. At least she hasn't consumed a single alcoholic beverage since that last remarkable, lamentable occasion. But as soon as the words have left her mouth, she realizes she *does* feel drunk — drunk on desperation. She lets out a string of profanity, and Moey stiffens.

"Oh, for Christ's sake, don't look at me like that!" she snaps. *Lord, I sound like Mei-ling,* she thinks. "I'm not mad at you. I'm mad at myself. Because I envy you. Hell, I envy everybody! I'm pathetic. Pathetic, pathetic, pathetic. I don't have the gumption of a boiled banana. I just go through life doing what's expected of me, doing whatever it takes to be the perfect mother/wife/parent-committee member, and the entire time I'm completely denying the little voice inside my head that's shrieking, 'Get out! Get out while you still have the chance!'"

Raindrops patter softly against the windows.

"Get out of what?" Moey asks warily.

"Me! Get out of me! Don't you ever wake up in the morning and say, 'Oh, shit, not Moey still! I can't believe I'm still Moey'? I get up every single morning thinking, Karen — *yuck*!"

She sucks in a deep, wild breath. "And don't tell me I have no reason to feel that way. I *know* I have no reason to feel that way. I have a house over my head and food in my cupboards and healthy kids and a husband, and I live in one of the most affluent cities in the world. I *know* I should be busting a gut with happiness, but I'm not! So what does that make me? Pathetic!"

More soft raindrops splatter against the window.

"I don't know what to say," Moey murmurs, repositioning his duffle bag so it looks more like a shield than a dying dog. "I've never thought of you as pathetic."

"What *do* you think of me then?"

He shrugs. "Creative. Industrious. I don't know. Look, did you mean it when you said you don't want me to dance here anymore?"

Karen plucks lint off the armrests of her chair. "I have absolutely no idea what I want." She glares at him. "It's the fault of that damn hart we saw. Until then everything in my life was going just fine. Maybe I wasn't thrilled about certain things, but I was in control. Now everything is *different*."

"You're talking about the white stag we saw? By the creek?"

"Stag, hart, whatever. Yes. I mean, haven't you felt things have been a little bit weird in your life since then?"

Moey nods. "But in an all-right kind of way. Magical even."

Karen snorts. "Magical! Since then you've lost your job and received an eviction notice from your landlord! Tell me what's magical about that?"

No raindrops now, just wind against the windows, soft and crack-seeking.

"Nothing," she says, leaning forward in her chair, feeling as if she's pinning a live butterfly to a corkboard and finding a malicious glee in it. "I mean, I *know* what you want me to say. You want me to say, 'Moey, that hart made me think about my dreams. Moey, that hart made me realize I've been robbing my husband and kids of myself.' But I'm not going to say that, okay? Because you don't know, *you don't know*, what my dream is."

She sucks in another deep breath and plunges on. "Your dream is a little odd, granted. But men do ballet, men dance ballroom stuff, so it's not that outlandish for a man to enjoy belly dancing. But you don't know how weird *my* dream is. You don't know how it would destroy my family, how it would humiliate them and expose them to all sorts of teasing and humiliation. I'm *not* going to fulfill it."

"So shut up and die miserable."

She gapes at him. "I beg your pardon?"

"Commit suicide."

"What?"

"What's your dream, Karen? Is it really as bad as this slow suicide you've set yourself up for?"

"You're angry."

"No. A little. Yeah. Yeah, I'm angry. Damn right I'm angry. You've invited me to dinner so you can fire me, even though I work only for tips, and all you can do is whine about yourself."

She flushes. "Sorry. I ... sorry."

She sits back in her chair, deflated and humiliated. Hemlock trees sway and groan outside her house, and muted Chinese opera wails from her living room. *Splitter-splitter pat-pat* — a small gust of wind blows a volley of raindrops from the boughs of the hemlocks onto the Footstop roof.

Raucous laughter bursts from the living room, followed by silence. Even Mei-ling's tape falls silent; it has either reached the end or someone has finally turned it off. Behind Karen's house, deep in the canyon, Lynn Creek thunders over cliffs, churning cold green water into white froth. For a moment the dull rumble is audible. Then a bus drives down Peters Road, a dog barks, and the music and laughter start again in the living room, blocking out the sound of the creek.

Karen licks her lips. "I owe you an apology," she whispers without looking up. She hears Moey shift, though he doesn't respond. He isn't going to let her do this easily. "Do you know the Christian bookstore at the foot of Lonsdale?" she asks timidly.

"Yes."

"Have you ever been in there?"

"Once. To get out of the rain."

"So you know what it's like." Her heart begins to pound harder. "Warm. Bright. Good music in the background. Fridge magnets and books and candles on the shelves. All with a religious motif."

"Like here with feet."

"Yes." She coughs to clear her throat. "Like here with feet. See, the thing of it is, I want to open my own shop. Like that. Like this. Only more like that than this."

"A Christian bookstore."

"Not a bookstore, no. And not Christian. Spiritual." She is getting breathless and dizzy. And her birthmarks are tingling like old scabs that need scratching. "A non-denominational store embracing Old World mythology and New Age fantasy. Elves and angels and Artemis."

"Selling *what*, though?"

"Sex toys. I want — I have *always* wanted — to open my own Spiritual Sex Store."

Spiritual Sex Store. Moey can't picture it. A vision of Miranda's steel dildo with wings and a halo pops into his mind.

Moey lets Karen talk. He doesn't have much choice — he would have had more success convincing Master Zahbar to put on a crop top and sequined skirt than to get Karen to stop talking. And as she talks he begins to see where she is coming from.

"Books and paintings and music and incense. Sexual aids, statues, water fountains, and glass ornaments. I want everything to be a work of art. Handmade. Celebrating the sacredness of sex. I don't want the aggressive, raw gadgets churned out of Japanese and American factories. I don't want to treat sex like other sex stores do, like a drug or a party commodity. I mean, there are hundreds — no, *thousands* — of people out there who have serious questions about sex, but where can they go? To a psychiatrist who'll tell them they have a father fixation? To a love shop that'll sell them a battery-operated novelty? No, Moey, no. They want to experience the magic, the *transcendence* of sex. I know. I used to feel that magic with Morris long, long ago."

Magic. Okay, the picture is getting clearer now.

"Orgasm is like, like a religious ecstasy. When you touch

the skin of your lover, you change. You go into another state of consciousness that deepens your awareness and sharpens your emotions. Unicorns and Jedi knights and the Hogwarts School of Wizardry — they all exist, Moey. In sex. And I want to give people the ability to see that." She leans forward in the chair, eyes shining, cheeks flushed, lips parted, hands balled into defensive fists on the armrests. "So what do you think?"

He coughs. Swallows. Croaks out the only thing that comes to mind. "I can see why your shop would be a success."

"Yes, but my *family*, Moey, my family. What about them?"

As a rule of thumb, Moey has discovered that in such situations the best response is to rephrase the question back to the woman and let her answer it herself. "Good question. What about your family, Karen?"

"I can't just abandon the Footstop, can I? It's my husband's life."

"Then why isn't he looking after it? You aren't him. You've got a life of your own."

She grimaces. "But imagine being the child of a parent who owns a sex store. Think of what it'll do to Andy and Candice."

Is she serious? He glances at the foot fetishes surrounding them. "If your kids have survived what you're doing here," he says slowly, deliberately, "they'll survive a sex store."

She stiffens, then glances at her hands. "I can't do it. I owe my family more than that. And ... and I owe you an apology. For not being honest with you about our arrangement here."

Oh, yes, *that*. He experiences the same rush of emotions he had when he first arrived and she told him he couldn't dance at the Footstop anymore: despair, fear, and anger. Now another emotion enters the equation. Determination. "I accept your apology," he says coolly. "But if your invitation to dinner is still open, I'll take you up on it. I'm starved."

Chapter Twenty

Before saying grace the reverend surveys the people gathered around the dining-room table with immense satisfaction. To his immediate left sits Lingy, resplendent in a purple satin Chinese sheath. Karen is beside her, flushed and distracted, wiping an errant drop of gravy off the tablecloth. Andy and his boisterous friend Kyle jostle each other at the end of the table, giggling and making *sotto voce* quips about the gynecological position of the roasted turkey's legs.

On the other side of the table, directly across from Karen, Sarah Kay is deep in a one-way conversation with Clara, who keeps turning away to shoot flushed looks at the new arrival — Moey something-or-other. Candice is between Clara and Moey, right across from the reverend — a furious, consumptive Madonna with red hair. Beside her Moey is engaged in earnest dialogue with Morris as he has been ever since appearing. Morris sits at the head of the table, listening attentively. To the reverend's right is Mr. Osaban, busy sketching the engine of his 1949 James Young Bentley onto a paper napkin. Morris's mother has fallen asleep on the couch. By tacit consent no one has woken her up.

My family, my friends, the reverend thinks expansively. *The bounty of this feast lies not on the table but around it. Truly, we are all blessed.*

He clears his throat, waits for silence, and gives thanks to the Lord for what they are about to receive.

"Pass the peas, please."

"Try some of this Gruyère-and-walnut pie. Karen makes it every year. It's really quite good."

"Stop it, both of you, before you knock something over!"

"Stripped down the carburetor and you know what I found?"

"This is totally disgusting. Isn't there a single vegetable on this table without half a pound of butter on it?"

"Zero percent down and a no-interest loan."

"It's one of the best hotels in Java, and they always keep a room reserved for Njai Loro Kidul, the goddess of the South Seas."

"Can you see the cranberry sauce? Is that it over there?"

"Involves complicated footwork and a good sense of timing."

"White meat or dark, Clara?"

"I'm sure your mother doesn't let you do that at home, Kyle. Andy, don't you copy him!"

"A seat on the New York Stock Exchange went for $515,000."

"Knows I'm a belly dancer but has no idea I'm making this proposition."

"Let the boys alone, pudding. They aren't hurting anyone."

"I think I heard the back-door bell ring."

"I'll get it!" both Karen and Candice cry in unison, scrambling to their feet.

Everyone at the table falls silent.

"No, that's the front door," Sarah Kay says as a

definitive *bing-bong* comes down the hall from the front of the house.

But then a *rat-a-tat tat* is heard immediately from the back door.

"Sounds like there's someone at the front *and* the back," Clara says.

"What?" Karen asks, a confounded look on her face.

"What?" Candice echoes, equally flabbergasted.

"Why don't you get the back door?" the reverend suggests, pointing at Karen with his fork. "And Candice can get the front. Simple solution."

After a pause, everyone resumes the busy work of piling carrots and stuffing and tofu sausages onto their plates.

"Has a fourteen-gauge chassis and a steel inner body cage."

"Church in the Czech Republic has a chandelier made of human bones ..."

Karen knows it is Egret even before she answers. How she knows such a thing she isn't able to say, but she can feel his presence against her skin as tangible as the heat from the kitchen stove. So she is more than a little taken aback at the sight of the teenage girl on her back-door step, muffled in an outlandish pink faux fur coat.

"Gloria said to come round to the back door. Said you guys are weird about using the front. So, like, is Candice ready?"

"I'm sorry?"

The girl jerks a thumb behind her and cracks her gum. "We're all waiting in the car. Double-dating. For the dance."

"Oh! The Thanksgiving Dance! She said something about that earlier."

"So is she ready or what?"

"No. We're in the middle of dinner."

"Oh. Yeah, well, I guess we should've called first. Sorry 'bout that."

Karen softens slightly. "Come inside. I'll get her for you."

"I'll wait out here. The smell of turkey makes me puke. Just tell her it's Sabine Mason."

Karen closes the door on her and goes to find Candice.

Candice stares at the flakes of shellac peeling off the front door. She is certain Gloria is standing on the other side — Gloria and her odious brother and his rancid friends, all here to make Candice bend to their collective will. Bend or break.

Shit. Now what?

Bing-bong!

"All right already!" Candice says, pulling back the deadbolt and opening the door, heart jack-hammering against her ribs.

A guy from her new school — she can't remember his name except that it's something dorky like Albert — stands on the doorstep. His eyes widen at the sight of her.

"What are *you* doing here?" Candice demands. "You don't hang out with Gloria's brother, do you?"

"Gloria who?"

"Vermicelli."

"I don't know her."

"Then what are you doing here?"

For a moment he looks as if he doesn't know the answer to that himself. "I, uh, was just on my way to the dance. And ..." He falls silent, then slowly reddens.

"And?" she prompts.

"Look, this is a shot in the dark, but do you want to come to the dance with me?"

Is this guy for real? She doesn't even *know* him except in passing in the hallways.

"Candice?" her mother calls from the kitchen.

"Shit, is that your mom?" He shoots a panicked look beyond Candice.

"Yeah. So what?"

He steps to one side, out of view and away from the light spilling from the hall. "I don't think she should see me here."

"Why not? I *am* allowed to date, you know."

"Candice, your ride to the dance is here. A Sabine Mason," her mom shouts from the end of the hall. "Who's at the front door?"

Sabine Mason — the most popular girl at school. Most popular *and* most cruel. Gloria and her brother will be with her.

Then, as breathtaking and brilliant as a bolt of lightning, Candice sees a solution to *everything*. It is so awesome that her knees weaken with relief. She clutches the doorframe for support.

"Sure, I'll come to the dance with you," she tells the guy on the front doorstep somewhat breathlessly. "Stay here while I get my coat." And she shuts the door on him.

"Who's at the front door?" Karen asks, limping down the hall.

"My date. Can I go now? I'm not hungry."

"But you haven't eaten anything! And why is your date at the front door if this Sabine girl is at the back?"

"It's a *joke*, Mom. You wouldn't understand." Candice fumbles in the hall closet for her jacket and thrusts her feet into her Doc Martens. "Look, can you stall Sabine for a couple of seconds? Just till I get onto the driveway?"

"What for?"

"I told you. It's a joke. You wouldn't understand. *Please?*"

"Candice ..." Karen doesn't know what to say. She is still muddled after having the faulty premonition about Egret standing at her back door.

Candice quickly leans towards her and pecks her on the cheek. "Thanks a million, Mom. You're the best." And then she is gone.

Candice isn't sure where her idea came from — maybe from some TV sitcom — but it's a totally spectacular solution. Her mind ticks overtime, working out the details, the wine she consumed acting as a lubricant for her thoughts.

She links an arm through Albert's and marches him quickly down the dark, overgrown path to the gravel driveway. At the end of the drive, crammed into an idling car pointed right at them, she can see Gloria, her brother, and two of his oafish friends.

Candice pulls Albert into the glare of the headlights. "Kiss me."

"What?"

She plants her lips on his.

They are warm, they are wet, they are firmer than Gloria's. And not very participatory.

She pulls away a fraction and hisses, "Put your arms around me and kiss me properly, goddamn it!"

After a pause, he complies.

Boy, does he comply.

Candice pulls away slowly, somewhat stunned. *God, that kiss was good.* It is somewhat disappointing then to surface to the face of Albert and not Sarah Kay. Candice struggles to regain her composure.

"Look, can you wait here a second for me?" she gasps. "I've got to talk to those people in the car."

He nods, equally breathless. "Sure, whatever. They pulled in the drive just after I got here. Friends of your Mom?"

"No. Just wait here." She approaches the car.

Candice doesn't give Gloria an opportunity to say anything, not even the chance to open her mouth. She just yanks a door of the car open, leans in, and starts blubbering maniacally. The tears come surprisingly easily, or maybe it isn't so surprising, everything considered.

"I'm so sorry, Gloria. I didn't want you to find out like this. I wanted to tell you, but I was so afraid of what you'd say. Please don't be angry at me, please!"

She turns to Gloria's odious brother, who sits gaping in the driver's seat, his red bull neck nicked with shaving cuts. "I'm so sorry ..." Shit, she can't remember his name, only ever thinks of him as Gloria's rancid brother. She uses a spout of blubbering to cover up. "I shouldn't have led you on like I did. I should've told you I was already going steady with someone else!"

"You're going steady with *Van Gorder*?" Rancid says in disbelief.

Fear flickers in Candice. "You know him?"

"I know *about* him. Shit, he's only the best fuckin' athlete on the Lower Mainland. The guy's going to the Olympics!"

"Shit, Van Gorder!" both of his oafish friends echo from the back seat.

Jocks, Candice thinks in disgust.

Gloria finally finds her voice. "But why didn't you *tell* me?"

Candice stares at her, tries to remember the answer to that. "Because I'm pregnant!" she wails, but not loud enough for Albert to hear at the top of the drive, then turns on the eye tap again.

"Shit!"

"No way!"

"Pregnant!" Gloria cries. "*You?*"

Candice feels supreme, watching the disbelief flood Gloria's face. "I wanted to tell you, but I was scared to, so I said all those wild things the other day instead! Please don't tell anyone. Don't tell people at school ..."

"But, *Candy*, I'm your best friend. You can tell me anything. You know that! I wouldn't ever blab bad things about you!"

This is such a whopper that for a moment Candice completely forgets to blubber. Then she regains her ground by snuffling, "I'm sorry ... I was scared to."

"Scared of *what*?" Gloria presses.

Damn it, won't the girl just give up? "Of ... of ... because ... you know ..."

"What?"

A blank. A total and complete blank.

"Were you afraid I'd convince you to get an abortion?"

"Yes!" Candice cries in relief. "Yes, that's it! Yes!"

"I'd *never* do that!"

"I'm so sorry!" More blubbering, during which Candice tosses a harried look over her shoulder at Albert. Sabine is picking her way down the path from the back of the house.

"So what are you going to *do*?" Gloria asks.

"Go to the dance with Albert, but at my new school."

"*Albert?*" Rancid says. "Is that Van Gorder's name? I thought it was Egret."

"I *said* Egret," Candice insists fiercely, then instantly regrets it. What if Rancid is wrong? What if her date's name *is* Albert?

"I meant, what are you going to do about the ... you

know ... baby?" Gloria asks, fluttering her hands around her own belly.

"What?" Candice shoots another look behind her. Sabine is approaching Albert/Egret. If those two start talking ... "Look, I'll tell you everything later, okay? I'll phone you after the dance."

"Hey, why don't you and Van Gorder come down to the canyon with us?" Rancid proposes.

"What?" Candice says, eyes glued on Sabine and Albert/Egret.

"Yes, come with us, Candy," Gloria begs. "It's a pre-dance party. Everyone from Sutherland and Argyle will be there."

"Yeah, okay," Candice says. "I'll go get Al ... him."

She slams the door shut and sprints up the driveway. Sabine is running a hand through her hair, trying to look cool and bored in front of Albert/Egret.

"So, like, you two are going to the dance at Sutherland, hey?" she says as Candice comes panting towards them. "Why not come with us to Argyle?"

Albert/Egret shrugs. "Whatever. We could check it out."

"No," Candice says sharply. "I'd rather go to Sutherland."

Sabine narrows her eyes. "Why?"

"'Cause, like, it's my new school and I have friends there. New ones. And they're *expecting* me ..." She can tell that Sabine isn't buying it. "Look, it's no big deal, okay? I mean, we *are* going to the canyon first, like everyone else. So what difference does it make which dance we go to?"

Sabine shrugs. "Fine. I'll see you at the canyon." And she strolls down the drive to the idling car.

Candice turns to Albert/Egret. "Shit. Now we have to go to the canyon first."

"Big deal."

"What were you talking to her about?"

"Nothing …"

"Did you tell her we were dating?"

"Well, I didn't phrase it like that."

"But she *does* know we're together tonight, right?"

"Yeah."

"Good." They both watch the car pull out of the driveway and head towards the canyon parking lot. Candice faces him. "What was your name again?"

"Egret."

"I hope you like to kiss a lot, Egret. I mean, I hope you're not shy necking in front of people."

He opens and closes his mouth a few times.

"'Cause I really like to kiss," she says. "*A lot.* Is that okay?"

"Uh, yeah, sure." He pauses, then leans towards her.

Candice quickly puts a hand on his chest. "Not *here.* Wait until we're in the canyon with the others." And then, because that sounds weird even to her, she adds, "It's so uncool doing it in front of my parents' house."

Andy and Kyle churn through dinner like two gophers. They ask to leave the table without any pumpkin pie, giving the excuse that Kyle has to be home soon and Andy wants to walk him partway there.

A lie, that.

They have plans, though Andy isn't altogether comfortable with executing them. The act of creating said plans has been far more thrilling than the prospect of enacting them, and yet Andy still can't help but experience a delicious frisson at the thought of creeping into the canyon and trying out the Ark, which is the code name for the bomb he and Kyle have created. He's never deliberately done anything so naughty in all his life. The explosion of his first bomb at his old school didn't count. That was more accident than intention. He has never before put so much forethought into disobedience. And though his stomach is currently doing the hula, he feels positively giddy with anticipation.

"We'll explode it behind some trees at the Thirty Foot Pool," Kyle whispers. "Freak everyone right out of their minds."

"Are you *sure* people are going to be there?" Andy asks.

"Positive. That's all I've heard my sisters whisper about all week — the pre-dance party at the canyon. That's how I got the money for all the stuff for the Ark. They had to pay me to keep my mouth shut. You should try that sometime. It never fails. Find out a family secret and then use blackmail to rake in the cash."

Andy glances at his mother, who is picking at a sprout and nodding at something Sarah Kay has said. He immediately dismisses the idea of blackmail as far too ulcer-inducing.

They leave the table and put their coats and shoes on in the bedroom, with the door firmly closed. Andy hesitates before pulling on his coat. "I'm going to look like such a dweeb in this thing," he moans.

"Who cares? No one'll know you're hiding the Ark underneath it. Just forget what the coat looks like."

"Why don't *you* wear it then?"

"It doesn't fit, does it? And besides, it's *your* coat."

It is his coat, true, though Andy has worn it only twice in his life. Thankfully, his mother has seen the folly of her purchase and hasn't insisted he wear it again.

It is bright orange and quilted and massively stuffed, so that when Andy pulls it on, he looks as if he's encased in a giant pumpkin. The thing was a Zellers clearout special. His mother bought it with subzero temperatures in mind.

With a sigh Andy struggles into the coat.

"Don't worry about it," Kyle reiterates. "Once we're out of here, no one's gonna see us, anyway, right? This is a covert operation."

The bomb — a large can filled with the requisite materials — fits snugly against Andy's stomach. Kyle giggles as he zips the coat up. "Perfect! You can't even tell! You could park a truck in that thing and no one would notice!"

Andy grins lopsidedly and shivers. "Gotta make sure I don't fall, though. This thing's for real."

"*I'll* carry the Ark once we get away from here," Kyle says magnanimously. "You're such a klutz."

Andy nods agreement. He most certainly doesn't want to be tripping and killing himself or something.

Egret takes Candice's word literally. As soon as they are among her friends in the canyon parking lot, he starts kissing her. And kissing her. And kissing her.

Oh, God. No! Not in his pants!

Good thing it's dark out.

They stand in front of the massive three-panel billboard at the foot of the trail that leads to the suspension bridge. While Candice and Egret neck to one side, Gloria and Sabine read the billboard and try to outdo each other with smart remarks. Gloria's brother draws penises on the graphics accompanying the billboard messages. The messages read as follows:

> Please be advised that the water temperature of Lynn Canyon is 10 degrees

Celsius. Prolonged exposure = fatigue, hypothermia, loss of motor control, and drowning.

Use of controlled substances is strictly prohibited. Heels should not be worn in the park. When your friends ask you to do something dangerous, don't bend to peer pressure.

Water hazards: large rocks move through the canyon pools during flood season. At all times, logs and debris rotate underwater in the pools below waterfalls.

Small waterfalls flow into pools with enough pressure to hold a person underwater against the bottom or sides of the pool. In 1991 a hiker was trapped in this position for 5 days. The force of the water was so great he had to be pulled away from the canyon wall by a team of commercial divers with ropes and pulleys.

Do not stand too close to the narrowing waterway at the top of a waterfall. Victims have been caught in the current and swept over the falls. Many swimmers have died this way over the years.

Loose rock forms an unreliable foothold. Rocks covered with algae and moss are extremely slippery. In July 1992, a victim fell to her death from an algae-covered rock.

There are many hazards to jumping from cliffs. Failure to clear protruding outcrops has resulted in injury or death. A jumper suffered severe injuries this way in 1990.

> Another jumper suffered a broken leg from striking an underwater outcrop in 1982.
>
> Severe impact with water after a high jump has also resulted in casualties. The force of such an impact tore the running shoes up the legs of a jumper in 1970; they had to be cut from around the jumper's thighs with pliers. The victim suffered debilitating back injuries.

Karen can't eat. She attributes her uneasiness both to the unexplained presence of Clara and her husband's rapt attention to Moey — *what are they talking about?* She forces herself to play hostess.

"Pumpkin pie, Dad?"

"Good Lord, no."

"Mom?"

"Just a slice. A little bigger than that. Bigger. With a bit of that cream, please. Another scoop ... perfect."

"Clara, Sarah Kay? Would you like some —"

"People, people," Morris interrupts. He rises from his chair at the head of the table, beaming. "Perhaps we could all move into the living room for dessert. Moey and I have arranged a little surprise for you."

Karen freezes and stares at Moey. He smiles and winks at her. She drops the pie server.

"Oh, a surprise," Sarah Kay says, pouring herself more wine. "Don't you just love surprises?"

As everyone stands up from the table, Clara murmurs that she does indeed.

He's going to dance, Karen thinks, stunned. *Somehow Moey has convinced Morris to let him dance for us.*

Moey remembered what Karen said to him upon his first visit to the Footstop, about the cinnamon spread she sells at an exorbitant price to tourists — the revolting brown stuff she calls Foot Butter.

I had to call it that, otherwise Morris wouldn't let it in the shop. I had to convince him that as part of a balanced diet, essential oils and fatty acids maintain the health of the foot.

So during the Thanksgiving dinner Moey convinced Morris that as part of a balanced lifestyle, dancing improves the flexibility and coordination necessary for the health of the foot. He now holds within his grasp the opportunity to dance full-time at the Footstop *and* get paid for it.

But first he has to give one hell of a persuasive rendition of the completely fictitious Middle Eastern Foot Dance.

Darkness has descended with the totality of oblivion. Andy can't see where he is going. The bomb rests against his stomach like a metal tumour. With every footstep its liquids slosh back and forth. Andy doesn't like the sound. Sweat fogs his glasses.

Overhead, hemlocks and cedars groan and squeak in the rising wind. Moonlight splashes across ferns and rocks, creating shimmering shadows and black caves. Twigs rasp against tree trunks; pinecones patter to the floor. Unseen movement surrounds him.

Sharp, cold smells envelop him, too: mud, rotting wood, fungi, mushrooms, wind, wet rock. The thunder of the creek in the background is incessant and all-powerful; spray from the waterfalls mist the air, beading Andy's face and hair. He stumbles on a smooth root, trips over a rock, and squelches and slides over a mound of mouldering maple leaves. The bony fingers of a salmonberry bush snag his coat and drop dew down his nape. He staggers again over another unseen root.

Kyle grabs him by the elbow. Not too far away someone howls and hoots. Raucous laughter drifts up from the Thirty Foot Pool. "Jesus! You're going to blow us sky-high! Give me the Ark now."

"You sure?" Andy gasps. A leaf splats against one of the lenses of his glasses, covering it like a decomposing eye patch. He pries it off.

Kyle unzips Andy's coat and plucks out the tin can. "We're close enough to the pool, anyway. Let's go uphill where no one'll see us. It's time to light this baby."

Candice clings to Egret's side like butter to a slice of bread. She is afraid to leave him alone for even half a second, because she knows Sabine and Gloria will descend on him and start grilling him with questions. Questions to which, of course, he has no answers.

As everyone inches over the seamed, mist-slicked boulders that form the banks of the Thirty Foot Pool, Candice begins to seriously doubt the wisdom of her alcohol-inspired actions. How can she keep up the charade of being Egret's pregnant lover without someone discovering the truth sooner or later? Okay, sure, she can take a day off school to pretend she is having an abortion, but that won't solve the problem. Just a few well-placed questions to Egret by one of the jocks ...

I'm going to have to have sex with him, she realizes dismally. She slips on a rock and almost falls.

"Whoa!" Egret says, grinning foolishly. "Want me to carry you or something?"

Yeah, carry me away from here, she feels like saying. Instead she mumbles, "I'm okay."

Three small, weak fires flicker at different places on the boulders, sending gusts of thick smoke and the occasional spark into the horde of teenagers milling around the pool. Music booms from a ghetto blaster; beer cans and empty mickeys of vodka rattle across the creek rocks. The thick, sweet smell of marijuana hovers over everything, more powerful than the wood smoke and miasma of perfumes.

Candice doesn't want to be here. These people aren't her people. She doesn't know who her people are — is terrified she might not *have* people — but she is suddenly certain she doesn't want to be here among Gloria's clones. She stops and pulls on Egret's hand.

"Let's go downstream a bit where it's, like, more private."

Egret pauses, eyes flashing orange from the flames of a fire. He glances over his shoulder at everyone else — a couple of guys have spotted him and are calling his name like a rugby chant. Turning back to her, he says, "You sure?"

Her throat constricts; tears are too damn close. *Fuck this miserable world, fuck this miserable life.* The sooner she gets this over with the better. "Yes."

Chapter Twenty-One

Matches are the one vital thing neither Kyle nor Andy remembers to bring.

"We'll just have to go down and get some," Kyle says glumly. "That'll ruin the surprise. They'll *guess* we're up to something, especially if my sisters see me."

"We could pretend we smoke," Andy says. Kyle gives him a withering look. Andy studies the black and orange silhouettes gathered around the fires on the rocks below. Shafts of smoke glint through the trees, eerie and blue from wind and moonlight. "Or," he says, desperately trying to erase that withering look from existence, "we could steal a burning twig from one of those fires."

"Yeah, *right*. As if no one'll notice us."

"No, look, really. That fire there on that ledge. No one's around it. If we hike through the bush, up the back of that hill, then climb down the cliff, we can grab a few sticks without anyone noticing us."

"We might be able to. Maybe." Kyle contemplates the adventure, then nods and grins. "Sure. Why not? Let's go for it."

Moey dons his costume in Karen's bathroom, thinking furiously. What dance moves, what music, can possibly accentuate footwork? As he mentally rifles through the cassettes in his bag, he knocks his elbow on something while stooping to pull off his socks. The something beeps. Still bent over, he turns and peers at the object. He is eye to eye with a microwave.

A microwave in a bathroom. What strange purpose does that serve? He doesn't know. But the appliance heartens him. If this household can keep kitchenware alongside a toilet bowl with impunity, then Moey Thorpe stands a good chance of pulling off this whole Foot Dance thing.

As Candice lets Egret lead her downstream, away from the party, she feels exposed and isolated. The failure of being unable to connect with those around her is crushing. She knows now that no matter what lies she spins or clothes she wears, she will never belong among her peers. Certainly not among that cluster of Budweiser stallions near the fire, nor that huddle of indifferent, oh-so-cool girls hanging off their elbows. Not with the couples necking in the shadows, nor those three girls sitting on a nearby outcrop taking ludicrously small, obviously unwanted puffs from a shared cigarette.

Everywhere she looks Candice is aware of status and attitude and labels. The need to belong, the *effort* of belonging, is tangible and all-pervasive, more powerful than the wind bending the cedars around them.

I'm always going to be alone, she thinks, and then realizes what that thought embraces: she *is* a lesbian, just as she declared melodramatically to Gloria the other day. She really, really is. *For life.*

Her stomach lurches, and sour red wine rushes into her mouth. She gags, about to vomit, and stumbles on another crevice in the massive, seamed hump of rock Egret is leading her across. He clutches her hand tighter, as if that alone can hold her upright.

Until now Gloria has held her hand, has acted as her ally, her mask, her mirror, her release. But now Gloria is gone from her, leaving Candice to make a journey to an unknown place without the one person she thought would make the journey with her.

And it dawns on her that the way she feels now — the despair, the loneliness, the inability to connect with anyone — is a massive dose of how she has always felt. She has tried to starve it out of herself by dieting, has tried to clean it from her surroundings by removing all the garbage she has come across. She has tried to wash away the strangeness with multiple showers, has tried to find the Holy Grail of acceptability in the stacks of *Cosmopolitan*s and lipsticks on her desk.

With this revelation comes the inane need to tell the truth to everyone. But there is no one around, save her and Egret, for by now they have hopscotched downstream from everyone else.

So she tells Egret.

The music begins. From her seat in the living room, wedged between her father and Sarah Kay on the couch, Karen shivers. The music is unlike any Moey has played in the teahouse.

It is mournful, lonely, full of unspoken emotion. A wooden flute whispers; a harp weeps. A bell tolls once, twice, thrice. Slow. Funereal. Karen glances around. Everyone is mesmerized, eyes glued on the doorway, awaiting Moey's entrance. In their faces Karen can see exactly what they are feeling. It is an eerie out-of-body experience charged with certainty.

The music reminds Mei-ling of windswept, barren landscapes and bombed temples and monasteries. The music reminds her father of Petra, caskets, and last goodbyes.

Sarah Kay is thinking of poverty and hunger. Clara sees a fireless hearth in an empty house. Mr. Osaban is reminded of the rusted skeletons of abandoned, once-loved cars.

And Morris ... he hears the music and sees a river, specifically, Lynn Creek. This knowledge — divine, irrefutable, and inexplicable — stuns Karen. The creek? Why does the music remind Morris of Lynn Creek?

And then, as if looking through fog and blue moonlight, Karen glimpses what image the music has invoked for him. Not just Lynn Creek, but also the ghosts of all the men and women and children who have died there over the years.

They scramble, they crouch, they crawl, they slither. The creek thunders beneath them through the narrow gorge that opens into the Thirty Foot Pool. From their current vantage point the teenagers below are muted black wraiths. Only the bass of the ghetto blaster is audible, booming like a tribal drum.

Kyle breathes heavily. The excitement and the wood smoke from the fires have irritated his asthma. And Andy can't see properly. The mist spewing up from the crashing falls coats his glasses like damp cotton wool.

They are both exhilarated and terrified, pulled onward by the irresistible lure of adventure. Andy has never felt this alive.

Candice feels dizzy and distant from herself, hears her own voice as though she is holding her breath underwater and is listening to someone else speaking. Her heartbeat races so fast she coughs repeatedly from the pressure on her ribcage.

Egret watches her in astonishment.

When she is done — uncertain of what exactly she has said, though the word *lesbian* hangs in the air like the mournful blare of a foghorn — she melts to the ground, unable to stand any longer.

Egret sits beside her, staring. "Shit," he finally croaks. "I mean, are you *sure*?"

She nods, can't trust herself to speak again.

"But all that kissing stuff ..."

She waits and lets him figure it out, using what he knows of high school and the rigid, vicious laws of fitting in.

"I'm the first one you've told?" he says, and this time his voice squeaks, which makes Candice want to laugh, but she doesn't because she's afraid she might shatter.

She nods again. A tear slides down her cheek.

"Shit," he says again, looking at the creek. A muscle in his cheek twitches like the disturbed withers of a horse. He picks up a rock, tosses it in. It is immediately lost in the foamy white rapids hissing and churning over each other. "Greg Louganis is gay," he eventually says.

"Who?" The word comes out as a gasp for air. She has been holding her breath without realizing it.

"Greg Louganis. The diver."

"Never heard of him."

Disgust flashes across his face. "Fuck, where have you been? The guy won a silver medal at the Olympics when he was sixteen. He's won a ton of stuff since — four Olympic golds, six Pan Am golds, five world championships ..."

"Really? And he's gay?"

"Yeah." He gazes at her strangely. "What? You think gays can't be athletes?"

I'm on the wrong end of this conversation, Candice thinks giddily. "No. It's just that, you know. I mean, I thought ...

I didn't think gay people were ... are normal ..."

She can't hold back the tears now, is, in fact, bawling her eyes out. Great rivers of snot flow from her nose as she sobs into her hands. She wipes them repeatedly on her pants.

He shifts about a bit, then clumsily pats her back a couple of times. "Don't sweat it. Chill out before someone hears you."

She stifles her sobs with a series of gags and hiccoughs.

"Shit, you gotta start hanging out with other dykes," he says.

Dykes. He says it so casually. Suddenly, she is filled with bitterness and rage. "And where do I find them, huh? And how do I survive high school? They'll *crucify* me at school. You know that! Sabine and Ashley and Hierza —"

"Then don't tell anyone. Just stick with what you've already told them. *I* don't care if they think we're going steady. Another year and we graduate, anyway."

She can't believe her luck. Doesn't dare hope that what he says is really true. "So, like, you won't tell anyone?"

"*No.* Guys don't gossip the way girls do. Fuck, women are like a bunch of hens or something. Always clucking at each other."

"It doesn't bother you that I'm ... a lesbian?"

"Believe me, I'm not *thrilled*. I liked it better when I thought you were necking 'cause you wanted to, not because you *had* to."

"Sorry," she whispers. "You *are* a good kisser, though."

"Yeah?" He perks up. "You think maybe you're bisexual? Or this girl thing is just, you know, a phase?"

She pauses, then slowly shakes her head.

He sighs. "Well, whatever. But if you get the urge to test yourself on a guy or something, you gotta come to me first, okay?"

Just like that. He's accepted her incredible disease, her outrageous deformity. "You still want to be friends with me?"

He snorts. "Yeah. Haven't you been listening?"

She nods, then starts crying again, differently this time. He lets his arm slip down around her shoulders.

Moey dances. His muscles ripple, his feet flash. Raw emotion billows from him. He creates an internal storm within each of his watchers.

They feel transported. Numinous. At one with the mystical forces that create life. That control death.

Andy slips. He knows fear. It balloons under his diaphragm, snatches away his breath. Moss and slick rock rake beneath his outstretched fingers as he slides down, down, down. His glasses bounce off. Pain flares across his collarbone. Something rips open his shinbone, tears his coat partially off.

Then a drop. Cold. Silent. Airy.

He screams.

And hits water.

The music finishes. Moey falls still, arms raised above his head as if beseeching ancient gods to bring the dead back to life. Everyone holds their breath.

Then Morris leaps to his feet and wallops Moey on the back. "Stunning! Marvellous! Unbelievable!"

The mood breaks. Sarah Kay calls for an encore. Clara stammers effusive, bashful praise. The reverend pours wine for everyone and bellows to Mei-ling to put on some more music, while she quotes various scriptures concerning the power of dance. Mr. Osaban laughs and laughs, throwing back his head and displaying an alarming amount of bridgework. Even old Mrs. Morton smiles and nods approvingly, with more vigour than she has shown over the past few years combined.

Only Karen sits motionless and silent. She shivers all over uncontrollably. Sarah Kay presses a glass of wine into one of her hands and pulls her upright. Karen plasters on a smile and begins to dance with Sarah Kay to the powerful, turbulent music surging again through the room.

Muffled against Egret's chest, Candice doesn't hear the single, high scream or the violent splash and the shouts that follow, doesn't hear anything but Egret's heartbeat and her own ragged breaths. Until Egret pulls away and jumps to his feet.

"Shit!" he shouts. "Someone's fallen into the creek!"

She stands and sees an orange balloon coming down the creek towards them, pummelled by hissing rapids. The balloon disappears under an angry froth of white water, followed by one thin extended arm, one small white hand.

Egret whips off his jean jacket and kicks off his shoes so fast she is barely aware of what he's done. Then he dives into the water.

It is a shallow, flawless, Olympic-gold dive.

People run downstream, leaping over rocks, shouting to one another, calling for help. Candice can't move, can't speak. She stares at the place where Egret has disappeared into the rapids.

The Thirty Foot Pool is wide and deep, the largest pool in Lynn Canyon. The water entering it flows through a narrow ravine; the water exiting the pool flows over a series of boulders and rocks, along a wide creek path that slowly, inexorably, narrows again to a steep gorge. Here the water gathers speed, becomes swift and frothy.

On the western side of the creek, downstream from the Thirty, is another pool. It is more a shallow eddy than a pool. In the summer it is completely dry. Logs, Styrofoam cups, beer cans, and drowned raccoons get snagged here on rock and clay. A scant few hundred feet away, dead centre in the creek, the gorge drops.

Just drops.

An

abrupt

sheer

cliff.

The creek thunders over this precipice, hurtling down to a churning white-water pool. Massive logs roll endlessly in this vortex, stripped of all bark from the roiling waters, trapped until smashed to splinters. Boulders the size of wheelbarrows tumble round and round, pulverizing branches, smashing creek rock to sand. The sound of the falls is deafening. The spray reaches clear up to the suspension bridge some 150 feet above.

This is what the tourists love to see.

The first person who reaches Candice is one of the jocks. He grabs her by the shoulders and shakes her wildly. "Was that Egret? Did he go in there after the kid?"

He releases her without waiting for an answer and continues running downstream, slipping on rocks, bellowing for help. Girls scream at the Thirty Foot Pool.

They should turn off that ghetto blaster, Candice thinks.

More people converge on her, all breathless, their terror palpable. Too many people talk at once.

Then Gloria stands before her, shrieking, crying, shaking Candice.

But Candice can't hear her.

"Shut up, everyone!" Sabine screams, and for a moment they all obey.

"Up on the rocks," Gloria gasps. "His sisters are trying to get him down right now. Oh, Candice, I'm so sorry! Andy, oh, God, Andy!"

"What?" Candice says, blinking at the creek, at the rapids where Egret dived in after that bubble of orange and that thin arm and small white hand.

"Your brother fell into the creek," Sabine says sharply. "Christ, do something about it!"

Candice turns towards her. Slowly. Carefully.

People are still shouting and screaming and stumbling downstream. No one has switched off the ghetto blaster yet.

"It can't be Andy," Candice says. "He's walking Kyle home."

"Kyle's up on those cliffs back there!" Sabine screeches, pointing behind her, back to the Thirty Foot Pool where some girls still stand and scream. "Are you fucking deaf?"

"You're wrong," Candice insists, glancing back at the creek again, back to the spot where that hand sank beneath the churning white foam.

"Shit, someone else deal with her!" Sabine yells, turning away.

Sobbing, Gloria gropes for Candice's hand. She strokes Candice's fingers the way she used to when they were in bed together. "Candice? Candy? Listen to me, okay? Ellen and Ariel are back there telling Kyle not to move. He's freaked out, says Andy was with him. Candy, we all *heard* him fall."

"You're wrong," Candice says.

"Candy ..."

Candice pushes her away, then turns and runs. Away from the creek. Home.

Karen can't dance. Her heart is beating strangely, irregular and too fast. And her vision is odd.

Her joints feel ice-locked. Her limbs won't move properly. She feels she's a parody of a human, a marionette in disguise.

Karen is terrified and she doesn't know why.

Candice bursts into the living room, splattered with mud and leaves. Her eyes are black with mascara, black tears stream down her flushed and mud-splattered cheeks. Her hair is wet, and a strand of it is plastered across her lips. Her lower lip is cut, as if she's fallen.

No one has noticed her except Karen, who moves swiftly and snaps the music off. Suddenly, the room is filled with the gasping, jagged breaths of her daughter's sobs and breathless words. "Andy ... in the creek ... fell ... Mommy!"

Karen crushes Candice to her chest. That's all she can do. There is nothing else.

Her husband tears out of the house. Her mother searches for flashlights and blankets. Her father picks up the phone.

And Karen holds her remaining child — her baby, the flesh from her own body — against her chest. And rocks her.

That's all she can do. There is nothing else.

Chapter Twenty-Two

Karen stares at her closet. She doesn't know how to reach for that new black dress in the filmy clear plastic, squeezed between her regular clothes and Morris's suits. She can't find the strength to pull it off the rack and slip it from its padded coat hanger.

And if she could, how would she put it on? Pull it over her head, let it engulf her in blackness until she bursts through the neck, gasping for air? Or step into it and wriggle it up past her birthmarks, hips, and breasts to zip it shut like a black body bag?

She stands there, heavy-limbed, so weary, so very, very weary ...

Morris finds her an hour later. By then gooseflesh has replaced the shower droplets on her skin.

"Karen?" he says. He crosses the room, touches her bare shoulder. His fingers are hot; his dry-cleaned suit smells inky, like a Magic Marker. "How long have you been standing like this?"

She shrugs. Doesn't know, doesn't care.

He leans closer. The buttons of his jacket brush against her bare back, smooth and cool like polished river pebbles.

"Karen, we're going to be late if we don't leave soon."

The dead can wait forever, can't they? There is no time, no urgency, for the deceased. Late for a funeral — the idea seems impossible.

"You're cold as marble," he murmurs, running his hands down her back. "Get dressed. I'll help."

"I wonder if that was his last sensation," she says, her voice mechanical, eyes still on the black, newly purchased dress trapped under the clear, airless film. "Cold. As marble."

"Don't. Don't."

"Why?" She stiffly turns her head to look at him. "Why can't I? Don't tell me you don't think about what his last moments were like, what he felt, what he heard, what he thought. Don't tell me you don't wake up at nights clawing the air, trying to swim to the surface."

"Stop it!" His hands shoot out with a speed that startles her, shoot out and grab either side of her face and squeeze as if her skin is Plasticine and he's trying to mould a different face into it, new life. "Don't do this, don't!"

His face contorts and he pulls her cheeks harder. It hurts. She welcomes the pain, welcomes the flame of anger it provokes. Then Morris abruptly transfers his hold, crushes her against his chest. He starts weeping into her hair.

"He's *alive*, Karen. He's *alive*. You have to keep telling yourself that every moment of the day, every second of the night. Our boy is *alive*."

"But someone else's boy is dead," she whispers.

She buckles under Morris's weight, and they both sink to the floor, a puddle of black clothes smothering creamy white skin.

There is a coffin, even though there is no body. Two days ago Karen learned from the six o'clock news that the "retrieval team" — that's how the newscaster phrased it, as if it was some sort of football game — suspended all efforts to free the trapped body until the heavy rainfall ceased and the water level in the canyon dropped. "A spokesperson on the team said it might not be possible to reclaim the body of the victim until early spring," the newscaster said with the generic soberness that was supposed to pass for professional concern.

People keep staring at Andy. They pause on the church steps, they stop in the church aisle. They turn in their pews. They whisper. Karen holds him protectively against her, fingers white against the dark navy wool of his suit jacket.

"Are you sure you want to be here?" she whispers, lips brushing his slicked hair.

"Stop asking me that!" he hisses. "I told you, yes!"

She has to stop asking him that.

"Are you sure you want to be here?" she asks several minutes later, forgetting.

Andy purses his thin, blueish lips and stares lock-jawed at the front of the church.

He is shivering. Still. He says he's freezing all the time, even though the hospital released him two days ago, his vital signs are normal, his collarbone is in its proper place, and his hypothermia has reversed. Plucky lad, the intern said. No permanent damage done.

No permanent damage.

Karen examines the impeccable, extravagant coffin — *white, why white?* — and wonders how the intern defined permanent damage.

She adjusts her sunglasses on the bridge of her nose, fumbles in her coat pockets for the Tylenol bottle, and swallows two more pills.

Her migraine just won't quit.

"And we must not mourn today for Kris Van Gorder," the presiding Lutheran pastor intones, "for although he has departed from us in the flesh, his spirit shall remain with us always ..."

Kris, Karen thinks. *His name was Kris. I never knew.*

She feels as if someone has punched her in the stomach, as if something has been stolen from her.

I never asked him his real name.

The pallbearers don't carry the coffin out. Karen doesn't know what they will do with it until the body is recovered. (The body. Not *Egret's* body, but *the* body, as if depersonalizing it can lessen the tragedy, reduce the reality.)

Do churches have a basement for this sort of thing? A waiting room for expectant coffins? What about funeral homes? Or will the Van Gorders take that exquisite empty casket with them as a sort of surrogate son until the real one is dredged up from the creek bottom, all rotten and bloated and grey?

Mrs. Van Gorder is wrapped in a thick mohair blanket that looks as though it came from the trunk floor of someone's car. Karen assumes she is dressed expensively underneath that blanket, as expensively as the Porsche she stepped from, as expensively as the house she lives in, but Karen can't be sure. All she can see is that hairy beige blanket.

Karen spoke to her outside in the parking lot, among all the slim, sombre athletes and coiffed, weeping relatives. Andy insisted, and Karen couldn't refuse him. But one look at Mrs. Van Gorder's waxy face and her husband's bewildered, swollen one and Karen wanted to flee.

"I'm Andy," Andy said then, his voice small and thin. A half-dozen flashes snapped across the street where the police cordon held newspaper reporters and TV cameramen at bay. "Andy Morton."

That was enough. No explanation needed. Mrs. Van Gorder reached out a black-gloved hand and stroked Andy's head. "So young. I didn't realize you were so young."

Mr. Van Gorder grabbed her by an elbow and tugged. A chunky gold ring glinted on one of his knuckles. "Come, Dolinda."

Karen moved an involuntary step forward. Mrs. Van Gorder's eyes snapped towards her. Karen felt as if a fist of ice was being rammed down her throat.

"You're Mrs. Morton, yes?"

Karen, my name is Karen. You don't fuck a woman and then call her by her mother-in-law's name.

"Yes," she rasped. "I'm Mrs. Morton."

Mrs. Van Gorder nodded and drew the mohair blanket tighter around herself. She gazed skyward into the clouds. "Egret was a pale boy at this age. The first time he stood on a diving board, so white, his legs like little twigs, he shone like a pearl. His coach named him Egret. I had to look it up in a book. My English was not good then. Look how it's raining. Still."

"Dolinda," Mr. Van Gorder said hoarsely, and Karen's eyes flicked to him. The man's beefy, florid cheeks were damp despite the huge umbrella he held. His hair, his coat, his forehead were all dry. But his cheeks and chin were damp.

"I'm sorry," Andy said, voice tremulous. "It's all my fault."

Mrs. Van Gorder released a long, thin wail and swayed. She collapsed like a snuffed candle wick sinking in a pool of wax. She seized Andy on her way down, took him with her, so that as her knees thudded against asphalt, he was forced into a kneeling position, too.

You'll displace his collarbone again! Karen wanted to cry out, but she couldn't. Her throat wouldn't work.

"Dolinda, for God's sake! Dolinda!" Mr. Van Gorder cried. People stopped in their tracks and glanced at one another uncertainly. *Flash-flash-flash* went the cameras across the street.

Mr. Van Gorder looked around desperately. Two tall athletes wearing Brazilian flag pins on their lapels stepped forward and pulled Mrs. Van Gorder upright.

But still she clung to Andy, and Andy held tightly to her, his face obscured beneath her mohair blanket. His whole thin body shuddered. He cried.

Karen started forward to rip her son free.

He's mine, he's mine, he's mine!

Only Morris's hand on her elbow stayed her.

They file out of the church, moving in a polite shuffle that conceals the desire to run. As they pass the last pew, a long-haired, gap-toothed man on crutches rises in front of Morris.

"Hey, Doc. Didn't expect to see you here."

Karen's eyes instinctively drop to the man's feet. She recoils from the sight of the empty bottom of his pant leg.

"Ah, Mr. Chapman. How do you do, how do you do?" Morris says.

He steps out of the stream of people, bringing Karen, hooked onto his arm, with him. Candice and Andy continue out the vast church doors. Karen panics as the river of bodies pushes her son away from her. She jerks her arm free from Morris and begins to go after Andy, but —

"This is my wife, Karen," Morris says. "Mr. Chapman is a patient of mine."

She mumbles something vague and appropriate and

glances over her shoulder to where her children have disappeared.

"Mr. Chapman is quite an interesting case. Contracted Madura foot while touring the south by motorbike. Unfortunately, I failed to cure him."

"Shit happens, Doc," Mr. Chapman says, and Karen looks back at him. He rolls something around in his mouth, a large purple blob that might be grape bubble gum. "Shame about the kid, eh? Christ almighty, I still can't get over it. I knew him since he was a tyke."

"Very tragic," Morris says hoarsely. "Nephew?"

"Naw," Mr. Chapman says. "No blood relation. I live in the Van Gorders' basement. Tenant."

"You're the Man! That's your Virago!" As soon as the words leave Karen's mouth, her head swells into a helium balloon. It slowly rises and floats a foot or so above her. To her left she senses rather than sees Morris stare at her.

"I didn't realize you two were acquainted."

Mr. Chapman studies her in mild confusion. Then his eyes widen, his eyebrows lifting slightly. Something akin to a smirk spreads across his face.

Oh, God, Karen thinks. *He knows about me and Egret. Somehow he knows.*

"We don't know each other, not really," she babbles. "We've never met before. Egret spoke of you. The night he came to pick up Candice for the Thanksgiving Dance — that's when he mentioned you. And your Virago."

Her teeth are dry wood chips, her tongue rough bark. She can't swallow. Her heart booms against her eardrums.

"Really?" the Man — Mr. Chapman — drawls, looking her up and down, the half leer still on his creased, razor-nicked face.

"Yes, you know how boys are, always trying to impress

girls. I heard him talking about how he wanted to ride a motorbike, a Virago, just like his tenant's. He was talking to my daughter. Picking her up for the dance. The Man, he called you."

"The Man in the Basement," Mr. Chapman says, tonguing his gum while he speaks, his blood-veined eyes riveted on her. "That'd be me. That was all he ever called me. Goddamn tragedy, losin' him like this. Goddamn shame."

"Yes," Morris says huskily. "It was ... my son he went after in the creek."

The Man cocks an eyebrow at him. "No shit? Well. Small world, ain't it?" He transfers his gaze back to Karen. "Real small world."

He extends his hand towards her. It is callused and hairy, and dark half-moons of dirt crown each fingernail. Karen fumbles in her purse for bribe money. Then, with a hot flush that feels like flames searing up her ears and across her hairline, she realizes he wants to shake her hand. She places hers into his, and he squeezes as if wringing the neck of a trapped ermine.

The hairy hand leaves hers and slaps Morris on one shoulder. "See ya around, Doc. We should talk one day soon." He readjusts his crutches under his armpits, turns, and hobbles down the church aisle, against the flow of the crowd, towards the casket where Mr. and Mrs. Van Gorder stand.

Morris steers Karen back into the stream of people leaving the church.

On the drive home, Candice abruptly asks her father to stop the car. She pushes the door open, leans out, and vomits into the gutter.

A little later Morris pulls into their driveway and turns the ignition off. No one moves. Rain *splitter-splats* on the roof. Steam rises from the engine hood. The smell of burning rubber drifts up through the rusted floor. Still no one budges.

Splitter-splat. Splat, splat, splitter-splitter splat.

"I want to sell the house," Karen finally whispers, staring straight ahead. "Move."

"Yes," Morris says hollowly. "I've always hated that creek."

"I hate the teahouse," she says. The words come out by themselves, and Morris stiffens.

Karen feels uncannily calm, devoid of fear, but is unable to look at him. She clears her throat and continues. "It's not what I'd planned on doing for the rest of my life. I'm sorry. But I really hate that teahouse."

A gust of wind shakes Douglas fir needles over the windshield.

"You should have said something before," Morris says.

"I know. And there's something else I should tell you." Deep breath. "I want to open my own business. A Spiritual Sex Store. Sell crystals and harps and vibrators and condoms."

Morris sits straighter. Karen catches the movement from the corner of her eye, but she remains face forward, gazes only at their tree-shrouded, rain-veiled house.

"I'm a lesbian," Candice announces breathlessly from the back seat.

Morris's collar rises an inch from the top of his jacket. "I hate my trumpet," Andy says in a small voice. "And I'm not crazy about karate, either."

"Kickboxing," Karen says hoarsely, a tear sliding down her cheek. "You mean kickboxing."

"Yeah."

"I'm a *lesbian*," Candice says more loudly. "Didn't anyone hear me?"

"Yes," everyone in the car says in perfect unison.

Splitter splat-splat.

"I have a foot fetish," Morris whispers, enunciating each word as if English is a second language.

A silence so long, the windows of the car steam over.

Then Andy starts to giggle. A light, bubbly sound that grows and grows. Karen's lips crack into a smile.

The giggles increase in volume, expand into helpless belly laughs.

"What? It's not funny, you little twerp," Candice says to her brother. "This whole family is totally *weird*."

But then she, too, begins to laugh.

Chapter Twenty-Three

Karen lies awake in bed long after Morris falls asleep. Sweat slicks the nape of his neck where they made meek, desperate love to each other. His heartbeat feels like a small rubber mallet against the drum of her cheek; his chest moves up and down, easily, gently.

From the living room her father's snores roll and rumble with the rhythmic force of waves crashing on a beach. Both Andy and Candice reclaimed their bedrooms; the reverend and Mei-ling now sleep on a large, flock-lined air mattress on the living-room floor. The snoring isn't a soothing sound; Karen doesn't know how anyone else in the house can sleep.

She rolls off Morris's chest and gazes at the ceiling, painted black by night. She stares until her eyes become dry as peanut shells.

She can't cry, not anymore. She has wept herself dry, retching on her own mucus, gagging on the thick ropes of saliva in the back of her throat. Her grief isn't unseemly for a mother who almost lost her son. Her shock is to be expected. But what about the guilt and the gratitude she feels because Egret was taken instead of her son? What about the horror, the self-recrimination, is this, too, expected? *I caused his death,* she tells herself a million times a day. *He was punished for* my *adultery.*

She has to believe that; she has no choice. It is necessary

to assign blame to herself because that makes the world an ordered place. If Egret's death is a random, senseless thing, an accident of nature, a result of the indifference of the universe to the plight of those alive, then the world is a very cold, unpredictable place in which to live. A place where she has no control, where next time her son might be the one washed over a waterfall and crushed beneath a hundred tons of raging white water. Better Karen believe in a vindictive God with an incomprehensible divine plan than to believe that a young, healthy boy with his life ahead of him died for no reason at all.

Slowly, Karen disentangles herself from Morris's limbs. She crosses the room, pulls a thick sweater from a drawer, and tugs it over her head. She hasn't visited the canyon yet, not since Andy was found splayed on the western clay bank of the creek a mere three dozen feet from the waterfall.

"Where are you going?" Morris asks.

She whirls around, heart slamming into her ears. "Jesus! I thought you were asleep!"

"You're going out, aren't you? To the creek."

Karen hesitates, then nods slowly.

"I'll come with you." Morris throws back the bedcovers and rises.

"You don't have to —"

"Of course I damn well do." He snatches his pants off the back of his desk chair (the pants from his funeral suit, as uncreased as when he first put them on this morning). "You expect me to lie here and wait for you to return, listening to the creek, wondering if you've fallen in?"

"I'm sorry. I didn't think."

"Don't apologize," he snaps. "This family is doing too much of that lately. Why can't we just say what we want without asking to be pardoned all the time?"

"Because we're afraid to hurt each other's feelings."

Morris whuffles in the back of his throat, sits on the edge of the bed, and slips on his socks.

Karen watches his long, slim wrists moving deftly about their task. "Are you having an affair with Clara?"

His hands freeze. He turns an incredulous gaze up at her. Karen flushes, knowing immediately how foolish and wrong the fear is.

"Clara? My *receptionist*?"

She nods, mute.

"Good God, what gave you *that* idea?"

"I don't know. You've never invited her to Thanksgiving dinner before. And you're always at the office these days, staying late, sometimes going in even on Sundays. And you and I ... we haven't been close. Lately."

He jams his feet into his shoes and stands. "No. We haven't. And I blame myself for that."

"It's not your fault."

"You despise me for ruining you. For getting you pregnant."

"What?"

"I was older than you. I should've known better. The responsibility was mine to provide adequate contraception. I apologize."

She gawps. "But you did!"

"I didn't."

"You put on a condom! And gobs and gobs of spermicidal jelly. You used up the whole tube. It was yellow, like butter. Don't you remember?"

His scowl melts and is slowly replaced by a stunned expression. He looks like a man who has just discovered religion. "That's right. I did."

"How could you forget such a thing?"

He shakes his head, dazed. Then his eyes clear. "But how did you ...?"

"Get pregnant? Jesus, Morris! I got pregnant *purposely*. It was *planned*. I bit a hole in the condom and sucked all the jelly off during foreplay. I thought you *knew*."

He peers at her with the face of a man who, after only recently discovering religion, meets a *Playboy* bunny in a nun's habit.

"I was afraid you'd get tired of me and move on to someone your own age," Karen says. Seventeen years together and he *never knew*. "I got pregnant to keep you."

"Keep me?"

"I thought you knew all this! You can't tell me that's why you've been so angry with me all this time!"

He blinks, jerks back as though she's thrown a glass of water in his face. "I've never been angry with you, Karen. I've been angry with myself."

They stare at each other, he in his pants and socks, hair damp and tousled, chest bare, she naked from the waist down, a thick fisherman's sweater covering her torso.

"We don't really know each other, do we?" Karen whispers in wonder. "I've got a strange man in my bedroom."

He crosses the room in three strides and crushes her in his embrace.

They make love again. Differently, this time. Fiercely, freely. Their emotions raw and open.

Teeth bared, they claw, they slap, they push, they pin down, they pull up. Fingers rake abdomens. They can't stop.

They twist and stretch. They snarl and bite. They bruise themselves and each other, slamming elbows and heads against the headboard. She makes him bleed, tastes the salty copper of his blood on her swollen lips. He wraps his large hands around her feet and slowly tightens until she can't breathe, until everything goes soft and deliciously black.

He thrusts into her then, and she clings to him, gasping for air, pushing back, crying out because the feeling surging through her has been absent for such a long, long time.

After it's over, she hurts, feels like a cheese grater has been rammed between her thighs and down her throat and dragged across her breasts. It is wonderful. She takes each breath carefully, wincing, ribs creaking.

Morris lies on his back beside her, both of them on the floor, halfway in the open closet, among all the sensible, beautiful shoes he purchased for her a long, long time ago. Seventeen years of ache lie between them.

Karen stares up the skirts and trouser legs of the clothes hanging above her head, all a uniform grey from the moonlight straining through the dusty closet window. In the gloom she can't discern her funeral outfit from the rest of her dresses.

"You lied to me," Morris whispers.

She thinks of the Man, and alarm spurts through her. "About what?"

"You allowed me to believe your pregnancy was an accident."

"Oh." Sharp relief. Then she says, "Wait a minute. I never lied to you."

"You did. Through omission."

She props herself up on one elbow. "I told you already. I thought you knew why I was doing all that sucking and licking and nibbling. If it was a lie, you were a conspirator."

"Then why bother putting the condom on at all?"

"*You* didn't even remember you were wearing a condom, so what difference does it make?"

"Accountability."

"Accountability," Karen snorts, getting up, thwacking the clothes out of her face, stumbling over a jumble of shoes.

He follows her, groaning as he rises. "You don't seem to understand how I've condemned myself all these years." He limps over to the bed and lowers himself gingerly onto it. "How I've felt unworthy of you, how I've been afraid to touch you for fear of ruining you further."

"So I'm ruined, am I?" she says, snatching up her sweater. "Flabby and loose-loined after two births? Thighs laden with cellulite, a few folds under my chin?"

"I didn't mean it that way."

"I don't see what other way you could mean it."

"What are you getting dressed for?" he says, incredulous. "You aren't still going to the creek, are you?"

"I am." She yanks open a drawer and pulls out a pair of musty-smelling jogging pants. "You don't have to come."

"I want to." Moving like an old man, he fumbles through the bedsheets for his pants. "Though I don't know why you want to go there."

"I want to see where you found Andy."

She pulls the chair away from Morris's desk, sits on it, and works socks onto her feet. Anger spumes inside her, born from the knowledge that perhaps Morris is right. Perhaps she *did* mislead him. Yes, her whole intent was to trick him into impregnating her, to ensnare him as a husband with the net of her life-bearing womb.

She jams her feet into her Birkenstocks and sighs. "You're right," she says in angry resignation. "I should've told you. I should've been up front about the whole baby-wanting thing."

He stands and zips his pants. "And you're right, too, of course. Maybe I suspected what you were doing and all these years I've psychologically blocked it out."

"Really?"

He shrugs, looks away. "It's possible."

"You're just saying that to make me feel better."

He turns back to her, spreads his hands. "I don't want us to fight. Not now. Not for something that happened seventeen years ago, that we've ridiculously allowed to cloud our relationship."

Tears spring to her eyes, and she suddenly realizes how sore and tight her throat is. "I don't want to fight, either," she whispers.

"But why didn't you *tell* me back then? That you wanted a child?"

"Because I thought there wasn't anything admirable in being a mother at eighteen. It was so unambitious of me."

"There's nothing unambitious about bringing a life into this world," Morris huffs. "It's a very weighty responsibility!"

"And I thought that if you knew how much I was afraid of losing you, you wouldn't love the quivering mess of fear that was me."

"That's the most preposterous thing I've ever heard."

"Oh, really? Then tell me, Morris Morton, why has it taken you so long to tell me you thought pregnancy ruined me? And why has it taken you just as long to admit your career is only a way to indulge in your foot fetish?"

He opens his mouth, colours, and starts to whuffle.

Karen cuts him off. "*I'll* tell you why. Because you're afraid that if I and other people knew what you were really like, we'd all reject you as bizarre. If we all knew your deepest thoughts, we'd go screaming into the night. *That's* why you've hidden behind your silence and your medical degree all these years."

He sits back on the bed, studies the wall in front of him. "I suppose my medical degree has ... afforded me a large measure of respectability and protection. And you're quite correct, of course. I should have asked you seventeen years ago whether you hated me for impregnating you, rather than assuming it."

"So we're no different."

"Well, I wouldn't say *that*."

"Why not?" she challenges.

"Oh, fine, have it your way."

"Don't sulk. It's unbecoming."

"I'm not sulking, Karen." He glances up, shrugs dismally. "I'm just sad that we're both so ashamed to be ourselves with each other. We've hidden our feelings all these years from the person we should trust most in our lives, and I think, I really do think, it has cast a terrible pall over our marriage."

She instantly feels crushed and old.

"That's why you never told me about ... about your desire to open a sex store, isn't it?" Morris presses. "Because you were afraid of how *I'd* react."

"Spiritual Sex Store," she whispers, nodding. "And because I was afraid — am *still* afraid — it might make our children targets for ridicule."

"Well, I think I've got *that* fairly well established already," Morris says bitterly. He groans and plants one large, slender hand over his face. "Do you think it's my fault Candice is ... believes she is ... what she said today?"

"A lesbian? Because of the Footstop?" Karen sucks in a swift breath. "I hope not."

Morris looks up at her pleadingly. "It must be a stage she's going through, yes? The teenage years can be so difficult ..."

Karen wants to agree. She really does. She wants for her daughter a wedding with flowers and a cake and a dashing young groom with broad shoulders. But something in Candice's voice when she made the announcement in the car today negated the possibility that her current sexual preference is just a stage.

"I get the feeling she meant what she said," Karen says slowly.

"But how does she know? She's too young, hasn't had enough experience with boys! She can't know she's a ... homosexual ... until she's played the field a bit."

Karen arches an eyebrow. "Have *you* ever slept with a boy, Morris?"

"What? Of course I haven't."

"Then how do you know you're heterosexual? If you haven't 'played the field a bit?'"

He opens his mouth, closes it, then bends over and fusses with a shoelace. "It's not the same thing. And why are you defending her?"

"She's our *daughter*. And besides, not five minutes ago you said that a person shouldn't hide her feelings from the one she trusts most in her life. *We* did it and you think it's hurt our marriage. So let's give Candice a little support for trusting us enough not to make the same mistake."

He nods at his socks. After several moments, he blinks owlishly at her. "One wants life to be joyful and carefree for one's children. One harbours the hope their lives will be easy and perfect. Homosexuality ... She's going to come up against a lot of nasty remarks, Karen. She's going to get hurt, and I won't be able to protect her."

"But we can be here for her."

He swallows, nods again.

Karen sighs and gets to her feet. "I have to admit

I'm awfully disappointed, too. I was hoping to jiggle a granddaughter on my lap in another ten years or so, and now it looks like *that* isn't going to happen until Andy gets married."

"Well," Morris says, attempting a smile, "I suppose motherhood for Candice isn't entirely out of the question. There *is* always the turkey-baster method."

Curtains of hanging moss. Torturous roots. Slippery, sloping logs lush with swordfern and fungi. Yellowish green alders clustered between huge hemlocks. Great-girthed cedars, grooved and fractured boulders. Tangled undergrowth of licorice fern and salmonberry. Delicate dew-laden spider webs stretching like platters of lace between trunks and branches. Animals, microbes, plants, and insects all rustling, squirming, growing, burrowing. Lynn Canyon.

Karen and Morris walk close to each other, arms linked like chain fencing. The dark splendour of the forest resonates with the thunder of the creek. The noise vibrates against Karen's throat, presses against her chest.

"Lynn Creek," Morris says, his voice loud enough to carry above the roar of the falls. "That's what the pioneers named this. Not Lynn River, but Lynn Creek."

Not creek nor river, Karen feels for the first time in her life, but a raging power that hisses and boils and seethes through the cliffs like an angry bull bucking against a holding pen.

Karen heads for the suspension bridge, but Morris shakes his head. "No. This side of the creek. We found him on this side."

They pass the blue garbage can that is rusted at the cocked-height leg of a dog. They descend the slime-slicked wooden stairs behind the garbage can, shoulders brushing against the mossy cliff. Without speaking they step onto the wooden walkway that leads to the trails along the western creek bank.

A piercing east wind gusts over the treetops and separates the clouds above. A knife of moonlight cuts across the creek, highlighting a muscle of water lathered with foam. Karen clamps her teeth to stop them from chattering.

Morris halts in the middle of the boardwalk. "There. The kids found him there."

Karen sees only a hump of water, frothing white at the crest.

"The rock's underwater now," Morris says. "From all the rain."

The blistering flow of that water — all gushing towards the powerful, sinuous chute three dozen yards away — mesmerizes Karen. She can't tear her eyes away. "Do you think Egret saved him?" she whispers, eyes on the drowned rock embedded in the clay bank where her son, less than a week ago, almost lost his life. "Do you think Egret pushed him up there?"

"I'd like to think so, yes. I wouldn't like to believe he died in vain."

"Andy can't swim."

"No."

She turns away from the creek and buries her face in the cool, smooth polyurethane of Morris's yellow rain slicker. He wraps his arms around her.

"Home?" he asks.

She nods.

On the way back up the trail's slimy wooden stairs, Karen abruptly stops and points. "What's that?"

Morris shifts, clears his throat, bends closer to the shiny heap at the base of the stairs. "Flowers. Roses, mostly.

Wrapped in plastic film."

"Oh, God. For Egret."

Still stooping, Morris pokes a finger into the leaf-spattered pile. "There's a few cards here, a picture or two —"

"Don't touch it!" Karen says, pulling him by one elbow. She flushes, embarrassed by the revulsion shooting through her. *It's not his body rotting there,* she tells herself.

Morris straightens. Another gust of wind sways the crowns of the surrounding Douglas firs. A shower of raindrops patter against the plastic-covered bouquets.

Her husband starts up the stairs again, but Karen remains where she is in front of the mildewing shrine. "I hate it when they do this," she murmurs, twin rivulets trickling down her face. "The plastic breaks down and ends up as litter. And the photographs fade until you can't tell what the person looked like, as if the person's been erased from memory. The flowers turn black and slimy and they shrink as they rot ... Why doesn't the park ranger ever clear it up? Why does he just *leave* it here to decay? Doesn't he realize this is somebody's child?"

Morris descends and hugs her until she pushes away because she's choking so hard on her sobs she can't suck in enough air. He bends abruptly, knees popping like a car backfiring. Instantly, Karen is transported back to when she first met Moey on this creek bank, when they glimpsed the white hart. Moey's knees backfired like that while reaching to pick her up.

Two months ago. Only two months ago.

With careful, precise movements, Morris scoops up the mouldering bouquets and cradles them in the crook of his arm as gently as if holding a baby. A glistening worm sluggishly humps along the bare patch of ground he leaves behind.

"I'll take them to our compost heap," he says. "In the spring, whoever's bought our house can lay the compost over the flower garden around the roses. There won't be any litter, Karen. Nothing will be erased."

Chapter Twenty-Four

Andy can't sleep. Grampy Woodruff's snores sound like a Rottweiler growling outside his bedroom door, and despite the hot-water bottle at his feet and the electric blanket wrapped like a cocoon around his body, he is cold.

According to his bedside clock, it is 3:21 a.m. His parents tiptoed out of the house almost an hour ago. Andy can hardly breathe for fear. He clutches his ivory Buddha so hard it feels like a diamond.

Please let them come back, he prays. *Please.*

Prayers are powerful things. He knows that for a fact. Prayer killed Egret.

How many times has Andy lain in this bed, with this Buddha in this position in his hands, and relived the horrible moment of watching his mother bounce naked on top of the Teenager in the teahouse workshop? How many times has Andy prayed the Teenager would never return, that he would be flame-broiled in hell for messing with his mom?

As of today, Andy has decided the Teenager was Egret. He doesn't know for sure what has led him to this revelation, but he is fairly certain he is right. The way his mom looked beside him in the pew during the funeral service. The way she jerked when the pastor said "Kris Van Gorder." The words she whispered: *I never asked him his real name.*

And, of course, the pictures everywhere of Egret himself — in the newspapers, on TV, at the funeral. If you imagined the eyes screwed shut and the head thrown back and the neck muscles knotted in sexual concentration, then everything else matched the Teenager Andy saw beneath his mother. (The everything else being, namely, the head of blond hair and the lean, muscular diver's body.)

Andy prayed for the Teenager's death, and Egret died. Great swarms of guilt buzz around him, stinging relentlessly.

The back door opens. Andy hears it between a couplet of Grampy's snores. Footsteps come down the hall, slightly uneven, heavy on one side: his mom, still limping on her bad ankle. Andy's door creaks open an inch, and her dark silhouette appears, backlit by the hall light.

"Where's Dad?" Andy whispers.

The silhouette jerks. "What are you doing awake?"

"I heard you guys go out. Where's Dad?"

"In the garden. He'll be in shortly." She enters his room and rearranges his bedsheets, patting them here, tweaking them there. A pocket of green-scented night air surrounds her like a bubble. "Do you want me to refill your hot-water bottle?"

"No, it's okay."

"You sure? You're still shivering. Here, let me turn up your electric blanket."

"It's on as high as it goes."

She sits beside him and picks up one of his hands. Her fingers are cold and wet. When she speaks, Andy hears a frown in her voice. "I'm taking you to the doctor tomorrow. You shouldn't be cold like this all the time. There's got to be something they can do for you."

"Did you know Egret?" Andy bursts out. His pulse races. He's glad it's dark.

His mother doesn't answer, and Andy has to break the silence because it's too hard to breathe and he has to say something, has to tell her. "I think maybe I saw him here with you one time. You weren't wearing anything."

Her hand tightens around his, but still she doesn't speak.

"And I think it's my fault he drowned. I mean, I know it's my fault 'cause he went into the creek to rescue me, but that's not it. It's the other thing, the thing no one knows about. I *wanted* him to die, Mom. I didn't know who he was. I thought you might divorce Dad and leave us, and I even prayed to God he would die ..." He starts to cry.

"Oh, Andy," Karen says, lying down and folding herself around him, her hair rasping against his pillow. She cups his head in her hands and presses her forehead against his. "Oh, Andy," she says again and again, her tone making him cry all the harder. "Shhh, Andy, shhh," she whispers. "It's not your fault. You didn't kill Egret no matter what you prayed for. It was an accident. That's all."

He shivers and shudders, his forehead jerking against hers spasmodically.

"Andy, enough. I want you to listen to me," she says sternly.

He sucks in a quavering breath that makes his nose burn, the way it does when he jumps into a swimming pool and forgets to blow out. He frees one of his arms from beneath his blanket and swipes at his nose, gasping unevenly. She keeps her forehead pressed against his, both hands firmly on either side of his cheeks.

"I made a mistake," she almost hisses. "A terrible, terrible mistake. I was very unhappy with myself and I made things worse by hiding behind a fantasy. I'd sooner have lost an arm or a leg or my eyesight than have you witness that mistake. But I never considered leaving you and Candice and Daddy for Egret. Never. Do you understand me?"

He nods and hiccoughs, her wedding ring pressed into his cheek.

"I love your father very much, and you and Candice. Without you all —" her voice thickens and becomes hoarse "— my life would be as flat and brittle as a mirror." She slowly releases his cheeks and moves back a little so they can see each other. "What happened to Egret," she says, weighing each word like an anchor, "was an accident. No one caused it to happen, either by prayer or by making a terrible mistake. Gravity and nature killed Egret, and those things are blind and deaf and dumb and completely without feeling and thought. Understand?"

He nods.

"I think ..." she says slowly. "I think I didn't realize that myself until now. That his death was an accident, nothing more. When I saw that creek just now with Daddy, I think I realized that. Understand?"

He digests that, sniffles a couple of times, then nods again. "Are you going to tell Daddy about ...?"

She doesn't answer right away. "One day. Yes. But not now. We have too much ... healing to do already. But I will. Soon."

"He'll be angry."

"Shhh." With a thumb she rubs the fresh tears on his cheeks as if erasing a wrinkle in a bedsheet. "Yes, he'll be angry. And hurt. And all sorts of other things. But I owe him the truth. If I'd been honest with him a long time ago about what I felt for the Footstop, I wouldn't have made such a mistake with Egret in the first place."

"D'you really hate the Footstop that much?"

She sighs. "Hate's a pretty strong word. No, I don't *hate* it. But I think if I have to spend another year working in there, I'll end up dancing on tables and wearing a turban on my head like Moey."

Andy giggles a little, just small ones, more vocal shivers of relief than anything. "He's weird, Mom."

"He's a nice man."

"I think Dad's receptionist likes him."

"You think so?" There is genuine surprise in her voice, and her eyebrows, at least the one not squashed against his pillow, rises into her frizzy hairline.

"Geez, it's kind of obvious."

"Well, that's interesting."

"What's he going to do when we move? Where's he going to dance?"

"I don't know." She shifts restlessly. "But I'm sure things will work out. I'll do my best to make sure they do. And I *promise* I won't make things worse. Okay?"

"Okay."

She pats his cheek and slides her other hand out from under his face. He snuggles against her, breathing in deep her salty, wool-sweater smell, her apple-shampoo scent. Maybe she *can* make things turn out all right. For once.

"Can you sleep with me tonight? Just tonight?" he asks.

"I would be honoured to."

He giggles as she squirms and wriggles under the bedcovers.

"Wow, it's hot enough to bake bread in here!"

"It is kind of warm," he agrees, and for the first time he realizes it's true.

She wraps an arm around him. "You've stopped shivering."

"I'm warm now."

"So you don't think we have to go to the doctor tomorrow?"

He closes his eyes, and sleep descends on him in a muzzy sort of way. "No," he whispers against her chin. "I think it's going to be okay now."

And he does. He really thinks it's going to be okay now …

Karen lies in the dark, feeling Andy's ribs rise and fall beneath her arm. So frail, so tiny, carrying such a secret on his shoulders … Karen knows she won't sleep now, not with this new burden of guilt.

Not long after Andy falls asleep, Morris peeks in. Even from where he stands in Andy's doorway, the pungent manure smell of the compost box emanates from him.

"He asked me to stay for the night," Karen whispers.

"Nightmare?"

"Something like that." She flushes from the half-lie. She'll tell him the truth one day soon. But right now she wants to stay here, pressed against the sweet, small warmth of her son.

Morris nods, looking stooped and alone in the doorframe. "Do you think I'll wake him up if I have a shower?"

"If he can sleep through his grampa's snoring, he'll sleep through your shower."

Morris nods again. "Good night then," he whispers.

Karen's guilt mushrooms larger. "Do you want me to join you? He's fast asleep."

"Nonsense. Stay with him."

"I love you," she calls out. Kind of throws it out, hoping he'll catch the words and all the complexities they entail.

He pauses. "I love you, too," he says almost bashfully.

"Sleep well." And he shuts the door.

But Karen can't sleep. She listens to the *thrum-splatter* of the shower interspersed with cloudbursts of snores from her father in the living room. She listens to Morris pad down the hall and imagines him climbing into bed, exhausted and damp and smelling of Pear's Transparent Soap. She listens to the wind feather through the hemlocks and cedars outside. She thinks about leaving Moey high and dry without the Footstop, thinks about the torment her son has endured from witnessing her adultery. (*Mistake* — if that isn't a slick euphemism, she doesn't know what is.) She thinks about how she owes Morris so much more than what she's given him, and she thinks about what the Man knows and the way he looked at her and his last vaguely threatening words ...

The red numeral three on Andy's digital clock clicks into a four. Karen turns her back to it, then twists around again when Andy starts to twitch in his sleep and begins to grind his teeth. They squeak against one another like cubes of fresh, wet cheese. *Squeak, squeak, squeak.*

The glowing red four on the clock changes into a five.

I might as well give up on sleep, Karen thinks, extracting herself from the blankets.

That's when everything falls into place. That's when she gets the Idea.

She lies still, lest by moving she scare the Idea away. She lets her mind ruminate, lets it churn and rumble and digest the Idea. Then she sits up.

This isn't the same sleep-deprived epiphany she had while on the back-door step the night after Andy's attack. This isn't about delving farther into fantasy in an effort to redefine reality. No motorbike riding or kickboxing lessons in this idea. No, this is a solid, workable idea.

She slips out of Andy's bed, tiptoes down the hall, and wakes her father.

Mei-ling watches the apparition creep into the living room. The hall light falls across its face in one thin yellow slice, briefly illuminating a thick rope of hair, a single eye, one gleaming tooth.

Om hum phat! Mei-ling thinks with a shiver. *It's Ekajata, the one-eyed, one-toothed, one-breasted goddess!*

But, no, it's her daughter, Karen.

Now what the hell is she up to? Mei-ling thinks, sour with disappointment. *Doesn't anyone in this house sleep?*

Karen crouches beside her father and touches him on the shoulder. "Dad? Dad?"

"What? S'boiler on fire?" the reverend burbles, humping around on the air mattress like a beached whale.

"Shhh," Karen hisses. "You'll wake everyone!"

Mei-ling rolls off the mattress and out of the way. Her tailbone thumps hard against the floor. "As if anyone can sleep through that snoring," she snaps.

"What?" the reverend says, groping in the dark to shut off a nonexistent alarm clock.

Mei-ling slowly gets to her feet, one hand on the small of her back. She hasn't felt this sore since hauling rocks for the Chinese army when she was seven. She staggers to the couch, lowers herself onto it, and draws about her the foot quilt lying across the back. "We can't go on like this," she mutters. "We're too old to camp on the floor."

"What's wrong?" the reverend says, heaving himself into a sitting position. "Am I snoring again?"

"Was the Buddha born perfect?" Mei-ling grumbles.

"Yes, you were snoring," Karen says. "Loudly. But that's not why I woke you up. Well, it is, but not really."

"Oh, dear God," the reverend groans, rubbing his hands over his face as if trying to strip car grease off it. "Could you please try to be a little coherent at this hour of the morning? What time is it, anyway?"

"Five something. Look, I've had an Idea."

Mei-ling shivers; she heard the capitalization. "'Inspired by the mystic wine of Night,'" she murmurs. "'Sable-vested Night, eldest of things —'"

"Lingy," the reverend says reproachfully. "No Milton."

"I've had to listen to you snore for the past six hours. You can listen to me quote a little poetry."

"Mom, Dad, *please.*"

"Go ahead, go ahead," Mei-ling says irritably. "And that wasn't just Milton. It was Louis Untermeyer, too."

Her husband grunts.

Karen inhales with self-importance, and Mei-ling stifles a groan. *What now? She's going to confess she's a closet necrophiliac or something. As if this family hasn't made enough wild announcements today.*

"Morris and I are going to sell this house to you at a price you can afford," Karen announces. "And Moey's going to rent the Footstop to help subsidize your mortgage."

Mei-ling stares at her.

"It won't be the Footstop anymore, of course," Karen rattles on, "and we'll have to renovate the workshop a bit. Moey will have to share the kitchen and bathroom with you, but I don't think you'll mind, will you? I was thinking he could call it the Shimmy Shack, the Footstop that is, and sell Middle Eastern jewellery and bongo drums and belly-dancing costumes and what not. He could hold dance classes. I'm sure it'll attract as many tourists as the Footstop — "

"Whoa, whoa, whoa!" the reverend interrupts. "Slow down a minute. You're making my head spin!"

"This is only a suggestion. An Idea."

"'The imaginatio,'" Mei-ling quotes sombrely, "'is a physical activity that fits into the cycle of material changes and brings them about.' C.G. Jung. So do not belittle your ideas."

"Good God, don't go off on a tangent." The reverend waves a beefy hand at her as if trying to stave off the Holy Ghost. To Karen he says, "Are you *serious*? About selling this place?"

"I told you we were going to."

"Yes, and you also told me you were going to open up a Christian Sex Store, but I didn't quite believe that, either."

"Oh? And why not?"

"Well, for heaven's sake. What are you going to sell — Bibles in the shape of phalluses?"

"Sandy," Mei-ling says warningly.

"It's just a little much, don't you think?" he says, shifting to look up at her on the couch. From that angle his large jowled face and misshapen, blanket-wrapped bulk remind Mei-ling of the dwarf Black Lord who guards the teachings of Karma Kaju.

She shakes her head to clear away the vision. "We need some lights on in here if we want to think this through properly."

"What's there to think through?" the reverend says, but Karen gets up and turns the light on. Everyone briefly shrinks from the glare, like worms from the beak of a robin. "I don't want to discourage you," the reverend continues peevishly, "but I really think a Christian Sex Shop won't go over well with your target market. Namely, Christians."

"I never said a Christian sex shop," Karen snaps. "I said a Spiritual Sex Shop. And that's not open for discussion. It's what I've always wanted to do and it's what I'm going to do."

"Good girl," Mei-ling says. "You've finally discovered your destiny."

"Don't encourage her."

Mei-ling glares at him, which is a difficult expression to maintain since his grey hair is clumped about his head as if smeared with honey, and fluff balls from the green flock-lined air mattress cling to these clumps like small emerald bees.

"Dad," Karen says firmly, "I'm not Petra. This isn't the beginning of my moral decline. It's the opposite. *I'm not Petra.*"

Ah, Mei-ling thinks. *She's seen straight through his protests to the heart of his fear. Good girl.*

The reverend swallows, closes his eyes briefly as if in pain. "Of course," he whispers. "Forgive me."

"There's nothing to forgive," Karen says.

Mei-ling leans forward and rests a hand on one of her husband's broad shoulders. "As it is said in the *Jevajira Tantra,*" she intones, "'With the very portion of poison which slays all others, he who knows the essence of poison removes poison. With the same savage karma which binds all others, he who has the Means is freed from the bonds of being. The world is bound by passion, and by passion it is freed.' You've seen the birthmarks on your daughter, Sandy. You know she has to do what she has to do."

The reverend opens and closes his mouth a few times, then mutters, "There are a hundred appropriate responses to that. But without a drop of coffee in my blood, at this hour I'm quite unable to come up with a single one."

"Then be silent and let your daughter finish what she has to say," Mei-ling says. "I believe it might work, this Idea of hers. I believe it might just be a Splendid Idea."

Karen beams at her. "Thanks, Mom."

Mom. The way she said it ... why, for the first time ever Mei-ling feels Karen really meant it. *Mom.* The ghost of Petra has finally been laid to rest.

Something warm and soft swells deep in Mei-ling's gullet.

The world is bound by passion, she thinks, *and by passion it is freed.*

Chapter Twenty-Five

It is spring. The buds at the ends of salmonberry twigs glint like tiny drops of pale lime-green glass. Crocuses turn their purple and golden heads to the sun; daffodils unfurl their frilled snoots. Dew sparkles on the tender green needles at the ends of massive hemlock boughs, and the skirts of cedar trees wear hems of golden green. The drained, bare look of winter has been tucked away, replaced by the clear, airborne energy of new life.

Karen pulls into the parking lot of the Lynn Canyon suspension bridge and toots her horn. From the back seat Scott and Andy each burst out of a door. Thankfully, Scott has taken the place of Kyle, who promptly abandoned Andy after the tragedy in the canyon and now shows more interest in kids his own age.

Andy and Scott go racing up to the Footstop; only it isn't the Footstop anymore. Where once a large white ankle dominated creamy pearl-ended toes, a woman's naked midriff reveals a pierced navel. The Shimmy Shack is calligraphied across her coin-studded bra.

"You coming in, or are you going to wait in the car?" Karen asks Candice, who has come along on this Family Project reluctantly. These days Candice spends most of her spare time downtown in Kitsilano at a recreation centre for gay youth.

Candice toys gingerly with her newly pierced eyebrow.

"Forget it. I never want to step foot in that house again."

Karen nods. She kind of feels the same way. "Right then. I'll fetch your father and we'll be off."

But Morris isn't inside. Clara is there, bustling around in Mei-ling's kitchen, helping Moey pack the mountains of food Clara's mother has cooked for the picnic. Mei-ling and the reverend are there, proud new owners of the house and Moey's equitable landlords. They are arguing over how best to load their ancient, rusted bicycles into the back of Moey's Plymouth. Scott and Andy are there, too, tearing through the house and making fart noises with their hands cupped under their armpits. But Morris isn't anywhere to be found.

"He sent me home," Clara says. "He's still at the office, said he'll take a cab back here."

Karen's heart sinks. Only a few months into his promise of working half-days on Saturday and already he's lapsing.

"Oh, don't worry. He's not working," Clara says quickly, seeing Karen's crestfallen face. "He's chatting with his last patient. He'll be here any moment now."

"Oh," Karen says, only slightly mollified. "What's so important about his last patient?"

"It's that Mr. Chapman, the amputee." Then, to Moey, she says, "Don't forget salt and pepper. Over there, by the teapot."

Karen goes cold. "Mr. Chapman? The Man?"

Distracted by Moey's inability to locate the salt and pepper shakers, Clara merely nods and repeats, "He'll be back soon."

Suddenly, the day isn't so bright. The trees are cold and wind-creaking; clouds flit over the sun. Like an automaton, Karen helps load the picnic baskets into

Clara's car, her mind at Morris's office, running over exactly what the Man might be saying to her husband, how Morris might be reacting. The shock, the hurt, the disbelief, the anguish ...

I should've told him by now, Karen thinks, pressing her head against the cool metal of the car hatch as she rams another box of food into the trunk. *Why did I wait?*

"There he is!" the reverend booms behind her.

Karen glances up to see Morris stepping out of a taxi. A swirl of cold wind neatly parts Morris's hair as he pays the cabdriver. A white ribbon of skull is briefly revealed. Then the wind drops his hair back into place, a dense black cloud lumbers over the sun, and the taxi drives away. Morris comes towards them, looking grim and weary.

"Hope it isn't going to rain," the reverend mutters. "Forecast is for sunshine."

Karen feels weak and ill and hot. She tries to form words as Morris approaches her and instead forms tears.

"Who's riding with me?" Moey asks, and Scott and Andy immediately leap towards his derelict car and start fighting over the passenger seat.

"Looking mighty serious there, son." The reverend claps Morris on the shoulder, and he winces.

"How did it go with Mr. Chapman?" Clara says brightly, stuffing the last cardboard box of boiled eggs and tofu salad into Karen's car.

"Not good." Morris rubs his temples, then sighs and looks directly at Karen.

She staggers back as if struck and bumps into her father's chest.

"He's leaving town," Morris continues. "I hate losing a patient, especially one like this. It's such an unusual case."

"Maybe he'll keep in touch," Clara says.

"I doubt it. He's travelling across America with his brother's circus. He wouldn't even take a referral list of specialists with him."

Clara clucks sympathetically.

"A circus?" Mei-ling says, chewing her tobacco vigorously. She is dressed in spandex cycling pants and an oversize maroon sweatshirt with a green lizard on the front. "Animals in captivity. Not a good thing."

Morris shrugs. "There aren't that many animals in this circus. That's why Mr. Chapman's going. His brother can't afford to pay any roustabouts."

"What kind of a circus is it if there aren't any animals?" Mei-ling asks.

Morris frowns at her. "There used to be animals. But a group of protesters from Greenpeace released them all back in the fall."

"Can we cut the chatter and get going already?" Candice shouts from the front seat of Karen's car. "Some of us have a life to get back to, you know."

Moey executes a complicated shimmy and finishes with a mock bow in her direction. "The lady is right. I have to be back here at 3:30 for two students. Let's get this show on the road."

The reverend and Mei-ling follow Clara to her car, while Moey gets behind the wheel of his Plymouth. Morris checks the straps pinning their bicycles to the Tercel's roof rack, then asks Mei-ling for the keys to the house.

"I have to use the bathroom before we go," he says, striding towards their old house as if approaching a sullen mule.

Karen follows him, heart trip-hammering in her chest. "What else did Mr. Chapman say?" she asks huskily as she follows him through the swinging kitchen doors and down the hall.

"What? Oh, not much. Went on and on about his brother's circus, wasn't paying much attention to the instructions I was giving him about proper care of his stump ... Are you coming in with me?" Morris asks incredulously, stopping short on the threshold of the bathroom.

"Huh? No, no. Sorry, go ahead."

He shuts the door. Moments later she hears the *splash-tinkle* of urine in the toilet bowl.

She clears her throat. "So he didn't mention anything else? At all?"

"Like what?" Morris asks through the door, sounding a trifle irritated. "He doesn't blame me for his foot, if that's what you're asking. Nor Andy for what happened to the Van Gorders' boy. That's not why he's leaving."

She sighs and nods at the hollow, pressed-wood door of the bathroom. Relief and gratitude and a million other emotions flood over her.

Today, she thinks. *Tonight. I'll tell him tonight and say goodbye to Egret once and for all.*

It won't be easy. There will be tears, anger, repercussions that will bleed into the future. But not to tell Morris would be worse. Her conscience says so.

And she has to diffuse the power the Man holds over her, eradicate the fear that, despite his lack of proof of the affair, the Man might one day send her a blackmail letter. Yes, she'll tell Morris tonight.

The bathroom door opens, and Morris appears, wiping his hands briskly on a purple towel. "Mr. Chapman did mention one peculiar thing. I don't know if he was joking or not."

Karen freezes. "What?"

"He asked me to keep my eyes open for a white stag. Said there have been a few sightings of one in this area."

"White stag?"

Morris carefully hangs the towel back up, squaring it neatly along the chrome bar. "Seems the Greenpeace protesters released the most valuable animal in his brother's circus. Somehow it made its way over here." He turns and faces her, then gives a vintage lopsided smile. "But I told him we don't live in the canyon anymore, so there wasn't much chance of me sighting his stag. Coming?"

And he links an arm through Karen's and propels her down the hall.

After thundering and bucking through Lynn Canyon, Lynn Creek widens into a purring ribbon of content green water. On its final leg to the ocean, it meanders past an old dump site where, despite the mile-high hillocks of garbage buried under lush blackberry bushes and stately lupines, it is illegal to allow your dog to defecate. The fine for not picking up after your canine's colon earns a fine of $200. But as there is no one to enforce this law and the area is rife with dog walkers, all cyclists, joggers, and hikers using the trails that border this portion of Lynn Creek must keep an eye out for any offensive brown piles.

Therefore the convoy of Mortons, supplemented by Moey, Clara, and Scott, shout warnings to one another as they cycle beneath the sun-jewelled cedars and moss-cloaked maples: "Dog doo on the left! Dog doo on the right!"

"Oh, for God's sake," Candice says from her position at the rear of the bicycle convoy. "This is totally embarrassing."

Andy almost ploughs into a jogger, swerves his bike at the last moment, and crashes into a rotting log. "Geez," he says, wiping mud off his glasses. "That was close. I need a bell or something."

"Bell-schmell," Mei-ling says, wobbling on her squeaky steed. "Use what God gave you. Use your voice."

So Andy does. "Ding-dong!" he shouts as he rounds each bend. "Ding-dong!"

Scott joins in enthusiastically. "Ding-dong, ding-dong, ding-dong!"

"Oh, *God*!" Candice groans. "This is the *worst*."

Karen grins at Morris. Moey winks at Clara. The reverend booms out "Ding-dong" in his volcanic voice, and Mei-ling pipes up with a "Ding-dong" of her own.

Soon they are all ding-donging at the top of their lungs. Even Candice throws back her head and joins in, figuring what the hell, what has she got to lose?

Across the waters of Lynn Creek, surrounded by brambles and alders, a white stag snorts. And the bright spring air reverberates with the sound of merry "Ding-dongs."